the
Step
Mother

CLAIRE SEEBER

Bookouture

Published by Bookouture

An imprint of StoryFire Ltd
23 Sussex Road, Ickenham, UB10 8PN
United Kingdom

www.bookouture.com

ISBN: 978-1-78681-050-2
eBook ISBN: 978-1-78681-049-6

To ALL my family – every single last one of you, however step you may be!

Mirror, Mirror, here I stand
Who is the fairest in the land?

Wilhelm Grimm, *Grimm's Fairy Tales*

PROLOGUE

Once upon a time there was a king who married a lady, and so she became his queen. Soon after their wedding the new queen gave birth to a beautiful daughter. The queen looked at her baby and saw that her hair was black as ebony, her skin as white as snow and her lips as red as the roses climbing around the window. The queen liked the pure and pristine snow best, so she named her baby Snow White.

Not long after the baby's christening, the queen died of a mysterious ailment.

I wonder what that was.

(Though isn't it true that some women – many women perhaps – don't like other beautiful women – especially younger ones? Or is that a fairy tale too, probably made up by men?)

Anyway. I digress…

The king was sad and lonely on his own, as men of a certain age tend to be, and so, sometime not so long after the queen's death, he married a most beautiful woman, who seemed quite nice. She became the new queen – and, of course, the young Snow White's stepmother.

And we all know about stepmothers, eh?

Oh yes. We know all about them.

Don't we?

MARLENA

This is not the story, is it?

It's not *meant* to be the story – for either of us.

My breath sobs out of me as I run off the train and down the platform, up the footbridge stairs, past people going calmly about their daily business: travellers who glance away like I am deranged.

I *am* a little deranged, in my desperation.

Down the other side, I stumble through the barriers, out into this unknown city.

Where the fuck is the taxi rank?

I bundle myself into the first yellow cab I see, praying the whole time as it drives out of the city, so slowly – torturously slowly –

and into the countryside.

Who made all this countryside? I hate the countryside.

Out across the fields, into the small town, through the orchards, up to the hill. It's the longest drive I've ever been on, it seems – it goes on and on…

And all the time I'm praying this is a dream.

All the time, I can't quite catch my breath: it stops all jagged in my throat. I can't believe it. I can't, I won't, I can't.

They still have no answers when I get there, and so I put my head back and I do something I've never done before. I scream to the sky, to the heavens, to the world. I have always kept it in, my fear and rage, but now I scream it out.

And it doesn't even touch the sides; not even remotely, not even a tiny little bit.

And later, when more becomes clear, I vow to sort this whole sorry mess out – to find the truth. Oh yes, I will. They can't hide from me, oh no.

There is nowhere for this wickedness to hide.

JEANIE

28 NOVEMBER 2014

The old house is like a living thing. I felt it the first time I came here: as if the very cracks between the bricks were breathing quietly, as if the building were actually sentient. As I stand now before the great front door with its sturdy old locks, the keys for which I hold for the very first time, I struggle to believe it's *my* home.

Grey bricked, square and squat, mullion windowed, the first parts of the house were built in Elizabethan times. It has been added to along the centuries and modernised: a new drive curving before it, wrought-iron gates to keep outsiders firmly out. But still its age seeps from the walls. Old creepers twine around the sills, climbing up the old brickwork; red and white roses round the thick wooden door. Built onto one side, a single pointed turret reaches desperately to the darkening sky, as thick cloud scuds across a shadowed new moon.

I will never forget my first sight of it. I remember most distinctly the first time I crossed the threshold, following nervously in Matthew's wake. How in awe I was, and how my heart thumped.

Now, apparently, I am home.

* * *

Yesterday afternoon, at the estate agents squeezed between the old arcade and the chippie on the seafront corner, I detached my battered old 'Virgo' key ring – proudly presented to me by Frank on his tenth Christmas – and handed back the keys to 9 Marine Buildings with an almost-lump in my throat. Almost, but not quite.

Despite my nerves about what was coming next, I can't say I was entirely sorry to say goodbye to the dingy hallway that always smelt of cat wee, despite my best attempts with air fresheners or potpourri. (Last year Frank was so desperate to mask the smell from a new girlfriend, his joss sticks almost burnt the whole place down.)

I definitely wouldn't miss the patch of mould shaped like a polar bear above the bedroom window, or the shower that inevitably turned icy halfway through a hair wash – but for all its faults, it had been home for a long time. It was what we were used to, Frankie and I.

Sure, the second bedroom wasn't big enough to swing a mouse. The balcony was small and never chic, despite valiant efforts with greenery and two stripy deckchairs – but just having it enabled me to sit and watch the sea, sometimes for hours that slipped by unmarked; the sea that I both feared and loved in equal measure.

But in my heart I'd left already. I closed the flat door more resolutely than I felt and knocked on Elsie's. When she didn't answer, I left the yucca and the peace lily on the landing, unsure if she'd gone to her niece's – or if she found the idea of goodbye as painful as I did.

I shoved the last bits of mail in my bag – the redirection would kick in tomorrow – and closed the street door behind me for the final time.

The speed at which my life was changing felt surreal and astonishing – only this time in a good way. I just couldn't quite believe it was true.

After I'd dropped the keys off at the estate agents, I drove towards Shoreham for my last night on the south coast. In Judy's dingy first-floor flat we sat below a curling print of someone French's lilies, toasting new beginnings with warm Sauvignon Blanc. It took quite a bit of 'jokey' sniping that wasn't very jokey for me to gather I'd upset her. Hanging in the cramped hallway, my wedding dress had apparently become a red rag to a bull. I wished I'd left it in the car – but I'd been scared it was too tempting for light-fingered locals.

'Fantastic pulling grounds, weddings.' Judy sloshed wine into her half-full glass, topping up mine with the end of the bottle. 'I could be meeting my own Mr Right if you'd asked me.'

'But there won't be any Mr Rights there.' I covered my glass with my hand so the dregs trickled between my fingers. Only Frankie and Marlena were coming – and the twins of course. 'There's no party or anything, Jude, really. It's not like that.'

It was the truth. It *was* going to be tiny – and private. Just our immediate families – of which there wasn't much, for either of us; the families that we were going to integrate, bring together, in my imagination, like the Brady Bunch – only considerably smaller.

'Your prince has come then, eh? Let's just hope he's a bit more charming than the last one,' Judy slurred, draining her glass too quickly. 'Let's hope *he* doesn't sell anything to the press. Or that he hasn't got a mad wife in the attic. God, imagine that!'

'I don't think it's like that.' My smile was becoming fixed. Matthew did have an ex-wife – that much was true – but as far as I knew, she wasn't mad or living in the attic.

I'd been teaching *Jane Eyre* again for A level this term, covering for a teacher on maternity leave at a comprehensive out by Stenning, only slinking beneath the wire because my old head of department was there now and, desperate to fill the post at the last minute, took pity and hired me.

No, there were no parallels between the fiery little governess and my life. None at all.

It was definitely time to hit the saggy sofa bed before Judy got started on all men being bastards and the bottle of mouldering dessert wine she'd produced from somewhere. She didn't need me to rub my good fortune in – or to remind her of all the trauma I'd already been through that made this new adventure all the more special and extraordinary.

And I definitely didn't need to start thinking about what I hadn't *quite* told Matthew yet. I could deal with that later.

Couldn't I?

I woke early, sore and stiff from the cheap sofa bed, and crept out of Judy's with indecent haste, leaving a thank-you note and a rather sour taste in my mouth about our friendship.

I'm not sure it's one that will withstand the move. It's been floundering since my sudden, forced departure from Seaborne last year. I suppose I was just grateful Judy didn't turn her back like many of my other colleagues. (Let's just say there was definitely no whip-round when I left.)

Frankly I took friendship where I could get it during those awful months. Judy had cleaved to me a few years before at Seaborne, after I'd taken pity on her isolation when the staffroom hadn't warmed to her Tory views. We shared an occasional warm cider after I left, although I suspected it was largely because the depths to which I'd fallen made her feel better about her own life.

I pulled the door quietly behind me.

Outside I felt the air, damp and salty, on my face. I paused for a moment, savouring it, listening to the seagulls cry like kittens. The sea was only at the end of the road, and I contemplated the walk down to the beach for a last look – but the day was grey, and glancing at my watch, I thought, *I've got somewhere new to be*. Frankie's train was getting in at 11 a.m.

I turned away from the sea and got into the car, and despite my resolution, it felt very final.

To a soundtrack of Joplin and Joni, I took the M23, my tummy rolling with nerves and excitement. Still, there was more than a tinge of sadness, despite what happened here eighteen months ago. Brighton had been our sanctuary for the past twelve years, ever since Simon meted out his punishment. I'd miss it badly.

But it was time to push those thoughts away; it was time to start afresh. Not everyone gets this second chance at happiness, I reminded myself firmly and cranked up Janis's top notes.

At Berkhamsted Frank's train was delayed, so I sat outside the station, nursing a coffee and contemplating this new place we were coming to. Such a neat and tidy town compared to the tangy sprawl of the south-coast town that burst with gay bars and hen parties, the busy little Lanes and the neon fairground on the Pier. Berkhamsted, on the other hand, is not Bohemian, cool or chavvy in any way: it is proper, grown-up suburbia.

As I watched from my seat, neat little families poured out of 4 x 4s and a clutch of affluent older couples in beige headed to Waitrose. Across the street, yummy mummies ran in and out of the coffee shops in Uggs and fake fur, glued to smartphones. It was all so nice: we might just end up being the sore thumb, my son and I.

The truth was I didn't want attention any more; no more whispers and sniggers, no more covert looks across the street.

But what is nice anyway? Nice is so often only on the surface in my experience. The debris usually lies beneath.

Frank's arrival curtailed my musings. He didn't see me as he loped out of the station in his skinny jeans and scuffed Converse, an old parka falling off his narrow shoulders, and I watched him with joy.

'Oh gosh, I've missed you.' I hugged my son hard, shocked at how tall he was – taller even than when he'd left for Hull three months earlier, breaking my heart as he left the nest entirely empty: only me left.

'Don't say it, Mum,' he grinned.

'What?'

'All grown up!'

So I didn't – I just grinned at him. But it did cross my mind that day, yet again: would I have given into Matthew with such abandon if Frankie hadn't packed and gone north?

Now he released himself from my hold and swung his rucksack up, and I noticed a new tattoo poking from his jacket sleeve. 'New ink?' I teased, and he swiped my hair.

'Yeah, something like that.'

In the car he told me about his new mates, about his halls and then finally that he wasn't convinced he was doing the right course. 'I'm thinking of changing to music production,' he said. 'More me.'

And despite his chatter, as we neared Malum House, my stomach turned over again. I was looking forward to showing Frankie his new home. The prospect of giving him something more than we'd ever dreamt of was tantalising – but I was suddenly terrified.

What if they didn't get on?

Sure, they'd been all right the few times Matthew visited Brighton; they got on fine, that was true. They chatted about football, and a bit about music, though their tastes differ vastly. But – what if…

Matthew flung the door open wide before I even knocked, soothing my nerves, all smiles, damp dark hair and faded old jeans. He'd been waiting for us with fresh coffee and croissants in the big white kitchen. Leading us in, it was obvious he wanted us to both feel at home, kissing me and giving Frankie a jovial back slap.

'Welcome to Malum House,' he said, his hazel gaze on me. My stomach flipped over – with excitement this time.

'Nice.' Frank took his cup to the French windows. 'Cool view. What's Malum when it's at home?'

'The house was built on the site of Malum Farm's old orchards, in the seventeenth century.'

'Oh right; well old, then.' Frankie nodded sagely.

It was Matthew's turn to grin. 'Malum's the old Latin for "apple".'

'I see,' said Frank. Then he grinned and admitted, 'I never did Latin actually. One year of Spanish just about did me.'

'Well I don't think many of us did Latin.' Matthew was kind.

Whilst Frank was in the bathroom, Matthew scooped me to him, kissing me with vigour. When I came up for air, I felt oddly shy, and I pushed my head into the neck of his cashmere jumper. He wrapped his arms tightly around me.

'I can't believe I'm actually here,' I whispered. 'It feels like a dream.'

'I can believe it,' he murmured into my hair, 'and I thank God you're not going anywhere again.'

'Really?' It was like I needed to pinch myself. No man had ever made me feel like this before. Not even…

Not even the devil still haunting me now.

'Really, hon.' Matthew kissed the top of my head. 'You are so good, Jeanie. You are going to be the saving of me – I know it.'

And I revelled in it for now. For now, I would let myself revel in this unusual, addictive and exotic feeling. Because I knew, for all my high hopes, I knew it probably couldn't be sustained. But I wouldn't think of that now…

When Frankie slouched back into the room and swallowed a croissant practically whole, Matthew released me and suggested a tour of the house. 'We ought to show Frank his new home, eh, Jeanie?'

'Cool.' Frankie eyed another croissant, and I propelled him gently towards his rucksack.

'Do you want to see your room?' I asked.

'I've given you the end bedroom on the first floor, looks out onto this—' Matthew gestured at the great sweep of lawn that led down to woodland on the other side of the high wall. There was no way over that wall.

I was surprised by a sharp feeling, like a weight on my chest. *Come on, Jeanie!* I couldn't crave the openness and enormity of the sea already, less than two hours in. Could I?

Don't fuck this one up, for Christ's sake! Marlena's voice was in my ear. *This is your big chance.*

'Sounds good to me.' Frank hitched up his jeans as we watched Matthew open the 'secret' kitchen door with a flourish, showing off the twisty hidden stairwell.

'The Cavaliers hid their allies in this stairwell during the Civil War.' Matthew was ahead of us. 'I saved it from Kaye's terrible architect when we did the extension. There's a priest hole behind it from Elizabeth I's reign – when the Catholics were persecuted. They'd have torn it all out if Kaye had had her way.' I couldn't see his face, but I sensed the roll of his eyes. 'It's listed now, so it's safe.'

'Awesome, man.' Frankie loped behind his stepfather-to-be. 'Can you get in the priest hole?'

'No, it's bricked up now – but it's there behind the wall.'

And they were up and out of the stairwell.

Alone, I paused in the dimness. I ran my hand across the cold, bumpy wall, salvaged from the demanding ex-wife who was so rarely mentioned. I wondered whom exactly it was who hid behind the bricks. Did they listen in terror to Elizabeth's soldiers or Cromwell's Roundheads tramping through the house, ready to pull them apart? They must have feared for their lives.

The wall was very cold beneath my fingers, and I realised I was holding my breath, my ears straining for sound.

It sounds silly, but once or twice, I'm sure I've heard voices, late at night, whispering in the hallways and on the landings, when there's been no one here but Matthew and I.

And it's strange, because I don't feel like the house is hostile – but it has unnerved me.

Matthew always assures me the odd noise is quite normal; just the creaks and groans of old timber – but I'm not so sure. It makes me horribly uneasy.

It makes me feel someone else is here. And it's too soon for that.

Isn't it?

About six weeks ago I was woken from a deep sleep in the early hours by a noise I couldn't distinguish. The twins weren't staying that night. They'd been here earlier in the day, and we'd gone to the cinema to see *The Maze Runner* before taking them back to their mother's after tea.

Lying awake in the dark, my heart pattering, something moved near me. The swish of material against wood – a skirt, a petticoat, a curtain, I wasn't sure – but it was enough to force me bolt upright in bed.

'Listen!' I clutched Matthew's arm. 'I can hear someone...'

'It's just the wind,' he muttered, without opening his eyes. 'Lie down, hon.' He threw a protective arm over me and fell straight back to sleep.

I lay awake for at least an hour that night.

And are there voices here too, I wondered now, in the stairwell? Today? Behind these cold walls...

'Jeanie? Are you coming?'

I jumped slightly, despite myself. Then I went on up to marvel along with Frank at his new bedroom, which was complete with a sound system beyond his wildest dreams, speakers attached to the walls.

'Is this a Sonos?' he was crowing. 'Linked to the whole house? God, that's amazing!'

There was only one tiny blip during the 'tour' – and probably it was only my imagination again anyway; what Marlena would call my 'over-thinking' – and what I might just term slight anxiety. Frankie had put his hand in mine as we climbed the turret stairs, and as Matthew turned at the top, a slight frown crossed his face, his eyes flicking towards my son's hold on me. I felt it like a dart.

My eighteen-year-old son, it has to be said. The thing was we were used to having to hold onto one another, Frankie and I, but maybe now, maybe it had to change a bit – and that wasn't a bad thing, given what we'd been through in the past few years. Frankie was growing up and away from me, and it was time for a new time.

I slipped my hand out of Frank's and moved up the last few stairs to join Matthew in the circular room.

It was his daughter's bedroom: girly in the extreme, frilly and pink. The sickly smell of rose and vanilla pervaded the air – from cheap candles on the windowsills, I thought. Carefully, I avoided looking at the display of family photos on the ledge. I looked out of the other window, towards the town.

'Blimey.' Frank opened a casement and leaned out. 'It's like Sleeping Beauty's castle or something. You wouldn't want to get an attack of vertigo up here.'

'Careful,' I couldn't help myself saying.

'It's quite something, isn't it?' Matthew clapped his hand onto Frank's shoulder, leaning out too to survey the view with a trace of pride. I was glad Frankie had shown his approval, and I was sure it would be all right between them; this might even be the beginning of a bond. 'Makes all the long hours at the office worth it.'

The creepers creep-creep-creeped around the windows – the red roses didn't make it this high – and peering through the window behind them, down at the street, where a small figure was running towards the fields, onto the Chiltern Hills, I thought Matthew and Frank were quite right. It was magnificent: the views were immense.

I looked at my son and my lover standing together, gazing out, and then Matthew turned and smiled at me – a smile full of what I could only read as love, and I felt my skin tingle.

Or was it tingling because of the figure I'd seen scurrying away down the road?

I turned to Matthew.

My husband-to-be.

This time on Saturday, I would be Mrs King.

My home.

If you'd told me six months ago I'd end up here, the day before I met Matthew at Jill's terrible office party, I'd have said you were a fantasist. I'd have said the same the week after. Two weeks after.

But here I was.

In the distance a motorbike revved, and then it sped away.

MARLENA

I meant to make the wedding. I did, really.

Oh come on! I bet you've had to miss an important occasion for work; we all have, haven't we?

What?

All right, it wasn't *entirely* work. I mean, it was, but it was kind of more like a hunch, and I was hoping it would lead to bigger, better things, as I inched my way out of the wilderness I'd found myself in four years ago. I had a lot of ground to make up, a lot of apologising to do, a lot of proving myself journalistically, all over again.

The wedding photos looked lovely, really. She looked gorgeous, so gorgeous, my Jeanie, and I could see why exactly, despite all his money and his posh house and flash car, Matthew would've fallen for her.

The most pure of heart, my dear Jeanie. Wouldn't hurt anyone; really, truly, wouldn't refuse anyone. Would always manage to be kind, even when times were hard.

As she learnt to her huge cost.

But she's paid for that shit, hasn't she? More than once.

This was her once upon a time all over again. This was the happy ending she'd been longing for since Simon's worst betrayal had lacerated her. Since the days of Uncle Rog and his pissed-up paedo mates at the Star & Garter off Peckham High Street. Since the subsequent inflicted damage. Jesus.

Let's leave that for another time, yeah? It sours everything.

Happy endings? In my book, they're what you get down the massage parlour on the Old Kent Road. They are *not* real life.

I stared at the wedding picture my big sister had just emailed me.

Jeanie in her white velvet dress and big fur hood, eyes shiny and huge with hope; Matthew very debonair in an undoubtedly expensive dark suit, looking down at her with – I couldn't dispute it – something definitely akin to love. Not that I'm an expert though.

Still, there was something about the picture I didn't like: something I couldn't quite put my finger on immediately.

Something about the look on his daughter's face, perhaps – a teenager whose name escaped me, whom I hadn't met yet. Slinky, skinny little thing: too much black eyeliner, wearing a long, tight purple dress and wedge-heeled boots.

Pudding brother, not nearly so handsome as his twin, but at least his smile was benign.

And lanky Frank, freckled and mop haired, in his borrowed suit and old black Converse, grinning lopsidedly. Probably dying for a roll-up if I knew anything about the boy.

I looked at the twins, these kids that Jeanie had met only a few months ago, who were taking a while to warm up, apparently, despite all her best efforts. Well the girl was, by all accounts. The boy was quite chilled, at least. But they weren't ready for a stepmum, it seemed.

Jeanie had even bought a book, bless her, when we met in London in September for a lunch soon interrupted by a call from my new editor. (I dare not leave work calls unanswered these days.)

After I'd hung up, I'd accompanied my sister to the self-help section in Piccadilly's Waterstones and watched her root the book out from the bottom shelf.

How to be the Best Step-parent or some crap – that's what she chose. 'Confront the challenges head-on,' read the tag line.

She'd been worried about Frank too. Worried he'd feel left out and not the 'only one' any more. Worried that the twins wouldn't accept her; worried they would compare her to their mother. Hoping to make a 'new family'.

What did we know about family though?

I'd told her to stop over-thinking – as usual.

'Just get on with it,' I'd instructed again, a fortnight ago, over Jeanie's hen-night cocktails in the Covent Garden Hotel, when she said it was still 'a bit sticky' with the girl. 'How can anyone not like *you*, Jean?'

'Quite easily.' She ate her olive morosely. 'I can't get Scarlett to smile at me at all. I offered to take her clothes shopping last week, and she just left the room without speaking.'

'Horrible age, babe,' I reminded her, licking the salt from my hand and downing my tequila. 'Think what we were like at fourteen.'

Not helpful, actually, that last comment. We were hardly today's typical teens, my sister and I. Too busy fending for ourselves to have hissy fits about potential step-parents.

Too busy with the business of survival.

Matthew came to meet Jeanie after our cocktails. They were going to stay the night in the hotel – and when I saw him scoop her off her feet outside the main doors, her cheeks flushing with pleasure and excitement as she disappeared into his embrace, at least I could relax a bit.

This man was besotted by my sister – that much was obvious.

Strange match they might seem, but then stranger things have happened. He treated her like she was made of glass; he seemed to see her as precious.

And she is. Infinitely precious.

When I couldn't make the wedding at the weekend, when I texted to say I had to follow up a lead on a story about corruption in the back benches – Cameron's lot and their sense of entitlement – that if I didn't, my job would be on the line – Jeanie insisted it was fine. But I knew it wasn't really. I sent the biggest bouquet of flowers Interflora did, but I still felt shit about it.

Especially when my 'big story' turned out to be a complete dud. Maybe I should have examined my own motives for not attending the wedding more closely. Maybe.

Now I closed the wedding photo down to read the directions to the sixth-form college I was visiting this afternoon. I was giving a talk on social media, responsibility and digital journalism. I was trying to do my bit; trying to make amends.

I also had to tell Jeanie I wasn't going to their New Year's Eve party. Matthew might be good for my sister, but wild dogs wouldn't have dragged me to mingle with his money-market mates. I was a little hazy on what exactly his job was, but bankers really didn't do it for me. Bankers had nearly been my own professional downfall.

Maybe, though, maybe I'd leave telling Jeanie that till tomorrow.

JEANIE

31 DECEMBER 2014

3 p.m.

The party is starting in less than four hours. I'm behind already and horribly anxious as I arrive back to find an elderly lady hovering just outside the drive. Our drive, I should say.

Except nothing feels like 'ours' to me yet, whatever Matthew says.

The lady ignores my polite beep, refusing to move more than an inch, but eventually I manage to squeeze carefully around her, parking my old car behind the phalanx of shiny, far grander vehicles.

Trying to avoid her eye, I drag Matthew's dry cleaning out, along with a big box of wine glasses I bought this morning, before my cursed trip to the hairdresser's.

My hairdo, as my Nan would have called it, is truly awful. I don't know why I let the girl keep going when I could see the disaster it was becoming – but I just grinned at her manically in the mirror as she turned me into a bouffant Miss Piggy.

Or rather, I do know why I let her carry on. It's because I didn't want to upset her. Can't say boo to a goose me.

And it was because I was distracted.

Whilst the girl cut and curled, I had a cup of tea and scanned a copy of something glossy – maybe it was *OK!* magazine; I'm not sure. Mid-read about Kylie's love life, I sensed eyes on me – but it was just a couple glancing at the price list in the window. They walked on.

I finished the magazine and looked for something else to read. I avoided the newspaper rack – I don't like newspapers any more – but I did catch the *Daily Mail*'s front-page story – about that girl who'd disappeared from London on Christmas Eve. Apparently they thought she'd quite likely flown to Turkey, planning to travel on to Syria in what they call 'hijrah': jihad by emigration.

Then I opened yesterday's post that I'd stuck in my bag earlier.

At first I thought the hard-backed envelope was a late Christmas card, and I studied my name written in swirly black writing across the front, wondering which friend had tracked me down so soon.

But of course I was wrong.

After I saw what was inside the envelope, I couldn't move for a bit. The hairdresser's that had seemed so noisy a moment ago suddenly seemed very quiet, and everyone in my peripheral vision seemed to be moving in slow motion.

I sat staring at the picture. It wasn't a good picture of me anyway, and it had been doctored with black biro: the artist had had to go over his 'work' a few times, by the looks of things, to make the noose really stand out.

The noose around my neck.

When I'd calmed myself a little and put the horrible picture away, I realised what I had to do.

Something I should have done weeks ago. Something I should have done before the wedding.

Now, on the driveway, all I want is to get inside and make sure the scary caterer's doing all right on her own before I take Matthew aside.

I need to talk to him quietly and tell him the truth. Before all his smart friends – I imagine they're smart anyway – before they all turn up and see me for the fraud I am.

Before it all implodes.

But before I reach the front door, the elderly lady, who I recognise now as Miss Turnbull from next door, bears down on me like a Rottweiler on a squirrel in the park.

'Hello there.' My jolly smile's meant to say: *please let me go; I'm sorry, but I'm pushed right now.* 'Just dashing inside to see—'

'I think these are yours.' The stolid lady is already halfway up the path. She extends a woolly-gloved hand; she's holding something.

'Sorry,' I say. 'The postman must have gotten the house numbers confused.'

Or maybe it's because Miss Turnbull lives in a bungalow called 'Heaven's Gate', and the postman doesn't recognise that celestial address as being located in suburban Hertfordshire.

She waves a wodge of envelopes held by an elastic band. My redirected mail. I see the handwriting on the top one.

I don't want the letters, but I don't want her to have them either. I stick my hand out as best I can, given I'm holding a box of glasses under one arm and trailing a man's suit from the other.

Reluctantly Miss Turnbull relinquishes her cargo.

'Thanks,' I say as I move off. I refuse to look at them this time. Later. Later will do.

She's still hovering. I realise she's waiting, her whiskered chin quivering with some sort of emotion I can't quite make out.

'It's odd, you know.'

'What is?' I am bright, fumbling for the key.

'I thought I recognised your name…'

'Oh it's a common-enough name,' I say, trying for breezy. 'Well thanks so much. I'd better get inside before I drop this lot.'

It's not enough apparently.

'*Where* exactly did you say you moved from?' the old woman asks.

Nowhere. *I moved from nowhere*, I want to shout.

But she knows already, if she's looked at the forwarded mail. And I'd bet my last pound she has.

'Sussex,' I mumble.

Please go away now, I think fervently. God, I wish I was more like Marlena. I'd just turn my back, forthright and assertive with my boundaries.

But I am not like my sister. I am the least assertive person I know – except with my students. The only place I ever came into my own was in front of my class.

Back then.

Pushing the thoughts down, finding the key, I move to the door – but she's still there.

'Thanks again,' I say.

'Having a do?' Miss Turnbull glares at the catering van parked next to the bashed-up old Fiesta Marlena bought Frankie for his eighteenth. The only other rubbish car parked on the curved drive.

I couldn't afford to get Frankie anything much last year – but at least Marlena saw him proud.

This year I can do better.

'I don't know why people bother seeing New Year's in,' Miss Turnbull sniffs. 'I do hope it won't be too loud.'

'I'll make sure we keep a lid on it.' The key's in the door now, thank God. 'It won't be too noisy, I promise.'

A rash promise to make, if my Frankie has anything to do with it – but we're so detached in this big old house, I doubt The xx will reach Heaven's Gate.

The New Year's Eve bash was definitely not my idea. I don't know anyone locally, not yet, and I've invited no one apart from

Marlena and Jill. Honestly I'd be happier nodding my head along to Jools Holland with my new husband, accompanied by a glass of Cava and a tube of Pringles – but my new husband (God, how odd that still sounds!) has different ideas.

'I want to show you off,' Matthew said when he first mentioned the idea, ever the gallant – and secretly, despite my innate shyness, I'm bursting with happiness. Despite knowing that, at the grand old age of forty-two and a half, I'm hardly a young bride worthy of being flaunted.

Second time round the block for him, and a lot of water under bridges. Whole oceans full, in my case.

And of course, I'm slightly ashamed to say, Miss Turnbull's not invited – not as far as I know anyway. Matthew said something like, 'That old bat will never darken my door again,' when we saw her outside one day, sweeping up non-existent litter.

I vaguely remember a story about her complaints to the RSP-CA, saying Scarlett's puppy barked excessively; so much so that the RSPCA had come round and checked on the Kings.

What *is* that expression on her saggy face as she looks at me now?

Concern?

No – it's worse than that. It's disapproval.

'I mean we don't want any more shenanigans, do we?' Miss Turnbull says. 'I really don't want to be calling the police again.'

'*Again?*' I stop, key in door. 'What do you mean?'

'Less said.' She purses bloodless lips now as I gaze at her.

'Please *do* say,' I prompt. '*What* police? When?'

The old lady glances up at the house and then away. She's not going to tell me anything else; she's decided apparently.

'Well I don't want to be out here in the dark,' she harrumphs, although it's a pleasant, if cold, afternoon: there's even a glimmer of sun in the washed-out sky. 'You never know who might be around.' She shoots a look down the road, as if we were in downtown LA, the Bronx – or even central Peckham, where I was hauled up. Here I'd hazard a guess a couple of dog walkers are the worst she might encounter.

'Thanks so much, Miss Trunchbull—' Horrified I stop, thinking of Roald Dahl's horrid old headmistress – and my last boss.

'*Turn*bull,' she corrects crossly. 'I must say'—she gives me a final once-over—'you're quite different to the last one.'

Last round to her then.

I watch her sensible lace-ups squelch through the last leaves, not cleared from the foot of the drive, disintegrating in all the rain we've had recently.

Glancing down at the mail, I feel a familiar squeeze of fear.

I shove the lot into my coat pocket and lug the wine glasses and the suit into the house.

My tentative 'I'm home!' rings false in my ears, and although I want to see Matthew – I always want to see Matthew – I feel a surge of overwhelming relief when silence greets me.

Dumping my wares in the hallway, I stick my head round the kitchen door. The scary, super-efficient caterer waves from the central island where she's counting something called smoked salmon blinis, and I'm just wondering where Matthew is when full-blast techno pumps through the house: The Prodigy's 'Firestarter', I think.

Frankie's got the sound system up and running then.

'*Back soon, I ♥ you*' says the note stuck on the front of the fridge with an Aston Villa magnet. Matthew's gone to fetch the twins.

It's not his weekend, but as far as I can tell their mother – 'the last one' as Miss Turnbull would have it – or the only other one, in fact, plays hard and fast with the rota.

'It's our gain,' I'd reassured Matthew last night after his phone had started to ping with texts. Feeling flushed and giddy with the romance of my new life, when he'd announced that she'd asked us to have the twins for New Year's Eve, I'd been quite happy to agree. 'It'll be fun to party with them.' I'd dolloped more chicken chow mein onto his plate and topped up his glass of red. 'I'm looking forward to seeing them.'

But actually that was a lie.

I am only looking forward to seeing one of them this week-end. Frankly the other one alarms me quite badly.

Despite my best efforts, Scarlett's proving a tough nut to crack. I'd met the twins about six weeks in, against my slightly better judgement, but I'd never anticipated such hostility from her. And I can't help feeling partly responsible: the speed at which Matthew and I married, almost six months to the day we met, hasn't helped, I guess.

But I couldn't wait. 'Do you need help?' I shout over the music to Julie, who shouts back that she's fine and it's all underway (I think, though it's hard to tell as Keith Flint is still yelling something about a bitch someone hated), and I think how strange this is, to be in this smart, large house whose inside doesn't match its outside at all.

Inside it's all ultra-modern and blank, neutral tones; matching three-pieces and plush rugs and every electronic mod con I could wish for – and a few more I'd never heard of before.

How very different to where I was this time last year – entirely different, in fact. I'd never have dreamt I'd be this happy; a year ago I thought I'd never see the light of day again. I'd certainly never dreamt I'd be paying a lady to make canapés for guests I don't even know.

All right, correction: I'm not paying her. Matthew is.

Everything's happened so fast. The issue of my finding a job now that I live in his house, in this town, hasn't arisen yet, and it's another subject we need to discuss soon.

There are a few things that have been overlooked – the most important of which I know I need to rectify immediately.

The letters crackle in my pocket as I push by the kitchen counter.

But I've missed my chance today. When Matthew returns, it'll be with his kids – and I can't tell him when they're here.

I just need to get through tonight – to pass the initiation test, I suppose…

What if I don't pass though?

What if…

I head upstairs. When I get to the master bedroom – *our* bedroom – I close the door firmly and sit on the bed.

I stare out into the huge back garden, past the bare old apple trees, their lichened branches sprawling towards the bedroom window, down to the great lawn sloping into a cluster of old trees at the end: big oaks that provide a canopy of dark and dappled light I've not explored yet and other naked, December trees. Beyond them is the high wall that keeps us in.

Someone's strung up fairy lights around the terrace this end, planted outdoor candles along the path. Silver lanterns adorn the lawn's edges. It's very pretty – magical almost – perfect for the theme of tonight's party.

It's my home – and yet I feel like a fish out of water still, and I fear my days might be numbered if I'm discovered *before* my confession.

Pulling the new mail from my pocket, I feel sick with fear.

One's from the bank. One's from the TV-licensing people. One's a mail-order catalogue for clothes I'd never wear.

And then, in a rush, I tear the last one open.

It's even worse than I feared.

7 p.m.

From the percussive *thump, thump* through the floor, it is apparent that the countdown to the party has officially begun.

I need to hurry, or I'll be late for our guests – but I'm dawdling. I can't bear to leave the sanctuary of the room.

I'm terrified that Matthew's friends will see I'm not worthy of him, that I'm not what I purported to be. Terrified of people seeing through me, thinking I'm not good enough. Terrified that I don't match up to the great Kaye, she of the long legs and tumbling blonde mane and the hard body, honed whilst her husband was away making money – money she was very good at spending.

I haven't met Kaye yet, but I know what she looks like.

Forget that now.

I take a huge breath down into my diaphragm, and I check my reflection in the mirror one final, anxious time, my clammy hands smoothing the sparkly skirts of my dress.

The mirror says I look nothing like normal. I look odd, outlandish even, my feathery headdress so tall I have to bend to see the top of it.

Do I dare walk out of this room? What if they laugh?

Worse, the gremlin taunts, *what if someone recognises you? There's always a chance…*

They won't laugh surely? Luke helped me choose the costume last weekend. He was looking for his own on a fancy-dress website, and when I saw the dress, he positively encouraged me – unlike his sister, who didn't want to look at all.

I imagine she'll be in her usual denim hot pants and holey tights.

Just get on with it, Jeanie.

I remember Matthew's assurances, murmured into my hair early today – before he slipped out of our rumpled bed to play a round of golf. My fears were forgotten; always forgotten during the times I am in his arms, when I'm warm and sated.

Still, the thing lurks in the corners of my mind, that squat little beast called memory, its sticky fingers covering everything with a thin layer of slime.

And it seems strange I've been found out so soon, doesn't it?

After I opened Miss Turnbull's bundle earlier and pulled out the contents of that first envelope, hands trembling and head spinning, I studied the front as I had on the other envelope in the hairdresser's.

My 'old' name typed above the address; postmark London, Central.

Why now? I thought.

But I know really.

Looking around the room now, I feel that I always knew it wasn't right anyway. We don't belong here, Frankie and I: we are proper misfits.

We belong in our old rented place, with damp patches and mould and mismatched furniture; gaudy cheap curtains and plastic bath suites; Elsie knocking on the wall when Frankie played his music too loud. Not here, in this opulence. It's all pretend.

I ought to go back before I'm found out...

It's been so stupid to have not told Matthew, extremely stupid – a far bigger risk than I'd normally ever take doing anything.

I fear I'm going to pay the price.

But – I do have some hope still. No man has ever made me feel like he does. Not even the devil. So my hope resides there: in our feelings for each other, our new passion, that might make it all right.

Please. Let it be all right.

Banging dance music fills Matthew's house again, the floors shaking with the huge bass beat. I imagine the old house's disdain at the intrusion, the things it has seen. Now the invaders are all too evident, it sighs…

The knock at the door makes me jump.

'Are you ready, hon?'

I glance at the dresser drawer where I shoved the envelope when Matthew arrived back with the kids – one of whom was loudly truculent and rude.

'Just coming.' I lock the drawer, hide the tiny key in my make-up bag, and open the door. All the little things I've been worrying about – the glitter with which I've liberally powdered my cleavage, the brilliant shade of my emerald eyeshadow – are forgotten again in the light of my recent fears.

But, stepping out to be judged, the way Matt looks at me calms me.

'Wow, Jeanie! You look beautiful,' he says wonderingly.

It's like warm water washing over me, like sinking into a bath that's the perfect temperature. A soup of love, almost.

'Come on, hon.' Matt holds out a hand, and the expression on his face is one I can't read. No, maybe I can. It's one of pride, I think.

Cheeks flaming, I'm proud to inspire this reaction. 'You…' I look down at myself shyly. 'You don't think it's too much?'

'You're beautiful,' he murmurs. 'Lovely girl.'

'God, Mum!' Frankie bounds up the stairs. 'Are you wearing *that*? You look—'

'What?' I'm nervous all over again. 'Ridiculous?'

'Like you're about twenty-five!' His freckly face breaks into a grin.

'Ah, get away with you,' I scoff, sounding like my Great Aunt Margaret from Enniskerry – but inside I'm glowing. How could this not be addictive – approbation from my two favourite people in the world?

'Yeah, right.'

Another imaginary whisper?

Halfway down the attic stairs stands Scarlett, wearing the tiniest dress I think I've ever seen: yellow shiny skirt just skimming her thighs, sequined blue bodice glittering in the low lights, long slim legs in fishnets, chunky silver and black heels higher than my headdress.

My stupid awkward headdress that hit the top of the bedroom door as I came out to be 'observed'.

And who on earth am I kidding? Mutton dressed as lamb.

'Blimey,' Frankie mutters, the air between Scarlett and him crackling uncomfortably. Slowly she blinks.

'You look very pretty.' I smile at her, feeling the heat creep up my chest. I'll be all blotchy within the minute.

'You look very – silver.' Scarlett is blithe. 'Like a big piece of tinfoil.'

'Scarlett Bianca King!' Her father's solidarity warms me. 'That's *bloody* short.'

I realise the reprimand is for the outfit, not for the way she spoke to me.

'It's a fairy-tale dress, Daddy,' she pouts, giving a twirl. 'Just like you ordered.'

The look on Frank's face is one I recognise from days gone by: days of forcing him to eat his greens. It is almost mutinous.

'Really?' Matthew's sigh is hearty.

'I'm Snow White, Dad. You can hardly object. It's your theme – fairy tales.' The whine creeps into Scarlett's voice. 'You *said...*'

I hear Marlena: *I'll give you tinker, you little...*

I glance at Frankie. I wouldn't like to guess what's going through his head right now.

'Oh, but I *can* object.' Matthew really frowns now. 'And I do. Go and put a proper dress on immediately. People are about to arrive.'

Scarlett flicks me a look. One chance...

'Leave her.' I put my hand on his arm. 'She looks gorgeous. And it's a special occasion.'

She steps towards us, and I see our reflections in the great gilt mirror. Scarlett and I held together like a photograph in the curling frame.

Who is the fairest of them all? I think wryly.

Of course it's Scarlett, without any doubt. She does look gorgeous – and far, far older than her fourteen years. Matthew's right – it's entirely inappropriate. The whole look is almost pornographic: shiny red lips glistening above a low-cut Snow White bodice, laced to within an inch of its life; face young and wide-eyed as a fawn's; a creamy cleavage most would die for.

She's about as innocent as Hannah Montana in her reincarnation as Miley Cyrus.

Before anyone can move, Luke canters down the stairs, almost shoving his twin sister over as he skids to a halt.

'I can't get my stupid quiver to stay on.' He leans over his shoulder awkwardly. 'It keeps slipping down.'

'Robin Hood, Robin Hood, riding through the glen!' Frankie winks at the boy.

Luke. Slightly overweight and solid where his sister is svelte, not so handsome – but amiable where she is spiky. Always worried whether everyone is all right, used to soothing the neuroses of the female egos around him, I'd imagine.

'Here.' Frank adjusts the strap for him. 'There you go, Mr Hood. Nice costume, mate. Very cool!'

Luke beams. I think he rather reveres Frankie. 'Thanks a lot.' No edge to him. 'I like your costume, Jeanie!'

'Thank you.' I smile at the boy fast becoming my favourite stepchild, and he tips his pointy green hat to me. A most gallant Robin Hood.

It goes without saying that Frankie hasn't bothered with a costume, but he's scrubbed up well, my boy, in a white shirt, his freckly face open beneath artfully tousled hair. But he's less than friendly again now, still mutinous, refusing to look at Scarlett at all.

'Dancing Queen' suddenly belts out of the conservatory.

'Jesus! Abba? I told George not to let anyone tinker with the system!' Frankie is incensed. 'For God's sake…' He thunders down the stairs. ' "Royal Blood" is our first track.'

Scarlett tries to slink down after him as the doorbell rings.

'Hey!' Matthew barks at her. 'You're not going anywhere.'

'*Please*, Daddy.' She drops her head, lower lip trembling. 'I'll make it up to you…'

'Matthew,' I say, gently.

For a moment Matthew looks at me as if he doesn't know me – and then he smiles, the kind of smile that still makes my tummy flutter.

'Ah, Jeanie, all right, you win,' he sighs. 'You've got your step-mum to thank, Scarlett. Just *don't* tuck into the mulled wine, okay?'

'Course not.' She smiles prettily, tugging her skirt over her neat little bottom. 'Thanks, Daddy. Thanks, Jeanie.'

But I'm sure the look I catch in the mirror as her father guides her downstairs isn't gratitude.

Plodding behind them, Luke's look of sympathy doesn't entirely placate me either.

'Is Mum coming?' is the last thing I hear from Scarlett as they disappear round the staircase's bend.

Mum? Oh God. I really, really hope not.

7.15 p.m.

Alone on the landing, outside the room that's always locked, I hoick my corset up in the ostentatious mirror. My cleavage certainly doesn't look so eye-catching now I've seen Scarlett's.

But is anything ever what it seems at first sight? Isn't there always more beneath the surface than we are capable of first imagining?

The big mirror is out of place here, fitting so badly with Matthew's minimalist style I don't know why Kaye didn't take it – especially as she seems to have fought for so much else.

Perhaps it didn't match her new décor.

Décor that's cost Matthew at least one limb, in a two-floor penthouse apartment in a gated estate on the other side of town.

But we don't dwell on the past much, he and I. Matthew is all about fresh starts. Which has suited me, of course – up to a point. Sometimes though it's bewildering to live with someone I know so little about. I'm learning on the job.

A new wave of fear washes over me, and I struggle against it. I'll sort this all out in the next twenty-four hours – then we'll be safe again.

Still, I wish passionately that Marlena was coming tonight. But why would my little sister, no doubt seeing the New Year in with the great and good – or, more likely, the malign and glamorous – eschew swigging Cristal in the capital's most fashionable haunts to drag herself out to the sticks for curling canapés – even if they are made by a top-notch firm called Classy Catering (yes, really).

No, I realise Marlena won't abandon the bright lights to dance with a sweaty accountant who'll get too close after one glass too many; to sing a tuneless 'Auld Lang Syne' at midnight with a load of drunk suburbanites she'll never see again.

And if Marlena *isn't* in high society tonight, she'll be on the trail of someone from low society, pursuing her next story.

Perhaps I could have been more honest about why I need her now…

'Jeanie!'

I jump again.

Matthew's waiting at the foot of the stairs. Quickly I switch on my smile and walk down to meet him.

'Come on, *Mrs* King.' He holds a hand out.

I greet the first arrivals awkwardly in the doorway: the Thompsons from number 52 whom I met over Christmas drinks – he a jovial solicitor, she a dowdy housewife. They hover in their coats, uncomfortable with their gaudy costumes – too early, they've just realised, too late.

Are they comparing me to Kaye?

Don't be such a drip, Jean, Marlena's voice resonates in my head.

I am a drip though. The good girl: always the staid, boring one, that's me.

This is your home now! Don't be scared, for Christ's sake.

I draw myself up to my inconsiderable height, push my shoulders back and slip my hand into my new husband's.

'Hello.' I smile at Anne Thompson. 'Can I take your coat? Oh you *do* look nice.' She looks entirely ridiculous as a crêpechested Cinderella in pink satin, wearing so much foundation it's collected in her wrinkles. But I see trepidation in her eyes, and I feel sorry for her. 'That shade of pink really suits you. And where did you get your lovely cape?'

MARLENA

Okay, so I know what you're thinking – but come on!

I already said I wasn't going. And, I mean, would you have gone, in my position?

Sure, I love Jeanie, like I love no one else really – but trawling out there? That would be one step too far. New Year's Eve in the home counties, all Crimplene and fake Barbour – or, even worse, flouncy WAG hairdos and spray tans. Most fun to be had: warm Chardonnay, sweaty husbands and a spot of fantasising about swapping wives for the night? No ta.

To be honest, I had better things to do on New Year's Eve 2014. Biggest night of the year: bigger fish to fry, I could say.

There was Levi, first off. He's cute – like properly cute. He's what the kids call 'buff'. Body like Brad Pitt's back in the day, pretty face to match. All smooth caramel-coloured skin and muscles where they're meant to be, you know, where you want to stroke 'em. And whilst we're not official – I don't do official, you know – I suppose I kind of like him. We are more 'Netflix and chilling', as Sharon on reception likes to say when she's swiping left on her Tinder. Horrible expression maybe, but it suits me just fine right now. I don't need complication in my life.

And then once that was done, once I'd seen Levi, and the single malt was drunk, and the itch was scratched, there was the small case of the girl named Nasreen.

Nasreen, who I'd met at her sixth-form college just a month ago when I'd given a talk on the pros and cons of digital journalism; Nasreen who had upped and disappeared from her home in Hounslow, just before Christmas. Done her Christmas shopping, left it all neatly wrapped in the wardrobe she shared with her little sister, under her winter jumpers – and then just vanished, without a whisper to her distraught family. No note. Oh yes, sorry – a text. One text to her sister, saying:

Don't worry, sis, I'm fine ☺

And that was it.

I felt it was my duty – very much my duty, all things considered – to find out what had happened.

So please don't blame me for not noticing right there and then that Jeanie needed me.

And anyway, at that point, I'm not sure Jeanie even did.

At that point, NYE 2014, she was still basking in the warm glow of new love and lots of sex. You know what it's like, that first year: can't get out of bed, can't get them out of your head – like Kylie said. Okay, well, the first six months at least. That's the longest I've ever managed without getting bored. Without having to run.

At that point, it hadn't all hit the fan. Not yet anyway.

So. Don't look at me like that. Please.

Cos what I'd also say is this: family – they'll either make you, or they'll break you.

As an adult, of course, you get to walk away – if you have the courage. As a child, you have little choice. Generally you're stuck right there.

So. You can have that nugget of wisdom for free – Marlena Randall, 2016.

And here's one more: *keep your best friends close; keep your enemies closer*. Now I didn't make *that* one up: some old Chinese general did – according to Wiki anyway. Wise words, my friends, wise words. That's what I told Jeanie when she was worrying about Scarlett.

Keep her close.

Because how do you know *who* has it in for you? How do any of us really know?

JEANIE

31 DECEMBER 2014

9 p.m.

Despite all the dancing, the smiling at new faces, the shaking of hands and kissing of cheeks, I never shake my feeling of unease.

I try my best to feel like I am part of something in a way I haven't been for a very long time. Or ever maybe. I really do try.

I *had* felt ready to face the bigger world officially, for the first time since we'd married at Berkhamsted Town Hall a month ago. Not a white wedding, more a foggy grey one – but definitely a whirlwind, winter one. I was so happy on the day – I thought my heart might burst. Frankie and I, we were part of a proper family now, I told myself, and it didn't even matter when Marlena didn't come.

I was happy, despite Scarlett scowling her way through the ceremony, chewing gum then drinking her one glass of champagne too fast at the French restaurant, meaning she felt so sick she had to sit outside with Matthew for a good twenty minutes. And Luke spent most of his time texting – his mother, he said, when I asked. When Matthew returned with Scarlett, dropping a kiss on my head, it was quite obvious she'd been crying.

Inside Frankie had just told me he was dropping out of Hull, that art wasn't for him. He'd reapply to do music production the following September. It was for the best, he kept saying, and I found myself downing my own champagne pretty fast too.

Despite all of that, I kept telling myself it would be okay. It wasn't just the two of us any more; it was all of us. And it'd be fine.

How wrong could I be?

10 p.m.

By ten o'clock – a bit tipsy, as Nan would have said – I've managed to dash away any thoughts of being recognised. Matthew, chatting to his golf mates, grins at me, as Sylvia Jones from the cul-de-sac, pink cheeked from too much Prosecco, asks if I fancy a stab at Nordic walking. 'Scandi stuff is what it's all about! I do love IKEA, don't you?'

I am relieved at how relaxed Frank seems, joking nearby with his mate George, whom he met recently at a local gig. They've chosen their playlist together carefully, no doubt frustrated by the limitations of old fogies who prefer Coldplay to Kurt Cobain. I look at him, and I think: *It will be all right.*

Before I can go and say hello to them, the caterer signals from the kitchen door.

'A delivery just came,' she tells me. 'The man said sorry it's so late – the traffic was bad. I think it's more fireworks.'

'Oh they'll be Matthew's.' I peer over her shoulder. 'Just leave them with the other boxes, by the back doors. Thanks.'

'Of course. Actually, though, it's in your name…'

I feel eyes on me and am distracted by Scarlett's cold stare. She is talking to a red-haired, eye-patched pirate, an awful lot of eyeliner on the visible eye, regarding me with a look I can't read.

Bravely I go over.

'Hello,' I toast them with my half-full glass. 'Are you from Peter Pan?'

The pirate peers down at herself as if she is surprised to see her costume. 'Yes, I suppose I am.'

'I went for Wizard of Oz, myself, which isn't strictly fairy tale, of course,' I confide. 'But I didn't think anyone would mind.'

'It's not fairy tale at all, is it – Oz? But it *is* your party.' The woman is very serious. 'So you can do what you like.'

Her tone throws me a little. I wait for Scarlett to introduce us, and when I realise she isn't going to, I stick out my hand. 'I'm Jeanie—' I was going to say Jeanie Randall, but of course I'm not any more, and saying *Jeanie King,* especially standing next to Scarlett, still seems presumptuous. So I say, 'I hope you're enjoying yourself…?'

Nothing.

'Sorry,' I flounder on. 'I don't know your name…'

'Alison.' Finally the woman takes my hand, gingerly, as if it alarms her. 'Alison Day.'

'Very nice to meet you, Alison. I'm enjoying meeting all Matt's friends at the moment.' Another pause. I feel myself start to sweat slightly – but I plunge on anyway. 'How do you know—?'

'Through Kaye. And how's Luke?' Alison pulls a sad face at Scarlett. 'Is he better?'

'Better?' Scarlett swings back on her giant heels, eyes darting round the room. 'Er, yeah. He's fine – he's over there.'

'I bet your mum's missing you, if you're both here.'

I take an involuntary step back.

'Not really.' Scarlett shrugs. 'She's out with Yass tonight.'

'Typical Kaye.' Alison's single eye fixes on me. 'Always the life and soul, eh? She loves a party herself, doesn't she?'

'Yeah, s'pose.' Scarlett twiddles her glass round by the stem. 'But Dad didn't really go in for this sort of thing then, did he?'

'Oh I don't know,' Alison says. 'Your mum certainly knows how to throw a party.'

Scarlett shoots her some kind of look, and she stops.

I don't look down, but I know my chest will be flushing horribly.

'Not this type of party though. She likes a bit more – glamour. I guess this must be your influence, then, er – *Jenny*,' Alison says. Why can't I read her tone? 'The fancy dress?'

'Jeanie,' I mumble. 'It's Jeanie actually.'

'Sorry.' She smiles now. 'I'm terrible with names. And it's hard when I was so used to Matthew and Kaye. So sudden…'

Scarlett's lower lip trembles again.

'Oh, pet.' Alison pats her. 'Don't get upset. How's Daisy by the way? So awful. Is she any better now?'

Scarlett lets out a stifled sort of sob, and then Alison looks really worried.

I think I remember hearing about Daisy – a pet dog who died recently.

'Scarlett,' I begin rather hopelessly, and then suddenly Matthew is by my side, thank God. Scarlett wipes her nose on the back of her shiny blue sleeve, reminding me how young she really is.

'Matthew,' Alison says coolly, offering a cheek to be kissed.

'Alison.' Matthew obliges. 'No Sean tonight then?'

'He's in Dubai. On business.'

'Really?' Matthew is equally cool. 'Strange time of year to leave you alone.'

'Yes, well. He's very busy.' It is Alison's turn to go pink. 'And not *all* men aren't to be trusted.'

'I wasn't suggesting you shouldn't trust him, Alison. Please send him my best. I have to say, it was really him I was hoping to see tonight.' Matthew smiles. 'To talk business, I mean, of course.'

'Of course.' Alison manages a tight little smile herself.

'Now, if you'll excuse me'—Matthew puts an arm around both mine and Scarlett's shoulders—'I'm stealing my girls away. I've got a toast to make in a bit. Where's Luke?'

'Dancing with that stupid Joe.' Scarlett scowls and slinks off to refill her glass – with the non-alcoholic punch I hope. Judging by the smell of whisky wafting around her, I am pretty sure she's been at something stronger. I should tell Matthew. But if I do, how is that going to help things between me and her?

So I keep quiet.

Matthew guides me through the throng, past Luke and his schoolmates. We wave at them as a portly man with suspiciously black hair and too many ruffles for his fat cheeks greets Matthew cheerily.

'Good do, King. Great vino. Fucking uncomfortable costume though.' The man runs a fat finger round his sweaty neckband. 'Only wore it cos the missus said I'd be rewarded later if I did, eh?' He gives a horrible wink. 'Fancy the shooting range soon?'

'Perhaps.' Matthew grins. 'If my lovely wife will spare me for an hour. This is Detective Chief Inspector Peters, Jeanie, otherwise known as Kipper.'

'Don't ask.' Sweaty Kipper winks lasciviously and I smile back.

'I wasn't going to,' I assure him. *Shooting?* Did Matthew really think that was fun?

'Good to see the kids doing so well. Enchanted, my dear.' He bows over my hand, and I blush.

'Nice to meet you, er – Kipper.'

They chat about clay-pigeon distances, while I watch Scarlett move over to the decks, loitering by Frankie and George. Frank gives her half a polite smile and carries on chatting. Still, she lingers there, staring into the crowd, sucking an ice cube provocatively as Frank puts on a remix of Little Richard's 'Good Golly Miss Molly'.

'So was she being vile?' Matthew kisses my forehead as Kipper is whisked away to do the twist by his tiny wife.

'Who?' I ask, surprised. He's never acknowledged Scarlett's behaviour before, but it'd be a relief, actually, if we could discuss it...

'Old Ali Baba!' Matt shakes his head. 'She seems to be getting worse in her middle age, I'm afraid. A bit... bitter.'

'Well she was a bit – unfriendly maybe. Who is she?'

'Alison? Scarlett's godmother unfortunately. Old school friend of Kaye's.'

'Oh I see. Of Kaye's.' Even saying her name makes me feel a bit funny. My warm glow of earlier has dissipated.

'Husband Sean's a decent bloke though. It was him I was hoping to see actually.' Distractedly Matthew checks the time. 'Whizz with figures. I wanted to tap him up about some stocks someone's selling. Fancy a spin round the dance floor?'

Some time later, when Matthew goes to sort out the fireworks, I notice Alison intercepting him by the patio doors. I don't have my glasses on, so I can't make out the conversation, which is animated. When I look for her later, she's gone.

It is annoying – I am annoyed with myself – but I can't quite regain the happy feeling I had earlier.

Perhaps I am still chasing the buzzy feeling I had when I met Matthew six months ago: the feeling I'd landed the jackpot.

And meeting Matthew had been a complete fluke.

Unusually I'd been in London for the weekend when my old friend Jill rang out of the blue, begging for company at a work do.

'Corporate speed dating,' she'd coaxed. 'I emailed you about it before – remember? What's not to like? Men with jobs *and* money.'

'Great,' I'd sighed. 'Now they just need their own teeth and hair too.'

Jill and I had been friends since I'd done my PGCE, about five years after Frankie was born – and just after I'd met Simon. I'd pulled myself out of the hell that ensued and plodded on in education – but Jill had quickly given up teaching. Never loving it like I did, she cited lack of 'prospects' for her decision to work for a big City bank.

On this particular visit, I had noted her prospects appeared to be stressing her badly. She had terrible skin for the first time, and she was lonely since splitting with her husband a few years before – but she was also working all hours.

I only went to her party because she'd needed solidarity. I was lurking in the corner, nursing a warm margarita and watching Jill heroically tackle a hedge-fund manager with two chins and hairy ears, when Matthew honed in on me – to my enduring surprise and much to the hilarity of his laddish mates.

When he asked for my number, Jill was gallant about it, despite the fact it was her who'd noticed Matthew, prior to Two Chins. I felt bad though and tried to make amends by buying her a horrendously expensive ticket for *Gypsy* a few weeks later.

When Jill had heard we were getting married, she'd sent a nice card. But she couldn't come to the New Year's Eve party, she'd said.

Just before twelve, Matthew makes a charming speech, welcoming Frankie and me to the family. He kisses my lips as the crowd toasts us; I flush as scarlet as my stepdaughter's name, to Frankie and George's whoops. Luke's shy hug delights me. Maybe this is it now.

I look around for Scarlett to share the moment with us – but she is nowhere to be seen.

They are about to set off rockets to mark the New Year; George is making a big hash of fixing the fireworks into the flowerpots set out for them. Perhaps Scarlett is out there too?

But she isn't.

I search all the rooms downstairs. No Scarlett.

Perhaps the alcohol has taken its toll. Perhaps she's conked out somewhere.

I have a duty of care now, don't I? I want to forge this relationship properly, to look out for her. And I've already ignored her possible drinking once...

I find Scarlett sitting on her bed in her pink turret room, which is still decorated for a much younger child. The girl is sprawled on her frilly double bed, all eyes and legs, glued to her phone.

She doesn't look up – but she knows I am there.

'Hi, lovey.' I stay in the doorway, feeling suddenly shy. 'Everything okay?'

'Why wouldn't it be?' she asks, staring at her screen. The fluffy bathrobe over her little dress seems both babyish and incongruous as I look away from the silver frames of Kaye and Scarlett hugging on the beach in Ibiza, on a hill in the Lake District, on a boat somewhere with a very blue sky.

Of Kaye and Matthew, kissing on a sunlounger.

'Well you weren't there when Daddy—'

'*My* dad, you mean?' She does look up now, her eyes narrowed.

'Er, yes. Your dad. When – when Matthew made a little toast.'

'I heard it.' Scarlett's voice is flat. 'Then I came up here.'

'That's a shame.'

'To get away *actually*.' She couldn't be more pointed if she tried.

'Oh I see.' I am well used to dealing with teenagers, but she makes me feel anxious. Still, in for a penny, etc. 'Luke's downstairs, having a whale of a time. And I just thought – well it'd be nice for us all to be together, don't you…?'

Do I sound like I'm telling her off? I take a small step into the room, and she looks at me like I've just violated something.

'No one comes in here. Apart from…' Her eyes are huge, her eyeliner melting below them. 'Apart from me – and Luke – and *Daddy*.'

Outside her small window, a golden firework explodes in the dark velvet sky. Together we watch the brilliant sparks falling back to earth.

'Happy New Year!' I muster as much enthusiasm as I can. 'I love that picture, by the way. Did you do it?'

I point at the small, framed painting of an old window, surrounded by snow, a red rose growing around the ebony frame. There is a dash of blood in the snow on the sill.

'It's total shit,' Scarlett says flatly, without looking at either the picture or me. 'I did it in Year 7. Can you tell my dad I want him?'

'Oh – why?' I can't help myself.

She looks up at me again. 'I just do.' We stare at each other for a moment until she begins to pout. 'To come and tuck me in of course.'

Really? Then I think, *She's just being silly. Childish. She* is *a child.*

'All right.' I back away. 'I'll tell him. And I'll… I'll say goodnight myself then.'

'Night.' She is fixated on her phone again. I am sure I've glimpsed a packet of Silk Cut in her dressing-gown pocket – but I leave it. Enough for one night.

On the way back downstairs, feeling rattled, I catch my reflection in the horrible gilt mirror.

Don't be ridiculous. She's just a little girl, Jeanie, I tell myself. *She's not a threat.*

Still, I don't dare rock the boat any more tonight. I am tired and a bit drunk; she is suddenly cross about something. Or rather *more* cross.

I don't tell Matthew about the cigarettes – or the tucking up, because when I get downstairs, Frankie is looking for me.

'You missed the fireworks,' he says, and he is frowning, 'and there's something odd about one of them.'

'What?' I feel exhausted, my feet aching in the rarely worn high heels.

He walks into the kitchen. People are starting to leave, which relieves me, because I've had enough excitement for one day, enough smiling at strangers. I don't really like parties.

'This one.' Frankie kneels by a box. 'It's called a time bomb apparently.'

'Oh yes?' I plonk myself down on a stool and ease my heels off. He shoves the box towards me. Amongst sawdust nestles what looks like old-fashioned sticks of dynamite with a hand-written tag attached.

'Yeah.' Frankie pulls it out. 'Only it's not a firework at all. I think it's real.'

'Real?' I am confused. 'Real fireworks?'

'No, real dynamite.' He looks worried. 'And it's addressed to you, Mum. The box has got your name on. Look.'

I do. It's the box the courier brought, and it says my name, *Jeanie Randall,* and in smaller letters after it: RIP.

JEANIE

1 JANUARY 2015

8 a.m.

A whole new year! A new start. I look out at the bare apple tree nearest the window, at the miserable wet day, and I huddle closer to a gently snoring Matt.

If it's all a fresh new start, why is my stomach rolling with anxiety?

I turn my head from the mail locked in the dresser and from Miss Turnbull's, '*I thought I recognised your name*' of yesterday. It's only a matter of time. I've got to tell Matt before someone else does, but…

I can't bear to shatter the illusion. I can't bear to knock the light out of his eyes when he looks at me.

As if he's sensed me watching him sleep, Matthew opens his eyes and pulls me closer.

'Come here, you,' he says, kissing my neck, and I shiver and snuggle into him, thinking, I *will* deal with this – only not just now…

Half an hour later I leave Matt sleeping again and slide out of bed. It is miserable and grey, and I am definitely a little hungover – unusual for me. One glass too many last night.

George has stayed, as well as Luke's friend Joe, and I thought Matthew might have put one of them in the spare room – but they are on the sofa bed in the living room.

'Still haven't found the key,' Matt had said absently when I'd talked of making up fresh beds yesterday, and I'd had another look through the key drawer in the kitchen with no luck. 'It'll turn up', he added. 'Or we'll have to change the lock. Use the sofa bed for now, in the study.'

The key had been lost by one of Matthew's sister's kids, visiting from America in the summer. They'd lost it playing hide and seek apparently. When I asked Matthew what was in the room, he laughed and said it was the second spare room, full of junk, and I was welcome to look if I could just find the key.

But I can't. I've searched everywhere for that key since I moved in: everywhere. The locked door unnerves me every time I pass it.

Downstairs is deserted, although the cornflakes are out on the side, and the TV is chatting away to itself.

A huge cooked breakfast would be perfect now, a nice way to ease everyone into January. Then perhaps a walk, or a film in front of the fire – *The Sound of Music* perhaps, or *The Wizard of Oz* – something cosy and family oriented, in honour of last night.

The news comes on. Debt, death, the Pakistani media accused of pandering to extremists, followed by someone from the Metropolitan Police talking about the schoolgirl who vanished on Christmas Eve. She'd taken only her passport and one small bag of clothes and was last seen on CCTV catching the Heathrow Express. The fear is that she was headed to Syria; they think she might have been enticed out there to marry a Daesh jihadi. A few photos are shown of a pretty, head-scarfed girl and then one of her with her English boyfriend, laughing on a fairground ride. The police spokesman goes on to say that this relationship had possibly been a decoy, planned to throw her family off the scent. Her older sister makes a plea for information and then starts to cry.

Poor family, I think, imagining my own sixth-formers. They were such babies: not ready for the world, let alone war.

It is too early in the day – in the year – for such bad news. I turn it off, clutching my tea for warmth.

The house is strangely silent, considering all the people sleeping in it, and I have that sense again that the old walls are whispering.

Whilst I'm looking for the eggs, something creaks nearby.

Then I hear it – I definitely hear muttering, coming from outside.

'Frank?' I call. No answer. 'Scarlett? Luke? Is that you?'

Nothing.

I'm just not used to old houses that creak with age – that's the truth. I'm used to newbuilds and council flats.

I've cracked the eggs into a basin and begun to whisk them when I hear footsteps running somewhere above me and whispering.

In my fright, I slop the batter everywhere. Whisk in hand, I stare at the ceiling – and then there is another noise. The crash of breaking glass.

'Matthew? Frank?'

For God's sake, why does no one answer? My fear makes me irritated. With an action braver than I feel, I pull open the lopsided door at the back of the kitchen that leads to the rickety stairwell.

'Hello?' I call up the dark little stairs. 'Who is it?'

There is no answer. I turn the light on – and something explodes. My own cry resonates in my ears.

The light bulb has blown.

Don't be daft, Jeanie! Old houses, old electrics…

I go back into the kitchen and switch on my phone's torch.

Gingerly I walk up the first few stairs until I see something in the shadows: a picture, I think, lying smashed halfway up the staircase.

Shaking the broken shards of glass away, I hurry back downstairs with it.

It is our wedding photograph, I realise in the daylight, my heart sinking. Only a month old, in an elegant silver frame that the children had bought us – and it is completely smashed.

I look down at my stupidly smiling face, gazing at the camera with all the hope in the world, Matthew's arms around me on the happiest day of my life.

The last time I saw this photograph – last night probably, before the party – it had been safely on the dressing table in our bedroom.

Hands trembling, I clean up the glass on the stairs as quickly as I can. Then I drink a pint of water with a couple of aspirin, hoping I'll feel more human soon, and realise from a single drop of ruby blood on the white worktop that I've cut my finger on a shard of glass.

Sucking the blood away, it strikes me once again this marriage might not be as welcome to all as it was to me.

As I am flipping the first batch of pancakes about ten minutes later, Scarlett appears. In her baby blue tracksuit and matching beanie, mascara smudged below her eyes, she looks her real age again. It is odd how that happens, the years fading away – and I find her rudeness more forgivable when I remember she's only a child. A rather lost one, at that.

'Morning!' I don't want to show anyone I am rattled. 'Sleep well? How do you want your eggs?'

'I hate eggs.' She swipes her phone. 'Disgusting chicken mess.'

'Oh.' I keep smiling. 'Well there's pancakes, American style. Do you like them? Frankie says maple syrup and bacon's the best; I like blueberries. What do you reckon?' Nothing. 'You could flip some if you fancy?'

'I don't want anything,' she says dully. 'Mum's picking me up now.'

I feel it viscerally.

'She's not actually.' Matthew comes in, yawning, looking slightly the worse for wear. 'She just messaged to say her car's got a flat. I'll give you a lift in a minute.'

'I want to go now. Where's Luke?'

'Gone to play football with Michael and Joe.' Matthew sifts through the fridge, gulping orange juice straight from the carton.

'Matt!' I reprove with a smile. 'Do you want a glass?'

'Too much cheap champagne.' He winks at me. 'And not enough sleep, eh, honey?'

I blush, thinking of last night, after everyone had gone and he'd taken me to bed.

'Can we go now?' Scarlett mutters, texting again, and I wait for him to say, *Yes, after breakfast*, but he doesn't.

He says, 'Have you seen my car keys, love?' as he rifles through stuff on the side.

I look at all the food, the piping coffee, the stack of pancakes glistening with syrup, and for the first time since I've lived here, since I've been confronted with Scarlett's obvious hostility, I feel a small flame of anger.

I bite my lip. *Good girl, Jean.* 'By the recipe books?' I suggest. 'In the Piglet bowl?'

'Aha!' He holds up his keys triumphantly. 'Come on, tiger.' He ruffles Scarlett's hair. 'Stick mine in the oven, would you, Jeanie? Won't be long.'

'Sure.' I smile brightly. 'No problem. Bye, Scarlett! Have a good day.'

Scarlett doesn't look back as she leaves the room; she doesn't say goodbye, still glued to her phone.

'Matt,' I say quietly, as he waits for her to get her bag. 'Our wedding photo – the one in the bedroom…'

'What about it?'

'Did you move it?' I can't remember if I saw it there yesterday, during all the party hullabaloo. 'It seems to have got broken…' I couldn't say, *Someone seems to have thrown it down the stairs,* could I?

'Oh, hon! It's fine if you broke it, really! We can get the glass replaced, no sweat.'

'No, but I didn't—'

'Dad!' Scarlett commands from the front door.

'Coming!' he practically salutes.

When I put the pancakes in the oven to keep them warm, I bang the door very, very hard a few times, so that Frankie, sloping in wearing last night's clothes, holds his head dramatically.

'Blimey, Mum. Hold it down, would you?'

It couldn't be helped, I suppose, as I think about Matthew driving over to Kaye's new place. The amazing Kaye. Matthew has to put his children first – that is the right thing to do, I know. But the thought of Kaye galls me this morning.

About a month before I moved in, before I brought Frankie here to live – when I was unsettled still, trying to get my bearings – when Matthew was out one morning, I took the opportunity to seek out his past a bit.

The truth was I needed to know what my predecessor looked like. The not knowing was torturing me. And so I discovered the framed photos of her in Scarlett and Luke's rooms. Well why wouldn't there be? I picked each one up and stared for a while, trying to imagine what it was like to be this immaculate woman. Then I replaced them exactly where I found them and shut the doors behind me.

So I'm aware not only that Kaye looks amazing but that she also seems to have been extraordinarily good at spending Matthew's money to achieve that look. Still *is* good at it, judging from the mentions Matthew's made of the hefty maintenance he pays.

But it's all part of a healthy divorce apparently, these photos: keeping the other partner present in the child's life. My parenting book is explicit: after a split, allow the other parent to still exist. It shows the children's welfare is more important than your own.

That same day I found the photographs, I'd also contemplated climbing into the attic that ran the length of the roof, suddenly paranoid, anxious I might have missed something vital – but Matthew came back just as I was about to attempt it.

I shoved the ladder back up and rushed back downstairs again, feeling guilty and sordid for my intentions. It *was* paranoia.

But in all honesty, I tried *all* the doors that day. I told myself I wasn't prying; I was just sizing things up before I moved in. I'm not naturally nosey, or even particularly curious – unlike my little sister, who makes a living delving into the lives of others. I just wanted to understand my surroundings and what I was coming to. It was so alien to my old life.

The only room I couldn't look into was the locked one on the first floor. Unsurprising, though, that a key is missing in a house with two spare rooms, four used bedrooms, a study, a utility room and a tiny gym – weights, running machine – behind a partition in the double garage.

I live in a place the likes of which I'd barely imagined.

Some time during New Year's Day, as the rain lashes the windows and we turn the designer fire up, I remember to ask Matt what has been niggling me since last night.

'Who's Daisy?' I ask, and he looks surprised.

'Why do you ask?'

'Alison. She asked Scarlett how she was.'

'Oh I see.' He moves a cushion irritably. 'Daisy was Scarlett's dog.'

'I thought so!' I grin sheepishly, feeling guilty I'd thought anything else. 'Is that the puppy old Miss Trunchbull reported?'

'Think so…' Matthew moves again and then winces. 'Can't get comfy. Think I sprained my wrist slightly at squash the other day.'

'I'm sorry,' I say. 'Do you want me to look at it?'

'No, it's fine, hon.' He smiles as the phone rings; I leave it for him to answer. No one really has my number here yet.

'Hello? Hello?' He frowns. 'Can you hear me?'

I look up. 'Who is it?' I mouth.

'Hello?' he repeats and then tosses the receiver aside. 'Bloody cold callers.'

'They're a pain, aren't they?' I look for the remote to turn the sound back up.

'Especially when they just heavy breathe down the phone.'

I glance at Matthew again, unsure whether he is joking. But he is laughing at Jimmy Carr now, and I leave it alone. I don't mention our wedding picture again either, because I know Matthew thinks it was me, covering my misdemeanour up.

But cold callers on New Year's night? Seems unlikely somehow.

JEANIE

5 JANUARY 2015
10 a.m.

Matthew's gone to Manchester for a business meeting. I've written various thank-you emails to people, done some final changes of address. Now I'm packing up the Christmas decorations, the drone of daytime TV in the background – and I'm thinking about work. Or worrying rather.

If I don't get a job, what on earth will I do with myself? I've worked really hard all my life – too hard, often, crawling in and out of bed, completely exhausted, getting through the days. Two jobs when I was at college, juggling childcare when Frankie was little and I was alone...

I've certainly never had a choice before whether to work or not. And if I don't, I will feel useless.

But after what happened at Seaborne last year, I feel useless anyway. Redundant and afraid. What I thought I had to offer no longer feels so tangible. Despite my new happiness with Matthew, I don't know which way to turn. And I feel increasingly on edge.

On Sunday I went for a January run, which meant I had about another four weeks of forcing myself round the local streets before not running again until next January. I was panting home, listening to a podcast of a show about Joplin's life, when a white Range Rover pulled around the corner too fast, nearly taking me with it.

I jumped back quickly, banging my ankle on the kerb.

'Hey!' I called crossly, but the car disappeared round the corner, oblivious to pedestrians.

At home, the television was blaring away to itself.

'Did you check the roast?' I called, planning to slip straight upstairs before I was spotted for the red-faced sweaty mess I was.

'Jeanie?' I heard Matthew from somewhere deep in the house.

'Just getting in the shower!' I ran up the stairs. There was a strange exotic smell in the air: definitely not roast beef.

Matthew appeared silently above me on the landing.

'Oh hi!' I'd been rumbled. 'Don't look at me please!'

'Why?' He was shoving something into the back pocket of his jeans.

'Oh nothing, just being silly.' I sniffed. The smell was stronger up here. 'What's that smell? Like – roses, or something...'

'I don't know.' Matthew's jaw was very set as I drew level with him.

'Has something happened?' Fear shot through me.

'Has Mum gone?' Luke appeared in the hall below us. 'My tablet's in her car. I've got homework I need to look up.'

'Mum?' I was surprised to see Luke. I didn't remember Matthew telling me they'd be here, but...

'No, she's gone.' Matthew gave me a quick squeeze as he went down past me. 'I need to check the potatoes, hon.' Which meant he hadn't checked them earlier. He didn't like cooking – that was becoming evident, though I didn't mind. It gave me something to do; I quite liked feeding everyone.

'I thought she was still with you.' Luke sounded plaintive. 'I heard you up there.'

Upstairs?

'Lucas, she's gone, all right?' Matthew disappeared into the kitchen, the door banging loudly behind him.

'She said they had stuff to sort out.' Luke looked up at me apologetically. 'They were talking in the kitchen, so I didn't want to disturb them – but then they went up. Dad gets a bit cross if I interrupt.'

'Don't worry, love.' Something about his worried round face reminded me a bit of Smudge, the old dog we inherited as kids from Gloria along the stairwell when she moved back to Trinidad. That was before my mother gave up on us, pets and home for the last time.

'Perhaps you could use Frankie's iPad? It's probably in the front room on the bookshelf.' Too late I prayed Frankie hadn't logged into anything like the Kardashian sex tape, as I'd caught him doing a few years back on our ancient PC in Hove. I didn't want to be responsible for my stepson being corrupted in any way.

'Thanks.' Luke looked cheered. 'I want to look up the ghost of Malum House.'

'The ghost?'

'Yeah.' His round eyes brightened. 'Hasn't Dad told you? About the Grey Lady? She died in the old turret, and now she walks the corridors at night – and you can smell violets too.'

'Oh wow!' I said. 'Violets, eh? No, I hadn't heard about her. I'll keep an eye out…'

'I've heard her because I'm sympathetic,' he said gravely, disappearing into the lounge. 'But Dad says I'm imagining it.'

* * *

Getting in the shower, I couldn't quite place the reason for the heavy weight in my stomach – but I did feel most uncomfortable at the idea of Kaye being in the house when I was out.

It was daft though. Obviously she'd lived here for a while before the divorce, and I'd always known that. They'd bought the house together when Matthew got his promotion to partner, the job he had now. She'd redesigned the interiors using some swanky architect – and then got bored, apparently, leaving Matthew to decide on everything.

When I moved to Berkhamsted, Marlena said, 'God, don't you think it'll be strange to live in another woman's trappings? Redecorate why don't you?'

But I put that comment down to therapist rubbish. Frankly I was used to rented places, and I didn't give it much thought.

I had more important things on my mind.

At lunch Scarlett was in a strange mood, more garrulous than usual, rattling on about things I didn't understand to do with her maternal grandma up in Cambridge and her mother's friends. She'd stop mid-subject and ask what I thought about her grandpa's dog or the new car her aunt had just got. I tried to enjoy being included – but of course I could have no opinion, really, on anything she said. My conversation was punctuated with, 'Oh goodness,' or, 'I don't know, I'm sure that's very nice though.'

After that Scarlett turned her attentions to Frankie, telling him about some nightclub she and her mate Gemma had been to last week, until Matthew raised an eyebrow and she realised the story wasn't appropriate. Luke plodded through his beef, glancing up every now and then to cast me his hangdog look, as if to apologise.

I thought Scarlett seemed younger again, picking at her food, twisting her hair round and round her finger, silver glitter nail varnish chipping away as she gazed at Frank.

In response Frankie was polite but quiet – strained, even, as he concentrated on eating.

I steered us on to a new, safer subject: favourite films. This was a topic beloved of Frankie ever since his film studies A level.

'Hitchcock's my favourite.' He was typically enthusiastic now. 'He's a proper master of his craft.'

'But – *Psycho*?' Matthew pulled a face. 'That's a horrible film, isn't it?'

'It's brilliant,' said Frank. 'But I prefer *Vertigo*. Or *Rebecca*. God, the atmosphere he creates in that.'

'I really hate *The Birds*.' I shuddered. 'I mean, it's a great film – but I do actually hate birds.' Something to do, I suspected, with Uncle Rog's manic mynah bird who'd tormented me and Marlena as kids, swearing at us, pecking at our heads and hands – until Rog's starving Alsatian tore it apart one day.

'All beaks and claws and…' I shuddered again and fetched the apple crumble.

'We're thinking about getting a dog,' Scarlett was saying as I returned.

Matthew pulled a face. 'Is that really a good idea?'

'Dad-*dy*,' she said in her best cross voice, and he sighed.

'Well you'll have to keep it at your mother's this time.'

'Blimey, is it raining inside?' Frankie said, wiping drips off his face. We all looked up.

'Shit!' Matthew leapt to his feet. Water was cascading through the ceiling. We ran upstairs to find my mistake.

Apparently I hadn't turned the shower off properly when I got back from my run – though I could have sworn I did.

I was quite sure I did.

'It's buggered, hon,' Matthew said later, after he'd cleaned up and I'd apologised profusely. 'The grout's so wet at the base it's not safe to use. Use the spare bathroom for now.'

* * *

'What exactly *did* happen to that puppy?' I asked Matthew tentatively later, half watching a boring costume drama.

'What puppy?' He was half asleep, drowsy with food and wine.

'The one Miss Trunchbull complained about.'

'Oh. It got out. It got run over.'

'How awful.' I thought of Smudge and how distraught I was when he died. 'Did you get a new one?'

'No.' He reached over for the wine. 'That's the only pet they ever had. That and Luke's hamster he had aged six, who lasted about two weeks. Two animal tragedies was enough.'

11 a.m.

I call the plumber about the leaking shower, and then I lug the Christmas box into the spare room that *isn't* locked, trailing tinsel behind me.

As I drop the box onto the bed, I see an earring on the carpet – a big silver hoop. It must be one of Scarlett's, because it's definitely not mine.

I sit for a minute to catch my breath, and it's then that I spot the handwritten envelope with my name on it, leaning against the dresser mirror. *Jeanie...*

Matthew, I think joyfully. A love letter? He's surprisingly romantic for a businessman. Tickets for something maybe, judging by the size and padding of the envelope. I remember my surprise on our third date – tickets to see Kings of Leon, after an early, expensive supper at Mark Hix's place in Soho. I'd never heard of Mark Hix before, but I'd gathered this was a place you got taken if your partner wanted to impress you.

Am I meant to open the letter now?

I struggled with presents as a small child – probably because they were so rare. I got walloped if I got caught squeezing packages, and it wasn't long before I learnt they were always disappointing. Something cheap and plastic, something out of hock, something that got stolen back or broken.

I hate surprises now – that's the truth.

I pick the earring up and put it on the dresser, staring at the envelope.

I can't resist it.

I take the envelope downstairs to the kitchen and switch the kettle on.

Feeling like George Smiley, I steam it open, grinning to myself. After I've read it, I'll reseal it and pretend I never saw it.

Unfolding the A4 sheet, I see it's a photocopy of something. A picture, a clue? I turn it over.

It's a bad, grainy copy of…

Oh Christ.

I sit heavily on a kitchen stool, hands shaking.

It *can't* be from Matthew.

I could make a guess at who it *was* from, except…

This time it is *inside* the house.

Panicking, I run upstairs, thinking I'll replace it – and then of course I realise I can't. If I leave it there, he'll see it eventually and…

Obviously I need to get rid of it – but before I can think, I hear a car in the drive. I find the key to the dresser in my make-up box and shove the envelope into the drawer, along with the other mail that Miss Trunchbull gave me and the first card.

Out of breath, I lean against the dressing table as if that will stop the nightmare from starting again.

Someone here knows what happened last year.

'Hi!' Matthew shouts up the stairs. 'Where's my gorgeous girl?'

For a moment, I think he must mean Scarlett.

'Jeanie?'

It's with something like relief I realise he means me.

'Up here, sweetie.' I go out to greet him. I'll get rid of the evidence later. For now I'll just enjoy my husband's company.

'The trains are up the spout because of the snow, so my meeting's cancelled,' he says. 'I'll just work from home.' But he doesn't look like work's on his mind as he kisses me and leads me back to bed.

That's all right, isn't it? It's all right just to be with him – to keep the world out, for a tiny while longer at least.

Afterwards he holds me in his arms, and I find that I am crying. 'What's up?' He looks worried.

I wipe my eyes and say, 'Nothing.' It is overwhelming, this feeling of love I have for him.

It terrifies me.

When I take a shower later in the spare bathroom, I run it so hot it burns my skin.

The bathroom is misty from the heat when I get out. As I stand dripping in front of the basin – circumspect about the taps really being off this time – condensation bobbles like strange wet growth on the mirror before me, obscuring my reflection.

And as I squint at myself, words form slowly in front of me, materialising out of the steam.

I blink at them: once, twice.

Go home, they seem to say, followed by another word I can't read.

But it's nothing, really, I think. Just old words that someone's written here in this unused bathroom. Still, I'm disquieted as I wipe them off.

It's nothing.

JEANIE

17 JANUARY 2015
2.30 p.m.

I'm studying job-application forms that threaten to overwhelm me. But I must act. I'm also overwhelmed – after a lifetime of supporting Frankie and myself – by becoming what I can only describe as a kept woman.

I'm getting organised. I registered with a doctor two days ago, now I need to find a dentist for me and Frank, and then that's us – all settled. As if it's really home.

Like noticing a quiet scratching at the door, I start to become aware of something in the next room. I realise it's Matthew's voice, rising querulously – on the phone, I guess. It's hard not to listen, though I do try not to – but he's getting louder.

'For fuck's sake,' he's saying.

Furious. He sounds furious. Perhaps it's work?

'You can't keep doing this – it's just impossible,' I hear him say, and I put the radio on loudly so I can't hear any more, because I feel like I'm snooping – though honestly I'd quite like to hear too.

I have a suspicion it's Kaye on the other end of the line.

Originally I'd suggested – having read it in my book – that we all met, for civility's sake. So we could all be cordial for the children.

But I wonder now if I'll ever meet her, and I'm not sure I want to any more.

Half an hour later Scarlett arrives on the doorstep, angrier than I've ever seen her.

'I don't want to be here,' I hear her say to Matthew. 'I just want to go home.'

'This is your home,' he's saying as he carries her overnight bag up to the top of the house. Up to her princess-in-the-tower room, where she has everything she'll ever need: a flat-screen TV, an iMac, a walk-in wardrobe – albeit a small one – and more, I expect, because her father's so frightened she won't come back if she's not happy. 'You've got two homes, you lucky thing.'

'I don't want two homes,' she says angrily as they turn the bend on the landing. 'Why can't you and Mum stop arguing and just make it up?'

'Ask your mother that,' I hear Matthew say levelly.

My stomach plummets as they disappear. I am left, mouth open, staring into the void.

Does he wish he was still with her then?

It is a shock. I'd never suspected that before, not really. I thought their marriage was long over, done and dusted. But – does this mean there's something unresolved? Matthew's quite reserved when it comes to talking about Kaye and his past. It's a man thing, I remind myself; most men don't reveal emotions easily or encourage discussion of their past.

Still, I don't know enough, I realise now, with a thud.

Neither of us knows the first thing about each other: that is becoming evident.

I wipe my clammy palms on my jeans.

I remember the writing on the steamed-up mirror.

Impostor, I think that last word might have been.

* * *

4 p.m.

Matthew and Scarlett haven't come down yet, and I can't concentrate on the silly application I've half answered, so I go up, sticking my head round the bend on the stairs to look up at her room.

Scarlett's door is almost closed, but I can see from their feet that they're both sitting on the bed.

'Hi,' I call brightly. 'Shall we have tea soon?'

Matthew jumps up and opens the door. He looks unusually flushed. It's very hot in the house, I suppose, the heating on full blast as ever.

'Just coming,' he says. 'Thanks, love.'

I walk down alone.

When they arrive in the kitchen five minutes later, I suggest cheese toasties in front of *Doctor Who.*

Scarlett looks at me as if I have small green antennae growing out of my head. No – worse. As if I have dog mess smeared all over my face.

'I hate *Doctor Who*,' she says flatly. 'It's for geeks and babies.'

Matthew kisses my forehead and rolls his eyes at me, opening the fridge for beer.

The kiss inspires me. 'Fair enough,' I say. 'How about an episode of *The Voice* on catch up?'

'I watch *The Voice* with my mum.' Scarlett just stops herself at 'you idiot'.

'Okay. Well I'll make the toasties then.'

'I'm not hungry—' she starts, and her father interrupts with a low warning.

'Scarlett, you'll be polite, thank you.'

She glares at us both, about to stomp back up to her room, when the front door opens and Frankie bundles in, bringing the chill with him.

'Afternoon all,' he says, and I am filled with love and gratitude for his generally cheerful demeanour. 'What's for tea? I'm Lee Marvin.'

'You're *what*?' Matthew's confused.

'Starving!'

'Cheese and ham toasties and banana smoothies?' I suggest. 'Or vanilla milkshakes?'

Frankie grins. 'Are we back at nursery again?' He winks at Scarlett. 'She's such a softie, my mum. That's why I love her so. You're not sliding off, are you?'

So Scarlett comes back down and eats a toastie with us and thaws out a little. Once or twice she even smiles at Frankie's jokes.

But not at mine. Still. It's a start.

The letter to 'Jeanie' crosses my mind, and then I manage to cast it out again.

JEANIE

18 JANUARY 2015

In the morning Luke, who has been at football camp, is dropped off, and Matthew appears in the kitchen in a waxy Barbour and a flat cap, announcing that he and the twins are going to shoot some clay pigeons. I can't decide if his new look's sexy or just silly.

'If you fancy a lesson, I'll let you touch my gun.' He winks.

Marlena and I used to party in Peckham in clubs where people sometimes shot each other when they were pissed off. Not my idea of a good time, recreational shooting.

'I'll touch your gun later,' I murmur and flush at my own daring. It's good for him and the kids to hang out without me, the book says. 'I'm going to take Frank shopping. He needs new jeans. You have fun.'

'Okay.' Matthew selects a set of keys from the drawer, kisses me on the lips and clomps out to the garage.

I wave them off from the lounge window about ten minutes later and wonder what it is that Scarlett's holding as she climbs into the back of Matthew's big car.

I squint over the dead palm I was trying to save, its leaves reaching into the room like dead men's fingers.

The thing she holds in her right hand is a shotgun apparently, the metal glinting as she pulls it in with her – and it's almost the same size as her.

JEANIE

30 JANUARY 2015

I haven't told Matthew about the job interview – I want to wait and see if I get it. I really want him to be proud of me.

And it's Friday thank God! I always look forward to the weekend with Matthew, to having some proper adult company for a few days. Frank's on his way back from Hull, where he went to collect his stuff, but when he's at home, he's not really – he's out most of the time, working at the bistro in town.

I definitely miss company in the week, rattling round here on my own – but today Matthew came home early, with Luke in tow.

They're just finishing a game of FIFA on the Xbox when I walk in, about to get on their way to Luke's football match. I debate going along to show my support, but I think it's good for them to have time on their own. Scarlett takes up a lot of Matthew's energy when they're all together, so it's nice for Luke to have his dad to himself.

I'm pottering upstairs when the doorbell rings. Peering down from the window, my heart sinks – it's the red-haired pirate from the party: Kaye's friend – Alison, I think.

But maybe this is a chance to set my mind at rest.

Running to open the door, I'm shocked by a loud explosion from the direction of the kitchen.

Confused, I don't know what to do first.

'Hang on!' I shout, rushing into the kitchen. I can smell burning, and the lights on the stairs start to flicker on and off.

It takes me a minute to understand that the baked potatoes I've put in the microwave have exploded. There's a fizzing and banging and the lick of actual flames behind the glass door. The smoke alarm is beeping frantically by now.

I unplug the microwave, and then I open its door and chuck a glass of water inside.

It's a stinking, potatoey mess that I start to clean up as best I can. When I've chucked the potatoes away, I realise there's something wedged in the back of the microwave. A metal fork has slipped down behind the glass plate, along with a piece of soaking-wet, folded wax paper.

In all the drama, I've forgotten all about the knock at the front door.

When I return to open it, the woman has gone.

I'm worried – especially after the overflowing shower the other day. Did I really leave a fork in the microwave? How stupid. But I hardly ever use it, anyway.

Frank breezes in and breezes out again as I finish wiping up.

'You didn't leave this in the microwave, did you?' I indicate the bent fork and the wax paper on the side. 'It could have been a disaster.' I shudder to think what would have happened if the whole thing had caught fire. It's almost like someone put the stuff there deliberately.

'Er, no.' He ruffles his hair in the mirror. 'It's much more likely to have been you, Mum.'

'It isn't,' I protest, and he grins widely.

'Yeah and the rest. You're getting worse in your old age.'

'Oh.' I'm taken aback. 'Thanks very much.'

But – maybe I did forget then.

I offer Matthew a beer when he returns.

Leafing through his post, he doesn't answer.

'Everything all right?' I sidle up to him. 'How was the football? Did Luke score?'

'It was just training.' He chucks the post down and gives me a hard peck, throwing me off balance rather. 'Why didn't you answer the door to Alison?' He opens the fridge.

'What?' I'm distracted by the oven timer beeping. Too much beeping. My head's throbbing as I turn it off.

'She texted me to say she knew you were here, but you refused to answer the door. Bit weird, no?'

The microwave looms in the corner.

'I was upstairs. I didn't hear her at first,' I lie. If he's already in a mood, I don't want him to think I'm really incompetent. 'She'd gone by the time I'd got down.'

'Seems a bit rude, don't you think?' He slams the fridge. 'I'd really rather not wind her up, you know.'

'Sorry. I didn't mean it to be, I was just…'

'What?' he snaps. He's getting more riled, not less.

'I just – I burnt something actually and…' Ridiculously there's a lump in my throat now. 'I was embarrassed.'

Matthew gazes at me as if I'm a stranger for a moment, and then he seems to come to.

'No, *I'm* sorry, love.' He softens. 'It's just I *really* need Sean on my side at the moment. I know she can be a bit of a tricky customer. We should ask them round for a meal. Sweeten them up.'

'If you like,' I say brightly. I thought he hated her – but whatever he wants.

'Shout when dinner's ready.' He drops a kiss on my head.

I haul the battered fish out of the oven. *I* feel battered. I drink a beer, which normally I wouldn't touch: I drink it in about four gulps.

It's time Matthew and I got some things out into the open.

It's time to bite the bullet.

9 p.m.

'Matthew?' I ask as we curl up on the big leather sofa later. 'Can I ask you something?'

'Yep.' He starts flicking through the channels.

'And then I'll tell *you* something…' I'm a bit tanked up. Now seems as safe as it's going to get; he's relaxing again…

'If you must.' He grins.

'I'm not entirely sure you'll want to discuss it.' I trace a pattern on the palm of his hand.

'Well don't ask then.' His smile isn't as wide now.

'It's just – I feel I know so little.' I draw his initials, then mine.

'About what?'

'About you. Your past really, I suppose.' And it's true. Things happened very quickly between us. Once I'd given in, he'd swept me off my proverbial.

Why wait? he'd said, back then. *We're not getting any younger.* So I'd listened; I'd done something rash for the first time ever.

Well. The second time ever, if you like.

I plough on. 'I mean, I don't even *really* know why you and Kaye split up? You said you'd had enough of the marriage but, apart from that…'

'Do we really have to talk about this now?' He pulls his hand away. 'I'm knackered. Work's crap, and the markets are in bloody turmoil. Can we just chill out tonight please?'

'It's good to talk,' I say lightly, mimicking the old BT advert, but he's definitely not smiling now. 'It's just...'

'What?' He fixes on a channel, although I'm fairly sure he's not interested in whatever it is Kirstie Allsopp's about to make with a load of old cotton reels and some pipe cleaners.

I gaze at the screen absently. 'It's just...' *Shall I go on?* He's obviously uptight – but I'm just the wrong side of drunk, and I can't stop; I need to know. So I press on. 'It's just you've never told me exactly why it wasn't working, I don't think. And it just – it seems odd not to...'

'I kicked her out, okay?' Matthew stares at the presenter's slightly smug expression. *Here's one I prepared earlier.* His words sound harsh. They *are* harsh.

'Oh I see.' I don't see. 'So – why?'

'If you really want to know...' He stops.

'Yes, I do, please, Matthew.'

'I kicked her out because she was shagging her personal trainer. Her *twenty-four-year-old* personal trainer.'

'Oh, God,' I stare at Kirstie too; I can't bear to look at Matthew's expression. 'That's awful.'

'Yeah well.' He finishes his beer. 'It was only once or twice I think, but when I caught them at it...'

'Caught them?'

'Yeah. Came home early, that old chestnut, and found him upstairs. And afterwards she said she wanted a new life – as well as a new body.'

I feel sick.

'Not my body anyway. So I told her to choose.' He bangs the bottle down and looks at me. Is it a challenge? 'And she did. She chose freedom.'

'Oh.' The word seems – discordant. Freedom. 'I'm sorry.'

'Don't be.' He stares at me for a moment. 'Glad you asked now?'

'It – it must have been very hard for you,' I stutter. 'I'm sorry to have, you know… opened a wound up.'

'Oh, God, don't be silly.' Remorse creeps in apparently. He edges towards me. 'I'm sorry, hon. I could have told you before, I suppose. But I also think it doesn't have much to do with us and our future. It's you I love, Jean.'

'Were you gutted then?' I have to know.

He sighs heavily. 'Not really. I was pissed off, of course. But we hadn't been getting on for a long time. She'd changed. I reckon she was just waiting till I got my next promotion. Holding out for a better settlement.'

'Blimey.' I laugh, but there's not much humour to my tone. 'You really think she's that mercenary?'

'Kaye? Bloody hell, yeah.' His own laugh is hollow. 'I *know* she is.'

'I'm sorry,' I repeat.

'Stop saying sorry.' Like the tide, his irritation ebbs and flows. 'It's not your fault, is it?'

'No, of course not, but—'

'Can we drop it now please?' He grabs my arm and pulls me to him. 'Let's talk about something else. Like how nice you look in that blouse…'

I glance down. It's totally unlike anything I'd normally wear – all fussy and lacy – but it was a Christmas present, and Scarlett helped him choose it (so he said). I felt I should wear it at least once.

'Thanks.' I'm ramrod stiff; I can't relax in his embrace at all.

'It's very sexy,' he murmurs into my hair, which normally would make my tummy go to jelly but this time has little effect. 'Mrs Schoolteacher, you might have to reprimand me…'

'What?' I pull back. 'Why say that?'

'That's what you remind me of, with your hair pulled back and that outfit. Very tempting!'

My chest tightens, and I have to stand. 'I'll get you another beer.' I head to the door.

'I'm fine.' He looks puzzled. 'What have I said wrong?'

He holds a hand out, and reluctantly I let him pull me down again, thoughts of him and Kaye buzzing in my brain like angry wasps. Kirstie's saying goodbye now on the screen as Matthew nuzzles into my neck.

'When was all this, Matthew?'

'What?' His breathing has quickened.

'When exactly did you split up?'

He stops. 'Early this year.'

'What?' I pull right back from him.

'I mean last year. Just after Christmas really, in 2013.'

'Oh,' I repeat like a stupid parrot. Shit. 'I see.' But I still don't see. 'I'm sure you said it was longer ago than that…'

'It was, in spirit.' He moves away irritably. 'In body it was last year. Now can you drop it?'

We spend the rest of the evening watching a terrible film about a prison break in Siberia, but I can't concentrate. And for the first time when we go to bed, I turn over and away from him, listening as his breathing changes and he slips quickly into sleep.

I'm still awake when Frankie comes back a bit later and bashes around in the kitchen – leaving all the pots out no doubt – before going to bed himself.

I'm still awake when the old grandfather clock on the landing chimes midnight, then one, then two.

It has come home, properly, that I've married a man I hardly know. My own secrets seem far darker at this time of night. I didn't even get *near* telling him anything I meant to.

How could I when he was already so annoyed?

I stare into the darkness, and I hear the walls begin to whisper again. What exactly is it in this house that's being hidden?

Get a grip, babe, Marlena would say, *and get on with it.*

Tomorrow we need to drag it all out in the open, every last bit of it – and then we will be all right.

I get up and sit on the side of the bath in our en suite. I text Marlena, but she doesn't answer. Eventually I rummage round the medicine cabinet, take a headache pill and go back to bed.

Finally I sleep.

MARLENA

Really, Jeanie?
This is starting to alarm me a little now.

JEANIE

1 FEBRUARY 2015

8.30 a.m.

Matthew brings me tea in bed this morning. I overslept and was woken by my phone pinging.

Marlena:

You were up late. Or should I say early? What gives?

I call her.

'So are you coming to stay? I've got a lovely spare room with its own bathroom and all.' I stretch luxuriously, but I don't feel very luxurious actually. I'm starting to hate this house; the whispering walls feel less than benign now. I don't belong. I am an impostor – as that word *might* have said.

Might.

Yesterday I was sure I heard voices on the stairs again – a sort of muttering in the ether. I tore open the small door and shone the light up there – but the staircase was empty. Of course it was. But I didn't relax for the rest of the day.

'And everything's okay, is it?' Marlena asks suspiciously.

'Yeah of course, it's great.' Why do I feel like I'm lying?

'I mean – you've told him?'

I don't speak.

'Jean! For Christ's sake – what are you on?'

'Okay, okay! Look – if you come up one of next few weekends, I swear it'll all be sorted by then.'

'Okay – deal. I could do with twenty-four hours in the country. It's mental in London right now,' Marlena says, followed by a snappy: 'Watch out mate!' I hear the frantic beeping of traffic around her. 'Gotta go. Gotta see a man about a dog. Get on with it, Jeanie. I'll text you a date.'

Matt comes in as I hang up. He's been working out downstairs, and looking at his tousled hair and his muscular arms in his white V-neck, I feel the familiar, addictive wash of emotion – a surge of what Marlena would no doubt call lust.

Last night's demons disintegrate in the weak morning light.

'Is it okay if my sister comes to stay?' I ask as he goes to take a shower – now all fixed. He frowns.

'You don't need to ask. This is your home too.'

I don't say I've already semi-arranged it, because frankly Marlena is less than reliable with social arrangements. I'm so pleased she's finally agreed to come: I want Matthew to meet her properly, to get to know her like I do.

They've only met a few times, briefly; she took us out for lunch in London the week after the wedding she missed. She drank quite a lot and was funny and bitchy about celebrities. I wasn't sure what Matthew made of her, but he laughed at all her jokes.

I'm sure they'll get on famously when she comes to stay.

MARLENA

No comment.

JEANIE

1 FEBRUARY 2015

10 a.m.

I listen to the shower as I drink my tea, watching the finches in the bare branches of the apple tree as they pick at the pale lichen.

I have nothing to feel guilty about, I must remember that; I just have to be honest with Matthew. I have to trust he knows me well enough by now, loves me deeply enough, to understand.

And he hasn't told me everything either, I remind myself, thinking of last night's uncomfortable conversation.

I feel both relief and terror about what I must do, still chastising myself for not having told him before. It's so stupid, I see that clearly now – but it wasn't so clear before.

Matthew emerges, wrapped in a towel. His physique is good for a man of nearly fifty: toned and fit. Again I feel a wave of...

'What are these, Jeanie?' He's holding something in his hand that I can't make out.

'What?'

'These pills?' He extends the packet. 'Xanax?'

'Xanax? They're not mine,' I say quickly, seeing his face. 'Where did you find them?'

'They must be yours. They were in our bathroom cabinet, and they are most definitely not mine.'

I get out of bed and pluck them out his hand, turning the packet over.

'See, they don't even have my name on.' I study the label. Then I lay my hand on his bare chest. 'Why don't you come back to bed for a bit? I wanted to talk to you…'

'I can't. It's already late.' He frowns again, pulling away to get dressed. 'I need to check my emails.'

'Just for five minutes?' I plead. It'll only take five.

'I'm waiting to hear from Tokyo.' He has that bullish look that I'm starting to recognise as stress. 'It's important.'

'Sorry,' I say, as he pulls on his jeans. 'Sorry, I didn't mean to annoy you.'

His face is inscrutable.

'I'll be down soon.' I try to smile, but I feel oddly like crying. When he leaves the room, I sit on the edge of the bed, pills in hand. I look out at the bare apple tree. There was a pair of blackbirds, but they've gone. All the birds have flown off, scared by something nearby. A cat? A fox.

The foxes are always prowling here.

I stare out. I can't shake my feeling of unease.

Downstairs Matthew's on the computer.

I make some toast and then, nervously, I suggest a walk when he's finished, to the nice café near the woods. I'd rather be out in the open when I tell him. Neutral territory: isn't that what they always advise for difficult conversations?

I'm most worried about how angry he'll be that I didn't tell him before; that he'll feel I tried to trick him somehow.

If I'm honest, his anger would be justified.

I did *try* to tell him; I really did. I wrote him an email, a very long, painful one that took me about three days to compose.

He'd just told me he loved me for the first time. We had been seeing each other for a few months, and I was starting to feel so strongly about him that I thought, *I can't let this go any further without him knowing the truth – because if he can't deal with it, I need to get out before I fall any deeper.*

The other thing was that, back then, I kept expecting him to recognise me. Even though I'd been totally exonerated, I'd graced the front covers of most national newspapers for a good week or so.

But he never did.

My saving grace was that Matthew isn't a tabloid reader. His news intake is limited to the FTSE 100, which goes against all my left-wing principles (but I'd be lying if I said it didn't make life quite comfortable).

Anyway I wrote Matthew the email over those three days – and then I took a deep breath and, with a shaky hand, pressed send.

He was on business in Munich at the time. The next thirty-six hours were hell, waiting to hear – or not hear. Thinking that was it. I'd finally met a man who seemed good, who I could trust – and it was already all over.

When he eventually called from Munich airport, I was so pleased to hear from him, I nearly sobbed with relief.

It wasn't until the following weekend, holed up in a nice little hotel in the Chilterns, all chintzy wallpaper and champagne, that I realised, with horror, that Matthew had never read the email.

'So,' I'd asked shyly, head on his chest. 'You're – all right about it then?'

'What?' He stroked my hair. 'All right with you in my life? Yeah, definitely, hon.'

'No, I meant – about my email?' I sat up, feeling a shiver of anxiety. 'You – you did read it, didn't you?'

'Wellll…' He looked abashed. 'I was so busy, hon.' He pulled me down, kissing my neck, sliding his hand into my dress. 'I didn't have time for personal stuff.'

I froze.

'Do you want me to read it now?' He undid my top button. 'I can if you like…'

'No,' I said, panicking. 'Don't bother. Just delete it. Please.'

Checking the New York stock exchange, Matthew doesn't seem enthused by the prospect of a walk, but he agrees. 'It'll give me a chance to try out that new pedometer Fitbit thing I got for Christmas.'

I am the world's biggest Luddite: I barely know what an app is. I hate mobile phones; I hate everything about them, especially since the complaint and the spread of malice on the Internet. The great world wide web caught me in its sticky hold, and I hate it and what it means for us as a society. It's pernicious.

But I keep my opinions to myself.

'I wanted to talk to you about something.' I am full of apprehension. 'If that's okay with you.' I know I am ever more tense with him recently, less brave.

'Fuck!' He bangs the keyboard with ill feeling. 'This is shit.'

'Work?' I wish he'd concentrate for a moment.

'The Euro's shite because of all the Greek crap. It's knocking on to all the markets.' He shuts the screen down. 'Fuck, I wish Cameron and Osborne would get their heads out of their arses.'

'I'm sorry.' My stomach rolls with nerves as I sit beside him. 'The thing is, Matt…'

'Shall we wait till the kids get here?' He stretches and checks the time. 'To walk, I mean. Get them away from their screens.'

'The kids?' My heart sinks.

'Yeah. They love the woods. Well, they did when they were little anyway.' *Now* he looks enthused. 'I worry about all that computer shit sometimes. What effect it's having. Get 'em outside.'

Apparently I have forgotten it's our weekend. But it was our weekend *last* weekend too. This doesn't seem quite right.

But this is their home, of course; it was their home long before it was mine. And I imagine how I'd feel if Frankie's dad didn't make him welcome – except, of course, Frankie's dad has never been on the scene.

'No problem.' I smile. 'Let's take them too. Only I just wanted to tell you something. I've been meaning to tell you for a while now, but...'

As if they've been summoned by my surprise and fear, we hear the crunch of tyres on gravel. That shiny white Range Rover is outside, the children's mother obscured by Scarlett in the passenger seat.

There's not enough time to do it now. We need to be alone. I need to steady myself.

'I'll just be a minute.' I slip out of the room; I don't need to witness the hearty hellos. They need time alone with their dad anyway.

Catching my reflection in the curly gilt mirror, I pull a face at myself. I'm going to ask Matthew to move the bloody thing. I hate it. Better still, Kaye could take it with her now.

Mirror, mirror... Kaye is the fairest of them all, no doubt. Even if she does pay a fortune for her blonde.

I am going to be bolder. I must speak my mind more.

In our bedroom I sit at the dressing table, staring at myself. I look washed-out and pale – well it's that time of year I suppose, where we all fade a bit.

If I look better, I'll feel better perhaps. Fumbling for my blusher, I feel panic rise, dropping make-up brushes, knocking the key to the drawer onto the floor clumsily.

Without thinking, I pick it up and slip it into the lock.

The drawer is empty.

I scrabble my hand around it frantically – but there's nothing in it. Nothing – apart from an old receipt for Opium perfume, bought at Heathrow airport, around two years ago. And a hairgrip with a little flower on it.

Someone – not me – *someone* has removed everything I put in here. All the evidence is gone.

Where the hell has it gone?

Mind racing, trying to think what to do for the best, I feel like I'm struggling to breathe – and then I think I might be about to have a panic attack. After Seaborne I had a couple of them. I had to learn to control my breathing and to… breathe deep, and to remember I'm still breathing, and…

I put my head between my knees, feeling like this is not reality, trying to remember to breathe, just breathe…

And I'm shocked when Matthew comes in. I sit up too quickly, shoving the drawer shut as he sidles up behind me and leans down.

'Looking for something?'

'No, sorry, I just felt a bit – faint for a minute.' I feel lightheaded and giddy and sick now; it's the truth.

'Well you smell gorgeous,' he murmurs. 'Are you coming down to say hello?'

He pulls me up and kisses me hard.

'Matthew,' I say, still light-headed, clinging onto him for literal support. 'Kaye's not here, is she?'

He says, 'Shhh!' and kisses me again, harder this time, and, despite myself, I find myself responding – until a small yap makes us both jump.

Luke is standing in the bedroom doorway, holding a tiny white puppy in his arms.

'Oh – how adorable!' I say, although the truth is I'm wary about dogs since Smudge. I was never that keen to be honest, having been badly bitten once by my Uncle Rog's Alsatian, Kaiser. Rog had been on yet another bender and hadn't fed or watered the poor animal for days. The smell of dog shit still reminds me of that horrible night.

But Smudge sneaked into my heart, despite my misgivings. What eight-year-old wouldn't have loved him, with his liquid brown eyes and the wet nose he pushed hopefully into my hand? The truth was I needed someone to love – or someone to love me – unconditionally. Without wanting something back.

When Smudge died, just before my tenth birthday, I thought I would die too – I was so devastated.

'He's Scarlett's,' Luke says. 'Yassine got him for her from his friend.'

'Who the hell's Yassine when he's at home?' Matthew looks thoroughly irritated.

'Mum's new boyfriend. He got scouted for West Ham when he was fifteen.' Luke looks so excited that I smile, but Matthew's face has set in that way it does whenever Kaye is mentioned. 'He can do one hundred keepy-uppies in a go.'

'Typical,' Matthew mutters. He scratches the little dog's fluffy head. 'He's cute – but we don't want him here, mate. We're not set up for dogs.'

'But Mum's going away for the weekend.'

'She is, is she?' Matthew looks even more pissed off.

'Yeah, and she said we had to bring him.' Is Luke's lower lip trembling now? These children are so vulnerable it seems.

'Oh we'll manage, won't we, Matt?' I say quickly. 'It's okay, Luke.'

'I suppose so.' Matthew sighs again. 'Well tell your sister that if he craps on the carpet, she's cleaning it up.'

'It's fine,' I say. 'We can take him to the woods with us. What's his name?' I tickle his chin – but I won't look into his eyes. That was my mistake with Smudge.

'Justin,' Luke says.

'As in time?' Matthew jokes. 'Ridiculous name for a dog.'

'No.' Luke rolls his eyes at his father's stupidity. 'As in Bieber.'

12 p.m.

We wrap up warm and take the dog on the walk. He doesn't have a lead, so we stop at the pet shop on the high street, and the twins choose a purple suede one, as well as a dog bed and some toys.

As we amble through the trees, Matthew's arm around me, I'm pleased that even Scarlett seems to be enjoying herself – although the poor little puppy gets confused a few times and, by the end, has to be carried, none too enamoured with the brambles or the scary big trees.

Still, it's the most family-oriented time I've ever spent with the twins – and I haven't even worried about Matthew showing me affection in front of them. I'm ebullient as we drive home, singing along to Ellie Goulding – although there are some rumblings in the back about 'proper' music.

It's only when we get back and I run upstairs to change my muddy jeans that I remember the missing letters.

Downstairs Matthew is busy in the kitchen for once. He makes popcorn and hot chocolate for the kids, pours us a glass of wine and reveals a load of old home movies he's had transferred to DVD.

I perch on the arm of the sofa, my sense of security dissolving as reality sets in. Watching their old memories is hard.

The home movies are mainly of the twins, of course – holidays, special occasions, birthdays and school plays – but occasionally there are shots of Kaye, usually in huge sunglasses and a miniscule bikini or a radically cutaway swimsuit, lounging by a turquoise pool or watching a sunset. There's a whole five minutes of the twins shooting on the range at Gleneagles, high-fiving and laughing, and then Kaye in a stupid fur hat grinning into the camera.

Am I wrong to mind?

When eventually in one sequence she begins to turn faultless cartwheels on a tropical beach straight from a Bounty ad, I stand up.

'Burgers and wedges okay for tea?' I ask, and they chorus approval, their eyes firmly on Kaye's perfect behind flipping up, over and around, Scarlett following faithfully in her mother's tracks.

In the kitchen, alone, I bend double, trying to slow my breathing. In and out, in and out…

Luke comes in, looking for water for the puppy.

'Are you all right?' He looks concerned. 'Are you ill?'

'I'm fine, love,' I say. 'Just – feeling a bit tired.'

Matthew comes in for more wine as Luke leaves.

'Where's the bottle?' Matthew glances at me. 'Are you okay, hon?'

'Yeah, fine,' I say, and he kisses my forehead.

'You don't mind, do you? I thought it was important to show them that you're not bothered by seeing their mum. You're not, are you?'

'Course not,' I say with some relief. 'It's fine.'

'After all'—he hugs me—'it's you I love, hon.'

Through the open door, I see Luke making barfing noises at Scarlett, and I grin.

'Thanks, darlin'.'

I go up early to have a bath, leaving them arguing about whether to watch *Bridesmaids* or *Poltergeist*.

As I pull the curtains and flop into bed, all the lights flicker and then go off entirely.

'Hello?' I call urgently. Someone must have pushed the switch outside in the hallway accidentally.

I don't like the dark much – not much at all. There was the methamphetamine phase just before we went to live with Nan, when our distraught mother found the tiny cupboard under the stairs a useful tool for misbehaving daughters. It was small and dark and...

'Hello?' My voice sounds pathetically tremulous.

Whispering. Walls whispering – indistinct voices.

But no answer.

'Hello?' I repeat, swinging my legs out of the bed. 'Who is it?'

A door slams somewhere nearby – along the landing possibly. I hear laughing, high-pitched giggling...

I fumble my way to the door, stubbing my toe horribly on the bed: it is agony.

As I grope along the wall, the lights come back on.

I debate going back down, but I don't want to disturb them. So I go back to bed, but I don't turn my bedside light off all night. Even when Matthew comes up later and switches it off, I wait till he's asleep and then I switch it back on.

JEANIE

2 FEBRUARY 2015

The next morning, when I go down to put the kettle on, the little dog seems very lethargic. Trying to coax him out of his new bed, I see he's been sick; there seems to be blood in the bed too.

He won't eat or even take any water. We ring the emergency vet, and Matthew rushes him down there with the twins.

They come back without the puppy.

'It's your fault!' Scarlett screams when I ask how he is, her blue eyes narrowed and furious.

'Scarlett!' her father warns but without much conviction.

'How can it be *my* fault?' I'm shaken. 'What's wrong with him?'

'You said it was okay to take him out.' The girl glares at me.

'I didn't,' I say, although of course it *was* me that suggested the walk – before I knew any of them were coming of course.

'He hadn't had his full vaccinations apparently. They don't think he'll make it; he's too young,' Matthew says quietly. 'The vet says he probably picked up a virus in the woods. You weren't to know.'

'But…' I start – and then I think it's not gracious to argue now, and they are so upset and angry they won't hear what I say anyway.

All morning I pray that the little dog will pull through – but at lunchtime the house phone rings. It's not good news.

Scarlett is inconsolable, throwing herself into her father's arms, sobbing in his lap until I have to go and sit upstairs, I feel so awful.

Matthew drives the twins home. Kaye is coming back early, apparently, from wherever she was spending the weekend. Luke comes to say a muted goodbye, but Scarlett won't talk to me at all, even though I try to apologise. She won't even look at me, stomping out to the car, tears wet on her flushed cheeks.

I go upstairs to busy myself doing nothing, feeling wretched. Maybe I'll change the beds, I think, even though Matthew's cleaner normally does it – which makes me uncomfortable anyway.

Fetching sheets, I glance out of the landing window by the airing cupboard and see a man in the back garden, mowing the lawn.

I move slowly out of the window's sight line and peer down. He has his back to me as he cuts a straight line up the lawn – all dirty blonde hair, khaki trousers, headphones on. He reminds me of someone.

I'm too tired to do the sheets now; I decide I'll do it later.

I lie on our bed until Matthew gets back.

MARLENA

Jeanie hates strangers; she always did when we were kids. I was the boringly extrovert one; she was the one who watched those Government warnings: don't talk to strangers; don't get in strangers' cars.

Even if the old woman in the corner shop offered us a free lolly, Jeanie wouldn't take it. Boringly paranoid, my sister. Or careful, my Nan would have said. Sensible. Unlike me.

Me? I'll take anything for nothing.

As I've since paid the price for.

But Jeanie was the one who fell in love: so hard, too fast, no sense of judgement. It was after Frankie was born – he was about seven or eight at the time.

That bastard. He nearly brought her down for good.

JEANIE

2 FEBRUARY 2015

3.30 p.m.

I dream of the devil. I am running, and he is after me and I reach a door in the wall, but the door won't open, and I fumble with the catch, and when I get through it, the devil is on my heels, the heat of his stinking breath on the back of my neck. Sobbing, I can't shut the door after me, though I desperately try. Desperately I try.

When Matt wakes me, I realise I must have fallen asleep, and I'm not sure if it's because I'm so groggy that he seems a little... frosty.

'All right?' he says. 'You sounded like you were having a bad dream.'

'I'm okay,' I say, but my heart is racing still.

'Have you seen my grey tracksuit?' He's pulling stuff out of drawers like a child.

'Second drawer down?' When he turns back, I try to focus on his handsome face. 'Surely, Matt, *you* don't think it was my fault?'

'No.' He rubs his eyes tiredly.

I haul myself up to sit. 'I mean how was I meant to know about his vaccinations? I don't know the first thing about dog care.' I sound a bit like a teenager myself. 'Their mother should have made sure they knew the facts if he wasn't meant to go out.'

It's the first time I've ever criticised Kaye, I think later.

'No, I don't think it's your fault,' he sighs, but he seems remote: blank somehow. 'Not really.'

'Not really?' I feel a bubble of anger in my stomach. 'What do you mean – *not really?*'

'Look I just don't want to give Kaye any ammunition against me, that's all.' He pulls blue shorts on, changes his top. 'We've got the solicitors' meeting coming up…'

'What meeting?' I wish he'd confide in me more. What a bittersweet irony that wish is.

'To resettle the alimony payments. I don't want to wind her up.' He drops a kiss on the top of my head. 'Go back to sleep. I'm going to play squash with Sean. I'll eat at the club.'

Frankie comes home just after Matthew leaves and, oh God, I'm pleased to see my lovely boy. I miss him as he forges his own life – but I'm increasingly relieved he has so much wherewithal.

Frankie has been at George's all weekend, but he senses something's wrong immediately. I tell him about the puppy – but I don't say that people seem to be blaming me for its death. What's the point?

I put tea on a tray, and we sit in front of the fire. The garden is empty again: I've checked and rechecked. The gardener's gone.

'So was Scarlett as moody as ever?' Frank asks, turning on an old episode of *Sherlock*. The twins love it; own the whole series on DVD. 'She's such a little madam.'

'She was okay, actually, at first,' I stare at the screen absently. I seem to be doing a bit of that recently. 'She was thawing out a bit. Until the poor dog died.'

'Don't take it personally, Mum.' He helps himself to a stack of chocolate digestives. I can't be bothered to tell him off. 'Her not liking you. Jenna says that it's very common for girls to hate the women their fathers date. Or even their own mothers. It's called the electric complex apparently.'

'Electra, you mean?' I feel so leaden my smile is muted.

'Yeah, that's the bird. Girls who hate women who like their fathers. Something like that.' He loses interest in what he's saying as a pretty woman knocks on Sherlock's door.

'I see.' I do grin now. 'And who is this extremely knowledgeable young lady? I'm guessing she's a young lady anyway.'

'Jenna? Just a mate of George's.' Frankie turns a faint pink. 'From the pub. She's studying psychology.'

'And why were you talking about Electra complexes?'

'Because.' Frankie shrugs. 'I have noticed that Scarlett's not being exactly – friendly. It's hard not to. Notice, I mean.'

'Yeah,' I admit. 'She's not really. But she'll come round.'

I think about her furious little face; her screwed-up eyes, blue and hard as sapphires, as she looked at me earlier like she hated my guts. I'm not as convinced as I was a month ago that we'll ever be able to bond.

I think of her lying in her father's lap. Of them shut in her bedroom. I push away my discomfort.

'I suppose it's hard for her to accept the changes.'

Dr Watson is saying something silly and Sherlock is saying something clever. Frankie's distracted again. Then he turns to me. 'Well I do know it's hard to make transitions…'

'Oh-ho!' I'm amused, despite myself. 'Is that something the lovely Jenna says too?'

'Perhaps. But, it's just – I want you to be happy, Mum. You deserve it. After…' Frankie pauses. 'After everything.'

We never talk about 'it', about 'everything' – we have both been so glad to put it behind us, I think, since we came here.

But it was so bloody awful at the time; we both carry our scars – hidden, maybe, but definitely there. And yet it linked us in a way I couldn't explain to anyone else. We have a bond, Frank and I, that I share with no one else. And yet I'm realising I'm going to have to sever it soon, when he leaves again. I will have to learn to live without my beloved boy.

'I *am* happy,' I insist – but for the first time since I got married, I'm not being entirely honest. I *was* feeling a new happiness. A state that's fading rather quicker than I'd anticipated.

Something's not quite right at the moment: something is rotten in the state of Denmark.

'Did you see the gardener when you got back?' I glance out of the window, but it's already nearly dark. He must be long gone. I meant to ask Matthew about him, but I was distracted...

'Who?' Frankie's phone beeps. He glances at it then frowns, chucking it down again without texting back.

'Everything okay?' I recognise that belligerent look.

'Fine,' he shrugs.

'Frankie Randall!' I pause the television. 'What's wrong?'

'It's just...' He runs his hand through his hair until it sticks up on end. 'That bloody girl.'

'Who?' I'm confused. 'Jenna? But I thought you liked her?'

'Not Jenna, no.' He grabs for the remote, but I hold it aloft. 'Frank! What girl?'

'Scarlett,' he mutters, and my heart sinks.

'You've been texting?' This is the last thing we all need.

'Er, no!' He gives me what we used to call a 'Paddington Bear hard stare'. 'Hardly. She's been texting me more like.'

'How did she get your number?'

'I dunno. Can you just put the telly back on please?'

I do it slowly. 'Are you sure you didn't give her your number, Frankie?'

'Positive.'

'And – have you answered her?'

'Once or twice.' He shrugs again. 'But not when she texts things like that.' He nods at the phone.

'Like what?' Oh God.

'Like, "My mate Gemma thinks you're peng." ' He looks disdainful. 'She's just a kid.'

'Peng?' I'm none the wiser.

'Like, fit,' he says – and then he has the good grace to look embarrassed. Our eyes meet, and I can't help myself: I grin, and then he grins, and then we are both laughing.

'Oh dear,' I say when we stop. 'Maybe best not to say anything to Matt.'

At least she can't be quite so upset any more, about the dog.

'Don't be daft.' Frankie chews on a nail. 'As if.'

'I'll – try and have a word with her. Try and let her down gently.' But I think about the state she was in when she left – and I think it's unlikely she'll ever heed any advice I give her.

'Bring Jenna round for dinner, why don't you?' I change the subject. 'Or Sunday lunch. I'd like to meet her. And now explain to me exactly how Sherlock knows that woman's just been in a first-class train carriage on the way from Dorset?'

I try so hard to enjoy my night with Frank; I mean I *do* enjoy it. But now I am alarmed by this new Scarlett thing. *Please, keep away from Frankie*, I think. That's all we need.

JEANIE

9 FEBRUARY 2015

I've finally told Matt the truth. I can't believe it – but it's out in the open at last!

I told him because I was pretty sure that Scarlett had found out, and that she would tell him before I did. I was convinced that it must have been her poking around in my drawers – and probably her that had left the envelope in the spare room, along with her earring.

So I cooked the best dinner I could, fed Matt a bottle of Bordeaux (from his own wine rack, it must be said – I know nothing about wine) and a rare steak, managing to get his attention off the FT rolling news for long enough to tell him. It was obvious that he hadn't known – his surprise was evident.

I told him I've got a second interview for the college job – and he was pleased – and then I told him I'd been worried about applying to teach again. Deep breath: because of the Seaborne incident.

'Why didn't you tell me?' He put his hand over mine on the table after I'd finished talking. 'I'm sorry you went through that.'

The flood of relief washing through me was immense; tears sprang to my eyes.

'Poor Jeanie. What a nightmare for you, hon.'

Holding back my tears, I asked him if he remembered the email I'd sent to Munich. Fortunately, he did – and that he'd not read it.

'So – are you okay now?' He was tentative. 'It's all – behind you?'

'Yes,' I said, and I felt so relieved, so free and light that I started laughing, topping up my glass and his, wanting to get up and dance.

'What's so funny?' He looked confused.

'Nothing. Everything. I was just so worried – and I shouldn't have been. I knew you'd understand.' I threw my arms round him and kissed him all over his face and neck. 'Oh I'm so pleased, Matty. I love you so much.'

It took a lot to say those words.

JEANIE

11 FEBRUARY 2015

Matthew rings to say he is working late.

I go upstairs to put the bath on, freezing from sitting too long, finishing my interview notes for the morning. I am determined to get this job.

I run back down to find my glasses, and as I pass the great curly mirror, I hear a noise.

I stop.

Is someone in the house?

'Frank?'

But he is working tonight; I know that really.

Another noise, like chains rattling.

I go down a few stairs, leaning over the bannister. 'Matthew?'

In the mirror, I see the figure of a woman in a long grey dress, walking towards me, her face deathly white, a veil thrown over it, her eyes black behind the veil…

I start to shake.

I don't believe in ghosts – but this is the Grey Lady, and she is coming towards me, her hands out in front of her…

I run upstairs and slam the door of the bathroom, locking it. My chest is heaving, and I try to laugh at my own fear – but it's too real to be funny. I feel sick with it.

When Matthew gets home, I tell him what happened.

'Don't be silly.' He grins. 'You were imagining it. You're just tired.' He hugs me. 'Silly thing. Don't let Luke's stories scare you, hon.'

But I know what I saw.

14 FEBRUARY 2015

Valentine's Day – and we're going away for the night!

After all the stress recently, it's the perfect way to smooth things over. Plus Marlena's coming to stay next weekend. This all feels like a new start – everything's going to be okay!

I had the second interview at the college yesterday, and I felt an instant rapport with the head of department. She told me pretty much straightaway the job was mine. When I got home, they called to make the offer.

I didn't get the chance to tell Matthew because he rang to ask me to meet him in Berkhamsted for pizza with Luke and Scarlett: a late birthday meal for them. Matthew was upset he hadn't seen them on the actual day, but he and Kaye had decided to take 'celebrations' in turn – and so they spent their actual birthday with her.

We had an all right time. Scarlett even answered a question or two I put her way, mainly about school – although she's still angry with me, it's obvious. She was fed up Frankie didn't come – that was clear too when I sent her Frankie's birthday wishes.

At one point during the meal, I went to the bathroom, and when I came back, the three Kings all stopped talking.

'Don't mind me,' I joked, but no one really laughed. Matthew raised his glass to me, but I felt awkward from then on.

All in all I was relieved when the meal was over and we dropped them off.

There was something in Scarlett's steely little face that scared me a bit.

I'm packing my overnight bag when the house phone rings.

'It's Paul Harris here,' the voice says. 'We got the path results through for Justin.'

'Justin?' What on earth's he talking about? 'Sorry – wrong number I think.'

'Mr King's Pomeranian puppy?'

'Oh God, sorry!' Of course. I forgot the silly name – Justin. 'You should talk to my husband. It was his children's dog. Can I give you his mobile number?'

'Sure.' The vet takes it down. 'But you might want to do a quick sweep of your home. Check there's no more rodenticide around.'

'Rodenticide? Do you mean like rat poison?'

'Exactly. It wasn't the virus I suspected after all. It was blood poisoning unfortunately. A chemical ingredient called cholecalciferol was detected in his bloods. Lethal for dogs.'

I put the phone down feeling anxious. I'm sure we haven't put any poisons down in the house, and the dog was inside the whole time. Apart from in the woods, I suppose. But he barely walked; he was carried most of the way.

Our night away is far from the big success I've hoped for – the one we really need it to be.

The hotel is, as I expected, lovely. Five star, very luxurious in an understated sort of way, set in country grounds. It all makes me a little nervous to be honest, and I'm not planning to do anything but hang out with Matthew – but he needs to do some work when we arrive, as he left the office early.

I swim in the indoor pool. Gazing out at the Cotswold hills all swaddled in mist, I try to feel like this is just what I wanted to do – swim alone; have some time to myself.

Trouble is I have nothing but too much time to myself. Frankie's out more and more, and soon he'll go again for good. He's got a place in Leeds to study music production in the autumn, and before that a job picking grapes in France.

I'm gutted by this, though I try to hide it, and even though he's already been up in Hull briefly, I'm just not used to him being away. He's been my be-all and end-all forever it seems. He was what I lived for when Simon left.

At least it gives me an understanding of Matthew's sombre mood sometimes, when he seems a little – distant, missing his kids daily, although of course he does see them regularly, and it'll be years before they'll be off for good.

But when Frankie is away, I spend whole days talking to no one apart from myself – and Matthew when he gets home – often quite late.

At least that'll change now, thank God, with my new job!

At dinner Matthew keeps his phone on the table, awaiting a call from Tokyo.

I tell him about my job, and he seems pleased, if a little surprised. 'You kept that quiet!'

'I mentioned it the other night,' I point out. 'That I had a second interview, remember?'

'So when do you start?' He gouges a snail from its shell, sucking the greeny-brown flesh up with vigour.

Poor creature! I shudder. 'In about four weeks I think.' I crumble my bread roll, not very hungry suddenly. 'I've got to go for an induction, meet the other staff, stuff like that – but the teacher who's leaving finishes at the end of term.'

This is the time to tell him about the final piece of the puzzle I've kept to myself. I take a big sip of water and promptly choke.

When I recover my breath, the waiter arrives with the champagne Matthew has ordered and a big bunch of red roses.

'They're beautiful.' I am surprised and touched. Can I tell him now? I have to.

I neck my glass of champagne. 'Matt…'

His phone rings. 'Sorry,' he murmurs, glancing down.

I've seen the name on the screen.

'Please.' I put my hand out to him. 'I really need to tell you something.'

But he takes it. 'Might be the kids.'

Even from the other side of the table, I can hear her shouting down the line.

Eventually Matthew stands, walking out to the foyer to talk, pacing up and down.

He comes back tight-lipped. I gather it is more blame about the dog.

'Couldn't he have eaten something before he came to ours?' I say. 'The poor puppy?'

'Something like cyanide?' he snaps. 'I doubt it very much.'

'*Cyanide?*' I gaze at him. 'But I thought – I'm sure the vet said rat poison when I spoke to him?'

'Yeah he did – and now apparently this as well.'

Something about Matt's face tells me to leave it there.

We finish the rich, heavy dinner in complete silence.

Despite the lavish room and the draped four-poster bed, we are awkward as we get ready for bed. Matthew is exhausted after a hectic week at work, and I feel shaken again by the puppy and Kaye's shouting.

Why does she seem to crop up at such inopportune moments?

Lying on my side, watching Matthew descend into deep sleep without touching me, without coming near me at all, I feel ugly and unloved.

The sheer lacy nightie I bought especially for tonight stays forlornly in my case, as one hot tear after another squeezes out of my half-shut eyes.

* * *

In the middle of the night a phone starts to ring in the depths of my dream about trying to cross the river to reach Frankie.

Matthew fumbles for it, knocking his watch and keys off the nightstand with a clatter.

'Yes?' His voice is sleep filled and low.

I keep my eyes tightly shut. Calls in the early hours always bode ill.

'What?' He sits bolt upright. 'Jesus fucking Christ, Kaye! You should have told me earlier…'

Now my eyes are open too; I am wide awake, fingers clutching the sheet.

'I'm on my way.' Matt is scrambling out of bed, falling over as he pulls on his trousers.

'What is it?' My stomach is plunging like a fairground ride. 'Matt? What's wrong?'

'It's Luke,' he says shortly. 'He's been rushed to Hemel Hempstead Hospital. Where the fuck's my shirt?'

* * *

We race back down the empty motorway from tranquil Oxford-shire, driving straight to the hospital. There Matthew is rushed off by a nurse through paediatric A & E to the theatre, where they are about to operate on Luke for suspected appendicitis.

I don't know what to do for the best. I want to support Mat-thew – but I can't really see myself hanging out with a distraught Kaye. We've never even met.

In the end, after spending a lonely hour in the lobby with no news, I call a cab and go home.

JEANIE

15 FEBRUARY 2015

6.30 a.m.

The dawn is flat and unpromising. The empty house is cold. Frankie is in Glasgow this weekend with a group of friends, watching a local band they've started to follow.

'They're kind of grungy, Mum, like Drenge,' he'd explained kindly when I'd dropped him at the station. I was none the wiser.

I put the heating on and walk into the kitchen in my coat, staring out into the forlorn February garden. A few pathetic shoots struggle to reach the light from the pots on the terrace; further down clusters of snowdrops hang their pure white heads.

Everything else looks withered and dead.

Switching the kettle on, I see my Valentine's card to Matthew on the windowsill: a gaudy, soppy affair I made myself.

It feels wrong, misplaced somehow. I feel wrong and misplaced myself.

What is going on? Everything feels discordant suddenly.

Picking up the card, I put it in the kitchen drawer.

Then I pull my phone out and check for messages from Matthew: nothing. I send him one saying I love him and hope everything is okay and to let me know if he needs me.

Then I text my sister.

Everything's going a bit odd. Can't wait to see you next week.

MARLENA

A bit odd? This is starting to sound like an episode of *The Real Housewives of New Jersey* or *Dynasty* or some crap, don't you think?

I didn't really know what her text meant at the time, but I did know it didn't sound great for a newlywed.

And – a ghost?

I mean really?

JEANIE

22 FEBRUARY 2015

The good news is Luke's fine, thank God.

It wasn't appendicitis – in fact, after they put a camera inside him when he'd stopped being so sick, they couldn't find anything wrong, which was a relief all round. They didn't have to operate after all.

I couldn't help feeling then that maybe the degree of urgency had been unwarranted; that the screaming on the phone had been largely hysterical and not helpful to the poor boy.

I kept that to myself though. I appreciated that if something happened to Frankie, I'd have rushed down the motorway even faster than Matthew had: a parent's instinct kicking in – only natural. I loved Matthew even more for caring.

I just wish I didn't feel so – excluded. Like it's him and them, and him and me. Or me and Frankie, and him and them. I suppose that's normal in this set-up. My book on step-parenting says it takes years to 'blend' a family; it says women have overly high expectations. Ridiculous expectations, in my case.

But none of it says quite how tough it is – or how bad it might make you feel.

Matthew had stayed at the hospital until Luke was discharged.

We'd had a muted week, and yesterday he told me he was going to take Scarlett off to see her cousins in King's Lynn, did I mind? Luke was at home with his mum, and I was waiting for Marlena to arrive, so I said no – please go.

And then of course, just after Matthew pulled out the drive, my unreliable sister texted from Germany saying she couldn't come at all – she'd had a new lead; she had to file her copy, blah blah – the usual excuses. She'd ring when she got back.

Trying not to feel generally abandoned, I spent the weekend mooching, doing some half-hearted prep for my new job, but mainly watching rom-coms and eating chocolate, waiting to hear from Matthew. On Sunday morning, I forced myself out for brunch in town, but I felt so pathetically alone surrounded by couples and happy couples that I soon slouched off home.

Just before I went totally mad, my phone rang. Marlena – back from her trip abroad.

'What's up?' Marlena was typically frank. 'You sound like shit.'

'Thanks a lot! I'm just a bit – tired.' I explained the events of the past week briefly. 'He's okay now, Luke, so that's the main thing.'

'That's kids for you. And so?'

'So what?'

'You said things were "odd". Is that cos you've actually told your old man the whole shebang now?'

I nudged the coffee table gently with the tip of my toe.

'Jeanie?'

'No,' I admitted. 'I've told him some of it. Just not – quite all of it.'

She let out a long breath. 'Really?'

'Don't. I have tried, Marlena, honestly. Quite a few times, but it's just not very easy with all this going on—'

'For God's sake, Jean!' She'd been tapping on her computer whilst we'd been talking, I had heard her busy hands on the keyboard, but she actually stopped now. Ever the hack, my sister – never fully concentrating on her own life.

'Look, really, I didn't put myself on the line for you to fuck yourself up even further.'

'Yeah, all right.' I felt a surge of irritation at her selfishness.

She ignored my tone; she was in her stride now. 'I mean doesn't the man ever use Google? You know he's going to find out anyway some time, and it'll look fucking awful if it doesn't come from you…'

'Okay, okay,' I said meekly. 'I will. I'm just…'

'*What*?'

I sighed heavily. 'Scared he'll chuck me out I suppose.'

'Well if he does, he's an even bigger arsehole than I took him for.'

'Marlena! I thought you quite liked him?'

'Now, when, dear Jeanie'—I heard her lighting a cigarette— 'did I *ever* say that?'

It started to snow very lightly as I put the phone down, the flakes falling in sudden soft flurries past the window. I was depressed about being alone all the time, about my attempt to tell Matt failing yet again. Admitting my apathy to myself was hard.

Still, at least Frankie was on his way back; he'd been in Scotland all week. Now he was on some kind of Megabus, unlikely to be here before dawn, knowing him. I had no idea what time Matthew would be home; they'd stopped off to see friends in Cambridge apparently. I'd give this entire week up as a bad lot, I decided, and go to bed.

My legs had gone to sleep curled beneath me, and as I stretched them out painfully, I heard an odd rattle.

The hairs on my arms all stood up on end. Not that bloody ghost again…

I held my breath, listening.

God I wished this house wasn't so isolated. Tower blocks had never felt as unsafe as all this space.

Everything was quiet now. *I should get up and check out the noise,* I thought – and then the garden light sprang on.

I heard my own surprised gasp.

Don't be so stupid, Jeanie! I tried to laugh at myself – and then the noise came again.

I got up. Limping to the switch, I turned all the inside lights on as bright as they'd go. Taking a deep breath, I opened the kitchen door to investigate, thinking of Peckham or Hove's electric street lights with considerable nostalgia.

Crossing the kitchen, I could feel a blast of cold air. The sliding doors were very slightly ajar, the February wind blowing through the crack. Then I heard a woman's voice, murmuring from somewhere.

Oh Christ.

I ran to shut the doors – realising, with a sob of relief, that it was the radio talking.

The respite I felt at finding the source of all the noises was tempered by confusion as to why the doors were open. Sometimes the catch stuck and didn't slide in right; someone must have missed it. But I hadn't gone in the garden today; I hadn't noticed they were open…

Agata, Matthew's cleaner, might have been here earlier I supposed – when I'd gone to the shops. I could never remember when she came – but she *could* have left them open. Except – it was Sunday.

There's always an answer, Jeanie.

Fumbling with the handles, I heard a baby start to cry outside in the freezing night.

Just a fox barking somewhere nearby, Jeanie. There were so many foxes here, ruling the gardens. Quickly I flung the doors back to push them shut properly.

A flicker of light at the end of the garden perhaps – there, shivering across my eyes behind the lightly swirling flakes – and then gone again.

Instinctively I looked down, away from the light. That's when I saw them.

Two blackbirds, one much bigger than the other – a mother and a chick, maybe –together beneath a couple of glass bells, perfectly symmetrical on the decking outside the doors, an old wooden clothes peg next to one.

Snow speckled the cloches, and it would have been quite picturesque really – except both of the birds, sprigs of holly stuck into their guts, were absolutely and brutally dead.

MARLENA

Let me tell you a story, now I've got your attention.

Are you sitting comfortably? Then I'll begin.

Once upon a time there were two little girls born to a young mother who named them not for the rose trees in the Grimms' tale, *Snow White and Rose Red*, but for the beautiful film stars she would rather have been herself.

The mother was already sad, because she realised she hadn't married a king but a total tosser with a roving eye and a gambling habit – but she quite liked her two daughters. They made her smile, and the older one was very good at taking care of the younger on the days the mother couldn't get out of bed.

Only when the king disappeared with Lynnette from the Cordor estate, the mother was so distraught that she couldn't stop crying, and soon after she became well and truly hooked on pot and then on mother's little helpers.

Easily done. Valium was all the rage in the late 1970s...

When even the dodgy doctor on the high street refused to fill yet another prescription, she asked her Uncle Rog for help. He lit another fag and sniffed: *Go down the Breakspears in Brockley – you'll get anything there.*

Unfortunately that day the dealer in the pub wasn't the usual bloke but a new one: a handsome, stress-wise type, pretty eyes and sneering mouth. 'I can do Valium today, love, and if I ever can't, think about a hit of smack instead? Does the same sort of thing, don't it?' Then he gave her a kiss. 'You're very pretty, ain't you?'

And so it was that the mother fell for a man worse even than the horror dad of her two girls.

She kept off the heroin for a while – she wasn't daft. But when the pills began to not quite do their job, well…

And so the older girl – the quieter, gentler one – kept looking after the younger, who was a right little livewire, and somehow they stumbled through their childhood together – until they met the bear. But that's another story, for another day.

Bit clearer?

And make of that what you will, but just know this: if you grow up at the knee of a woman so out of it she can't remember to feed you every morning or take you to school; if you know that she kind of can't help it herself, but she's failing as a parent, except you're too young to actually manufacture that thought properly, so you just think, 'Oh that's our Mum, she's spaced again,' and you still love her anyway, though you couldn't define love if you were asked to; if you still hope she'll love you, despite the fact she's so off her head most of the time that she wouldn't know what love was if it jumped out and punched her on the nose – a broken nose, broken more than once from fighting with fellas or falling on her face – well if you go through that for a bit, it will affect you. Yeah, it will.

We are a product of what we grow up in. Not necessarily always our genes, it turns out – but a lot about our nurture.

Oh yeah, I see your face now. You're thinking, what the hell – how are they both walking and talking, let alone breathing, if they came through this?

Are you judging me? Well judge away, mate.

We were lucky. We had our nan. In the end she came and got us. Before the social got involved she took us away, and she did the rest of the parenting. We saw our mum occasionally, when she was clean, which got more rare until eventually she died. There was the terrible methamphetamine phase when Nan went on holiday with Sheila from bingo for a bit of a rest. We spent much of that week hiding in the cupboard beneath the stairs.

After that we saw our mum a few times a year – and our nan, and Great Aunt Margaret, made sure we were washed and fed, loved and schooled.

So. We survived. Just about.

But it made us what we are today.

I survived, largely cos of Jeanie. Because before Nan stepped in, Jeanie made sure we got food and got to school on the worst days, the days when our mum was comatose or had cried into her pillow all night till she couldn't see straight.

Now they'd call it 'bipolar' I guess or clinical depression or some such. There were reasons for her behaviour; she hadn't had a good time either. There were doubtless reasons she turned to the drugs and drink. But no, I don't want to go into all of that now.

Our dad? He was just a reprobate and a charming one at that. He took after my granddad, my nan's late husband – a sailor in the Merchant Navy and never at home till he died early.

Our dad literally had a woman in every tower block this side of the Thames, and that side too, along with many a scheme to get rich quick. In the end he offed and didn't get rich at all, as far as I know.

No. No idea – could be alive and kicking, could be six feet under. Do I care? Not really.

You don't miss what you never had.

Do you?

So. Don't look at us like that. We didn't do so badly, I don't think – but we didn't do relationships well, either of us. We didn't get it.

We couldn't get it.

The only thing we did get that was positive, thank God, was a little ambition. Our nan drummed it into us. 'Don't rely on a man.' Well there were none around to rely on anyway.

And we knew we wanted to get the hell out of Dodge.

And look at how that turned out for both of us in the end.

To return to the present, Jeanie *did* sound like shit on the phone that evening, after the whole Luke-in-hospital incident.

Sorry if that offends your sensibilities, but it's not what you expect when your big sister's apparently married the man of her dreams.

Except – as more than one bloody shrink's told me – I have zero expectations of love for myself, so why would I have more for Jeanie?

Not that she doesn't deserve love. Christ, if anyone does, if anyone deserves being adored, it's Jeanie. But as usual she put herself last and everyone else first.

That's just how she is... and now look what's bloody happened.

JEANIE

23 FEBRUARY 2015

9 a.m.

I didn't sleep well at all last night.

After I saw the birds, I pulled down all the blinds and tried both Matthew – whose phone went to voicemail – and then Frankie. He was still only near Birmingham, he said, waiting for a connection at the bus depot.

'Call the police if you're worried?' he said, but I decided that would be ridiculous, so I went to bed instead.

My dreams were filled with skeletons and bird beaks and tiny beady eyes, and at some point Matthew crept into bed, terrifying me even more when I opened my eyes and found him beside me.

I curled into him desperately. At least I wasn't alone in the house any more, though my dreams were still chequered.

In the sleety morning, all snow melted, I told him about the dead birds, but by the time he went to look, they'd gone.

'The foxes must have taken them,' I said, confused. But where were the cloches? 'They were definitely right there last night – like they'd been laid out. A baby and a mother.'

'There's hardly any foxes here at this time of year.'

That was rubbish, and we both knew it.

'I heard them, Matthew. Last night, I heard them. The foxes.'

'Well it's still not the right time of year for chicks. You must have imagined it,' he said. 'Probably tired – and maybe a bit drunk?'

'I didn't even have a drink last night,' I protested, and he looked at me oddly.

'*Really?*' He pointed at the recycling bin. A bottle of Sauvignon Blanc stuck out – my favourite – and an empty half-measure of Southern Comfort.

'Not mine,' I insisted. 'Honestly, I swear, Matt.'

'If you say so,' he said, with a half sigh.

It was obvious he didn't believe me.

When he left for work, I rang Marlena again. Frankie had a shift at the bistro, and I needed to see someone who actually knew me well.

'I'd – I'd really like to see you,' I said to my sister's voicemail. 'I should have said last night – I miss you.'

Need would have been a better verb.

Was I losing my marbles again?

11 a.m.

Marlena calls back to say she's on her way to Luton for a 'recce' and she could meet somewhere nearby for coffee.

We meet at a service station not far away, on the M25. She's in the coffee shop, scribbling on a notepad, transcribing something from her phone.

We don't kiss each other; we never do.

'Hey,' she says, not looking up properly. 'Won't be a sec. Grab me another black coffee would you? And a chocolate muffin. I haven't got long.'

I do as I'm told. It's easier, generally, I've found with her.

Sitting opposite Marlena, I wait for her to finish writing. She looks good; she always does. Her glossy black curls are bundled messily on top of her head; she wears a big fake fur, a leather mini skirt and high-tops that she manages to pull off, despite being thirty-six.

She finishes whatever it is she's been scrawling. 'So what's up?' My sister looks at me and grins.

'Nothing really.' I toy with my cappuccino froth.

'That's quite blatantly a lie.' Her nicotine-stained fingers are itching to light a fag. 'You look tired.'

'How's the no smoking going?'

She scowls at me like she did when I told her to brush her teeth aged five. 'It's not, as I'm sure you well know. Don't rub it in!'

'Sorry.' I try to stifle a yawn. She looks at me again, enquiry in her dark eyes, and I shrug. 'I'm not sleeping well.'

'I thought you were over all that?'

MARLENA

As I suspected, Jeanie didn't look like someone who'd just got married and was basking in her honeymoon period. Sure, she had a massive rock on her ring finger and a new navy coat that looked expensive – Hobbs or Reiss or somewhere sensible like that – but she looked really tired, big shadows under her warm brown eyes. When she said she wasn't sleeping, alarm bells sounded faintly.

Were we going down this route again?

'I'm okay.' She managed a half smile. 'Really. It's just…' She trailed off.

'What?' Surreptitiously I checked the time on my phone. The bloke I was meeting was meant to be here in twenty minutes. I couldn't miss the opportunity. If I could talk to the mullah of this group, he might have info on Nasreen's disappearance; they might have one tiny clue at least – God knows we needed it. The lead in Germany had turned out to be nothing; there was no evidence of the girl on any flight to Turkey at the moment, despite the CCTV to Heathrow – so *how* the hell had she got to Syria – unless she'd had a fake passport?

If she had got to Syria – that was what I was starting to think.

'Oh I don't know.' Jeanie pulled her hair back into a ponytail, and then she looked at me nervously. I always knew when she was nervous. 'I do feel a *bit* like I'm imagining things, but…'

'Spit it out.' I felt frustrated, partly because of my lack of time. 'Imagining what?'

'It's – someone knows, Mar. And it's as if they might be making things – well kind of hard for me.'

'Knows what?' I shook my head. 'Don't get it.'

'Everything. They know everything – and they've said so. And last night – there were dead birds outside. Only when I told Matthew this morning, they were gone.'

'Dead birds?' I felt myself frown. 'What do you mean?'

'There was a mother and a chick laid out, like someone had – I don't know. Made some kind of picture. I saw it, I know I did – but then it was gone.'

I saw her eyes fill with tears and I thought, *Oh shit, please don't cry, Jean.* I'm not good with tears; never have been. Make me feel – kind of angry inside.

Helpless, the shrink said. *They make you feel impotent, Marlena, so you get angry.*

'Sorry,' Jeanie said, wiping them on the back of her hand. She knows me so well, my big sis.

Frankly I was a bit worried by all this, but I wasn't sure how to play it.

'So let me get this straight.' I fiddled with the wooden stirrer thing, desperate for a fag. 'You *still* haven't told Matthew everything?'

'Most of it, I have. And I'm going to – I was going to the other night – but then his son got rushed into hospital and…'

'Shit.'

'He's okay – he's fine now. But someone wrote to me, Mar. They sent me a card.'

'What kind of card?'

My phone buzzed. It was a text from Ravi:

Twenty minutes!!! Outside Central Mosque.

'Oh God, Jean, I'm really sorry, but I'm going to have to go in a sec – I can't miss this bloke, it's pretty fucking crucial…'

I felt bad – but this might be life and death.

'No worries.' Jeanie gave a bright smile. 'I probably *am* just imagining things. It's been a big change, I suppose. Just need to get used to things. The house and things – it's so big, it's kind of – weird.'

Why did she say that? *No worries.* Why didn't she just say, *Stay the fuck here and listen to me*?

'I will come up soon, I promise,' I said. 'To stay in your nice big house. In a weekend or two. Tell him everything. Then it'll all be okay. And enjoy the house! I would.'

'Yes, I will try. I'm sure you're right.'

'I'm always right, aren't I, Jean?' I pulled a silly face as I picked my coffee up. 'How's Frank? Tell him to come and see me.'

I'm always right?

Jesus wept, Marlena. You fucking stupid cow.

JEANIE

28 FEBRUARY 2015

I feel a bit better now! It was good to see Marlena, even if it was brief – and Matthew was all normal when he got home. He ordered us a Thai curry for supper and told me about King's Lynn and the mad cousins. And I slept much better last night.

Frankie brings Jenna home for lunch. A curvy little brunette with a big smile and gappy teeth, I warm to her immediately. He was an early starter, my lovely Frank, always keen on the girls – and that's fine with me. I don't really get all that jealous mother stuff. It's beyond me.

As long as they are kind. I just want Frank to be happy.

That's *all* I want really.

But I don't think Matthew appreciated Jenna's rather left-wing politics. He's far more traditional than I first realised, and I've not told him yet about my misspent youth selling the *Socialist Worker*.

I'm starting to see it's best not to argue too much. The vein on his forehead stood out alarmingly last week when Frankie said he was a Marxist at heart.

'A communist?' Matthew spluttered. 'Well you won't want your subscription to the *Grand Prix* mag then, will you?' That had been Matthew's idea of the perfect Christmas present for Frank and not really up Frank's street at all – but I'd wanted Matt to feel that he was contributing emotionally as well as materially, so I hadn't demurred.

Matthew reacts very quickly to Frank and doesn't seem to get his humour. It's starting to occur to me that my husband and my son are clashing; tension's growing by the minute.

Luckily Jenna is sweet and perceptive, asking Matthew about his work, which goes down well. Although Matthew seems stressed recently, I have to say; far more so than when I met him.

'What's Malum House named for?' Jenna asks as I cut the cherry pie. 'It means evil, doesn't it – malum?'

'Evil?' Matthew seems shocked. 'No, it's the Latin for "apple". It was built on the old orchards. There are a few apple trees left in the back garden actually.'

'Oh I'm sorry.' Jenna smiles at him. 'I thought it seemed odd. I must have misremembered my Latin. It's been a while.'

'Custard, lovey?' I change the subject quickly. 'Hope it's not too lumpy. Not my forte, custard.'

Jenna leaves, and the headache that has crept up during the afternoon gets worse. I just can't shift it, so I go to bed early.

'I'll be up soon.' Matthew blows me a kiss from in front of *Match of the Day.* 'Take some more pills, hon.'

An hour or two later I wake up, needing a drink of water.

Matthew isn't in bed.

I can hear voices; maybe he and Frank are chatting? But Frankie is asleep when I peer into his room.

I realise the voices are coming from above – from Scarlett's room. I creep up the stairs, and the light is on.

When did she arrive?

Unsettled I creep back down and into bed.

I am relieved when, about twenty minutes later, Matthew comes to bed too. Reeking of alcohol, I notice, as I turn over to sleep. But at least he is here.

SNOW WHITE'S TALE: THE STEPMOTHER

Let us take a pause here in our story. Allow me to pose a question, if I may…

Why exactly do *you* think, dear readers, why do you think little Snow White's stepmother struggled with her so?

Was it merely because the girl was younger – and youth is always to be coveted?

Was it because the girl was the queen's daughter, who was first recipient of the king's great love?

Was it, perhaps, because the king loved her – his little Snow White, firstborn – more than he could ever love the stepmother?

Or was it because Snow White was a spoilt, precocious little cow, used to getting her own way all the time?

JEANIE

1 MARCH 2015

When I open the bathroom door, the blood in the basin is very red against the white porcelain. So red it shocks me.

I look at it, and then I run the taps – and it washes clean away.

Scarlett shocked me too today. She's friendly again, which is a huge relief. Well not even again – friendly for the first time.

I didn't ask why she'd arrived in the middle of the night, but I got the feeling she'd had some kind of altercation at home. She's got a new kitten apparently, a fluffy Burmese this time, called Bella, who is safely at Scarlett's mother's house – thank God!

At least, I thought, somewhat bitterly, looking at the photo of the kitten on Scarlett's iPhone, *if anything goes wrong, I can't be blamed this time.*

'Sam Smith, the singer, loves these apparently,' I said as we made smoothies together: peanut butter and jelly ones. I hoped Scarlett would appreciate my trivia knowledge.

'I told my mum how pretty you are.' Scarlett ignored the trivia, licking jammy fingers.

'Oh.' I was really surprised. 'Gosh.' I turned the whizzer on to hide my shock, the rush of sudden emotion.

'She wants to meet you.' She was intense suddenly.

'That was very nice of you, to say that.' I was flushing, I knew, but I was very touched. I didn't know what had changed – but it was nice.

I caught our reflections in the window opposite as I whizzed up the mixture again. We would never pass for mother and daughter: she was all pale skin and dark hair like Matthew, with her mother's blue eyes, I assumed. I was shorter, brown-eyed and – mousey? Dark blonde, my friend Jill used to tease. Mousey, I'd say.

And I didn't want to talk about meeting Kaye now. 'I think you'll like this.' I handed Scarlett a glass. 'And it's pretty healthy too. That's a win-win in my book!'

I'd have been happy to meet up with Kaye in the beginning. I'd even suggested it after I'd read my book. But now it felt too late.

Scarlett and I watched *Celebrity Big Brother* – and I thought it was one of the most awful, dystopian things I'd ever seen, with people sniping and snarling at each other like animals. Then they talked about how 'authentic' they were, '*telling it how it is*'.

Where was the good in this cruel, selfish kind of honesty? It was boundary-less. Talk about survival of the fittest.

But Scarlett enjoyed it, and for the first time ever, I enjoyed my time with Scarlett.

Afterwards I felt we'd both actually relaxed for once. We'd even chatted a bit about boys and school, although she was quite reticent about the boy thing. 'There's someone I quite like,' she said, painting her nails neon pink, 'but I'm not sure he likes me.'

When Matthew popped his head round the door, back from a screening of *Star Wars* with Luke at the local Odeon, his own surprised smile reflected the happy situation.

Do I trust it though? I asked myself as Matt brought us tea and kissed me. I snuggled into him, scolding myself for being cynical. Enjoy it, I told myself. It might not last.

I try to forget about the birds – but I keep seeing the holly stuck in their entrails.

Marlena texts to ask: am I okay? And I reply: yes.

I don't bring it up again with Matthew, but I know they were there. The wretched birds, like a warning.

If I don't come clean, it'll be the end.

MARLENA

Okay so the dead bird thing did freak me a bit – but to be honest, I just thought it must have been the neighbour's cat or something, and Jeanie was just tired and stressed about Matthew and overreacting.

And just when I was about to go up to Berkhamsted and stay for a night, I got another lead on Nasreen. A different type of lead that led me away from the fundamentalists. As I was still trying to clear my blotted copybook, I had no choice but to go with it. My career's been in free fall for the past few years. You know why.

Oh. You don't?

Look at the videos on YouTube.

It's all there. Google Leveson; search for 'iniquitous journalists'. You can see a clip of me, if it's still online, after I turned myself in. I wore a skirt suit and everything: trying to clothe my remorse correctly.

I gave evidence at the enquiry, racked with guilt over a case where I'd listened to the mother of a dead boy howling down the phone to her husband, maddened by the depths of her grief. Something no one should hear unless they are part of the equation.

Something no one should ever hear, in an ideal world, full stop.

So I 'grew a pair' – as Dave from the print room used to say – and came clean.

It took a week holed up in a Blackpool B&B, not sleeping, necking whisky, dipping into a bottle of diazepam – and, er, a gram or two of finest Peruvian. I played arcade games into the early hours like when I was a kid – but once I'd got the bender out of my system (never chopped a line since), I contacted the top bods at the Press Complaints Commission.

I asked for a meeting, and I struck a deal. Having done that, I told the truth about my misdemeanours over the past few years. A good few years.

It was hard. I had to take some of my mates down with me; I'd been taught by the best. The worst, if you like.

I avoided jail because I 'snitched'. You can make your own mind up about whether that was fair or not. I never lied or coerced anyone into talking, I want to say that much. I only listened, sometimes inappropriately.

I think I've paid my dues – I'm still paying them actually.

I sold one flat and downsized, moving to get away from the haters. Thank God I'd already bought, because I lost most of my immediate income – and of course I had few savings. Colleagues spilled their vitriol down the line. I received threats and a promise from my big boss that I'd never get paid for another word I wrote (I'll leave you to take a guess who that boss was. These days I never write *anything* down that might incriminate me).

I had the sneering public spitting in my face once or twice – and celebrities threatening to sue. The father of the boy came pretty close to thumping me outside the court when I tried to apologise; he'd have succeeded if a policewoman hadn't restrained him.

I'd like to say he couldn't have felt any worse than I did, but we all know that's not true.

I was truly sorry. I didn't sleep properly for months; I got thin, which was quite good, I felt shit, which wasn't. I broke up with my then boyfriend – who I actually quite liked, for once.

What else can I say? I was young when I got my first job on the *Star*; my career was everything. I'd not gone to college – I'd begged a job on the local paper. I'd worked so hard. I'd worked and worked because I was addicted to it: the money, the buzz, the belonging to something.

It was a way out of the gutter. I loved it; I loved the thrill of the chase, of a good story.

But I proved I was no better than the guttersnipes I worked with.

The trouble with 'fessing up' was that, whilst I might have cleared my conscience an iota, I also became public enemy number fucking one – and then Fleet Street's scapegoat on top of that. I was an easy target for all the wrongdoings of my profession. I could have everything laid at my door by unscrupulous editors trying to save their own skins. Even though the majority of the tabloid journalists had been at it, they certainly hadn't all owned up.

I was deeply unhireable for a while. At one point I looked at going to America; the *National Enquirer* would probably have welcomed me with open arms.

But I couldn't leave England in the end – I couldn't leave my family. Even though I hardly saw them, I felt tied.

So when I got the magazine job and then the other gig, through a sympathetic former sub-editor of mine, lecturing on the pros and cons of social media and the digital age of journalism, both were no-brainers.

At the same time, my appetite was whetted by the need to do good. After I met a journalist called Laila Shah at a gender and race conference, I started working with her and then on my own when she went out to Lebanon. I began looking into young Muslim girls in suburban secondaries being groomed by radicals. It wasn't scary – it was vital.

Except even that wasn't as straightforward as it first seemed…

JEANIE

4 MARCH 2015

8 p.m.

It's cracking now: for real, this time.

How naïve I've been – I'm so angry with myself for not seeing the truth. And for letting myself be caught out like this. I've been an idiot – an absolute and complete fool.

No surprise there, I hear my mother's voice saying. *You always were a bit wet, love.*

Piss off, Mum, I surprise myself by thinking.

Mothers and daughters. That's nearly always a tricky one in my book.

I listened to a radio phone-in earlier on mother love.

Unconditional, a woman was saying; a parent's love is unconditional, naturally.

The psychologist disagreed.

I disagreed too. *In your dreams, love*, I thought.

Some mothers can't do it. Some just aren't up to it. Many can't see past their own needs; they use their children as validation of something. As a mirror for what they need.

And some are too frightened; some – like Marlena – are too damaged to trust themselves, so they get out before the harm's done.

11 a.m.

I feel motivated and energised this morning when I get up: I go for a run around the Common, and as I run, I realise exactly how excited I am about starting my new job.

But I get back from my run– proud that I've kept it up for a whole two months, practically a first for me – to find *that* white Range Rover in the drive, the noxious smell of *that* perfume in the hall – and the lounge door firmly shut.

Kaye, apparently: cosily ensconced with Matthew.

In the hall mirror, I see my hair is damp and plastered to my face, puce from the exertion and the cold, the top of my coral T-shirt ringed with sweat. Hardly the pretty woman Scarlett had promised her mother.

I creep towards the stairs – but too late. Matthew pokes his head round the door.

'Come and meet Kaye, hon,' he says. 'She's here to discuss the Easter holidays.'

I pull a face that says: *Really? Looking like this?* A face I think he'll understand.

But he's a man – and men, I must remember (I never remember) don't do subtleties! I haven't spelt it out for him.

'Come on.' He holds a hand out. 'Don't be shy. She's going soon.'

I have no choice: I follow Matthew like an obedient child.

'So here she is at last.' Kaye lowers her coffee cup as I walk in, smiling to display impeccable white teeth. 'How lovely to meet you.'

'Hi!' I say. She is drinking from some very expensive-looking china I didn't even know we owned. 'Good to meet you too.'

'So you're the lover of babes.'

I freeze.

'What?' Matthew looks puzzled. 'Hardly.'

'Our babes, Matty! Just my little joke,' Kaye says, but one look at that alabaster face tells me she is sizing up the competition – or maybe just sizing up her prey?

Matty.

Actually she isn't as pretty as I'd feared. Her beaky nose is too big for her thin face, her pale blue eyes narrow and unflinching. Judging by her smooth forehead, she's had Botox. Scarlett is much prettier than her mother.

But pretty or not, Kaye certainly looks spectacular in a fur gilet and tight leather trousers, immaculate blow-dry tumbling over her shoulders.

'Pleased to meet you,' I mumble. 'Sorry about my appearance. I've been for a run. I'll just dash and change…'

'Oh please don't on my account. I'm in my old things anyway.' She stands languorously and offers me her hand. She is much taller than me, and I feel horribly dumpy: a clumsy little figure next to her blonde elegance. 'It's great to exercise when we're not feeling our best, isn't it?'

But Matthew always tells me he loves my body, I remind myself firmly. He likes my curves and my tummy.

'Okay.' I wish my hand didn't look so red knuckled and rough skinned in her pretty white one, her nails perfectly shaped and polished pearly pink. 'I like your outfit.'

'So – the next Mrs King! Enjoying married life? The kids have told me all about you.'

'Yes, thanks.' I try to smile. 'Good things, I hope.'

'Wellll…' She pauses. Her laugh is shrill when she clocks the expression I fail to hide. 'Of *course* good things!'

'Fancy a coffee, Jeanie, hon?' Matthew seems exhilarated somehow. 'I'll grab another cup from the kitchen.'

'Thanks,' I say, but what I really mean of course is: *PLEASE don't leave me with the predator.*

'I understand it's a first for you – marriage?' Her smile is tight. 'The old wedding bells. Except you must have done it civilly, no?'

'O-ho!' Hand on the door, Matthew laughs. 'Been doing your homework, Kaye?'

'Naturally.' Kaye's smooth face attempts the stretch to a wider smile. 'Obviously I wanted to know who *our* kids were hanging out with. Any mother would, wouldn't they?' She looks at me for agreement.

'I guess so,' I say carefully.

'Cos we all know about wicked stepmothers, eh? Poor old Cinders and all that. You just can't be too careful these days, can you?' The door swings shut behind Matthew, and I am sure her eyes narrow further. 'I mean you of all people should know that, shouldn't you, Jeanie?'

Please don't, I think. *Please don't.*

But she does. I've known it was coming from the minute I stepped into the room. She is a big, sleek cat waiting for the kill.

'So how did you two meet?' She sips her coffee through perfectly glossed lips. Kaye *isn't* perfect, I know that really, I know no one is – but she gives a good impression of being so. She has me over a barrel, and she is going to enjoy every last minute of it.

I can taste the salt of my own dried sweat on my lips. 'At an office party,' I say. I wonder what he's told her.

'It's a shame you managed to poison my dog.'

Jesus! As Marlena would say: *You can take the girl out of the estate, but you can't take the…*

'Joke!' Kaye guffaws. *Liar.* 'Your face!'

'I didn't poison your dog.' I stand taller. 'It was a horrible accident – and I'm very sorry he died.'

'It's hard to admit you were a bit – lax, I'm sure, when the kids were so gutted'—she pats my arm generously—'but I believe you if you say it was accidental.'

'Well it's the truth.' I meet her slit-eyed gaze. 'It was nothing to do with me. It was just unfortunate.'

'And you always tell the truth?'

'Yes.' We look at each other. 'What makes you say that?'

'I always Google new boyfriends. It pays to know who you're shagging. Do you think my ex-husband would do the same?'

'I don't know…'

'Men are such fools, aren't they?'

'Are they?' I say with all the dignity I can manage. 'I've never particularly found that.'

'I find girls much easier than boys. Luke's a pain.'

'Oh he's a sweet boy,' I object. 'Very well meaning and kind.'

'And a tiny little bit of a – dud. Let's be honest.' She stares at me.

God! Her own son. I am sweating again.

'I'm only joking, silly!' But her laugh is flat and fake. 'I'm glad you take step-parenting so seriously.' She nods at my book on the coffee table. I feel the heat rising up my back in shame. My silly step-parenting manual. *Why* have I left it out for all to see?

Because I thought I was safe here, I suppose.

'He's nice. Luke. They're both – nice kids,' I bluster.

'Oh I know, lovely. I know.' Kaye pulls out a slim packet of expensive-looking cigarettes. 'But kids are hard work, aren't they? Even for kiddie fiddlers, I expect.'

Breezily she clamps a baby-pink cigarette between scarlet lips.

'I've always enjoyed working with young people.' I find myself very calm. 'I like to think I've always taken my job very seriously.'

'That's good.' Kaye digs around again, producing a gold lighter from her trouser pocket. 'I suppose they always claim, "It's not what it seems, officer." But hey, we weren't born yesterday, were we, Jeanie? Can I call you Jeanie?'

'Sure.' If Marlena were here, she'd give me a kick up the arse for being so feeble. Summoning all my courage, I say, 'It's no smoking in here actually.'

'Oh?' The lighter in Kaye's manicured hand has an inscription on it; I can't quite read it.

'We don't like it.'

'*We?*' Her thick dark brows – very Cara Delevingne – would have shot up her forehead – if it could actually move.

'Yes – Matthew and I. *My* husband.' I warm to my theme. 'It kills, you know. Smoking. Very nasty.'

'Oh how things change.' But she drops her hand. Perhaps she doesn't look quite as confident as a minute before. 'Matthew was a twenty-a-day man. I must say, you don't look like his usual type.'

'And what's that?' Trembling, I plough on. 'Tall blondes?'

'Something like that. Skinny women usually. But then he's had all sorts – hasn't he said? Sounds like you two have got some catching up to do.' She gathers her Mulberry bag. 'That's the best bit of a new relationship, isn't it? Finding out stuff about each other. I'll leave you to it.'

'What does that mean – all sorts?'

'Whatever you want it to.' She yawns widely. 'Just be cautious please. My daughter's my best friend in the world. I'll protect her against anything. You know how it is.'

'Really?' I meet her gaze. 'Do you think that's a good idea – being best friends, I mean?' My voice has risen a little now, I realise too late. 'Kids need boundaries, don't they? Parents, not friends.'

'The mouse roars, eh?' She smirks.

I see the red blood in the white bathroom.

'To know where they stand. Kaye…'

'Sorry, ladies.' Matthew reappears. 'Got distracted by footie results.' He hands me a mug. 'I thought you might enjoy a chat.'

It is all I can do to not let my mouth drop open in disbelief.

'Yeah, we caught up on the goss, didn't we, Jeanie? I'd better get off.' Kaye's artful stretch reveals a well-toned brown midriff. 'Appointment with the masseuse. Very stiff at the moment; so much stress.' She rolls her head, demonstrating stress – probably at whether it was the Atkins or the 5:2 diet this week. 'Yassine's got the magic touch – but he's working with Arsenal today.'

My arse, I nearly say, grinning at the thought.

'I'll walk you out.' Matthew shoots me an inscrutable look. 'Finalise the holiday plans.'

'God I can't wait to get back to Barbados at Easter,' Kaye is saying as they leave the room. 'Daiquiris are calling! You remember Slow Joe's place? We had fun, didn't we, babes? Back in the day.'

Oh just fuck off, I find myself thinking.

Alone, shaken, I pour some cold coffee into the old mug Matthew has brought in, the mug that says 'World's Best Washer-Upper' on it. I wonder why I got this chipped old thing.

But it is obvious, I suppose – I get the homely mug because this is *my* home now. Kaye gets the best china to show off.

This warped civility confuses me. They didn't do things like this down my way – a middle-class sharing of kids after marriages collapsed. Generally the mothers were left to cope alone. Calling Matthew and Kaye friends was stretching it – but they were friendly enough to chat about arrangements.

And yet God only knows what has gone on between them.

When my mum and dad split up, we almost literally never saw him again. Once, I think, when he was trying to soft-soap

some landlord about back rent and tried to play happy families
– and once when he fancied some woman who worked in the
local nursery. Turned out she loathed kids.

My mum, when she could get out of bed, or wasn't slumped
in front of the old television, watching old Hollywood black
and whites, brought home a string of miscreants and no-hopers,
most of whom hated us, ignored us – or, on the odd occasion,
liked us a little *too* much.

I shudder.

Marlena has espoused therapy during the last few years, sev-
eral times – partly after her own spectacular misdemeanours and
then again when I had my 'incident' – but the truth is I'd rather
eat my own heart than pour it out to a therapist.

Through the window I watch Matthew open the car door for
Kaye – and then lean forward towards her.

Oh God he's going to kiss her, right in front of me.

Horrified, I can't tear myself away.

But he doesn't kiss her. He just peers into her eye as she
blinks, looking up to heaven. She must have something in it.

I walk away and sit slowly on the sofa.

Kaye's lighter is lying on the coffee table. I think about rushing out to return it, then think again. She deserves no favours
from me.

Picking it up, I read the inscription.

To my darling Queenie on her birthday.
Love, always.
Your King, September 2013

It was from him, from *my* husband. Matthew King.

Only ten months before I met him.

I shove it down the side of the sofa and wait for him to come back from bidding his ex-wife farewell.

This is it now. No more hiding.

There is no choice any more.

5 MARCH 2015

After meeting Kaye, I know I can't put it off any more. I can't let her be the one who mentions it before I do.

Matthew is in a good mood the day after she's been round because Aston Villa have won, so I think I'll seize the opportunity. We stay in bed late, and it is like when we first met, and I have real hope.

I decide to cook an amazing meal, slipping out that afternoon to the best butcher's on the high street to buy him veal, planning to make a huge cheesecake with chocolate and caramel sauce…

But someone gets to him before me.

When I walk in from the shops, my hands curled freezing round the basket, planning on a hot shower, a ton of subtle make-up and my most alluring outfit – that Ghost dress maybe, the clinging burgundy one that Marlena made me buy two summers ago in the Lanes – an ashen-faced Matthew is waiting for me.

Later I will cringe thinking about my crass naïvety; about why on earth I ever thought it would be all right.

'What is it?' I panic. 'Is it one of the kids?' I check for my phone automatically. 'Is it Frankie?'

'No.' He is terse. 'It's this.'

He shoves his own phone into my hand. I squint at the screen, but without my glasses, I can hardly read it.

'What?'

He grabs it back, propelling me through the kitchen towards his laptop, shoving me down in front of it like a naughty child. He brings up his email and the link…

And of course all the time I know really.

There is the headline on the article – and a big photo.

The photo of the two of us – me and Otto. The back of my head, my hair tied up. Otto leaning towards me…

An article about my affair with a fifteen-year-old called Otto Lundy, a pupil at Seaborne Academy – *my* star pupil. The photo that started it all.

'It's not true,' I say immediately. 'Why were you Googling me?'

'I wasn't.' Matthew sits heavily at the table. 'Someone sent me the link.'

'*Someone*? Who?'

'I don't know. I don't recognise the address.'

'Can I see?' I ask, but he shuts the computer.

'It's not really relevant. What's relevant, Jeanie, is: is it true? And why didn't you tell me?' He looks like he might cry.

I've never seen him like this before, and it is physically painful. It is all my nightmares rolled into one. 'Matt, please…' I lean towards him, but he ducks away.

'Why the hell didn't you tell me?'

'I did,' I mutter. 'Sort of. I tried, honestly…'

'You bloody well didn't.' He is getting angry now. 'You most definitely didn't. You said you'd had a breakdown after an allegation of misconduct. You said you were cleared—'

'I *was* cleared,' I say. 'Absolutely.'

'So why didn't you tell me the whole truth?'

'I – I tried. I really did. And it's not true anyway.' I am speaking with an icy calm – born of terror, I think. 'I swear it's not.'

'But I don't understand. Didn't you think I'd find out everything at some point?'

'Yes. And I tried, Matthew.' I try to take his hand, but he pushes me away. 'Please! I swear I tried.'

'Oh come on!' He grimaces. 'You're a liar, Jean.'

'I'm not.' I hear my voice crack. 'I tried to tell you months ago. Don't you remember the email I sent? You didn't read it, but I tried.'

'That was a feeble attempt.' He sits looking away from me.

There's something very disconcerting about someone refusing to even glance at you whilst you're pouring out your heart. But I ploughed on regardless. 'I thought you knew, *honestly*. And when I realised you didn't, I panicked. I didn't want to lose you, Matthew,' I say, my voice shaking. 'I couldn't bear it.'

Now he does look at me. It isn't reassuring at all.

I cry. I can't help myself. The tears are hot and strong and constant. 'I couldn't tell you because when I realised – too late – you didn't know, I loved you so much by then; I was so in love with you, I couldn't bear to risk anything.'

He still won't look at me, though I go to him now, try to make him meet my eyes.

'I was so frightened of losing you, Matt. I'm so sorry – really, I feel awful. I *know* I should have told you sooner – but apart from that, I've done nothing wrong – really. Not in the grand scheme of things.' The sobs that have wrenched me are passing a little.

The thing I can't say is that after the bloody devil that was Simon, I've never let myself love anyone except Frankie and Marlena the way I love Matthew. So the stakes were really high. So high. Too high. But I keep trying.

'Can you see that?' I am desperate for his approbation. For his forgiveness. For his understanding about what so nearly ruined my life. The thing that, until I met him, I thought was the end of me. 'I didn't do anything wrong at Seaborne. They just said I did.'

'So tell me now,' Matthew speaks at last, flatly, '*exactly* what happened. Explain it all please.'

The thing that may still ruin my life.

'I need a drink.' I wipe my eyes, dry mouthed with fear.

He pushes an open bottle of red wine across the table, but I want to stay sober. At the sink, I pour myself a glass of water, looking out into the darkness.

I don't know if I'll be packing my bags in the morning.

Once I've drunk the water, I turn to him, and in a low voice I tell him everything it would have been wiser to say *before* we made our vows. In a great long rush of a speech, I explain the series of events that led to the incident, in my last job but one, when Frankie and I still lived in Hove, near the sea that I both loved and feared.

'I see,' Matthew says after I've finished talking. That is all he says. I stare at him. Waiting. Feeling him processing.

But he doesn't say anything else. He just gets up and walks out of the room.

'Matthew…' I start.

'I need some time,' he says over his shoulder, the door banging behind him as he goes.

I hear the front door slam and his car screech away.

I sit at the table and think about what has been sent to his email.

Later I realise it is the same article that I'd been sent six weeks ago: the poor photocopy that I'd hidden away. It is exactly the same one.

The one that so mysteriously vanished from my dressing-table drawer.

10 p.m.

When he comes back, slightly calmer, when he asks a few more questions, I think Matthew *does* believe I am innocent; that I was unfairly accused.

He believes what I repeat, sweating with anxiety, pacing up and down: that the photo was taken by a student with a grudge, from the most incriminating angle.

And it is the fact he seems more sorrowful than angry now that is almost worse than when he'd shouted.

'Why didn't you just tell me?' he keeps saying, increasingly drunk as he ploughs his way through the red wine – until I want to scream: *Why do you think? Didn't you hear what I said?*

Eventually we go upstairs, very subdued, and when I get into bed, he rolls away from me as I try to cuddle up to him.

I lie sleepless again, staring blankly into the night.

Have I left it too late?

6 MARCH 2015

8.30 a.m.

When I wake, Matt's already left for work. I fell asleep so late, I'd not heard him leaving, and I feel disoriented as I haul myself out of bed. There's no note from him, no text.

Frankie has gone to London, I remember, to sort his passport out. He's leaving for France soon.

It's Agata's day to clean the house. I feel awkward and embarrassed when she's here – but fortunately I'm going into the college, so I'll miss her today. And at least that'll be a distraction.

I'm really looking forward to it actually.

10 a.m.

On the drive into town my phone rings.

It is the college: an extremely harassed-sounding vice principal on the line.

'Hi, Lesley,' I say, hoping she isn't going to reschedule. 'How are you? I'm nearly there actually—'

There is a slight pause, then she says, 'I'm going to get straight to the point, Jeanie. I'm so sorry, but I'm afraid we're going to have to withdraw the job offer.'

I feel like I've been gut punched.

'Hang on please.' I veer into a bus stop and turn off the engine.

Lesley is talking to the air as I pick up my handset again, trying to say the other teacher has decided to stay – but I know it is a lie. Obviously it is a lie – meant to spare my blushes.

'And this is definitive?' I ask, but I already know the answer.

When I hang up, having muttered various 'Oh don't worry, I quite understand' type platitudes, I switch off my phone and just sit.

What else is there to say?

Eventually a bus hoots behind me. Absently I restart the car, driving blindly into the countryside, following a road I don't know.

I don't know anything round here: anyone or any place.

I park the car beside the old canal. I walk down the towpath to the water's edge, past a clutch of houseboats in varying states of upkeep. I stand on the bank, staring into the murky depths.

How can I clear my name and start again properly when people believe something that isn't true? When *everyone* believes it, except those closest to me? I am tarnished forever.

And if I lose Matthew too, if that happens – how can I ever live a normal life again? How can I live with that loss?

When I finally go home, hours later, Matthew is back.

'You're early.' I reach up to kiss him, but he pulls away.

'I had to come back. The alarm company called, saying it was going off.'

'Oh?' I put the kettle on, overcome with lethargy. 'Agata must have forgotten to set it when she left. I'll remind her next week.'

'You won't. Agata's resigned.' He is grim. 'She's not coming back.'

'Oh, God, really?' I am surprised by the velocity of his statement. 'Why?'

Personally I'm not bothered. Telling Matthew I've lost my job before I've even started is worrying me far more than Agata's resignation. It seems like some odd admission of guilt to say they don't want me – especially as he's already so angry. And I'm more than happy to do the cleaning myself; my first job out of school was cleaning offices at nights, paying to put myself through college. Underpaying some Eastern European isn't high on my agenda of social arrival.

'Because of this.' He shoves a note at me, handwritten in a childish scrawl: *I cannot work here when this is okay!!*

'From Scarlett? What does she mean?'

Scarlett has obviously been here whilst I was out. Her pencil case and her fluffy pink pen are on the side; they weren't there earlier.

'No – it's from Agata.'

'When what's okay?' I get the teapot down. 'Do you want tea?'

'For Christ's sake, woman.' He slams the note down furiously, making me jump. 'We're lucky she didn't call the police.'

He has my full attention now. 'Why on earth would she do that?'

'Why don't you ask your son?'

'Why?' My skin has gone clammy. 'What's he meant to have done? I don't think they've even met…'

And Frankie isn't here anyway. He is in London, shopping for vinyl, staying for a few days with Marlena, as his passport is taking longer than he'd hoped.

'You don't want to know.' Matthew is about to leave the room. I scurry after him.

'No, I do! Matthew, what *is* it?'

'All right,' he says. 'But don't blame me when you don't like it.'

Grabbing my hand, he drags me up the stairs to Frankie's room, at the opposite end of the landing from ours. 'It'll make you sick, Jeanie.'

'What?' I cry, terrified now as he throws open Frank's door, his fingers still clamped round my wrist.

Below the huge poster of a dishevelled Kurt Cobain, the clown's face Frankie uses as a screensaver blinks and winks at us, and I shiver, jamming my feet into the carpet like a child would. 'Please, Matthew…'

'Don't say I didn't warn you!' Matthew pulls me across the room.

'You're hurting me!' I remonstrate. 'I won't run away; let me go…'

Dropping my wrist, he jabs at the laptop's keyboard.

The hideous clown disintegrates, leaving behind an image of a girl: peroxide haired, wet lipped and naked apart from some kind of leather thing wound round her waist, a girl who doesn't look much older than Scarlett, who looks barely conscious, having sex with a...

'Oh my God.' My voice is barely more than a whisper, so stunned am I. For a moment I can do nothing but stare in horror. 'Please switch it off.' I feel really sick.

'Too fucking right: oh my God.'

'But – I've *never* known Frank to use porn,' I say – and then stop. That isn't entirely true. 'I mean, he's just not the kind of boy to be into this type of – depravity...'

'Really?' Matthew's expression is scornful. 'And what kind of boy would that be anyway? What teenage son would divulge this little penchant to his mother?'

'But we're so close, me and Frank.' I stare at my husband, willing him to believe me. 'I trust him, Matthew, and you should too. I just need to talk to—'

'Oh come on, Jean,' he says. 'The evidence is irrefutable. Agata was hysterical! We all know your precious son can do no wrong in your eyes, but you're going to have to face facts.'

'That's not fair,' I protest.

'Isn't it?'

We stare at each other, and the feeling in my stomach is one of lead, a weight that says: this is not good; this is not good at all.

'Face it, Jeanie...' he starts again, but I don't want to hear it.

'All *right*, Matthew.' For the first time ever, I walk away from him, out of the room. 'I'll talk to Frankie when he gets back.'

'Yeah, you will.' Behind me the door slams, and Matthew stalks past me, down the landing, into his study. The threat in his voice shakes me. 'I think,' he says, over his shoulder, his voice seeming dangerously quiet, 'that's a very good idea indeed.'

Then he shuts his door in my face.

12 MARCH 2015

My psoriasis is flaring. The backs of my knees are a mess, and my nights are filled with strange images, as I lie half waking, half dreaming until the dawn.

I *am* used to stress: used to scrabbling to pay bills or working into the night to meet deadlines at schools; I'm used to the stress of exhaustion whilst studying and trying to parent a sleepless Frankie alone. I'm used to the worries that might have come with a teenage Frank – hence our move away from Peckham, down to the Sussex coast when he was still quite young. I'm used to the typical things parents of teens always worry about.

And, of course, my own childhood was stressful I suppose.

But this is different. Or rather, maybe, this is starting to feel a little like *that* time: a childhood I'd far rather forget. A time that went on and on with no control. A time where I lost trust in those who *should* have been trustworthy.

I'm suffocating: nets are closing in.

I want to sleep for a hundred years – but I can't. I daren't.

I've got to persuade my own Prince Charming that everything's all right in our kingdom – before I'm cast out forever.

I rouse myself.

My first action after Matthew's fury was to ring Frankie in London, leaving a message that we must speak as soon as possible.

Answering messages has never been his strong suit, and it was a day before he called back, by which time he was planning to come home anyway.

'What the hell are you on about?' he spluttered when I told him what we found on his computer, and something in his tone reassured me. Frankie might have smoked round the back of the art hut, and lost his virginity too early; he might have used a bit of eyeliner during his emo phase aged fourteen; he might have once taken a pen knife to school ill-advisedly, trying to be cool, and immediately got caught – but he was never a liar.

'Agata's resigned, she was so appalled.' I felt terribly weary again.

'And you're bothered about Agata?'

That annoyed me a bit.

'It's not me, Frank: it's Matthew. He's furious.'

'Why? Has he never looked at a pair of tits before?'

Fear sent its cold shaft through me.

'So you *did* do it? You need to be honest, Frank. I can't defend you if…'

'Do *what*? Look at girls being shagged by animals? Hardly, Mum. I've got more taste.'

'It's illegal, you know,' I said tightly.

He sighed and said, 'I'm sure it is. It sounds disgusting. But it wasn't me, I swear, Mum. I didn't do it. I really don't get my kicks like that. I don't know why it was on there, but it wasn't me. I'll see you tomorrow.'

And that had to be enough for me.

Of course it's not enough for Matthew though.

I debate asking Marlena for more help, but I can't deal with her lecturing me about being pathetic right now.

But I *do* do something somewhat out of character. Surprising myself at my own daring, I ring the college and ask to speak to Lesley Browning.

'What can I do for you?' She sounds harassed when she comes on the line. 'I'm terribly busy.'

'Please. I have to know – did someone tell you something?' I ask. 'Something about me?'

'I don't know what you mean,' she says, but I hear strain in her voice.

'I think you do,' I say quietly. 'It'd help me if you could tell me. Or if someone emailed you, then…'

'Sorry,' she cuts me off, 'I'm late for a meeting. Good luck, Jeanie. I'm sure something will turn up.' Tiny pause. 'Your references were very good you know.'

Small comfort.

When I get home, wondering if Frankie's on the next train, I don't know whether I feel angry or depressed – or maybe both.

I drag myself out of the car, and then I hear something odd.

I rush up the path.

My fears are confirmed as I open the front door: Frankie and Matthew are in the hall, standing opposite one another, and it looks horribly as if they might be about to have a fight.

'What on earth's going on?' I move in-between them.

'Ask your husband,' Frankie says. He's deathly pale, which is never a good sign. It reminds me of a childhood sickness he had when he was tiny; when for a night or two, I thought I might lose him.

I reach my hand out towards him. 'Frankie…'

'You know *exactly* what's going on, Jeanie.' Matthew's voice is loud, and unlike Frank, he's very flushed. 'I won't have that filth in my house.'

'I don't look at filth,' Frankie spits, and I can see that his rage isn't helping. 'It wasn't fucking well me.'

'Just who the hell are you swearing at?' Matthew is growing ever nearer apoplexy. 'I won't have that language in my house.'

'No? Well, strikes me you won't have anything much in your house.' Frankie picks up the bag he's just arrived home with. 'So I'll make it easy for you and I'll leave.'

'Frankie, please!' I plead. 'Don't go. We'll sort it out. Wait a minute…'

But he's already at the door – and one thing I know about my son is the sheer level of his determination when he's set on something. 'Frank—'

I follow him out to the drive.

'I'm sorry, Mum, and I don't mean to swear – but I think he's a proper wanker.' He is visibly shaken.

'Please, Frank…'

'He thinks the sun shines out of his own kids' arses – but he looks at me with contempt.' He swings his bag over his shoulder.

'He doesn't…' I begin, but then I wonder: maybe he's right – maybe Matthew does. Is it true?

What have I done? What care have I taken of Frank in the search for my own happiness? I think of my own mother, who cared nothing for our welfare whenever it meant she could have a bloke around – blokes who were always unsuitable, never the least bit interested in us.

Am I following in her footsteps?

Hardly! I hear Marlena say. *You've done everything for that boy. Everything. It's time you had a life of your own, Jeanie.*

Is that what she'd say though? Or have I simply sacrificed Frankie's happiness for my own?

Or maybe this is just normal life? Kids and parents battling it out for a bit of equality. I've never had a man around, not really; not since Simon, and it's hard to know what's normal…

'I'm going to George's,' Frank says dully, and he kisses me on the cheek. 'Take care, Mum. You need to take care.'

'Don't go, Frank, please,' I plead, but he's already slouching down the drive. 'I'll ring you later, darling,' I call after him, and he raises one weary hand in farewell, but he doesn't look round.

Slowly I turn and walk back into the house.

MARLENA

Now what are you looking at?

Okay, yes, that *is* what I'd have said about Frankie and Jeanie. She'd done everything for that boy – above and beyond the call of duty.

Everything. Which was especially difficult, given the early circumstances of his life.

But let's not discuss that right now, all right?

Yes, I'm getting upset.

Leave it there please.

And Jeanie did deserve happiness, of course. But when you've got no blueprint for a healthy relationship, how do you know where to find it? It wasn't surprising she thought her dreams would be wrapped up by finding her Prince Charming.

Prince Charming's a stupid old fantasy though, isn't he? He doesn't exist. You only need to look at the divorce statistics to know that.

JEANIE

13 MARCH 2015

Waking this morning, I feel a sense of dread that I can't quite place.

Then I remember: I've lost my job before I even started it, Frankie's not here – and the twins are coming for the weekend.

Frankie's still so angry about his row with Matthew, he's still refusing to come home. Last night I took a bag of clean clothes to George's, humiliated further when George's mum looked at me like I was useless.

I should be used to people looking at me like that.

It still hurts though.

The gardener is outside again, mowing the already shorn grass.

I force myself out of bed and downstairs, but I can't be bothered to go for a run. The running's definitely on the slide.

Someone on breakfast television is talking about subverting negative thoughts. 'It's so easy to get into a downward spiral. We've all been there, haven't we?' the glossy life-coach lady says cheerily to the presenter, her bright earrings jingling. 'But if we're feeling down, why not make ourselves think *up*!'

She makes it sound so easy – and she looks like she's never been *there* in her life.

They move on to an item about making your own pizza dough. I switch the television off and sit staring into space.

The gardener clomps across my sight line, and I duck out of view. I don't want anyone to see me like this.

The phone breaks into my thoughts about being more positive, about approaching the twins' forthcoming stay with positivity. If I can do that, it will be a positive experience for us all.

'Hello?'

'It's Kaye, Jeanie. How are you?'

'Oh,' I say blankly. 'Fine, thanks. Matthew's at work actually...'

'It was you I wanted,' she says. 'I just...' Slight pause. 'Well I wanted to apologise.'

'Apologise?' I feel my brows knit. 'Why?'

'I was a bit – hostile, maybe, the other day. I didn't mean to be. You seem like a really nice lady. And I think Scarlett needs all the help she can get, Jean. Would you be an angel and keep a special eye out for her?'

'Sure.' I am completely nonplussed by Kaye's camaraderie. 'But – why? I mean, are you worried about something in particular?'

'Oh you know, not really. It's just – it's a difficult time for her, isn't it? Puberty and all that! And everyone knows what teenage girls are like, don't they? I mean, we both were one once.'

'Yes, well, that's true.'

'And she's such a daddy's girl.'

'Is she?' I am cautious now. What's Kaye driving at?

'Of course she is! Although I'm so close to her...'

'I suppose...' This is my chance. 'I wondered, have you had any suspicions she might be cutting herself?'

'Cutting?'

'Like – self-harming? It's pretty common in girls of her—'

'Are you joking?' Kaye's voice is rising. 'Cutting? She's not doing that, Jean, I'm sure of it. I'd know.'

'Okay.' It isn't my place really. 'Of course I'll keep an eye out for her anyway.'

'Thanks, Jeanie.' She recovers herself. 'That's so kind of you. Let's be pals, shall we? It'll be better for all of us, won't it?'

'Of course.'

'Great. I'll drop the kids round in a bit.'

5 p.m.

Breakfast TV has been most helpful today: now I'm making home-made pizza for everyone. Cooking's always therapeutic I find; I have since I was a kid – something about providing for people. And all kids like Italian food – even the fussy Scarlett. I text Frankie and ask him if he might come home this evening. Please. I tell him how much I miss him.

He doesn't answer.

Whilst I'm assembling the margherita topping my mobile rings.

'It's Lesley Browning here,' the voice says rather anxiously. 'I just – it's a quick call. I thought you deserved a little more explanation.'

'Right.' I'm wary, balancing the phone between ear and shoulder as I tip tomatoes into the blender.

'It's just – your suspicion was right. Someone did send the head an email. I have to say'—a sharp intake of breath—'it was very vicious.'

'Oh.' Of course. 'Vicious?'

'It was a link to a Sunday-paper spread. It said you were…' Is her pause one of embarrassment? I'm not sure.

'Yes, I know what it said.' I keep my voice quiet. 'Could you tell me who sent it?'

'I don't know. I didn't see the actual email. But I believe it was anonymous. From someone who called themselves a well-wisher, that type of thing.'

A well-wisher.

'Okay. Well thanks for telling me.'

I put the phone down and turn the blender on, watching the soft red flesh spatter against the sides. Almost immediately, the landline rings. It's the twins' school this time.

'Just to make sure Mr King knows about the parents' evening a fortnight on Monday?' the woman coos. That's what you get when you pay for education: cooing. 'We've not had a reply to the letter, you see. It starts at 6 p.m. on the dot.'

Cooing and dots. Efficiency and timetables. Personal phone-calls. Not like my last schools.

'I'll make sure he knows.' I wipe tomatoey hands on my apron to scribble the details down on the phone pad.

Luke comes in just as I'm hanging up for the second time.

'Oh hello! That was your school on the phone,' I tell him. 'You've got parents' evening in a couple of Mondays' time.'

'Oh right.' But he's not much interested. 'Is Dad here? I need to order some new football boots online.'

'Not yet. I'm sure he'll want to go to your parents' evening.' *Positivity*, I think. 'He'll want to hear about all your achievements.'

'Maybe.' Luke pulls open the fridge, hanging heavily on the door. I bite my tongue about hurrying to shut the door. He takes a can of Coke, slamming the fridge so that the whole worktop judders.

Now Scarlett waltzes in, all skinny legs and overly made-up eyes and flyaway hair: dramatic as ever.

'Hello.' I smile at her. 'There's fresh orange if you fancy it?' She doesn't like sugar normally.

'I'd rather have a Coke, like Luke. I'm totally dying from star-vation!' Scarlett eyes my sauce dubiously. 'Can I have a snack?'

No, I bite back, *wait for supper* – like I'd tell Frankie. But I know I must be the nice guy. 'Yeah, sure,' I say. 'Crisps in the cupboard? Or a Kit Kat maybe?'

'Great.' She shoves her head into the cupboard like someone who hasn't eaten in days.

'Can you just move that for me, sweetheart?' I ask Luke, who's loitering, swilling Coca-Cola round his mouth noisily. 'That pad, before it gets all covered in food?'

He reaches out to move it and somehow – I don't know how exactly, because I'm stirring the sauce and trying to open the dried oregano at the same time – he's suddenly screaming in pain.

My heart nearly stops.

'Oh my God, Luke, what's happened?' I drop the herb jar, scattering oregano everywhere.

Coca-Cola runs in a sticky brown torrent over the floor, and Luke's clutching a hand covered in blood I think – or is it toma-to sauce? I can't quite make it out because I'm panicking – and he won't stop screaming.

'Luke, it's okay.' I try to calm him, trying to look at his hand – but his screams increase, as if he's being murdered, as if he's in the most agonising pain ever…

'You must show me!' I'm sick with fear. Maybe he's not okay…

'Luke.' Scarlett's little face is angry now as she drops her prawn-cocktail crisps and faces her brother. 'Stop screaming!'

He doesn't, so she slaps him – hard.

Now he does stop. He stares at his twin, and she says quite levelly, like a little grown-up, 'You're hysterical. Calm down.'

Luke's eyes are like an owl's.

I search for the cut that's caused all the fuss. It's tiny, on the fleshy edge of his palm, and I was right – quite a lot of this is tomato sauce from the utensils on the side.

'Can you stir the sauce?' I ask Scarlett, and I take Luke to the downstairs loo, wash his hand and find a plaster.

By the time Matthew comes home, I've cleaned up, the twins are watching *The Hunger Games* and the table is groaning with food.

You'd never know there'd been any drama.

I am also a little tipsy. Sploshing red wine into the pizza topping, I couldn't help but be tempted. It's been tough recently.

'Hello.' My husband smiles at me, kissing me with more enthusiasm than he has for ages. 'Something smells amazing, you clever girl.'

I lean into him, feeling his hand on my hair, and I feel a vast whoosh of relief. 'Dinner's nearly ready,' I say. 'Just going to get my cardigan. It's cold, isn't it?'

At the top of the stairs, I feel even more chilled as I walk past the mirror – and something catches the corner of my eye. A shadow that passes over the light—

Looking up, with a start I see the ghost reflected there – the Grey Lady. She's slightly different to before, wispier perhaps… but there's no doubt she's there. She's walking towards me, arms outstretched, eyes like black holes behind the veil, her mouth a vivid red slash in her deathly face—

'She's here!' I shriek, stepping back, so near the top of the stairs that I nearly overbalance. I grab the bannister. 'Matthew, quick!'

A sigh of air. A slamming door somewhere inside the house. Giggling, giggling nearby.

'It's only me, Jeanie,' a grinning Scarlett pops her head round Luke's bedroom door. 'I'm sorry if I scared you. It worked though!'

'What was you?' My heart is hammering so fast I can barely breathe. The ghost has gone, but I feel very lightheaded.

'Look...' She shows me the projector she's set up on the landing. 'It was for a school thing, in media studies. We had to create our own visual motif for our homes.'

'I see,' I say, still trying to calm down.

'I got the idea from *Sherlock*.' Proudly Scarlett shows me how she's projected the image from behind the door, into one mirror, where the reflection bounced into the other.

'Was that you then? Before? A few weeks ago?'

'Oh, when Dad said you thought you saw something? That's what gave me the idea actually,' she says. 'Honest, it wasn't me that time though.'

I don't believe her. But I don't have the energy to argue now.

Sitting down to eat, Scarlett is distracted, looking at her phone.

'Put it down please,' Matthew says. 'The phone.'

She does, reluctantly. 'Where's Frankie?' she asks with non-chalance. 'Isn't he coming down for tea?'

'Scarlett fancies Frankie,' Luke crows. 'Scarlett and Frankie, sitting in a tree...'

'Luke!' Matthew's tone is a low warning as the girl blushes the same colour as her name.

'I do not,' she mutters.

'K-I-S-S-I-N-G...'

'Leave it there right now, Lucas!' Matthew thumps his glass down.

Scarlett looks mortified – her ill-hidden secret's out. Matthew's face has darkened. I don't want to make things worse for Frank now.

'Luke, tell us about your football game,' I change the subject quickly. 'Did you score?'

'Durr!' he says. 'I'm a defender, not a striker!'

'Oh.' I grin. 'Sorry! I don't know the first thing about football really.' I'm about to say that this is because Frankie hates sport, but bringing his name up again won't help the mood. And then I feel like a traitor. 'So was the lovely Beckham a striker or defender?'

That night Matthew and I have sex for the first time in a week, and afterwards I almost cry myself to sleep with relief.

The rest of the twins' stay goes without incident, and I feel a little better – although I feel inordinately annoyed about the ghost thing, and, far worse, I miss Frankie badly. But he's answered my text, at least, and he's coming home tomorrow, thank God.

I need to broach the subject with Matthew, but I feel I'm walking on eggshells all the time at the moment. I'm biding my time, waiting for the right opportunity to clear the air. Perhaps we're getting a little nearer now. Perhaps I can bring everyone together safely, bring the boat safely in to moor.

JEANIE

30 MARCH 2015

Matthew is in a foul mood when he arrives home after a late meeting in the City.

'I missed the bloody parents' evening.' He throws his *Financial Times* down on the counter. For someone who doesn't like swearing, he's been doing a lot of it recently. 'Kaye says the school rang to remind me a few weeks ago. Why didn't you tell me?'

'I'm sure I did.' I feel a stab of guilt. 'I wrote it on the pad by the phone.'

But the work surface is immaculate – and empty. No pad at all. I can't blame Agata; she's long gone. And actually I don't remember telling Matthew. But usually *he* checks his messages on the pad. All the phone calls in the house are for him generally, and I've never forgotten anything before.

But I haven't told him Kaye rang either – and that is through choice. I feel really awkward about that conversation; I don't want him to think we were in cahoots or something like that. I do think I need to mention the cutting thing to Matthew – but I have no proof, only a suspicion. I've looked at Scarlett's arms every time she's been here, but they are usually covered up.

'What pad?' Matthew looks at me like I'm mad. 'We finished it didn't we, doing shopping lists for New Year's Eve? I keep meaning to remind you to get a new one.'

I remember that awful evening a fortnight ago, the way Luke got sauce all over everything, screaming and screaming, and I wonder – did I chuck it in the bin amidst all the drama?

'Kaye's having a fucking field day,' he says before I can answer. 'I can't afford to give her ammunition. Not whilst we're still waiting for custody and alimony meetings. I'm going upstairs.'

'Sorry,' I call after him, but he's already on the phone to his accountant. I was going to tell him about the job, but it's not the right time.

I seem to be digging myself in deeper without even meaning to. What a mess. My skin flames.

JEANIE

31 MARCH 2015
4.30 p.m.

Frankie's out when Scarlett arrives; I'm upstairs, cleaning the bathroom. We're not expecting her, as far as I know, and I wonder with trepidation if she's looking for Frankie again.

'Hi! Finish school early?' I say as she sticks her head round the door. 'Good day?'

She doesn't speak but stamps down the landing, calling for her dad like a much younger child. 'Dad, where are you? Dad-*dy*?'

Oh God, I think. Now what?

Matthew is in his study, working from home, as is becoming more usual.

The door clicks shut; they're ensconced in there for a while. I finish the bath and go downstairs to surf the web, looking for new jobs. There's something at the local adult institute I might apply for...

About half an hour later I'm just debating making them some tea when they clatter down the stairs – and leave. I assume Matthew's taking her back to her mother's.

When Matthew returns, twenty minutes later, he's monosyllabic as he looks for something in the drawer.

'Are you ready to go?' I try for jolly. I don't ask what might have been up with Scarlett. I kind of can't bear to know.

'Where?' He stares at me like I've got two heads.

'I booked tickets for the new Judi Dench film, remember?' I try to smile at him, but I sense something is really wrong. 'The one about living in India? I thought we could grab some noodles at—'

'Cancel it.' He bangs out of the room. Then he comes back. 'Or take someone else, if you want.'

But who would I take, my dear Matthew? I've made no friends here yet.

I follow him out into the hall. 'Sorry – what's wrong?'

'Oh come on!' He stares at me like he doesn't know me. Well he doesn't really. We don't really know each other at all. It's becoming more obvious by the minute.

'Please…' I say feebly.

'Oh, Jeanie.' His voice is quiet; he's calmer. We gaze at each other, and then he puts a hand out and strokes my face.

It *must* be going to be okay.

'I'm not sure how much longer I can do this,' he says, in that same soft voice.

Pain flares. 'What do you mean?' I ask stupidly. 'Do *what*?'

'It's not meant to be this hard, is it, love?' He sounds so sad, it's heartbreaking – and it makes me think of my dad, how he left and how sad I was and how I felt it was my fault. Is it all about to happen again? My fingernails drive into my palm. 'Maybe we've been foolish.'

'No, we haven't,' I say, trying to hold onto his hand, so desperate for warmth from him, for his touch – but he drops it, turns away.

'I'm going to take the twins away for a few days at the weekend.'

'Great.' I follow him. 'We could go to the coast? Some sea air would do us all—'

'Just me and them, Jeanie.' He turns back. 'We need to spend some time together. Me and my kids, I mean.'

'Oh.' It's like a mighty slap. 'Did I – have I done something wrong?'

Jeanie, Jeanie, Jeanie, I hear Marlena reprove. *You sound like a lost child.*

'Yes well maybe I do – but then where the fuck *are* you, Marlena?' I say.

I look up to see Matthew staring at me oddly.

'Who are you talking to?' he says.

'No one.' I shake my head. 'Myself, I suppose.'

'You didn't do anything wrong. Not really. I'll take them away, and you can see Frank. Get your heads straight.'

Frank's back – didn't he even notice?

'*Our* heads?' He makes Frank and I sound like some kind of mad gorgon. And what's the intimation anyway? That my son and I are mutually and tangentially messed up?

'Look, Scarlett found out about you,' Matthew sounds weary. 'She saw something online. She's refusing to come in the house if you're here.'

'Oh God,' I say. I feel sick.

'And you can see that might be a problem.' He walks away. 'For me.'

The bottom is dropping out of everything.

And still he won't tell me who sent that email.

JEANIE

3 APRIL 2015

Matthew and the twins have gone to Brussels for a long weekend. First class on the Eurostar, rooms at a five-star hotel, puppets at the *Théâtre Royal de Toone*, whatever that might be.

I think the twins might have preferred Disneyland Paris, or just a weekend shopping and eating in London – but still.

I have fought and fought not to mind.

Marlena's promised to come up, but I'll believe it when I see it.

Taking matters into my own hands, I've got another interview, this time at the Oaklands College in St Albans. I've spent a day out with Frank looking at local sights, like the Hellfire Caves near High Wycombe. Tentatively I mention the Grey Lady as we drive home and Scarlett's prank – and he just laughs. 'Typical teenager,' he says, and I resist saying, 'Takes one to know one.' I don't bother saying she denied being responsible for my first 'sighting'.

Now I've decided to look for a local friend. I used to have lots of friends, once upon a time. Lots. I need at least one here too.

I ring Sylvia Jones, the woman who fancied Nordic walking, and ask her for coffee.

'I'm pretty busy this week. I've taken up pottery and I'm hooked,' she breezes. 'Hoping to meet my own Patrick Swayze! Next week maybe?'

'Great.' I feel pathetically desolate. 'Yes, please.'

I debate ringing Anne from number 52, but she's got such a downturned mouth and deep frown lines to match, I can't bear to.

I ring Marlena's voicemail. 'I'm coming to London tomorrow,' I say. 'Call me back please.'

I wander round the house, feeling redundant, and then I hear the mail drop onto the doormat.

I pick it up and flick through. Nothing of any interest here – just brown envelopes for Matthew and a final reminder from the gas board.

Then I look again. There's a letter from the dentist – addressed to someone I don't know.

Someone called Lisa Bedford.

MARLENA

It wasn't that I didn't want you to come down and see me, Jeanie, okay? Honestly, you were always bloody welcome, you know that really – don't you?

I was just so immersed in my own crap at the time. And you know why; I know you do. You of all people realised just how badly I'd damaged my reputation, how much I had to repay.

It was so bloody important that I helped that girl Nasreen. She'd been so sweet when I did my talk at the college – and maybe, I thought later, maybe she reminded me a bit of you, Jean – her trusting brown eyes, her warm face.

So I was still looking for Nasreen, and I felt like I was getting closer.

After I met Jeanie on that freezing February day, the imam in Luton had greeted me politely, inviting me into his tiny office. He offered me tea in front of the glowing three-bar heater, which I accepted, despite already jangling with too much black coffee.

The imam seemed like a good bloke: straight-up and concerned. My instinct for liars is pretty good – like a radar after all these years.

He said he'd helped many kids wavering near the path to being radicalised. He was, by all accounts, dead set against this 'wickedness', as he called it.

'The truth is we can find no trace of this girl at all through our network in the Middle East.' He looked sorrowful. 'We always have our ear to the ground. But no one has seen or heard of Nasreen that we know of. I'm sorry.'

I left, not feeling much soothed. If there was no sign of her in either Turkey or Syria, why did her family and her English boyfriend seem so convinced that she'd gone that way?

I realised later – too late – I'd gotten a little obsessed. Again.

Yes, I was distracted – I admit it.

But you've always been so strong, Jeanie. When our fucking useless mother vanished to a commune in Morocco to 'cleanse her soul' just after your eleventh birthday – inspired present as usual, thanks Mum – leaving you in charge of both of us, you did such a good job, the social never even got a whiff of it.

You got me to school, and then you got yourself there too – and you got us home again. You made a few cans of baked beans, some spaghetti hoops and one loaf of thin-slice Mother's Pride (oh the irony) last for a week. The bag of sugar, that lasted too – that was our treat.

When we ran out of tins, you 'borrowed' some money from Mrs Wilmers downstairs. You said it was for the raffle at school, and she could win a hamper or a holiday to Butlins. You said it like it was Barbados – well it was to us – and she gave you three pounds.

You eked it out till our feckless mother returned, suntanned and hungover, not cleansed, with a bag of vodka, two hundred duty-free fags and a worse habit than she'd left with. She brought us nothing.

What a surprise.

But you never even grassed her up to Nan, and you made me swear not to either (though you'd have been doing us a favour if you had). Still, your sense of loyalty was too strong.

JEANIE

3 APRIL 2015

I stare at the letter to this stranger: it's from Hillfield Dental Practice.

Lisa Bedford.

Who is she, and why is she getting letters here?

I'm being jumpy again. It's nothing. No doubt she's just someone who lived here before the Kings, an ex-resident of Malum House. And who is there to ask anyway?

I walk back upstairs, past the locked door, and I peer into Matthew's study. It feels so empty in the house without him here. *I* feel empty without him here. Without his approval and without the love I felt so tangibly until only a few weeks ago.

His shiny silver laptop stares at me from his desk.

If I just checked through his emails, I might get some answers about the person who 'shopped' me.

I remember the devil's idea of control: reading everything that came into the house. I remember the results.

I'm *not* going to stoop to his depths.

But then I pass beneath the attic hatch. I've resisted it for too long now.

I move the Queen Anne chair from the corner of the landing and stand on it to reach up and pull the attic stairs down.

As I clamber up into the darkness, emerging into the dim light, dust motes swirling in the weak beams of sun that fall from one tiny skylight, I remember Judy's drunken ramblings, back in November, and I think: *She was right. There is a mad woman in the attic…*

Only the mad woman is me.

I nearly laugh aloud – except it would only prove my own fear: 'the gambols of a demon' as Mr Rochester noted of his first wife.

Now I'm up here, I can see it's pointless – there's nothing in the attic. A few racks of old clothes, boxes of books and some photograph albums I can't bear to look at.

I run my hand across the clothes, wondering who they belonged to – and something whirls up from the corner.

I spring back, emitting a higher-pitched scream than I ever thought I could make.

It's a bird, I realise shakily; a bird is in the attic with me – flapping furiously against the roof slats, making an unearthly sound – and oh God I want to get out too…

Running back to the ladder, I stumble against a stack of paintings and the top one falls: a cracked old print of the nursery rhyme 'Sing a Song of Sixpence'.

I climb down again, sweaty palms sliding on the ladder rails.

The walls haven't whispered for a while; they might be silent today – but the house is definitely haunted. I think of the Grey Lady who died here. I think of Scarlett's projection. I think of my terror.

Is that just me too?

On the landing, I perch on the Queen Anne chair and try to calm my breathing. The bird will have to stay there until either Frank or Matthew get home. Sorry, bird, but I'm not feeling brave any more.

I stare down at the spring garden. It's starting to burst with life – unlike me.

How has my life turned into this... uselessness? There's no point to me; I'm like some odd 1950s housewife, like someone out of *Mad Men*. I just need a pristine apron, a gold cigarette case and a vodka-martini habit and I'll be set...

Outside Matthew's study I turn my back on the laptop burning into my retinas and force myself downstairs. Today the sun has actually shown its face, and I need fresh air before I suffocate.

I'll tackle the deadwood in the huge garden, I decide. It's a beautiful space, a bit dark at the end maybe, and I've not really explored out since I've been here.

In the garage I root around for gardening equipment. The gardener has left the mower and the big spades and forks very neatly in the wooden rack, but I need the smaller stuff. There's a long, thin cabinet that's locked, but I can't find any keys to it.

Eventually I *do* find a box of gardening stuff. Choosing the sharpest-looking secateurs and some thick gloves, I walk through the garage and down to the back of the garden, past the jolly daffodils, towards the big trees at the end where primroses cluster shyly at the foot of their trunks.

I'll start here and work my way up towards the house.

Savagely I cut back brambles and old rose vines until my skin above the gloves is scratched and bleeding. I'm out of breath but enjoying it – feeling alive for the first time in days. Weeks.

I stop at months.

Standing beneath the two great trees, I pull and I pull at rogue tendrils snaking around each other, up the trees, over the old brick wall until I'm panting with exertion, until I can taste the salt on my lip, until I stumble and overbalance, smashing my knee on something in the undergrowth...

Bending, I see it's a headstone, some kind of grave; covered in moss, but properly engraved.

I step closer, and the toe of my boot meets something else with a bang.

A whole *group* of small graves – at least four or five. More, maybe, under the spreading ivy.

Heart thudding, I crouch down and scratch off the moss on the first headstone. The sun's gone in, and it suddenly feels very dark and gloomy out here.

The headstone reads: *Millie, much loved, barking in heaven*

Relief makes me laugh out loud. Animal graves! They must all be. But there are so many – too many really for a house that no longer has pets. *Only two pets,* I distinctly remember Matthew saying.

I think of poor little Justin, the Pomeranian puppy.

I stand again, and as I move to have a look at the next one, to see if a dog called Daisy is buried here, I knock against something else. Something that wobbles before toppling heavily.

I'm too slow. I don't move fast enough, and it falls straight onto my left foot.

'Ouch! Oh God…'

Behind me a twig cracks underfoot, and I try to kick the slab away, but I can't. I'm wedged – and it *really* bloody hurts.

The hairs on my neck go up as I sense someone behind me. But this garden is walled, secure – how can someone have got in unless it's through the house?

I crane round quickly, wrenching my neck painfully.

A dark-skinned man stands on the path, halfway between the house and me. He's holding something in his hands – some kind of bag, I think.

'Hello?' My voice comes out as a creak. 'What do you want?'

He doesn't speak but walks a bit nearer.

It's not the gardener, who, from my short-sighted peering out of windows, I think is fair haired.

'Can I help you?' I croak – and I'm praying, *Please, stop, don't come any nearer*. I crane round a bit more, so I can at least see half of his face. His brow is knitted in thought as he stares at me. 'Please…'

'I thought you were a gardener.' He grins. 'But you must be the wicked stepmother instead.'

Again a sort of relief floods through me – but I'm still worried. 'Who are you?' I don't want to show my fear. 'How did you get in?'

'I'm Yassine.' He moves nearer. 'Kaye's other half. Worst half.' He laughs at his own joke. 'I came through the garage.'

Like a fool, I must have left it open.

'I brought Luke's football boots.' He has a pleasant-enough face and a wiry physique – and I don't recognise him from Adam.

'But he's not here.' I'm confused. 'They're in Belgium.'

'Yeah – I know. But he's got a match tomorrow evening when they get back, so he's gotta go straight to the club. Or so I'm told by madame anyway.' He grins again. 'I just do what I'm told.'

I desperately want to move, but my foot is well and truly wedged, and I can't lift the stone from this angle.

I'm trapped.

'You okay?' he asks politely.

'Yeah. No, actually. I'm… sort of stuck…'

'Wait a sec.' He walks to me, putting the bag down. 'Lean on me, yeah?' He crouches – and I realise I have no choice. I put my hand on his shoulder, and he levers the stone away, using the weight of his whole body – but as he pushes it, summoning some gargantuan effort, he slips. He can't regain his footing, and he falls into the ivy – and the mud.

'Shit!' he swears loudly. When he stands again, he's covered from head to foot in dark brown mud, all down his right side, his face, his dark curly hair – the other side still pristine.

I try not to laugh, but it is quite funny – and then we're both laughing, despite my sore foot and my arms that are now aching from all the hacking earlier.

'You'd better come and clean up,' I say.

Inside, he takes his muddy shoes off by the French windows.

'I can use the downstairs bathroom,' he says, and I'm about to direct him when I realise he already knows where it is. He has a slight accent, freckles that stand out very clearly against his tawny skin; he looks like a decent man. A young man.

He must be much younger than Kaye.

I change quickly in the utility room off the kitchen, pulling on leggings and a hoodie of Matthew's, still not entirely comfortable that we're alone in the house together.

The top of my foot feels really bruised, but at least, thank God, my boots were thick. The damage could have been much worse.

In the kitchen I wash my hands and put the kettle on, wondering about the sheer proliferation of animal graves. Yassine appears – cleaner but dripping wet where he's sluiced himself down. He's got no top on and rubs his hair vigorously with a hand towel. I'm about to offer him a T-shirt of Matt's when a face looms at the window.

'Oh my God!' I hear myself exclaim.

'What?' He turns.

It's a woman with elegant silver hair, tapping lightly on the pane, and for a moment, I can't quite place her...

Of course! Sylvia Jones from the cul-de-sac. She must have changed her mind about coffee.

'Hi!' I wave. 'Hang on a sec – I'll open the front door.'

An expression I don't understand crosses her face.

When I open the front door, she's gone. I stare down the front drive, but the only sign of her is the garden gate slowly swinging back into place.

'I'll put these on outside.' Yassine makes me jump again as he comes up silently behind me, his own shoes in hand. 'Don't want any more mess.'

'Can I offer you anything?' I just want him to go. 'A cup of tea in gratitude?'

'Thanks, but I'd better do one,' he says. 'Got a client at four.'

'Okay. Well – thanks, again.'

'No worries. See you around.' He winks, and he's gone.

God knows what he sees in Kaye – though of course that's disingenuous. I can well imagine what he sees in her. Legs, hair, boobs, big car. Sparkling intellect maybe? Or sparkling diamonds maybe; I'm sure I saw one or two on her skinny fingers…

And then I think nothing more of him until later in the weekend.

JEANIE

5 APRIL 2015

7 a.m.

A strange text from Matthew wakes me.

What's going on at home? it says. That's it — no kiss, no 'how are you?' etc. Just a bald question.

Not much, I text back. *Just missing you. Xx.*

Who's been round there? he texts back. *Someone has!*

What? I text back. *Don't understand the question?*

No reply.

I ring him. The phone goes straight to voicemail. I feel extremely uneasy. What does he mean?

The only person who's been here at all is Yassine. Is that what he means? I try and call again to explain.

Still no answer.

I go downstairs, past the locked spare room. Then I walk back, and I try the handle.

Nearby Matthew's laptop is there, like a reproving silver toad.

I grab it before I can change my mind.

Downstairs, I open it and sit, looking at the black screen — and then I lean over and switch it on.

It needs a password to get in. I try our names, the address. I try his birthday, my birthday. Then I try the twins' birthday: it works.

Feeling curiously proud of myself as I watch the twirling icon on the wakening screen, I think, *I'm in*!

Then I remember *why* I'm trying to get in, and I feel less proud.

I am only looking for one email, I remind myself: I'm not looking at all of his correspondence. That's his business, not mine.

I skim through the inbox. I see a few from Kaye; I don't read them. I see a few from Scarlett, but I don't read them either, though I can't help seeing the header: **BIG BIRTHDAY KISSES.**

Resolutely I keep going until I get to the one that says: **JEANIE RANDALL – BEWARE!!!**

Beware. Like I'm a contagious disease or something.

Feeling sick, I look at the address. It's from *Helpful2001xav@ hotmail.com.*

I open it. It's just what I might have expected. A single line: **Thought you should see this...**

And a link to the article.

Helpful? Malicious, more like. I am flushed, my cheeks burning with anger.

Who the hell is '*Helpful2001xav*', and why are they making it their business to alert my husband to my misdemeanours?

As I go to shut the computer down, the cursor passes over a minimised document: **KING FAMILY, BELGIUM TRIP**. I click on it.

There are four passport numbers.

Four.

There, in black and white in front of me, is a passport number that I'm pretty sure isn't mine. Mine ends in twenty-six; I always remember, because it's the same as my birthday.

So whose is the number?

Kaye? I think. Is Kaye in Belgium with the twins – and my husband?

I am going to get ready to leave in a minute, to catch the train up to town to meet Marlena. But I can't move for a moment.

For some reason the nursery-rhyme picture I saw in the attic springs into my head: 'Sing a Song of Sixpence'. It keeps going round and round:

Four and a twenty blackbirds baked in a pie…
The king was in his counting house…
The queen was in the parlour…
The maid was in the garden, hanging out the clothes,
When down came a blackbird and pecked off her nose.

When I finally force myself from my seat, I have another thought.

I go to the key drawer, and I search through it, turning everything out on the floor.

Nothing new that I can see.

I am going to go up and get dressed in a minute.

In a minute, I will.

1 p.m.

I need help – badly.

I am used to acrimony after the Seaborne affair, but I'm not used to this.

I'm frightened. I have a feeling someone nearby really wants to damage me, and they are becoming more insidious. Relentless, even.

Or am I just like Bertha Mason in *Jane Eyre* – a madwoman?

At least Marlena answers me promptly now; her text suggests a new bakery place on Charlotte Street.

I thread through the back streets from Euston to a café that sells gluten-free cake and smoothies made of something called maca, where everyone looks studiously cool: the girls all with shaggy, two-tiered coloured hair, the young men all with self-conscious beards.

Marlena's on the phone; she raises a hand in greeting. 'Yeah, cool, got it. I don't like this bloke at all. I think he's lying, but the police don't seem bothered.' She agrees to talk later before hanging up.

'Hi, you.' She grins at me, and I think how glad I always am to see my little sister, pain in the arse that she is sometimes.

Marlena eschews the good stuff, of course, when we order; her one concession to the 'clean eating' fad the wholemeal bagel she chooses, along with black coffee. I plump for scrambled egg.

'So. What's up?' She pours sugar in her coffee. Real sugar from sachets in her bag, not the agave syrup they've put hopefully on the tables. 'Sleeping okay now?'

I stir my almond and kumquat drink dubiously and glance at her.

'Bit better, yes. It's just – I don't seem to fully relax on my own in that big house.'

'Why are you on your own?' She frowns. 'I thought there were bloody loads of you there? It's like Snow White and the seven dwarves, you and your entourage.'

'Hardly.' I am struggling to admit my perfect marriage is less than that. I have a big fear that she'll just say, *I told you so*. 'Matthew's away for a few days…'

'Where's he gone?'

I feel like a soldier dodging incoming flak as she fires questions at me. 'He's taken the kids away for Easter,' I say, and my voice changes, I know it does – despite my best attempt at control.

'Oh.' She frowns. 'Didn't you want to go?'

'No, it's not that exactly…' I hesitate. Shall I mention my suspicions about Kaye being in Belgium too?

'What then?'

I feel the tears spring now, much to my annoyance. It'll only wind Marlena up; crying's a sign of weakness in her book. 'He thought they needed some time alone. Since Scarlett found about – you know what.'

'About you, you mean?'

'Yeah. About me.'

'So you *have* told him?'

'Yes.'

'Oh, Jean.' And she reaches over, placing her hand on mine in such a rare act of warmth that I'm shocked. Her nails are black and glittery and chewed to the quick as usual. They remind me of Scarlett's. 'I'm sorry.'

'I'm sure it'll be okay,' I say bravely – but I wish I *was* sure.

'Well stepfamilies are never straightforward. We both knew that, didn't we?'

'Yeah, I suppose.' I sigh. 'It's definitely tougher than I'd anticipated.' What an idiot, I want to say, what an *idiot* I was. I believed I could bring it all together neatly – and just look what's happened. It's everything but neat. The Brady Bunch? Ha. It's a complete and utter bloody mess, and if I think about it too hard, it makes me want to howl.

'How are you anyway?' I change the subject. 'You look tired too.'

She still looks good though. My little sister – the newshound.

'Still atoning for professional misconduct,' she says tersely. 'It's taking a while. A lifetime maybe.'

'Well…' I try to summon a platitude.

'I really fucked it up. Big style.'

'Yeah,' I agree, 'you did.'

'Yeah, I did. Cheers for that.' She toasts me with a rueful coffee cup. The pouty French waitress slops down my scrambled eggs and kale, more interested in making eyes at the cool cats on the table behind, and Marlena and I grin at each other. 'Silly cow,' Marlena mouths.

We are different, Marlena and I, poles apart – but we both get it. We came from the same place, one few others will ever understand. Only Frankie maybe – though I've tried to protect him. We are different to the circles we move in; we've done well – and then we've both fallen from great heights. Now we are attempting to climb up again.

'I guess phone hacking was never gonna pay the rent, was it?' I say, peering dubiously at the undercooked egg. Give me a greasy spoon any day of the week. I don't belong in London any more. I am the wrong side of cool, the wrong side of forty. And I'm looking over my shoulder every second now.

I think of Samuel Johnson: 'When a man is tired of London, he is tired of life.' I am tired actually. Very bloody tired.

'It was paying the rent very nicely, thank you.' Marlena is tart. 'It was just my conscience I couldn't live with any more. Look, why are you really here, Jeanie? Do you need help again?'

'No.' I push my egg around. 'I just want your solidarity.'

'Really?'

Ever the cynic, my little sister. I suppose she has plenty of reason to be. And who am I kidding? Not her apparently. We both know what Marlena did for me last year when all the crap hit the papers. 'Well there might be one thing actually…'

'I knew it!' she crows. She hates being wrong. 'So. Spill.'

'It's just… Someone sent Matt an email – and they sent one to the college that offered me a job too. With a link to – the thing.'

'Fucking hell, Jeanie,' she exhales loudly. 'I warned you. I knew that would happen if you didn't tell him yourself.'

'Please, Marlena. No told-you-sos…'

She pulls a face. 'Okay. So?'

'Some idiot sent him a link to the first article about a week ago. The one from the *Sun on Sunday*.'

'And the job? You hadn't told them either? That you were cleared?'

'What do you reckon?' I look at her squarely. 'And now I'm more concerned with who's going around talking about me and saying they're a "well-wisher".'

'Have you got the email?'

I pass her over the printed email. She reads it.

'And I'm guessing Matthew didn't recognise the sender either?'

'He says not. But actually…' I feel uncomfortable again.

'Actually what?'

'He didn't want to say who'd sent it. I had to – look.' I feel overwhelmed and really, really sad. I haven't even begun on my other worries. 'But he said he doesn't know them.'

'It's going to be all right, Jean.' Marlena pats my hand again – like when we were kids. 'I know it is.'

'Is it?'

'Course. And have you got any idea at all *who* might've sent it?'

'I suppose I thought it could be – you know, Otto's mum.'

'Hmmm.' She stands suddenly, sending the chair skidding across the tiles. 'Can we go outside? I'm dying for a fag.'

' "Dying" being the operative word…'

'Our vices make life's crap bearable.'

I can't really argue with that.

Outside we huddle together under the awning. It is drizzling and grey – and generally depressing.

'Have you contacted her?' She lights up. 'Old Ma Lundy?'

'No way.' I shake my head. 'I don't ever want to see that woman again.'

That woman had been my biggest detractor for six months; she'd made it her own personal quest to take me down, even when both her own son and I had denied every charge; despite the fact there had been no evidence, nothing really to say we were guilty –nothing apart from that bloody, bloody photograph.

Marlena helped me then.

I knew for a fact the Lundys weren't good parents, and the only reason Otto and I had become close was because he was so overlooked at home.

I hesitate to say he was neglected, but it wasn't far off.

Marlena checked the parents out in the way that only a ruthless journalist would know how to do. Their own past wasn't pretty, and when they were threatened with disclosure about some of their own misdemeanours, they slunk off, tails between their legs – but it wasn't long before they threatened pressing their own charges, civilly. Thank God that never happened.

'I'll check it out,' Marlena offers now.

'Thanks,' I say. 'I'd appreciate it.' I watch her blow her smoke up into the city sky, and I feel like I can't catch a breath myself.

I have this feeling, all the time, that I'm paying for my brief happiness with Matthew, that I don't deserve it and never did – and so it's over, and I must pay the debt now.

'And if it's *not* her?' I say. 'What then?'

'You've really got no other ideas who it could be?'

Of course I do. But I shrug, non-committal. 'Someone who doesn't like me.'

'I'll see what I can do,' Marlena promises, flinging her cigarette into the gutter. Then, weirdly, she kisses me. She smells of fags and Chanel. 'Nice to see you, J, but I need to crack on.'

I sink my face into her shoulder till she struggles, muttering, 'Yeah, all right. Don't go all Jean Harlow on me.'

Jeanie with an 'ie' for the original blonde bombshell Jean Harlow: dead with suspect kidney failure by the age of twenty-six.

Marlena for Dietrich, only with an 'a' instead of the 'e' – because our mother was half-cut the day she registered her newborn.

Our names: constant reminders of our failure to attain their dizzy heights.

'I'm not,' I mumble – but I really don't want to let go of Marlena, and I don't want to go home to that big, empty house where things keep going wrong.

Where the husband I live with seems ever more like a stranger.

I walk back to Euston checking my phone, hoping for messages from him, but there are none.

There's one from Frankie saying he'll see me later. Something good, at least.

I catch the train.

7 p.m.

It is even worse than I expected.

Apparently Matthew had only just pulled into the drive when Sylvia Jones accosted him.

I wasn't back. My own train had been delayed, thanks to emergency engineering works, and I'd missed the connecting bus between stations – by which time I was freezing. I rang Frankie for a lift and took him for coffee and a chat on the high street.

If only I'd gone straight home, I'd have been able to defend myself immediately, before the thought was planted in Matthew's head – but I was listening to Frankie rabbit on about

Jenna, watching him discover love for the first time with some wonderment. I felt really happy for him, but I was conscious I still hadn't heard from Matthew since those strange texts first thing.

The phone finally rang as Frank drove us home.

'Hi, darlin'.' I felt a flood of relief when I saw Matthew's name. 'Are you back? I'm looking—'

'Yes, I'm at Malum.' Matthew was curt. 'Where are you?'

'We're just round the corner.'

His tone wasn't right.

'Well get a move on.' He hung up.

'What?' Frankie clocked my face. '*More* trouble?'

'I'm not sure.' I stared at the road before us.

Oh God, I prayed not.

When Frank pulled up outside the house, I couldn't bear to look at him.

'Give us a minute, would you, lovey? I just – I need to talk to him...'

'Really?'

'Yeah – and I don't want you to worry, so just let me do it on my own.'

'Fine.' He shrugged. 'I'll go round to George's.'

'You don't need to go...'

But he said he'd prefer to.

Thank God Frankie's made friends quicker than I have, I thought, watching his tail lights disappear round the corner.

As quickly, apparently, as I had made enemies.

I didn't bother with any 'Hi, honey, I'm home' jokes. I was the joke now I feared. 'Matt?' I called gingerly.

'In here.'

How much had changed in four months. Ruefully I followed the voice.

'Have you been going through my emails?' Matthew asked as soon as I walked into the kitchen. No 'hello', no greeting at all – he barely even looked up.

'Oh!' Should I lie? But what was the point? I'd left the laptop in the kitchen, where it glared balefully from the table, its owner looking no less malevolent. 'Well, not going through them exactly – I just…'

'What?'

'I just wanted to know who sent you that – thing – about me.' I moved towards Matthew hopefully.

He was unshaven, in jeans and a T-shirt, not quite as svelte as when we'd married, his stubble blue-black, his face dark with anger. '*Not* going through them?'

'I just wanted to see if I recognised the email address.'

'But I told you that I didn't.'

'I just thought that *I* might though. I am sorry – but that's all it was really.'

'All?' He put great weight on the word. 'That's *all*?'

'Yes. I mean I didn't look at anything else…' But that *was* a lie. 'Why are you so angry? What's happened now?'

'Apart from you snooping in my private affairs?' He looked at me. My first thought was how sickeningly handsome he was, despite his scowl; my second was a rare flash of anger.

'I wasn't snooping!' I was vehement. 'It was just the one email, and it was about me – and…' I had to bite the bullet again. 'And you've not been honest yourself.'

'What? Why?'

'Who did you take with you? To Brussels. Did… did Kaye go?'

'Kaye?' He looked at me like I was totally mad. 'Don't be so fucking stupid.'

'I'm not. I saw another passport number…'

'Yes. Yours.'

'What?'

'Yours, I said.'

'I-It's not mine,' I stammered.

He shoved the laptop towards me. 'Why don't you check?'

'I did. Mine ends with a twenty-six, not…'

He opened his briefcase and threw four passports across the table at me. 'Check it then.'

I picked them up. One of them *was* mine, it seemed.

'When I booked it, I booked it for all four of us. But it's all been so fucking awful, I just couldn't take you too. You knew that.'

'Sorry,' I whispered.

'You should have believed me.' He slammed the laptop lid.

I didn't know what to say, but I saw the bottle of whisky and box of Belgian chocolates on the side, very fancy, wrapped in gold ribbons, and I contemplated a joke about my chocolate addiction – anything to ease the tension. Only the look on Matthew's face suggested jokes would be unwise.

'Matthew, please. Try and understand. I *had* to look on your computer. I wouldn't normally have, but I needed to know,' I pleaded. 'I feel like someone's trying to…'

'Trying to *what*?'

'Bring me down?' In for a penny, I supposed. 'Like – as if someone might be, sort of – trying to come between us?'

'Don't be so bloody stupid.' He looked at me as if we'd never met. 'You know, Jeanie, I thought you were such a quiet little mouse – such a safe bet – but you're not at all who I thought you were.'

'A mouse?' I repeated dumbly.

'And if someone actually was trying to come between us,' he said irritably, 'which they're not – well you've only yourself to blame. If you're going to act like a tart, then…'

'What do you mean a *tart*?' I was aghast.

'Well, first the boy at the school. Then entertaining men here.'

'What do you mean "entertaining men"?'

'Sylvia told me she caught you with that guy.'

'*Sylvia?*' I had no idea they were such good friends. 'She caught me with *what* guy?'

'You tell me, Jean. She texted me, saying sorry to have to tell me, but when she came for coffee yesterday, some guy was getting out of the shower.'

'Oh, God – Yassine?' I actually laughed with relief. 'She means Yassine.'

'Who the hell's Yassine?'

'Kaye's boyfriend?'

'You're fucking joking.' Matthew stared at me in horror. 'So now you're shagging my ex's new bloke?'

'Don't be ridiculous, Matthew!' I cried. 'He dropped off Luke's football boots when I was gardening, and…'

'So he got in the shower with you?' he sneered. 'Oh come on.'

'No, of course not! I was cutting back brambles, and he came down the garden to talk to me. He slipped in the mud, so he went in the downstairs loo to have a quick wash. That was it. He was here about five minutes.'

'Luke's football boots?' Matthew interrupted. 'Why?'

'He said he had a match. Tonight. He said he'd been told Luke needed them.'

'First I've heard of it.'

'I'll get them,' I said eagerly. 'I'll prove it to you.'

I went rushing to the utility room where I'd put the boots on the shoe rack, still in the Sainsbury's bag they'd been wrapped in when Yassine delivered them.

But they weren't there. I searched everywhere, but of course they weren't there.

6 APRIL 2015

10 a.m.

I didn't want to fall in love with Matthew. I didn't want his money. In fact I asked him to stay away, soon after we met.

It was very much Matthew who pursued me, not the other way around.

I let him take me out to dinner once, to a fancy Lebanese place in Mayfair. We had a nice night, but I felt shy and awkward with a man of his looks and expensive confidence. I didn't see what I had to offer – apart from myself.

Still, he pursued me, driving down to Hove a few weekends later, where we walked along the coast path, chatting, for hours. I told him I was flattered, but I wasn't interested, despite my growing attraction to him.

I knew I didn't trust love. I couldn't do it again after the wreckage from Simon. It suited me to be on my own with Frank. It was safer.

I didn't trust love one little bit – but I didn't follow my instinct. I let Matthew drag me in.

Now look.

It's like someone's pulling out my heart; I'm being hauled into the sausage maker, and once I've been chewed up, I'm going to be spat out.

After I'd hunted high and low for the stupid football boots, Matthew phoned Kaye and asked her if she'd sent her boyfriend round with them. She said no.

I sat on the stairs, and I tried to think: *where* could they be? Had I moved them without remembering? I didn't think so, but…

And then I heard them. They were on the telephone, *laughing* about me. I was the joke.

'Maybe she's going a little mad,' Matthew was muttering, 'or got early onset – but she swore blind he brought them…'

Was I mad?

Possibly.

I went upstairs.

Frankie came back at some point and stuck his head round my bedroom door, but I pretended I was asleep. I was terrified my sanity *was* actually slipping away.

I remembered Frankie talking about Jenna earlier, and I thought: *I'll be so happy if he manages to find love.* Still, I had to admit something I was ashamed of: I was a little jealous. Because I didn't feel like that any more, and I knew Matthew didn't either.

Such a quiet little mouse.

The ground was increasingly unsafe.

For once I was glad Frankie was leaving soon – getting out of this mess.

Things were falling apart fast.

10.30 a.m.

Matthew gets up, barely speaking to me. Then he comes back in and reiterates that no one had asked Yassine to bring the boots round – the missing boots.

'Are you *really* all right?' he asks. 'Perhaps'—he stares down at me—'you need some help?'

'What kind of help? I'm fine, Matthew, really.'

'Well that's good, because Alison and Sean are coming to dinner tonight. If you can hold it together that long.'

'Oh right,' I say slowly. Had I forgotten that too? 'Shall I cook something nice?'

Matthew does his tie up in the mirror. He looks tired, I notice, and his shirt is slightly tighter than it was four weeks ago. He definitely seems more distracted recently. 'If that's okay,' he says gruffly, 'I'd appreciate it.'

'Of course.' I feel more enthused than I have done in days – in weeks. The kitchen is my domain; I'll prove I'm not as useless as he obviously thinks. 'I'll get my Delia out.'

'I prefer Nigella,' he says, and he actually smiles. 'Better tits.' Then he leans over the bed and kisses my forehead. He smells nice. 'I need it to go well, Jeanie. Sean's been a great help recently. I need to say thanks.'

Before I go shopping I knock on Sylvia Jones's door.

She doesn't answer, so I go back home and sit in my little car in the drive. I just sit there, waiting and watching.

About an hour later, just when I am going to give up, just when I am so cold I am getting cramp, Sylvia walks round the corner, her little dog in a matching coat, heading towards the woods.

My hands icy from sitting, my legs bloodless, I run across the road to confront her.

She actually flinches when she sees me.

'Why did you text Matthew?' I demand. 'Why didn't you talk to me first?'

'I hope you're not threatening me.' She squares her shoulders in her horrid pink Puffa jacket. 'I thought he deserved to know.'

Oh how blind I've been! I think. *She's jealous.* Of course! A widow, around Matthew's age, looking for her 'own Patrick

Swayze'. And then I come along and snaffle him. She's really annoyed.

We're all just looking for love.

'Deserved to know *what* though?' I stare at her pretty, saggy face. 'There was nothing to tell. Why are you meddling in our business?'

'I'll call the police'—Sylvia's voice is shrill—'if you don't go away.'

'Gladly.' I am shaking with anger. 'But I'd like you to keep out of my marriage.'

'I'm not the least bit interested in your marriage,' she retorts.

'Did you send him an email too? A very *helpful* email?'

'No, I did not,' she spits. 'I have better things to do than get involved with your sordid life. Poor man.'

'Poor man?'

'First that dreadful Kaye, spending all his money – and then that girl – and now you.'

'There's nothing "poor" about Matthew,' I retort. 'He's fine, thanks very much. As long as you stay away.'

Then I go to the high street, frozen and shaken, and buy all the ingredients for dinner, along with some flowers and some candles.

What girl?

At home, I start to make a casserole, but I find it hard to concentrate. On the radio they are talking about a new production of *Macbeth* in the West End.

What girl?

Something wicked this way comes.

7.15 p.m.

Alison and Sean are coming at seven forty-five apparently. I'm running out of time as I finish the food; I still need to get changed myself, and Luke has turned up for the night. Kaye and Scarlett are both ill with some sick bug, so he's hiding out here.

Frankie and Luke are playing FIFA in the lounge.

'Are you all right, Mum?' Frank looks concerned when he comes to get himself and Luke a drink.

'Of course,' I say breezily, but I'm not; I keep forgetting to add things to the sauce and finding them on the side. 'Why wouldn't I be?'

'What were you doing earlier? I heard you banging around upstairs this afternoon, didn't I?'

'I don't think so.' I move the bread. I'm getting quite good at lying.

'Oh.' He looks confused. 'Must have been next door then.'

'Must have been.'

'Marlena texted.' He's trying to read my face. 'Said to keep an eye on you for some reason.'

'Oh she did, did she?' I try to smile. I wish she'd get back to me about the bloody emails. I wish I didn't feel so – discombobulated. So seasick, with all this debris floating around.

Frank skulks off when Matthew comes in. They're still barely talking.

'Something smells good.' Matthew opens some red wine to breathe, gets a beer, checks the temperature of the champagne in the fridge. 'I thought we should use the dining room, as it's a special occasion.'

We never use it – not since I've lived here anyway.

'Whatever you think.'

'I'll get Luke to lay the table,' Matthew says.

I'm going to ask him about the girl, about Sylvia's assertion – but Luke comes in, moaning, corralled into making place names. He helps his dad get out the best silver and places the jugs of lemon water, candles, napkins and side plates on the table.

Then he returns to FIFA with Frank, pizza and ice cream.

I look at Matthew, and I think about this afternoon.

After I'd confronted Sylvia, gone shopping and returned to start the casserole, I'd gone upstairs to our room and had passed the locked door to the spare room.

So many secrets in this house. Instinctively I'd tried the handle; it had become a reflex, a habit.

Still locked. I'd bent to peer through the keyhole, but still I hadn't really been able to see anything: the edge of a bed maybe. The door was solid and wooden – but the lock was old.

Frankie had been ensconced in his room, probably asleep, despite the hour, so I'd gone out to the garage and rooted around the toolboxes until I found some galvanised wire, which I'd twisted into the shape I'd needed.

Standing in front of the impenetrable door, hands on hips, I'd seen myself aged ten. I'd done this throughout our childhood, when we were locked in. It's not hard if you know how, slotting the pick into the lock. Although, this particular one had been very stiff.

At some point, as I'd rocked back on my heels, Frankie had stumbled down the landing to use the bathroom, hair on end.

'I'm going to miss you when you're gone,' I'd told his departing back. 'Specially looking like that.'

But it's good, I'd told myself again. *I'm glad he's off on Sunday. Off to safety.*

He'd gone back to bed.

The door had opened, and I'd been in.

It hadn't been what I'd expected: oh no, not at all.

7.40 p.m.

The vegetables are all ready to go in their pans, the French onion soup's bubbling, cheese grated, croutons cut – and the casserole's in.

'Is it a special occasion?' I ask, as I take my apron off to rush up and change.

'New deal with Transregions.' Matt checks the champagne again; he's already on his second beer, keyed up and excited. 'Sean's given me free advice. There's some papers to sign actually.'

'Oh?' I check the temperature of the sauce. 'That's good then?'

'Should be.' He kisses me again and pats my bottom. 'Should be a whole turn of fortunes. Put that nice red dress on, hon. It's really sexy.'

I feel galvanised for the first time in weeks.

When I come down, there's a glass of fizz on the side for me and The Killers on the stereo. Matthew's outside, checking the garden lights. I should be excited, but the memory of Alison's hostility at the party makes me nervous. I've never even met Sean. They are Kaye's friends.

I cast away the image of what's behind the spare-room door.

Quickly I drink my champagne and check the dining table. It looks nice, classy – the room dimly lit, snow-white roses as a centrepiece, our home-made place names. It's almost like a restaurant.

The doorbell rings; Matthew answers it. I hear laughter, the rise and fall of voices.

The drink seems to have gone straight to my head. I straighten the napkins, feeling a little woozy. I drink some water.

'Hello.' I smile, coming into the hall. Sean is a small, wiry man with slicked-back grey hair. Alison looks completely different out of her pirate costume. Her curly red hair is tied back, and she wears a severe black dress.

Sean kisses me hello; Alison hands me chocolates from Rococo.

'Can't go wrong with truffles,' she says rather stiffly.

'No, you can't. I love all chocolate! Thanks so much.'

Frank and Luke say hello and trudge upstairs. I feel Matthew tense slightly as he watches his son chattering to mine, but I'm glad they're together.

'They get on then?' Alison asks. 'That's good, isn't it?'

I tense, waiting for Matthew to correct her, but he doesn't. He's very buoyed up about something.

'Champagne?' He propels us all into the lounge, where we sit and chat until I have to check the food.

When I come back, the men are looking at some papers and Alison is leafing through a copy of *House & Garden* from the coffee table. It must be one of Kaye's old subscriptions.

She looks out into the garden.

'You've had outdoor lights put in,' she says. 'It's such a lovely big space, isn't it? You could do so much with it.'

'Yes,' I agree. 'I'd like to get into gardening actually. I don't know much about plants though. I've never really had a garden of my own.'

'I could help you, if you liked,' Alison says, and I try to hide my surprise. 'I had my own business for a bit when I retrained.'

'Oh thanks. That'd be really kind. We've got a gardener who comes once in a while…'

'Yes, he's very handy.' Matthew comes over, papers in his hand, and kisses my head fondly. 'New guy, since old Bill broke his hip – Simon something,' He takes a pen from his pocket. 'Hired him a few months ago. Hon, can you—'

'Simon?' My skin feels suddenly icy. 'Are you sure? Do you know his surname?'

'Not off the top of my head. Now shall we crack on?' I hear irritation creeping into Matthew's voice. 'Can you just sign this please?'

'Of course.' I force a smile.

Matthew points at places in the documents marked with an X, and I take the pen he offers.

'Signing my life away,' I joke, and I sense Alison stiffen beside me.

Sean laughs and says, 'Signing up for life, more like,' and I look at Matthew, who seems so jolly tonight. I think, *Everything might be all right – if we can overcome what I know now.*

What lay behind the door.

My timer goes off, and we all go through to the dining room. The soup is very salty, and I apologise, but no one else seems to really notice. They chatter on about this and that: Matthew's kids, their godchildren, holidays yachting and skiing. I mostly just listen. I've never been on a ski in my life.

Quiet little mouse. A safe bet.

I feel very thirsty as I clear away, and I wheel the hostess trolley in with the casserole and the new potatoes, feeling like the impostor someone said I was, didn't they? But I feel quite woozy.

At some point during the main course, I start to feel really very odd, as if my head is too heavy for my neck and my eyelids are weighted down.

I stop eating and just watch the others, almost falling asleep, and then I hear Alison mention Kaye, and I say loudly, 'Oh, Kaye, the amazing Kaye of the unmoving face – she's wonderful, isn't she?'

'Jeanie, really.' Matthew frowns. 'Not now.'

They all look at me, and their faces are blurry and going in and out of focus, like the circus hall of mirrors. I start to laugh, and then I can't stop, and then I think, *Oh, God, I'm going to be sick.*

'Are you all right?' Alison asks, and I wonder why she's frowning.

And then I pass out.

JEANIE

7 APRIL 2015

8 a.m.

I wake in the bedroom alone with the worst headache I think I've ever had.

I can barely remember last night, but I know without doubt I have disgraced myself.

Matthew didn't come to bed last night. I think he said I needed space – but I also think, really, it's space of a different kind he means.

I lie here, sick and mortified – and, frankly, scared. I don't understand what the hell's happening.

8.45 a.m.

'What the fuck did you take?' Matthew asks before he leaves for work, his jaw almost rigid. 'More of that Xanax crap? You were talking complete gibberish you know. It was so bloody embarrassing – and I really needed it to go well.'

'I'm sorry.' I feel utterly wretched in every way. 'I swear I didn't take anything.' But why *do* I feel this awful? 'Honestly. It might just be the same bug Kaye and Scarlett have.'

'Maybe,' he says grimly. 'Whatever it was, we need to talk properly at the weekend.'

He leaves without a backwards glance.

He's right though. We absolutely do need to talk. There are a few things I need to say to him too.

10 a.m.

When I stop feeling quite so terrible, I haul myself out of bed to see if Frankie's here, but he's off visiting Jenna. Luke's gone to school; at least I don't have to face his embarrassment too. I vaguely remember his worried face last night at the foot of the stairs as I was carried up to bed.

My head pounds.

So.

I go back to the room that I looked in yesterday, which is now not locked any more – although Matthew doesn't know that.

It is like a shrine.

Cupboards of clothes. A flouncy white dressing table of perfume and make-up. Antique prints of old nursery rhymes on the walls: 'Baa Baa Black Sheep', 'Mary, Mary Quite Contrary', 'Little Bo Peep'. One's missing, a lighter square on the wall where it must have hung.

'Sing a Song of Sixpence' – *the queen is in the parlour, eating bread and honey.*

Matthew's Queenie.

Why did Matthew not just say he couldn't bear to get rid of Kaye's stuff? That that's why the mirror still hangs out there on the stairs too? That hideous mirror that reflects how I don't fit in every time I pass it.

He couldn't bear to move on, so he must have left it all there. Complete. And yet broken. Incomplete.

I stagger downstairs to get some water. The post is on the mat; I scoop it up as I pass.

A postcard to Frankie from his mate Saul, who's travelling round Thailand. A few more bills for Matthew.

And another letter to Lisa, from HMRC – only this time there's a full name on the front of the envelope.

Lisa Daisy Bedford.

In my bedroom, I ring Matthew. When he doesn't answer, I leave a message.

'Who is Lisa Daisy Bedford?' I ask urgently. 'And why didn't you tell me what was in the spare room? Why have you still got all Kaye's stuff?'

He texts me later:

I won't be back tonight. I'm meeting Sean in town. I'll stay there. We need to talk properly when I'm back tomorrow. I got another email. PS Stay out of that room please.

He doesn't answer either question.

All right.

If that's how he's going to play it.

I go to his computer again, and I log in quickly, before I can change my mind. He's not changed the password, so he can't be that worried about me, I think, with relief. And there's another bloody email from that bastard. It says:

You were warned. Why don't you do something?

Feeling sick but braver now – or just with nothing left to lose – I skim the other emails to see if Kaye's sent anything recently. Are they in cahoots? But there have been no emails from her for weeks. I feel inordinately relieved.

I get dressed, and I text Marlena: *Have you found out anything? He's had another one.*

She texts back, *but I'm on it, I promise. Hang in there.*

Then I'm overtaken by another huge wave of nausea, and I have to lie down.

I stare at the bedroom ceiling. I have to prove I'm not mad, that someone has it in for me, before I lose either my marriage or my sanity entirely.

And then I think, *Do I even want this marriage?* Do I want to be married to a man who has been lying to me?

Who might love someone else still?

Even if I'm not losing it, I know I'm on borrowed time now.

JEANIE

9 APRIL 2015

I can't help myself. It is wrong, but I do it anyway.

Around five, I get up. I scrub the work surfaces and the kitchen floor. My compulsion to tidy is getting worse; the CBT last spring stopped it for a bit, but it's definitely rearing its head again. I know now that it's about creating order when I feel I've lost control, but even that knowledge is not helping.

Once the surfaces shine, I get dressed, make a thermos of coffee and two ham, lettuce and mustard sandwiches – one for Frank, one for Matthew's tea when he gets home.

I wrap Matthew's very carefully. Inside the wrapping, on which I write 'M', I slip a little note. It just says, *Forever.*

Afterwards I'll remember the word I chose.

I'll remember the desperation with which I wrote it.

I drive south, back to where I came from, skirting London, out into the brown and green fields.

Somewhere along the way I get a text. I hope it is Matt, but it isn't. *Hope you're feeling better, Kaye xx*

I am driving too fast to text her back.

Nearing the coast, I wind my window down, thinking I can smell the sea.

I miss the sea. For all its danger, it's more benign than the scary old house I live in.

I loop my way up over the hills, through the lamb-filled pastures, and the sun comes out at one point, fingers of light dancing over the sea, and I think, *Maybe it will be all right.* Maybe.

I know where they live from before.

Their small terraced house is what they called 'bohemian', and what I'd just call a mess. Broken window boxes full of weeds; half a rusty bike, missing a wheel; and, plonked in the middle of the front garden, the pièce de résistance: a ridiculous pink and orange sculpture with a sagging middle, courtesy of the woman Frank called Mrs Twit or Ma Lundy. It is entitled, according to the hand-painted sign, 'Birth'. Not like any birth I've ever witnessed. And it only costs £235, if you care to ask.

I take a deep breath and knock.

In the grand scheme of things, I'm glad it is Pa who is in and not Ma. He is definitely the more sympathetic of the two – which isn't saying much.

'What the hell do *you* want?' He is bleak, though he seems unsurprised to see me. He really is the most unprepossessing man: dirty fingernails on the door catch, lank hair pulled into a ponytail, old food down his fleece. He looks like he smells; I try not to get too near.

'You're not meant to be anywhere near here.'

How such a man managed to father such a beautiful child I'll never know.

'Have you been telling people about me?' I say quickly, before he shuts the door in my face.

Pa Lundy looks at me like I am quite mad, a running theme of my life recently. 'What?'

'Have you been emailing people? About – what happened?' I feel dizzy. Have I eaten today?

'No, we bloody haven't.' He is ferocious. 'Why would we?'

'For the same reason you thought I had an affair with your son?'

There's a nick on his cheek where he's cut himself shaving; dark blood has bobbled up there. 'But you know exactly why we thought that.'

I feel so deflated I could just crumple up right there.

'You should go, before Sue gets back. She'll give you far shorter shrift than me.'

That I don't doubt – and Sue weighs at least three stone more than he does. I realise, too late, that even if they *had* sent the emails, there's no way on God's earth they'll ever admit it.

A mangy ginger cat winds its way round my ankles. Pa Lundy looks at it like it's some kind of traitor. 'Come *here*, puss.'

'How is Otto?' I can't help myself. 'Is he here? Is he okay?'

Otto's father would have slammed the door in my face, but the cat gets in the way, so he makes do with telling me to get lost.

I sit in the window of the dilapidated fish-and-chip shop on the seafront. Before me the sea rolls indolently up and down. *What a fool.*

I eat half the chips I ordered and a bit of the fish.

How has it come to this? I think, stirring my tea full of sugar.

The truth is it would be easier if it *was* the Lundys sending those messages. Because if it wasn't them, the truth is even more unpalatable.

I text Kaye back: *Hi. How did you know I was feeling bad?*

A few minutes later, a reply: *Luke told me. Poor you* ☹

As I finish my sugary tea, my phone rings.

'Frankie says you're down south?' Marlena sounds urgent.

'Yeah, I'm in Brighton.' I watch a seagull dive-bomb the bin outside.

'Why?' She sounds anxious. Most unlike Marlena.

'I wanted to know if the Lundys had sent that email.'

'But you're not meant to go near those stupid Twits, are you?'

'I don't know.' I'm not. 'But I just wanted to check.'

'Well don't bother with them. They're not the answer.' There's a pause while Marlena speaks to someone in the background. 'I'm worried about you,' she says when she comes back on the line.

'Why? What's happened?' My ears prick up. 'Did you find out who *did* send it?'

'No, but my mate Robo's on it. Are you going home now?'

'Home?'

'Back to Hertfordshire?'

'Yeah, I'm driving back soon.'

'Drive carefully, Jeanie,' she says. 'I'll be in touch really soon, I swear.'

Walking back to the car park near the Lanes, my heart stops and then soars when I see Otto, in the midst of a group of teen-age lads outside one of the arcades. They are as rumbustious as a bunch of puppies, piggybacking each other down the road, shouting and laughing, sharing rollies and cans of shandy.

I quicken my step and raise my hand, eager to catch the boy's eye – but when I get nearer, I see it's not Otto.

Or, if it was, he didn't see me. He slipped around the corner silently with his raucous friends.

I don't belong in Brighton any more, I realise, as I drive away from the town. Everyone was right – I should stay away.

I thought this was my true home, but I know now it's not.

I just don't know where home is any more.

If I ever did.

When I reach the house, I can't remember the route I took to get here.

Dusk is drawing in, and the house is empty. Matthew must be working late, I guess, and I feel that strange pulsating fear I remember from last year.

Somewhere along the way, I've started to feel angry too – only I'm really not sure *who* exactly I'm angry with.

Everyone. No one. Myself.

I lie on the sofa, thinking I'll just shut my eyes for five minutes…

An hour later I wake in the dark, sweating, from a nightmare that's slipping away. I scrabble to remember the field of small children – they kept running away from me towards a river – I was terrified they were all going to fall in, and I chased after them, frantically shouting, 'Come back,' but…

Still bewildered, I hear a clatter from the hallway.

'Hello?' I pull myself up to sitting. 'Who's there?'

A figure walks through the door, though the gloom, towards me. My heart speeds up, and confused, only half awake, I stare into the shadows. I knew it – I knew it was only a matter of time before he came…

And then I realise it's Scarlett standing above me. She's holding something high in her hand, and for a moment I think it's a knife. She's going to stab me. And then I laugh…

'What?' Her pretty little face is ugly with anger. 'Why are you laughing?'

'I'm sorry,' I say. 'I just had a silly thought. A really silly one.' I swing my feet to the floor and turn the table lamp on. 'I must have dozed off. How are you? Haven't seen you for a while.'

She shrugs. 'Okay, I s'pose.' But she doesn't look okay. She slumps down in the armchair opposite, holding her phone, Dr Dre headphones balanced round her neck. It was her phone in her hand, not a knife at all. I can hear music blaring out of it, something about not having a gun, I swear. *Nirvana,* I think, recognising Frank's favourite band.

I'm still feeling bleary, trying to rouse myself. Scarlett's distracted, messing with the phone as usual.

'What's up?' I ask. I haven't seen her since she wouldn't talk to me again.

'It's just – I dunno. Everything's gone weird,' she says eventually, not meeting my eye.

I wait, poised for her to say something about what she's found out about my past, but instead she says simply, 'I miss my dad.'

'Oh, love!' Pity floods through me. 'Well your dad's always here you know.'

' 'Cept he's not, is he?' She scowls. 'He's never here, and he never used to be either.'

'Oh?' I say. 'Was he away a lot before then?'

She laughs drily. 'Yeah, always away. Always working, so we could have nice things apparently. But I didn't want nice things.'

'Right,' I say.

'And then my mum was always busy, and then neither of them were here. We even had a nanny for a bit…' She trails off, biting her lip.

'A nanny?' News to me. 'Was she nice?'

'Oh it wasn't for long. But Luke didn't like her, and he was getting bullied at the time.'

'Bullied? About what?'

'Stuff. Too much coding club. Being a geek. Dad and Mum divorcing, that kind of stuff. So she… she had to go. Can I have a drink?' She changes the subject abruptly.

'Course. Must have been really hard for you both.' I stand, turning the overhead lights on now. 'I'm going to make some tea.'

I feel like my bones are heavier than they've ever been.

In the kitchen, I think about the manner in which Scarlett delivered this information.

This house *is* haunted. No, not haunted — no more ghost stories. Tainted. I didn't notice it at first, but I notice it more and more now: the air is dark and sullied.

The sandwich I made Matthew is still in the fridge I see as I get the milk out. The sandwich with the note inside.

I take it out of the fridge and throw it in the bin, and I'm wondering how I can rectify things between us when the telephone rings.

'Hello?' I answer without thinking. It's rarely for me.

'You stay away, you fucking bitch,' a voice says. I nearly slam it down again — but then I realise I recognise the voice.

Ma Lundy.

'How did you get this number?' I ask.

'It wasn't hard; you're in the phone book, love.'

'Phone book?'

'Or 118 — whatever you call it these days. So stay away.'

'Look, I'm sorry, but I only wanted to know if you—' I start, but she cuts across me, in her familiar raspy tone.

'Stay away from my boy if you know what's good for you.'

Sue Lundy is the archetypal jealous mother, despite neglecting her son badly.

When I tried to talk to her at the time of the allegations, she refused to believe my story; she refused to believe I hadn't pursued her beloved son to within an inch of his life. *She* loved him — her version of love anyway — so every other woman in the world must love him too.

When she was warned by the school that nothing had been proven, the woman made it a vendetta that she passed on to Otto's father. He posted on social media about me until the Facebook administration agreed to take the page down. Next the Lundys began to tweet about me, trying to get anything in the press.

By this time avarice had taken hold, I was sure; they were looking to sell their 'tragic' story – a story less tragic than farcical.

'I meant no harm – really. I never meant any harm, you must know that,' I say – and then I realise Matthew's standing behind me, staring at me.

'Who was that?' he asks suspiciously as I hang up abruptly.

'It's a long story.' If I try to explain where I went today, it won't look good, I know that – so what's the point? 'It's not important now.'

Matthew frowns, as if he doesn't believe me, but he leaves it. 'Where's Scarlett?' he asks. 'Is she here?'

'She's in the living room. It's nice to see her – she seemed fine with me,' I reassure him – but he's not listening.

'Scarlett?' He crosses the hall and pushes open the door, and I follow him.

The television is blaring, *Hollyoaks* or some teenage nonsense. Someone's shouting that they love someone else, but they know they shouldn't, and Scarlett's not there. Matthew turns it off – and the DVD player comes on.

Images of Scarlett and her mother fill the screen, on some open-air ice rink, Alpine perhaps: Kaye clad in beige cashmere and fur, skating well as she flashes smiles for the camera.

But it's Scarlett I'm more interested in. I stare at the expression on the girl's face. I realise what it was that I found so odd before.

'Scarlett?' Matthew says again. 'She's obsessed by these old home movies.'

'She's probably upstairs,' I suggest, my eye caught by a vivid blur outside the patio doors.

A big healthy fox runs across the terrace, something in its mouth. It's a muscular creature, and Matthew hates them with a passion.

'Bloody things,' he swears. 'One's just killed all Sylvia's chickens you know.'

Good, I think. *Good.* I have nothing against chickens, but I don't like Sylvia one tiny bit.

Matthew slides the patio doors open to chase the animal off, and I go to call Scarlett.

Above me I hear giggling and a burst of music as a door opens and shuts. Frankie's rusty little car is parked haphazardly on the drive, in front of Matthew's big black beast.

Frank must have come home whilst I was sleeping.

I call them again – and then suddenly Matthew's inside, face like he's about to kill someone, and he's pushing past me on the stairs.

'Get the hell off her,' he's yelling, taking the stairs two at a time. He's headed for Frank's room. 'I can see you, you little fucker.'

'Matthew, wait!' I cry, following behind him.

I reach the bedroom seconds after him.

He's got my son by the neck, against the wall, and he's shouting in his face, that vein throbbing in his forehead again, and Frankie's spluttering and trying to speak over the garage music that thumps out, and Scarlett's crying and pulling at her dad's arm, saying something that Matthew won't listen to.

'Get off him!' I shout. 'Matthew, let him go!'

'She's only fifteen,' he keeps blustering, and Frankie's going red now, struggling to breathe where Matthew's hands are around his neck. With the most tremendous effort, I manage to pull my husband off my son, and I stand between them.

'What's going on?' I literally can't hear myself think. 'Turn the music off please, Frankie.'

He does so with ill-temper, rubbing his sore red neck, the fingerprints visible, glaring at Matthew. 'That really bloody hurt,' he mutters.

My heart contracts. This man I love has left marks on my son. I move nearer Frankie. 'Matthew, this is unacceptable.'

'I could see him from the garden; I saw you pawing her,' Matthew says, and he's so angry, he's shaking visibly.

'I'm sure he wasn't—' I interject, but Frankie's angry now.

'She said she had something in her eye,' Frank protests. 'I was just having a look because she asked me to.'

That old trick. *Like mother, like daughter,* I think.

'Likely story,' Matthew jeers – and Frank explodes.

'I'm not interested in her, for God's sake, if that's what you think. She's a kid, and I've got a girlfriend.'

'I'm not a kid,' Scarlett interjects. 'I'm fifteen.'

'You're a bloody child – and you expect me to believe that?' Matthew switches his attention to Frank.

'Matthew, look…' I say, but he grabs his daughter by the arm and drags her out of the room.

Scarlett wails, 'Stop it, Dad!' He ignores her, whisking her away from us.

We hear a door slam – and then silence falls.

Speechless, Frankie and I look at each other.

'Mum?' he says, and he sounds like a little boy. I'd better not cry; he hates it when I cry – he always has. Like Marlena, it panics him.

'I'm okay,' I lie. 'Let him calm down. I'll talk to him later.'

But later I will think: *This was the moment I felt defeat.*

We are not going to get through this now, Matthew and I. We can't make a family. We can't force it.

You can't take two halves of two different things and try to make a whole. It just won't work.

God knows I've tried.

I sit with Frankie in his room for a while, but he's so angry, he won't calm down. And I don't blame him, not really. Poor lad. *I've let him down,* I think.

'Why would he do that? Why would he not believe me?'

'I'll talk to him, Frankie, I promise, lovey,' I say. 'I'll sort it out.'

'He didn't believe me. He didn't want to believe me, more to the point. God…'

He clenches his fists, and I feel a surge of panic. He's getting angry again, and I don't want that – I don't want them to fight again. I feel the tension in the house; it's palpable.

'It's her, Mum. Not me. She's the one coming on to me.'

And this, I think, might be the whole problem. Matthew can't cope with his daughter growing up, with her being sexually attracted to a boy. No parent can cope with any inconvenient truth. Otto's couldn't either…

'Let me talk to him on his own,' I plead, 'and we'll sort it out properly, okay?' I grab Frankie's hand and hold it tight. 'Okay?'

Frankie stares at me unseeing. I remember playground tussles when he was very small: brave little soldier, teased for having no dad. I can't bear the idea of him fighting now. 'Frank, okay? I don't want you to do anything stupid.'

'No, okay, Mum.' He shakes me off irritably. 'I won't.'

I feel the energy drain out of me as he agrees, my shoulders literally slumping where I stand.

'Mum?' Frank's worried, I realise, and I feel a wave of love for him, a great tidal wave of it.

'I'm fine, Frankie, really. I don't know why, I'm just really tired today. I got up too early.'

'If you're all right,' he says, 'I'm going to see Jenna now.'

'Great stuff.' I feel fresh relief he's found someone good. 'Off you go then.'

I walk down the landing to mine and Matthew's room – except Matthew's hardly slept here this past week.

The bed is big and empty.

Five minutes later Matthew and Scarlett pass the door. Matthew's taking Scarlett home apparently and is telling her to get her things when the doorbell rings.

It's Kaye. I listen from the landing.

'You didn't say you were coming here,' Kaye's scolding Scarlett, who's still sniffing as she gathers her things. 'I'm fed up with this running around.'

'Ah, leave her be.' Matthew sounds exhausted.

'Where's Jeanie?' I hear Kaye ask.

Matthew says, 'Not feeling too good. Having a lie-down.'

'Still not well? Poor woman,' Kaye says. 'Is she often ill then?'

I stay safely upstairs; I don't want to see that woman now, her perfection in my face. And I don't want her near my son; I don't want any more blame on us.

Matthew leaves soon after.

I'm so tired: bone weary suddenly. I've been fighting all my life, and this was meant to be the good bit – but it's not. It's stressful and fraught and full of emotions that fracture us and swarm the sky unspoken, and I can't take much more.

I force myself off the bed. I wash my face and go downstairs and into the garden. I walk down to the woodpile, and I pick up the axe.

8 p.m.

When Matthew returns an hour or two later, I am calm again.

But one look at his face tells me he isn't.

'So you bothered to get up again,' he says. 'I wouldn't want to tire you out.'

'Sorry,' I say quietly. 'I do feel particularly exhausted today. I'm not sure why.'

'No, I'm not sure either when you just sit on your backside all day.'

His words don't even shock me any more. 'But you know I've been looking for a job. I think I might have—'

'I wouldn't bother. I mean with your past, it's hardly surprising you've not found one, is it?' He slams the kettle on. Then he changes his mind and opens the fridge, pulling a bottle of beer out and slamming the door so hard everything rattles. 'You're almost as bad as Kaye.'

'That's not fair,' I protest, reeling slightly from the savagery of his attack. Kaye had never worked properly from what I understood – or at least I vaguely recalled there was a brief stint as some kind of TV extra or catalogue modelling: something like that. But really she just produced children and shopping and went to the gym.

'Fair? Fair?' Matthew's going puce again. 'Whoever said life was fair?'

'Matthew,' I say quietly, 'I'm not one of the twins. Please don't speak to me like that.'

'I don't actually.' He glares at me. 'I wouldn't talk to my kids like that, because they don't need it. And you…' I sense him deciding whether to say it.

'What?'

'I don't think you should be *near* my kids at the moment.'

As soon as it's out, he looks abashed – but he obviously needed to say it.

'Is that *really* what you think?' I'm wounded, but I'm also not thinking straight. I'm not sure what to say.

'I don't know what I think any more.' He's quieter now, and he looks terrible suddenly. 'I'm sorry, Jeanie. It just feels – horrible.'

'I want to ask two things, if I may, Matt.' I place my hands flat on the table to steady myself. 'One – why keep Kaye's room like that? And two – who is Lisa Bedford?' I look at him squarely.

'Who?'

'Lisa *Daisy* Bedford.'

Unusually for him, colour stains his face. 'Daisy?'

'Yes, *Daisy*. You let me think she was a pet dog.'

He looks embarrassed. 'Well – it – was just easier.'

'Why?'

'I just – I didn't need any more complications.'

'So who is she?'

'She's a – family friend. She looked after the kids for a bit when Kaye and I first split. I mean, I employed her.'

'I see.' I try to absorb this. 'Was she good with the kids?'

'Yeah, she was absolutely great. They loved her – she was a natural – unlike some…'

'Please, Matt, don't say anything you'll regret.'

'Who are you, fucking Oprah Winfrey?' he yells at me. 'Don't be so paranoid. And fuck knows if I mean it. I don't know what I mean any more…'

'Well don't say it then.' I do sound like a teacher. Like the teacher I am. Or was anyway.

'Oh why don't you just *fuck off.*' Without warning he lobs the beer bottle; it smashes on the wall behind me. Beer froths and trickles down the tiles, drip-drip-dripping onto the floor.

I've been holding on so hard for these past few weeks, but it's like our marriage has a life of its own now; a horrible being in its own right – an ugly little beast, scuttling around, scratching at everything, not satisfied by anything…

The truth is I'm not sure I even want to hold on to it right now.

'Sorry.' Matthew stares at the mess. 'That was daft. But I just – I don't know *what* I think right now.' The earlier colour has drained from his face, leaving him pale. 'You've got to admit this is pretty crap.'

'Yeah.' I stare blindly at the wet wall. 'It's pretty crap.'

He rummages in the cupboard for a dustpan and brush, and I get up and step over the mess and walk out of the room.

'Jeanie,' he says. But he doesn't try to stop me going.

A while later I hear him come up the stairs – and then I hear his bellow of rage.

'Jeanie! What the hell have you done now? Jeanie!'

I took the axe to the pain.

And I felt a little better afterwards, a little calmer for a while.

Now I've locked myself away from him – for the first time ever I've locked the door.

I don't come out until he leaves for work the following morning.

JEANIE

2 MAY 2015

10.30 a.m.

'Another one bites the dust.' As I put a box in the boot, Miss Turnbull is at the gate, bundled into her tweed coat, despite the warm day.

'You don't need to take everything,' Matthew had said awkwardly a few days previously. We agreed I'd leave some stuff in the garage whilst I worked out what exactly would happen next. I didn't have much to take anyway; I never have had. I'm not a hoarder; I've never had enough belongings to hoard.

'Perhaps we just need some time,' he'd said, but we both saw the smashed door every time we passed, and we knew the reality.

No time would heal this I fear. All the trust is gone.

Frankie moved out first.

I insisted on driving him to Dover to catch the ferry. Despite my worry, he was determined to hitch the rest of the way to his job in a vineyard at the foot of the Pyrenees, but he promised to take care.

'I'll be fine. But will *you* be okay, Mum?' He'd hugged me tight. 'On your own?'

'Yes, of course.' I'd been as bright as I could manage. 'It's for the best. Things just don't always work out, do they?'

Waving him into the ferry terminal, I'd felt so proud of Frankie. I hadn't done a bad job there at least. Something I'd got right.

'What do you mean?' I ask the old lady now, wearily, wedging the last box in and shutting the boot. 'Another one? After Kaye you mean?'

'He's getting through you like hot dinners.' She nods with an emotion hard to read. I could ask her to qualify that – but she's just a lonely old lady with nothing better to do than watch.

'You're probably better off gone anyway,' she mutters as she turns away. 'Get out while you still can.'

'Miss Turnbull…' I raise my voice to call her back, but she's rounded the corner already, nifty for one so elderly.

I don't have the energy to follow.

I take a final look at the old house. It belongs in a fairy tale, this place – or maybe a horror film, I've thought more recently. The roses that run across the grey stone, curling round the windows, meshed into the ivy, are starting to bloom.

It never felt like home; I won't miss it. But I *will* miss my husband.

As I back out of the drive the tears start.

Sylvia Jones is walking up the road in high heels and a skirt. She's carrying a dish under a cloth, as if it were a glass slipper on a royal cushion.

I'd laugh if my heart wasn't breaking.

As I pull out of the avenue, I think I see a figure emerge from the shadows, watching my car. But maybe I am imagining it.

12 p.m.

I've just sat in a lay-by off the dual carriageway, howling, for about half an hour.

Now I'm going to Marlena's to regroup. I can't stay around here in Hertfordshire. It's twee and bland, and I crave a real landscape again – the sea or the wild peaks of the North: Brontë land maybe.

As I drive out of the town, I think of little Jane Eyre, stumbling heartbroken and lost on the moors, homeless when she leaves the great Thornfield, leaves the man she loved.

But I'm not Jane Eyre.

I'm more like the mad woman in the attic – and my friend Judy's ramblings don't seem so crazy any more.

And maybe, I think, maybe the mad woman wasn't quite so mad after all.

MARLENA

Right, so at this point all I want to say is as follows.

You might think you've got Jeanie's number – but she's a master of chameleon deception, my big sister.

Not in a malicious or malevolent way, but in this way: she learnt to keep quiet when danger abounded at a very early age.

More cleverly, perhaps, she learnt to change to suit.

And she learnt to keep the hurt in. Unlike me, from whom it exploded like a shell from a shotgun.

Jeanie stored it up and stored it up.

Only it still has to come out somewhere.

JEANIE

8 MAY 2015

I'm on my own at Marlena's in London.

She's away on an assignment she won't speak about – but I gather involves dinghies full of migrants, the unstable little boats that head constantly over deadly oceans these troubled days.

I feel rather like a migrant myself right now: homeless and unwanted.

And I'm remembering the reasons I left the city years ago. It's so noisy, so hectic. The sirens wail endlessly; the people are a flood. The only benefit is the frenetic energy that at least galvanises me.

In Marlena's studio flat in Farringdon – once a tobacco warehouse, now all stripped-back beams and wooden floors – I phone anyone I can think of about work, emailing any acquaintance who might possibly help.

I need a job. I need the income, and it's the only thing to distract me from the disaster of Matthew.

I'm just glad Frankie's safely out of the way.

Sometimes I go to the cinema alone. If I can find them, I watch old Hollywood films; films I watched with my mother when she was home and could concentrate. She loved those films so much; they brought her solace, belief in another life beyond her own.

I try not to think too much of Matthew, although he's on my mind most of the time.

It's starting to dawn on me though that maybe it isn't *just* me.

Matthew was a man at a crossroads when we met. He was vulnerable and, despite his outer shell of strength, had actually been deeply wounded. He was looking to be saved – he saw me as his salvation.

And then I disappointed him, because I was me – just me, just plain Jeanie Randall – and not salvation at all.

So far I've managed not to contact him. I go to the cinema, and I switch my phone off – I hate it anyway – and I sit in the dark watching the screen's greatest lovers argue – and then invariably kiss and make up again.

I know, deep down, I'm hoping we might do the same.

JEANIE

11 MAY 2015

Good news at last! My old friend and colleague Jon Hunter got my email and rang me this morning. He's about to go to Tanzania doing the VSO thing, volunteering in an orphanage, and he wondered if I'd be interested in covering his job for a few months. He teaches at a small college just outside Derby.

'Nice folk,' he says, 'if a bit unambitious. Good place to lick wounds though.'

Jon sends me a photo of his small cottage on the outskirts of a small town called Ashbourne in the Peak District. Ashbourne looks quaintly attractive, perched in the dip of two dales, surrounded by fields and woods.

'It's like *The Good Life*; minus Tom, of course, but you can be Barbara,' he jokes, offering it to me for a peppercorn rent. 'If you've got some dungarees.'

I feel enthused for the first time in months.

And it's strange – I'm starting to feel a bit less gutted about Matthew. I'm sad, yes, really sad – but lighter, somehow, too.

Perhaps I am starting to come back to myself a little.

JEANIE

13 MAY 2015

Matthew has begun to ring me in the last few days. He misses me, he says. He's really sorry about how everything went, and he wonders if we can meet soon.

Yes, I say, we should meet – but I feel very wary. I don't know how much more hurt I can take. I remember how long it took me to get over Simon, and I think now this may be my chance to move on more swiftly than the last time.

I want Matthew back on the one hand, but on the other, I have to admit I'm not sure it will ever – can ever – work.

I mention in a text that I might be going up north for a bit.

I drive up the M1 to see Jon. We meet at a café in the old part of Derby, near the cathedral. This end of the small city is cobbled and picturesque.

Jon arrives on his pushbike as I sit outside in the spring sunshine. He's fit and tanned, looking infinitely better than when I last saw him in Sussex. Then he was drinking too much: puffy faced and overweight, in the throes of a bitter, acrimonious divorce.

'You look so well,' I marvel. 'You're like an advert for the countryside.'

'It's all the fresh air.' He grins. 'It's good to see you, Jeanie.'

He doesn't say I look well, and I know that's because I don't. I'm too thin – which is rare for me – but I've lost my appetite, and I'm not enjoying my weight loss as I might. My sleep patterns are shot again. But I am doing all right really. All things considered.

We drink cappuccino outside the café. White and pink tulips like cupped hands bob around us in the gentle breeze.

When I fill Jon in briefly, he reaches over and pats my arm.

'I'm sorry it went wrong,' he says sincerely. 'Personally I'm giving up on love. Had enough bullshit.' I have a memory of muted telephone arguments in the staffroom to his wife Lynne, vitriolic and tense. 'Hence the VSO.'

He's enthusiastic about the school; he is form tutor to what's described as a special-needs class, who he's grown quite attached to.

'They're more open up here, the admin. I know it's been tough for you since the Lundy thing.' He drops his voice slightly – in embarrassment I wonder? 'I don't know what I'd do if it happened to me.'

I think of that terrible day, the day Otto's arch-enemy posted *that* photo on social media. It went viral within hours – until the whole school was buzzing with it and soon after that, what felt like the whole town too.

It had been late afternoon, and I'd already got home when the bursar rang and said urgently, 'You'd better get back to school now.'

It had all been caused by a sad, embittered boy who, riven with jealousy at Otto's popularity, had tried to ruin Otto's life – and had partly ruined mine into the bargain.

The experience will shadow me forever – I know that now. There's no safe place from the memory of the scandal.

'But it's over,' I say now to Jon, shaking my head. 'It happened, and I have to be more transparent in the future. I tried to hide it last time I went for a job – and it backfired badly.'

'Well I can see why you wouldn't want to tell all.'

'But if they find out of their own accord – well I'm kind of doubly buggered.'

'Come on.' Jon looks for the waitress. 'Let's drown our sorrows in carrot cake.'

The college where I'll be interviewed tomorrow morning already knows about my past. I sent them a link to the report that thoroughly exonerated me – and Jon has spoken to the head too.

I owe Jon a lot right now.

After putting his bike in the back of my car, Jon and I drive through the green hills to the winding roads that lead to Ashbourne.

Home for Jon is a pretty little honey-coloured stone cottage, halfway up a gentle hill at the back of the small town. He shows me around and then leaves me to 'chill out', as he puts it.

I stand in the window of the top bedroom and look out. I can imagine living here a while. Whilst I try to decide what's next.

Later, over a glass of wine and home-made rabbit stew – delicious, despite my slight squeamishness about Beatrix Potter bunnies – we reminisce about Seaborne – about the good things. There were lots of good things, before it went so bad.

Neither of us talks about our marriages – and we don't mention for a second time the scandal that saw me leave, tail firmly between my legs. Jon's a nice man, I think; his wounds rather more healed than mine.

My wounds are scabby and recent.

I fall asleep listening to the owl that I saw earlier, sweeping like a ghost across the fields behind the cottage. Utterly free.

14 MAY 2015

I can't think where I am when I wake.

All I can hear is the cooing of a wood pigeon or two, and I lie there as it slowly comes back to me.

When I switch my phone on, there's a voicemail message.

I can't make it out at first – but then I realise it's from Scarlett.

'Why did you just go like that?' she is saying furiously. I'm baffled. 'Why did you run away too?' There's a pause – someone calling in the background. Then she hisses, 'Why do you all go?'

All?

When I call her back, it goes straight to answerphone. I leave a message apologising, saying I'll see her soon I hope.

But I don't think I'll see her soon. I think our relationship is over. She got what she wanted in the end.

JEANIE

19 MAY 2015

Marlena arrives back in London just as I'm making my final preparations to move up to Derbyshire. They've offered me the job, and frankly I can't wait. I feel a rare sense of purpose again.

We are like ships that pass in the night, my sister and I. She's keeping strange hours, and I heard her on a very odd Skype call near dawn yesterday, something about love for Allah – but this morning she'd left a note for me on the kitchen table that I read when I got up:

Meet me in Oxford Street Starbucks near Soho Sq, 9.30.
It's v. important.

'Important' is underlined three times.

I know my sister; I take it seriously when she says 'important'. I catch the bus to Tottenham Court Road, making my way through crowds already pushing their insistent way forward, despite the earliness of the hour.

I can't believe how many people throng the busy shopping streets here; everyone with somewhere vital to go apparently – more vital than anywhere you or I might need to be. No one so much as looks at one another as they duck and weave across dirty pavements, surging on and on and on. Drills vibrate the air; yellow- and orange- jacketed workers jostle in the building site that's currently the underground station. Infernal, eternal sirens pierce the air whilst enraged drivers jam their hands on horns.

It feels like Armageddon; I'm glad to get into the coffee shop.

Marlena's already in the corner, wedged in by a young mother and a toddler gearing up for a tantrum.

As usual Marlena's tapping and flicking on her phone. She doesn't see me at first, but when I call her name from the queue, I can tell straightaway from her face something's wrong.

I don't bother getting coffee.

'What is it?' I ask urgently as I reach her.

'Sit down, Jeanie,' she says.

The small child glowers at me as I do what I'm told.

Something in Marlena's bearing reminds me of the day she had to tell me our mother was dead. I feel a wave of nausea. 'What is it?' I repeat.

'I'm sorry, Jeanie. I know it's been a while, but I've been so preoccupied with trying to find Nasreen and now all this stuff in Greece…'

'It's okay.' I'm used to Marlena being busy. It's how she gets through life without being forced to think about herself too often.

'It's just…' She seems reluctant to go on, but she does. 'You know that email you asked me about?'

'Yes.'

'My mate Robo traced the IP address. Handy-to-know cyber dude, Robo.'

'And?' I'm impatient. 'What did he find?'

'It came from a machine that's…' Her phone pings; she looks down. 'This is weird, Jeanie. I'm sorry – but it's a bit – worrying.'

'Oh God.' My heart flips. It had been dawning on me as I walked to meet her. 'It's one of the kids, isn't it?'

'Yeah, 'fraid so…'

'Is it Scarlett?' My stomach plunges. 'It is, isn't it?'

'No.' She looks me straight in the eye. 'It's Frank. The email address is registered to Frankie.'

'What?' I stare at her. 'Frankie? It can't be. Don't be daft.'

'I'm not. Sorry, but it's true. Frankie Randall – in black and white. Robo managed to trace the IP address the email account was set up from. It's not hard, apparently, if you know how.'

I realise I'm gaping like a goldfish. 'But *why* would Frankie send that email to Matthew? Or to the college? It doesn't make any sense.'

'Maybe he hasn't forgiven you. Maybe he…' She trails off, looking really uncomfortable. Picks up her coffee cup, bangs it down again. 'Maybe he was jealous of you and Matthew. He could be. He was so used to having you to himself.'

I think of my son; my beautiful boy. I think of how happy he seemed when I started seeing Matthew properly – and how he gave me his blessing. Sure, he didn't want to leave Sussex particularly, but he was so grown-up about the whole thing, and I'd been really proud of the way he behaved. And he knew, I guess, that he was going to be leaving soon himself, so he took it on the chin. He was scared I'd be alone when he went – so it worked for him.

'I don't believe it,' I say stubbornly. 'Forgiven me for what?'

'For – choosing someone else over him.'

'I didn't. I just…' I hesitate to say *fell in love*. It sounds so chocolate-boxy, especially given everything that's happened since.

Could all the horror *really* have been partly of Frankie's making?

I don't want to think about how he and Matthew never really bonded – and how it got worse and worse until it imploded.

Did I push him to that point?

'I don't believe it,' I repeat.

'Well you're going to have to believe it.' Marlena's curt. She checks the time on her phone. 'It's there in black and white – it's indisputable. You need to speak to Frank as soon as possible. Sort this shit out, Jeanie. You don't want Frank getting into something bad like this.' She stands, dragging her leopard-skin jacket off the back of the chair. 'You need to sort it out now.'

I try to call Frankie in France, but his phone goes straight to voicemail. There's no denying I feel sick about what Marlena's just disclosed – but I also feel uncertain. How can it actually be correct?

Yet there's a part of me that thinks, *Well yes – Frank might just have been so pissed off with me that he did send those emails.*

And if that's true – then I deserved it.

6 p.m.

When Frankie calls me back that evening, he denies it all. He's horrified that I'd even consider such a thing to be true. 'Why would I do that, Mum? Do you really honestly think I would?'

And I say, 'No, not really.' I'm just so glad to hear his voice, and hearing it reassures me. I try to remind myself I'm bound to believe him, because I *want* to think he's innocent of the charge – but the truth is I can't help it. I do believe him.

I remember Simon accusing him of breaking something in the Brighton flat. I remember defending Frankie to the hilt. I remember what happened next. I will always defend my son. Always.

Except: Marlena had evidence. She showed it to me.

I tell him so.

'Well look at my computer if you don't believe it.' Frank sounds stressed. 'I don't want you to think it was me, Mum.'

It's in storage though, his old PC, waiting for me to decide my next move after Derbyshire. He begs me to search his history – and I remember all the arguments we've ever had about computers, which have long been a source of disagreement between us – his inability to switch off lights, TVs, computer screens.

'It's your generation who'll have to pay when the planet frizzles up,' I'd plead, and he'd laugh.

'Because your lot messed it up, right?'

If I go through his computer now, it'll be like searching Matthew's all over again – and Matthew's fury is hard to forget. I hate bloody computers at the best of times, the way they trap us savagely in the technological jaws of our age.

Especially since what happened with Otto.

I decide to believe Frank – and I'll leave it at that for now.

We swap news. He tells me about the vineyard and the smelly caravan he's sleeping in; I tell him about the job in the Peak District. He's happy for me. 'As long as *you're* happy, Mum.'

Jenna's going to visit him soon, he says proudly. He doesn't ask about Matthew – but he does say that Scarlett called him once.

It's not until later that I think, *I never did ask how she got his number.*

'I swear it wasn't me, Mum,' he insists as we say our goodbyes. 'I wouldn't do that to you. You can't even think that.'

But if it wasn't Frank, who was it?

SNOW WHITE'S TALE: HER FLIGHT TO SAFETY…

So Snow White escaped the dangerous court in the nick of time, where her father didn't seem to be helping much – too busy shagging his new queen perhaps.

Snow White lived in the cottage in the forest, although it meant that, after the hunter left her out there, she had to pretend she was dead.

The hunter had a deer's heart to show her arch-enemy that Snow White had been destroyed, and so our heroine was safe – for a while at least.

By the way, forget the funny little dwarves: they've got no place in our tale. It's not all about Sneezy and silly Dopey and that miserable old git Grumpy.

Snow White did have, before you start fretting, the animals in the forest for company. She had all her chores to keep her busy and from missing her home too much. And that was all all right – until the day her rival looked in the mirror – oh treacherous Mirror – and realised the hunter had lied. But he was long gone by then.

And so Snow White's life was in danger again, because the old mirror kept speaking its truth.

But I wonder who *exactly* was the nasty rival trying to hurt?

The king, the pure-of-heart heroine or the memory of the dead queen – the 'ideal mother'?

Answers on a postcard please. Address it to Walt Disney if you like.

JEANIE

25 MAY 2015

When I arrive at the cottage, Jon helps me inside with my cases and then makes himself scarce. He's flying to Africa in two days' time.

'Tying up loose ends, saying a few goodbyes,' he says – but I think he's actually giving me space.

He's stored most of his personal things, just leaving the pictures on the walls and the furniture. I've brought hardly anything: just clothes, books and some photos of Frankie, at all ages.

I've got the wedding picture of Matthew and I that was smashed on the stairs in January, but I leave it in my suitcase.

I think of my last 'fresh start' and how wrong it went.

But from my new bedroom window I can see the green that stretches out behind the house, scattered with cotton-wool sheep. I can see the orchards at the foot of the hills, and I grin at the sight of actual rabbits bounding in the field behind the garden hedge.

'It's so pretty,' I say when Jon returns with fish and chips for two. 'Sort of – magical. Very Walt Disney.'

'Isn't it? And another plus – the fish and chips are infinitely better than anything down south,' he jokes.

We sit on the wooden bench in his tiny front garden, next-door's black-and-white cat rolling in the sun, and I feel a sense of calm that's been missing for a while.

I could grow accustomed to this peace.

Marlena's promised to come up soon — but she's enmeshed in this story that she's keeping very quiet. She's not so quiet about her anger about the plight of the migrants and the lack of publicity they're getting.

'It's just not considered "sexy", so we can't make the front pages,' she complains on the phone. 'And I have a very, very bad feeling about Nasreen too. I'm waiting for the DSI at Hounslow to get back to me.'

She's about to go to Turkey. I asked her if it was anything dangerous just before I left London, and she promised it wasn't, but the way she fiddled with her thin silver bracelet meant I knew she was lying.

'Have you spoken to Frankie about those emails?' she says now, and I tell her he's flatly denied it.

'I believe him,' I confess.

'Hmm,' she says — but she is Frankie's greatest fan, and I know she'd far rather believe he was innocent too. 'I'll get Robo to look at it again,' she promises, but I know it's not top of her agenda.

Matthew wanted to meet me before I left London, but I didn't answer that call.

I'm not ready.

JEANIE

3 JUNE 2015

Sitting in the bedroom window, I go through my post. I have two letters – well a letter and a card.

One from Frankie, extolling France's charms. I thought I'd do it old-fashioned style, he writes, and anyway, the Internet connections are crap out here. Write back, Mum. It's awesome here – the mountains are immense.

The card is from Matthew; it's that Hockney print of a swimming pool – no imagination, Marlena would say. He says he's sorry. He needs to see me, he reiterates.

I send Matthew a brief email. I don't say I miss him, but I am polite. The truth is I'm glad to hear from him, but I won't admit it.

I eat spaghetti Bolognese outside, but it's cold when the sun goes down. Afterwards I sit inside to write a proper letter to Frankie.

Midway I hear the ping of an email coming in. I look, half hoping it's from Matthew.

But it's not. It's from *Helpful2001xav@hotmail.com*.

The header reads: **F*** OFF AND DIE.** My hands shake a little as I open it.

Dont you know when its best to leave things alone?

The punctuation's wrong, is my first thought.

My second is: *Lock the door.*

JEANIE

5 JUNE 2015

I settle into class quite quickly. They're a nice enough bunch of kids: not the special-needs group I was led to expect but more what we'd have called 'remedial' back in our day – or what Nan would have called plain naughty!

'They can be – challenging,' the head had said at my interview, pulling an 'I blame the parents' face, and during my first week, I can see what he meant.

But I have nothing to prove, and they don't alarm me. I'm just glad to be back in front of a blackboard – or, more accurately, a whiteboard. My mind is so occupied during the day, it prevents me thinking about other things.

I don't receive another email, and I don't hear back from Matthew.

JEANIE

11 JUNE 2015

When I get back from school, pushing the bike up the hill because I need to work on my thigh muscles a bit more – especially with a rucksack of exercise books on my back – a car is parked outside the cottage. A big black car that I recognise. My heart gives a lurch.

My husband.

I contemplate jumping on my bike and freewheeling down the hill into the town and out the other side – but it isn't a very strong urge.

The stronger urge is to find out what Matthew wants.

As I near, I see him leaning on the front wall, holding an enormous bunch of red roses and talking on the phone. When he sees me puffing up towards him, he rings off abruptly.

'Hi.' I feel shy – and out of breath. I should have kept the running up.

'Hi, you,' Matthew says.

I look at him, seeing him through the eyes of a stranger, sensing he wants to be conciliatory – but I trust nothing any more.

'Nice bike,' he says. His smile seems genuine enough. In fact, he looks almost nervous.

'It's not mine actually.' I lean it against the low wall. 'So this is a surprise. What are you doing here?'

'I – well the fact is I missed you.' Most unlike Matthew. 'I thought we should talk – in person. Can I come in?'

My immediate reaction is to not let him through the door. Once he is in my space, that will be it. His mark will be left indelibly, however short a time he is here for.

'I tell you what, let's go to the café down in the square,' I suggest. 'They do great cake. My cupboards are bare I'm afraid.'

'Fine.' He shrugs. 'These are for you by the way.' Seemingly abashed, he pushes the roses at me, rather like a schoolboy might.

'Thank you.' Overwhelmed, I bury my nose in the beautiful red blooms. They feel like velvet against my skin – but there is no scent at all. 'I won't be a sec.'

I put the bike in the hall and the roses in the kitchen. I look quickly in the mirror – and then I think, *Who cares?*

Together we walk back down to The Deli on the square.

Over a pot of tea and scones we make polite conversation. I ask about the twins, and he says they are okay. He doesn't ask about Frankie – but I tell him he's fine anyway, last time I heard.

'He's picking grapes like mad,' I say, imagining my son, straw hatted and ruddy cheeked beneath a southern sun. And I wait for Matthew to say why he's come – but he doesn't.

So I ask him why he's here.

'Because…' He shrugs for the second time. 'Us, I suppose.'

Is there an 'us' any more though? And if there is, is it right for there to be? I'm not so sure.

The last month has given me space to breathe.

I wait for him to say more – but he doesn't. He just looks awkward and asks for the bill.

'So is there a pub around here?'

'There's a pub around everywhere, isn't there? But aren't you driving?' I insist on paying my share of the bill although he tries to wave me off. 'You don't want to do a long drive after beer, do you?'

'Who said I was going to do a long drive?' He grins, and I see a glimpse of the charming man I fell in love with.

'Where are you staying then?' I am disingenuous, and he grins again.

'Come on. I'll buy you a pint.'

'I don't drink pints,' I say. 'You know that.' Does he though? Does he really know anything about me at all?

'Half of cider then,' he says, holding out a hand. I don't take it, but I walk next to him, feeling the heat from his body – and I feel a small flutter of something. I let him lead me across the square, into The George and Dragon on the corner. He orders at the bar and then brings the drinks to the high table I'm perched at.

'You look beautiful today.' He takes a deep breath. 'I'm sorry, Jeanie. I was very – hasty. I was horrible. Work's been hard. I've been – stressed. I can see it's been hard for you…'

I flush hotly as I take the glass of golden fizzy liquid from him.

'I miss you, Jeanie,' he says again quietly, and I say nothing.

We sit in the window and watch the world go by.

Does he think I am so easily bought?

I don't let Matthew stay; I don't even let him come into the cottage. And I am so proud of myself.

He walks me home, and then he leaves again.

It takes some strength of will – but I let him kiss my cheek, and then I close the door and lean on it, feeling like I've done something bad in rejecting him. But it is the right thing.

After he's gone, I try to do some marking, but it is half-hearted, and the cider has made me blurry round the edges. I've hardly drunk since that awful dinner with Alison and Sean.

I take a long bath, despite the balmy temperature. I need to think, but I must drift off, because the next thing I know…

Someone is battering at the door.

MARLENA

So yeah, okay, I was still trying and totally failing to tie up the Nasreen case. There was literally no trace of her, and that was really unsatisfactory. I was pissed off the bloody police weren't all that bothered ('Just another silly little Muslim cow getting her priorities all wrong,' the old-school DSI had said when he finally agreed to meet me.) I'd had another meeting with the far more sympathetic DI Stevens about interviewing Nasreen's family again, but I was taking matters into my own hands now.

I was leaving for the airport when Robo called.

'All right, mate? See, I looked again at that email address. There was something niggling me about it.'

'Like what?' I said. I was catching a flight to Istanbul and another internal flight on to Antakya in Turkey to speak to the consul, and I was late already, my anxiety levels high as that famous old kite.

'Well I think it was a decoy.' He sounded enthused, as only a computer nerd could. 'It was a fake IP address, rerouted through the original email address.'

'You're losing me, Robo.' I dragged my jacket on and locked my front door. 'Just talk English.'

'It's not from Frankie Randall's computer. It's generated by a different account altogether.'

'Oh.' He had my attention now. I stood, case in one hand, key in the other. 'Well whose then?'

'Someone called Scarlett King?'

JEANIE

12 JUNE 2015

When I wake the next morning, startled by something unknown, startled from a deep and dreamless sleep again, I don't know where I am.

Instead of the gentle cooing of the wood pigeons, I open my eyes to a big black bird perched on the windowsill outside: a crow, or a raven perhaps. Small shiny eye, sharp tapered beak, tap-tapping at the glass. Not pretty like the blackbirds. The dead blackbirds outside Malum House.

I must have forgotten to pull the curtains when…

When we…

I roll over and see Matthew's dark head on the other pillow, and my heart flip-flops.

Shit.

Blearily I realise it's his phone that has woken me. It's ringing and then cutting off and then ringing again.

'You'd better answer it.' I nudge his arm gently, shy despite what we'd been doing before we fell asleep; despite my faint hope that maybe, just maybe, it would be all right again. 'Someone *really* wants you.'

He'd come back last night. He'd banged at the door, and he'd even got tearful. He'd begged me to let him in, and when I finally relented, he'd said how sorry he was.

He'd brought expensive wine, a bag of late apples from the orchard's shop at the foot of the hill and a bottle of their cider. I'd said I didn't want any more alcohol, but he'd poured me a glass anyway; he'd chosen it because he thought it was my favourite.

Later, after we'd talked and talked, he'd said please could I sign something he needed me to – it was only to do with the bank accounts in my name that he'd opened when we married, which needed two signatures. I skimmed through the paperwork, and I couldn't see anything untoward, so I did; I just signed where he asked. I couldn't see any harm.

And when I did that, he was so pleased he kissed me.

I tried to move away – but he just took my face in his hands and looked down at me. And he smelt so nice, and maybe the drink had gone to my head, or maybe it was the sight of the tears in his eyes earlier – but I gave in. I let him kiss me – and then I couldn't help it.

I kissed him back.

Oh God, I hope I won't regret it.

'What?' he mumbles now as I shake him gently.

'Your phone. It might be urgent.'

He groans, and, eyes half open, leans down, fumbling for the phone on the floor somewhere near the bed. Eventually he finds it, just as it rings again.

'Hello?'

He's frowning. There's a silence whilst he listens, and I pull myself up now to sit, feeling dozy and uncertain.

What now, for us, I'm thinking when he explodes.

'You are fucking kidding me!'

I turn. 'What is it?'

'You are fucking joking,' Matthew repeats down the phone, glaring at me. 'Are you sure?'

He's pulling himself out of bed too and ignoring me, and I've got a bad feeling, a bad feeling that started a moment ago, and he's telling whoever it was he'll call them back in five minutes.

Then he's off the phone and grimacing right in my face. 'Did you know about this?'

'What?' I'm suddenly wide awake.

'I bet you put him up to it. That'd be right, wouldn't it?'

'Put *who* up to *what*?'

'I should have listened to my instincts about your son.' He grabs his trousers and pulls them on. 'So stupid, getting sucked in again.'

'What is it? What's wrong? Are you talking about Frankie?'

'Yes, bloody Frankie, Jean, well done. Where the fuck are my socks?' He's so angry. 'Have you bloody well hidden them?'

'Matthew, you're scaring me.' I see his socks beneath the chair and clamber out to give them to him. 'What is it?'

He grabs the socks, muttering to himself as he buttons his shirt.

'Please calm down…' I start, and he stares at me like I'm mad.

'I'm not at all calm. And I won't be any calmer when I find him,' he spits, and I feel an intense fear I've never really felt before, not even when the whole Otto thing erupted. 'You're a fucking liar, Jeanie. I saw all those bloody pills again – and now this. God, I should have known.'

'Please tell me what you're talking about?' I try to grab his arm, but he shakes me off like a dog would shake a rabbit, making me stumble so I fall against the bed. I crack my knee painfully on the wall, gasping with pain. 'Matthew?' I'm really scared, scrambling up again. 'Please!'

'And this fucking time I'm calling the police.' Frenetic in his haste, he scoops up the rest of his clothes, his shoes, his jacket and leaves the room. Then he sticks his head back round the door. 'You'd better tell him to get a fucking good lawyer. He's going to need it.'

'What's he done?' I follow him down the stairs as he fumbles to get his shoes on, swearing to himself. Has he found out about the emails? That Frankie might have sent them? But that was directed at me, not at Matthew…

'Matthew, just tell me what the hell's going on, for God's sake!'

My shouting surprises both of us, I think.

He actually looks at me now. 'Your bloody son. That's what's going on.'

'But Frankie's not even in the country.'

'Yeah, well he'd better stay away if he knows what's good for him.'

'Why? What's he meant to have done?' My heart's beating so hard I think it's going to come clean out of my chest.

'He's cleared out Scarlett's fucking savings account. There was thousands in there. Fucking thousands! Where the fuck are my keys?'

'What bank account?' Ice needles me now. 'How do you know? Was that Scarlett?'

'No, that was her mother on the phone. She's totally distraught.'

'Scarlett?' I say stupidly.

'No, Kaye. Scarlett doesn't even know. Christ, the thieving little bastard…'

'Kaye's rung you to say Frankie's taken Scarlett's money? Are you sure?'

'Kaye rang to say'—his tone is quiet and icy now—'that she's seen the account is empty.'

'Empty?'

'Yeah, empty.'

'But how does she know it's Frankie?'

He's out of the front door now, key in hand, into the car. 'She's got evidence, she says.'

I run out into the tiny front garden in my dressing gown, to the passenger door, but it's locked.

I rap at the window. 'Don't go like this please,' I cry. 'Please! We can sort it out together...'

What together?

And Matthew refuses to even look at me as he revs the car and pulls out and heads down the hill, his tyres squealing on the tarmac. He hits the wing mirror of an old Jeep further down the road, taking it clean off – but he doesn't stop.

Another squeal of tyres round the corner and he's gone. The only sign of him is the metal mirror rattling in the middle of the tarmac.

And it's only when I turn to go back inside that I see the note, pinned to the door by an old tack.

It says: This is not right is it, baby Jean? This wasn't how it was meant to go.

Frantic, I try to reach Frankie in France, but his phone doesn't even ring. Perhaps his pay-as-you-go isn't working any more.

Where is the email with the details of where he's living? I rifle through things, hands shaking, folders of bills and letters I'd brought with me, but I am so panicked I am just making a mess of everything and not finding anything I need.

Breathe, Jeanie. I sit down. What can I do that would be helpful?

I debate ringing Scarlett – but it might just make things worse. I don't dare make anything worse.

So I ring Kaye. She doesn't answer.

I ring Marlena. She doesn't answer either – but I leave her a message, half sobbing into the phone, begging her to call me back.

Then I go to work. I have no choice.

I limp through the hot, sticky day, thoroughly distracted, constantly wanting to check my phone.

By two o'clock the kids have sensed my lack of concentration and are really playing up. I set a composition on the topic of 'Suspicion' for the last half hour and warn them that if isn't done, there'll be consequences next week.

I don't go to the staff meeting after class. I plead a migraine and cycle home. The weather has broken, and it is drizzling a fine misty rain now.

But I haven't heard back from anyone, and Matthew isn't answering my calls either. I keep ringing until he messages me: *Stop calling – it's harassment.*

I eat half a sandwich alone at the old wooden table. It is humid and sticky and horrible despite the open windows. *I* feel horrible. I chuck the second half of the sandwich away.

How different this is to last night – last night when there had been some kind of hope again. God – what an idiot. What a terrible stupid fool I've been.

I opened myself up to him – and just look what had happened. I hate myself.

Tears threaten – but I think, vehemently, I will *not* cry about this. Action not tears.

I try Frankie again; still not even a voicemail to leave a message on. But I have at least found the web address of the vineyard. There doesn't seem to be a phone number, so I write an email in my poor French, asking them to *please* pass a message on to my son Frank Randall to call me '*immédiatement*'.

Marlena had sent a text as I'd pedalled home; I'd read it as I trudged in the front door.

Keep calm and carry on. I'm in Turkey, back tomorrow night – will call then x

She'd put a rare kiss at the end of the message.

Was it pity perhaps?

I go to bed early, wanting this day to be over. Before I do so, I check every door and window.

In the early hours, a noise wakes me from a broken sleep.

I sit up, listening intently.

Nothing – I've imagined it…

Haven't I?

The owl is flying, calling his mournful warning as he makes his regular sweep above the fields behind the cottage.

I lie back down.

The noise again – a kind of scrabbling on wood. A rat maybe? I hope it is a rat.

I get out of bed very quietly and stand at the top of the stairs, listening again. It's not a rat—

There is definitely someone down there.

I have no weapon – I have nothing. I am wearing only a T-shirt and pants; my phone's downstairs; there's no landline to call from up here.

So I have no choice. I pull my jeans on quickly and creep down a stair or two.

'Who's there?' I call bravely, trying not to let the tremor creep into my voice. Nothing – but still the scrabbling. Perhaps it is an animal after all.

I edge down a few more stairs. 'Is someone there?'

I can just make out the room, veiled in darkness, and suddenly a hand comes through the window and I scream – and then a voice is saying, 'It's me! Don't scream, Jeanie, it's only me.'

I turn the light on.

It is Scarlett.

When I've calmed down enough to let Scarlett in the front door – 'The sensible and normal way to come in,' I point out – I ask her what on earth she's doing here.

I don't mention the bank account or her father; I don't know if it is linked to this sudden appearance, but it all seems very odd.

'I'm assuming your parents don't know you're here?'

'I'm meant to be on a geography field trip,' she says. 'Part of my coursework. I'm starving, Jeanie. I ran out of money at Leicester. Can I have something to eat?'

'How did you get here?'

'I hitched.'

I make her toast and Marmite and save my lecture about the dangers of hitching for another time. I sit down opposite her at the table. I am oddly pleased to see her now my heart has stopped hammering – but I am worried too.

'Why have you come, lovey?'

She shrugs, eating her toast and avoiding my gaze. But I look at her again and I say, 'Frankie's not here you know.'

'I know.' She scowls, that familiar little expression. 'He's in France. It's not him I came to see.'

'Oh I see.' I feel strangely touched. 'You came to see me then?'

She nods.

'Well I'm honoured. But you do know your mother will be going mad. You will have to go back.'

'I don't care.' She flings down her final crust. 'I don't care if she's going mad. She doesn't care about me.'

'Oh, Scarlett, I'm sure that's not true – really.'

'Are you?' Her look is full of challenge – and then she yawns widely. Little girl that she is, she looks exhausted.

The little cuckoo clock Jon had left above the door strikes the hour.

'Let's go to bed, love, and we can talk in the morning. Have you let your mum know where you are?'

'Yes.'

But I don't believe her, so I text Kaye myself: *Scarlett just arrived at mine; she's fine. Will put her on the train to London in the am.*

I owe her nothing, but it's one mother to another.

Before I go to bed, I stick my head round Scarlett's door. She is reading a battered old paperback. Daphne du Maurier's *Rebecca*, I think.

'Can I ask you one thing that's been bothering me?'

'Okay,' she says, laying her book down.

'It's just…' I go into the room properly and lean on the bed-post. 'Well. You know you said you had a nanny?'

'Daisy?' She stares at me, fingers clutching the duvet. 'Er – yeah – so?'

'What exactly happened to her?'

Her eyes are really wide as she hesitates. 'She – she kind of got – in an accident…'

'What kind of accident?'

'I'm not meant to talk about it.' She scowls like the old Scarlett.

'Why?'

'It's – it was like a legal thing, they said.'

'Who said?'

'Dad and Kipper.'

Kipper? I finally click: the overweight policeman who liked guns.

'She got sort of – run over, but she was leaving anyway, I think. I can't remember,' Scarlett prevaricates.

'Run over?' I am horrified. 'Was she – killed?'

'Oh no.' Scarlett is more airy now. 'Not killed, no. Just broke her leg. And her back, I think.'

'Oh my God!' I gape at her. 'That's terrible.'

'Well…' Scarlett yawns again. 'Yeah, it was. But at least she wasn't paralysed. They thought she would be at first.'

JEANIE

13 JUNE 2015

I am up first, around six, unable to get back to sleep.

I keep thinking about the girl who was so badly hurt, this nanny, and why that had been hidden from me.

I make coffee and set the table for breakfast, and then I sit in the window and think about what to do.

I haven't reached any proper conclusions when Scarlett staggers downstairs in her oversized T-shirt, looking exactly like the child she is.

'You're up early,' I say, surprised. I pour her orange juice and make her sit. 'Are you all right?'

'Don't send me back, Jeanie.' She slumps at the table, and I push the cornflakes towards her.

'Eat up. And why not?'

'I don't want to go back. Let me stay here.'

'I don't think your mum and dad will like that much, love.'

'Who cares what they like?' Her bottom lip juts out. 'I don't.'

'You have to go back.' I feel exhausted already, and the day hasn't even begun. 'You know that, Scarlett. It's not up to me.'

She stares into her bowl.

'Why don't you want to go back?' I ask gently.

'Forget it,' she mutters, and I realise I've blown it. No amount of pleading will make her tell me now, though I do try.

Something is troubling me badly.

Having promised to let her know what train I put Scarlett on, I ignore Kaye's increasingly hysterical texts. When she begins to demand that Scarlett call her, knowing Scarlett will refuse, I switch my phone off altogether – though the reception out here is rubbish at the best of times.

Trying to cheer Scarlett up, hoping to maybe eke out a bit of what's making her so low, I suggest a quick walk round Ilam Park on the way to catch the train. It's in the wrong direction, but it's still early.

'I'll buy you a cream tea at the café.' I give her a big smile – but she just jams on huge sunglasses and glowers out of the windscreen without answering.

Ilam is in the dip of breathtakingly beautiful hills, and it's a clear morning, the sky a forget-me-not blue – apart from one ominous cloud over the mountain of Thorpe Cloud. It may or may not be headed for us – it's hard to tell.

We drive into the National Trust car park for Ilam Hall. It's only eight thirty, and the place is quiet, almost deserted. A few staff bustle around the main courtyard, setting up for the day, but really we have the place almost to ourselves.

We make our way down through the terraced gardens and towards the River Manifold. Scarlett makes a point of staying at least five feet behind me most of the way, swiping at the trees with a bamboo stick she's picked up.

As we walk I debate how best to broach the subject.

'I do see how hard it is for you,' I start eventually, as we near St Bertram's bridge. 'You probably don't want to hear this, but I came from a broken home myself…'

'No, I don't want to hear,' she says rudely, and I feel the heat in my face as we pass it, walking on to the next bridge.

'Look, you're not the first kid in the world who's had to put up with a stepmother.' I'm unable to control my sudden irritation.

'Really?' she says, even more rudely than before. 'It's not the stepmother I have a problem with,' she continues.

'Well good.' I open the small gate to the bridge that leads to the fields, talking over my shoulder. 'Because I do have your best interests at heart, whatever you may think. I'm concerned about you, Scarlett.'

'Why don't you just get lost, Jeanie?' she snaps.

I stride over the bridge, biting back another retort. About to swing my leg over the stile at the end, the black cloud over Thorpe Cloud bursts.

The sudden deluge is so hard it stings my face.

Blinded by the rain, I concentrate on clambering over the slippery stile. On the other side, I turn to offer Scarlett a hand.

She's not there. 'Scarlett?'

She must have gone off in a strop – a 'mard', as they'd say locally.

Quickly I scan my surroundings.

A couple of ramblers cower beneath an oak on the other side of the river, brandishing a now soggy map. A woman in a red anorak with a black Labrador is walking up the far hill.

No Scarlett that I can see.

Cursing quietly, I make my way back over the stile, rain driving into my face and dripping horribly down my neck.

The most blood-curdling scream shatters the still air.

'Scarlett?'

I rush over the bridge, slipping in my haste so that I go down hard on one knee. It's agony, but I am up again immediately, dashing water from my face. 'Scarlett?' I'm yelling now at the top of my voice. 'Where are you?'

Still no answer; no more screams.

I run along the riverbank for a few seconds. 'Did you see her?' I cry at the ramblers, but they just look stunned.

And then movement above me attracts my eye.

A dark, hooded male figure bolts, like a creature from Hades, out of the trees on the steep incline above the river, away and over the top of the hill.

'Scarlett!' I bellow, panicking, panicking—

And then a sodden figure launches itself into my arms, nearly knocking me down again. A sobbing Scarlett.

'What happened?' I ask frantically, trying to look at her face. 'Are you hurt?'

'He just grabbed me.' She can hardly talk, she's crying so hard. 'I didn't see him, and he grabbed me.'

'Who did?'

'This man. He came out of nowhere, and he held my collar tight, and he spat in my face.'

'Spat?' I can see red marks on her neck.

'He said, "You better get your arse back to Malum House if you know what's good for you".'

Shit. *Shit shit shit shit shit.*

'Okay, love, calm down.' I stroke her damp hair. 'Keep breathing slowly, okay?'

The ramblers are here now. 'Are you okay?' the woman wants to know, all twittery.

'She's fine thanks.' I take a tissue from her to clean up Scarlett's eye make-up a little; black rivulets stain her pretty face. 'Let's get into the dry.'

In the distance a motorbike fires up.

I lead Scarlett back to the car park, scanning the area desperately, but he's gone. Whoever it was has vanished into the peaks.

What better place to hide?

Over the horizon the clouds come, thick and fast now. The beautiful day is quite spoiled.

12 p.m.

Instead of going into Derby, we go home, so I can sort Scarlett out and change myself. I run her a bath so she can warm up.

About to go upstairs, she pauses, foot on the first step. 'How did he know where I live?'

'Jump in the bath, love,' I say. 'We'll talk about it later.'

Just as she's getting dressed again and we're preparing to leave, there's a knock at the door.

Oh God. Do I answer – or do I hide?

Another insistent knock.

No choice. Heart thumping, I look through the old spyhole – and I open up.

There on my slate doorstep, hiding behind an upturned collar and a huge pair of shades even bigger than her daughter's, is Kaye.

'Are they here?' She seems desperate.

'Who?' I am disingenuous.

'Oh come on.'

'You mean Scarlett?'

'Yes, my baby.' She looks over my shoulder into the dark little downstairs. 'And Matthew of course.'

I have to invite Kaye in. And once she's in she doesn't hold back, especially when she learns that Scarlett's still here – but Matthew is not.

'I thought he'd be here too.'

'Did you? Why?'

'He's being tracked.'

'Tracked?'

'Yes, and we guessed he'd come here.'

'Who did?' I'm baffled.

'I wanted to warn you.' Kaye ignores my question.

'Warn me about what?' I'm extremely uncomfortable that she's in my home at all.

'It's too awful,' she says. She smells of that nasty sickly scent and old cigarettes. 'And I can't talk about it now. Can you get Scarlett please?' Her eyes are enormous saucers in her unmoving face. 'I've been going out of my mind.'

I have to decide whether to tell her about the man at Ilam Park. If I don't, I guess Scarlett will.

But I don't think it's Scarlett he wants; so it's not relevant to Kaye.

'She's getting changed upstairs.' I put my hand on her arm to stop her running up the stairs. 'But look – warn me about what, Kaye? I don't understand.'

'I can't say any more, so please don't ask me.' She looks… strange. Bewildered. 'I have to protect Scarlett.'

'From what?' A feeling of nausea is washing over me. I've had hardly any sleep, the morning has been stressful in the extreme and I'm starting to feel quite peculiar.

'I had to tell him that thing about your boy yesterday. I had to get him out of here.'

'Hang on.' I'm trying to compute this. 'Get who out of here?'

'Matthew of course.'

'What do you mean you *had* to tell him?'

'I made it up,' she says dramatically. 'I'm sorry, but it won't harm him.'

'You made it up? About Frankie stealing?' My initial relief is overwhelmed by a huge flood of anger. 'But why? What if Matthew's gone to the police? What if Frankie gets in real trouble because of what you said…'

'Oh he won't call the cops.' She's dismissive. 'He's got too much to hide himself.'

'Matthew has? Like what?'

'Never mind. Please just let me get Scarlett.'

This time I don't stop her. I let her thunder up the stairs in her leather leggings, her expensive poncho slung elegantly over the top. She's still immaculate despite her trauma – and overdressed.

Listening to the squeak of the old boards and the murmur of voices above my head, exhaustion floods me. I don't understand anything she's said – except that she made up stuff about Frankie to get Matthew out of here.

Kaye reappears. 'She's just getting dressed, and then we'll be off.'

'Okay.' I'll be glad when they're all gone. I contemplate offering her tea, and then I think she can go whistle.

Kaye leans on the edge of the table, long legs in front of her as I pour myself a stewed cup from the teapot, just for something to do. I know she's about to launch into something. She does.

'You know he was just using you, Jean. You were a convenient cover for…'

'For what?' I frown into my cup.

'Oh never mind.' Busily, she searches through her voluminous bag, producing a bag of apples, raisins, oatcakes – and finally her cigarettes.

'What happened to the nanny, Kaye? The one that hurt her back?'

'Why do you want to know?' She fiddles with her cigarettes.

'Because I do. It sounds awful…'

'Scarlett!' Kaye cries. 'There you are!'

She holds out her arms, but Scarlett hardly rushes into them. Instead she drags herself down, not looking at her mother.

'Darling!' The woman grabs her daughter. 'We need to get going. Say thank you to Jean.'

'I don't want to go back,' Scarlett mutters.

'Don't be silly,' Kaye smiles. 'I've brought you some snacks, but we can stop at McDonalds on the way back as a treat.'

'I don't want McDonalds.' She shoves the proffered apple away. 'I want to stay with Jeanie.'

'Don't be so stupid, Scarlett.' Kaye looks furious.

'You're always welcome, lovey,' I tell the girl. 'Wherever I am. Maybe just let's plan it properly next time.'

Now is the time to tell Kaye about the stranger at Ilam. But Scarlett and I gaze at each other, and some kind of understanding passes between us. She'll be safe once she's out of here, I'm sure of it.

'I'm sorry you've even been involved.' Kaye stares at me, her blue eyes icy. She pushes a teary Scarlett out of the front door and turns to me again. 'You – you didn't know, did you?'

'Know *what*?' I feel tearful myself now with frustration. 'For God's sake…'

Kaye doesn't answer but propels Scarlett towards her big white car, slowly driving down from where it must have been turning at the top of the hill.

Standing in the doorway, I can see Yassine behind the wheel. When I catch his eye he looks away.

Scarlett is dragging her heels, turning to talk to me. 'Jeanie…' Her mother clasps her arm tighter.

'Thank you,' Kaye says without looking at me, opening the back passenger door. 'Get in, Scarlett.'

I sense Scarlett weighing up whether or not to make a big scene. In the end, she doesn't – she just submits to her mother.

'I'll see you soon,' I call. I catch my worried neighbour Ruth's face at the window as they drive off, and I try to smile to reassure her.

I'm sure they don't want trouble in this peaceful town.

6 p.m.

When Marlena's call finally comes – the call I've waited for all day – it brings no relief.

'Jeanie. You need to look at this website.' Marlena is terse, and I feel terrified as she tells me what to look up. 'Try to stay calm.'

I do as I'm told, my fingers clumsy on the keyboard.

I hear Marlena talking to someone, giving her address. A cab perhaps.

On my screen a news site opens.

The front page: a story about a boat sinking in the Aegean, drowning thirty-six refugees.

'What am I looking at?' I ask, feeling a warped type of relief. I mean I feel terrible for them – but it's not what I was expecting. 'Is that what you've been working on?'

'No. I mean, yes, something like that – but that's not what I mean. Type Matthew's name in the search section at the top.'

A chill envelops me. 'Why?'

'Just do it, Jean.' Her voice is tight, clipped, matter of fact. I know it well enough to know it means bad news. 'I am sorry, hon, but just do it.'

Hon. The name Matthew always called me.

I type in his name next to the icon of the magnifying glass, misspelling it twice. Third time lucky.

A photo of Matthew comes up. A very serious face that says 'trust me': a publicity shot from his work, I think, judging from the dark suit and the corporate logo behind his head.

I read the text underneath the photo.

'Oh my God!' My own voice shocks me – an ugly ricochet in the warm summer evening. 'Oh no, Marlena.'

'My God indeed.' Marlena's voice is grim.

'It can't be true,' I whisper.

'Can't it?' she says. 'Well you might know. I bloody hope not, for his sake. For your sake I mean.'

I read it again, the type swirling in my panic.

> *Matthew King, 51, business analyst and a partner at Challenger Holdings, has been arrested today. No official comment has been made yet by either the Met Police or any representative for King, but the allegations are believed to involve the mistreatment of a minor. A source suggests that the minor is someone well known to King.*
>
> *We reiterate that these are only allegations at this stage, and there is no substantiated evidence.*

It feels unbearable.

'And it was her you know,' Marlena says. 'I only just found out, but it wasn't Frankie sending the emails.'

Thank God. My brain's not computing properly though.

'Jeanie? Did you hear me? Those emails came from Scarlett.'

JEANIE

14 JUNE 2015

Only ever half the story: that's what we get. Half the story. Half a picture. Half an idea of what, say, a marriage is actually like behind closed doors.

Half a picture of *any* relationship. We jump to our judgements and conclusions from what we see; we think we know best from what we only have glimpses of.

Of this I am well aware.

This is the second time I've got my affairs of the heart so very wrong – and I'm still paying for the first time of course.

I already know he's found me. He found me at the start of last year.

After Otto.

I was a sitting duck. Easy prey. But of course he knew that about me already. He knew too much; he knew everything.

And now Matthew too. I'm so horrified I find I don't even want to ask him his side. I don't want to hear his story; I don't want to talk to him at all.

Marlena has tried to emphasise that there's no proof of anything yet, that these are only allegations at this stage.

But my despair is huge and absolute. It engulfs me. Shame rages through me to such a degree I don't know what to do.

I let Scarlett down; she was a kid who needed help, just like I was once a kid who needed help – and I left her in the lion's mouth.

I ignored the signs. I thought they were the signs of a loving father. I didn't know; I had no benchmark, and I suppose, looking back, I chose not to believe he could be capable of such an atrocity.

How can I live with myself now?

All the horrors are being reopened, relived.

Since I read this news story last night, I just want to sleep. It's Sunday, so I don't have to go into school.

I can't sleep though, not yet. I'm waiting.

When I crawled into bed last night, I thought I heard a light knock at the door, and I wondered if it was my neighbour Ruth. I pulled the covers higher, and I didn't hear it again.

There is a skinned rabbit slung over the cottage fence when I walk back up from the shop with milk and bread.

I'm not even surprised.

Daddy's gone a hunting reads the note around its poor neck. There are numbers on the back – coordinates. I take it all down before the neighbours can see.

I wonder how much time I've got. Not much, I reckon.

In the early evening I walk into the back garden and through the little gate and across the field. The moon is etched on the blue sky like it's been drawn in chalk.

By the far hedgerow I see what I imagine is a hare, running free, long back legs powering him along, and I think of the freedom of the wild. He reminds me of my favourite book as a kid, a little girl looking out of the window at the moon. We didn't have many books in our house, not many at all. It must have been the school's.

'What's in the moon?' I asked my nan when she came to see us, and she told me it was cheese.

I loved that book; I used to think that little girl was me, staring up at the moon so wistfully.

I can't reach the moon though. It's too late.

When Matthew was trying to hurt me a while back, when he announced it was over – for now – he also said I was a blank.

'You're like – you're not there, Jeanie, a no one. I thought I could really love you, and you could help me with my future, but you're blank.'

He couldn't read me, he said, because there was nothing to me: I hardly existed.

Or maybe I said the last part.

And now I think, *Perhaps it's true.* Perhaps I don't really exist. I never have, not since – I'm not even sure since when. Since my dad walked out the door when I was small and didn't come back.

Since no one believed in us, no one except our nan. She was our saving grace at least. She stopped us from falling totally between the cracks.

But I'm *not* a blank. I have feelings and emotions – and I'm not sure what to do with any of them now. It's like I've gone into free fall.

I thank God that Scarlett is at least safe with her mother. And Frankie's happy in France, and he has Jenna now and Marlena too, of course. Marlena will always be there for him, and she won't ever leave him, I'm sure of that.

It was always borrowed time for me. I've always known the clock was counting down.

6.30 p.m.

My phone rings as I tramp back up the field.

I avoid Ruth's friendly wave, bouncing spaniel at her feet, as I reach the cottage. I don't like to be rude, but I am beyond caring now, as I go not home but to the place I've been lent.

I drink the end of the bottle of cider Matthew bought, and I text both Scarlett and Frankie.

I tell Frankie how much I love him and to take care and to not drink too much wine in the vineyard.

I tell Scarlett I'm sorry I wasn't more help, and I hope she's all right – and that she's left her copy of *Rebecca* here.

Then I get in the car, and I put my glasses on to read the coordinates I was left, and I type them into my phone.

I drive out, towards Dovedale.

I might not have time to drink the whisky I've put in my bag, the half bottle Jon left in the cupboard, but at least I might have the option. It's some sort of pathetic reassurance.

I'm so tired – so tired of it all.

All I want is for this nightmare to be over.

Lying in bed last night, I heard the owl again. It was a strange, sad noise – but I find it oddly comforting to think of the owl out there now, his great wingspan pale against the night sky as I drive out of Ashbourne and into the wilds, towards the beautiful desolate peaks that I don't belong in either.

It really hurt when he said I was a blank, you know. It really hurt me.

So I surrender.

MARLENA

She can't be dead.

I am in the bath when the call comes.

She can't fucking well be dead.

I rarely get in the bath. Showers suit me: quicker, harsher; God knows I am not lily white and I need that blast, that sting, to be washed cleaner – but a bath allows me time to think.

True it's time I don't normally want, that I normally avoid, but right now I *have* to think – debating what to do about Nasreen.

Turkey brought no answers about her, though it did have interesting leads on other stories.

Back here, frustrated by the useless fucking police, I met Nasreen's boyfriend, Lenny, last night in the grotty pub on the corner of his road. I bought him a pint or two of Stella and chatted about how they met and how much he missed her. At one point I watched his dull eyes fill with tears.

'Nas's parents hate me,' he said, his top lip pulled back over his teeth in a snarl, and I thought, *I don't blame them really.* 'They wanted a nice Muslim boy.'

'Ah dear,' I said sympathetically, but what I was really thinking was, *Why did she want* you? Were you simply an act of rebellion? An ill-chosen symbol? Handsome – a catch, perhaps, in looks at least, for a naïve teenage girl – but sullen and tense beneath the surface. Not a good catch in reality.

I bought him a shot of tequila to go with his pint, and we played a game of pool. I'm really fucking good at pool actually; I can thank my misspent youth for that. I relish the look on men's faces when I smack the black in – but this time I let Lenny win.

Him having the upper hand seemed vital at that moment.

It meant I had to put up with all those pissed blokes grafted to their bar stools exuding pity, scorn and superiority – but it was worth it, if it got Lenny on side.

Halfway through the second pint, Lenny was sweating profusely, but it wasn't that hot. Not that hot at all in the air-conditioned pub.

There's still no evidence. They've questioned him; they've taken away his computer – there's nothing. It was him that told the family she'd been talking to someone in Syria online, that he'd caught her, and they'd been talking about jihad and Islamic State.

But if he thought that, if he was worried, why the fuck didn't he act whilst she was still around? I asked him that last night – but he couldn't really answer. 'I thought she loved me,' he whined. 'Me not Allah.'

I am just waiting for him to trip up.

So now I lie in the bath with eyes closed and ponder why they can't find the dirt on this bloke – and then my mobile rings in the other room. I ignore it. It never stops ringing.

Then the bloody landline rings. Now that *never* rings. Only Jeanie has this number – her and Frank.

The answerphone picks up.

'This is a message for Marlena Randall,' a northern female voice says: tentative, clipped. 'This is WPC Evans at Derby Central. We'd like to talk to you about your sister, Jeanie King. Please call me back urgently.'

I'm frozen in the steaming bath as she reads a number out, and I find I can't move my limbs; they are so heavy they are like wax. They won't move…

Then I manage to scramble out, slipping, dripping across the tiles and the floorboards in the main room, and I snatch up the receiver. 'I'm here,' I croak. 'I'm here…'

The voice speaks.

'She can't have done,' I hear myself say, and the echo is in the room, bouncing off the walls. 'Don't be so bloody stupid.'

When I put the phone down again minutes later, someone is yelling – and then I realise.

I realise it's me.

So.

I know what you're thinking; I do, really.

You think I really fucked up, don't you? That I should have been there, that I wasn't – that it's my fault.

Don't look at me like that please.

And you know this is what I'd say to anyone who asked. I'd say: *Fuck! I really thought I'd seen it all – but I hadn't.*

The next day

It's the simplicity with which she was living that kind of breaks my heart, you know, when I arrive at her cottage. It's kind of like something from a sweet folk tale or Beatrix Potter – Goldilocks poking round the three bears' stuff, Mrs Tiggy-Winkle, that kind of nice cosy lovely thing that childhoods ought to be made up of.

Honey stoned and blue doored, in the middle of a row of four, roses round the door and pansies outside in the terracotta

pots. Fields and fields of bloody green space out the back; a terrifying amount of space.

And what really gets to me now, what brings the fucking
lump to my throat, is how there's only one of everything in the
meticulous kitchen. She was always so tidy, where I am such a
messy cow. The little one, the baby, I got used to her picking up
my pants, cooking for me, sorting stuff – you know the score. I
got used to Jeanie being there. Jeanie's always been bloody there.

I'm not sure why it's her little pot of raspberry jam laid out
by her single plate, alongside her single knife – why it's that
that makes me cry. Why is it that? After all, there's only one of
everything in my place too. We are the original singletons: just
not à la Bridget Jones.

Indelible, the damage our parents did to us, etched into us,
marking us forever. Why would we *ever* want to place our hearts
in others' hands? I can't do it; I never have.

Jeanie is the only person I really trust – and now look what
she's bloody gone and done.

Don't. Don't even say it. I know now, too late, how remiss
I've been.

Except... She did do it, didn't she? That's been the whole
problem. She dared to put her heart in his hands – that tosser,
Matthew – and Jesus, now look. Just look at this mess.

I kick the washing machine. I kick it and I kick it.

Her neighbour, Ruth, found the note in the early hours,
alerted by the constantly banging front door, seemingly left ajar.

It's just Jeanie that's missing. Just the body that's not here.

I kick the washing machine some more until there's a huge
fucking dent in it.

And then the officer at the door coughs gently, and I turn
towards her.

We get in the police car, and we continue the search for my sister.

One, a special constable it seems, mutters to the other, 'Twice up here in two days. There was that biker last night…'

The other frowns.

The first one says, 'Did you see the blood in the bathroom?' and then the other casts a furtive look at me in the mirror, hushing her colleague.

We drive on in silence, only the crackling police radio for company.

The day is drawing in, just a thin line of light left across the horizon, when the call comes.

Apparently a sheep farmer from Castern saw a woman walking near the bridge over the river Dove late last night as he drove back up to his farm. He thought she looked a bit unsteady on her feet, but he was on his way to check his sheep after a call about a savage dog roaming the fields. In the ensuing drama the woman slipped his mind. But this evening he found a rucksack in another one of his fields, below Thorpe Cloud, near a shepherd's hut. And a pair of broken glasses.

They might be Jeanie's.

As we drive down the ploddingly windy roads, the radio crackles to say they've found someone.

'Is she alive?' I keep asking frantically. 'Please – is she alive?'

'Please, Miss Randall,' the WPC repeats, ashen faced as her colleague drives faster. 'Let's just wait till we get there, all right?'

Then she turns the radio off so I can't hear anything more.

By the time we get out there, the bewildered farmer is being led off for questioning. Halfway up the track, an ambulance is parked as near to the stone hut as it can get, and as I scramble up the hill, I see them carry a stretcher to the door.

'Jeanie, I'm coming!' I'm screaming, falling and righting myself and falling again. 'Jeanie! I'm here. It's all right!'

But of course it's not all right, is it? It really, really isn't all right.

They give me the broken glasses later, and the twisted frame breaks my heart. They are so pathetic. They are Jeanie.

Later.

When I can catch my breath.

When I've gone in the ambulance to Derby and they've taken her off and she's not moved a hair, an inch, a muscle, a nerve ending.

When I've felt like I should call someone but don't know who. When I've seen my big sister Jean looking very small; tubed up, gowned up, not breathing for herself any more but hooked up to a machine that's doing the breathing for her, her face as white as the sheets she lies between. When I've sat holding her limp hand, berating both of us for this sorry state of affairs – but mainly myself of course. When I've smoked fags out the front next to the women with bad roots and pink towelling robes, shuffling in slippers, I catch a cab, and I go back to the cottage.

I try to think logically.

They showed me the note earlier: it was baldly simple and written in printed capitals.

It just said:

I'M SORRY – I CAN'T GO ON.

But why? Why now, exactly?

Because of Matthew? Really? Would it affect her to this degree, the heartbreak?

But maybe it was the final straw, after the hell that was Simon, twelve years ago. And then the Seaborne business – and then Prince Charming – who turned out to just be fucked-up Matthew.

Given the crap we grew up in, it's amazing really how high functioning she was, how she kept going most of the time. Because she had to. Because one of us had to.

Would she really have left Frankie? That's what haunts me, more than anything. I have to tell Frankie – and soon.

I go through everything in the house.

It doesn't take long to find the diary in her bedroom, tangled in the bed sheets – but it's almost brand new I realise, as I tear through it; only been started this week.

So where's the one before? That's the one I need.

It'll all be there in black and white I imagine. Where are the secrets of her heart?

Some time after I start searching I stop and drink the dregs of a bottle of wine in the kitchen – acidic Sauvignon Blanc that I hate and she likes – and then I check the time.

It's dark outside now, but I walk down into Ashbourne and buy a bottle of vodka just before the off licence shuts.

I trudge back up the hill with it, spooked by the darkness of the countryside.

I sit at her table, and I drink the vodka neat, and I read the brief contents of the diary again, looking for clues.

There's hardly anything though.

When I finish I go outside, and I smoke a cigarette, sitting on the bench in the tiny front garden. The sky is very big here, and there are hundreds of stars, and all the space scares me. It's not natural.

I hear an owl hooting, and it makes me shiver. It's an unearthly noise, and I think, *God, where are all the people and the buildings and the light?*

I think of her life in the few pages I've just read, and I think, *Why the hell didn't she tell me about this campaign of terror she was living under?*

She did try though, didn't she? *Come on, Marlena,* I think, *you know she bloody did. Innocent Jeanie.* Always willing to believe the best of people – and letting them make her feel like shit.

I feel the tears start again, and I dash them away impatiently. I don't have time for this. I have to find out what happened.

Otherwise I will go as mad as…

As mad as Jeanie has. But what is it that pushed her over the edge in the end?

Okay – so that's a no-brainer. I wince as I think of the BBC news site. Presumably Matthew and the abuse allegation was too much for her.

I light another cigarette, thinking, thinking, thinking. The vodka has made my head a little fuzzy, but I'm well used to drinking on the job.

Why was the daughter here the other day? That really puzzles me. This girl who was so close to her mother that she hated Jeanie at first, that she blew this hot and cold.

Why would Scarlett come to Jeanie, all the way up north, when she hated her at times? When Robo had just found out it was her sending the poisonous messages, trying to take Jeanie down?

Did she come to destroy her?

I need to find her, this Scarlett, and talk to her. I need her to explain. And I need to know what was going on with her and her father. I fear that this is what has pushed Jeanie to this point.

But another thought is there.

The thought that Scarlett could be involved in a worse way than might seem obvious.

But it can't be that.

Can it? A fifteen-year-old girl couldn't try to kill someone, remotely... No, it doesn't add up...

And the police obviously don't think anything untoward has happened. All the pills and the whisky bottle in the rucksack were signs enough for them: the writing was on the wall. Or in the medicine cabinet, rattling with pills – above the fresh blood on the carpet.

And Christ, how bad do I feel that I didn't even know Jeanie had slid back down the slope?

I mean, I knew she started again after the whole Otto Lundy episode; I knew she was prescribed various things, that at one point she was taking all sorts of antidepressants. And that wasn't the first time. After Simon, things got so bad I had Frankie for a short time whilst she got well. And for years she was well. For years – until Otto.

After Otto she was seriously depressed for a while. With good reason: she lost her job. Her reputation. Her livelihood and her reason – other than Frankie – to be.

I helped her out, got her back on her feet. She had some savings, thank God, because she was always cautious.

In the main, it was the thought of Frankie that got her through – him just being there.

I did try, at one point, to get Jeanie to see a shrink, but she refused. She seemed better. 'I may be sad, but I'm not mad.' She even smiled about it, and I believed her. She thought therapy was 'trendy' and 'faddy' – and her response annoyed me, but she knew her own mind, my big sister, for all her kindnesses.

Then she did actually see that CBT guy, when her cleaning got compulsive again. I thought she was going to be all right.

I didn't like Matthew all that much when he came along; I thought he was smug – but harmless. I thought she was in with a good chance of a good life. I thought he really loved her, that he saw the goodness reflected back at him.

I thought we were past this now.

I think of his harsh words to her – the words written here in this diary.

And you know what else? It pains me to say it – but she kind of *was* a blank, my Jeanie. I've seen it written down – and I hate the man who said it – I knew there was a reason not to like him.

But there's a part of me – and I bloody well hate to admit it, I really, really do – that understands *why* he said it.

She wasn't always like that, not as a younger child. No; then she was vibrant, if always a little shy and retiring.

It happened later. And I blame our mother. Well, both our parents really – though my dad fucked off when we were so young, I barely think of him. I wholeheartedly and squarely lay the blame at our parents' door. But then why wouldn't I?

Don't have kids if you can't cope, I say.

Around two I fall asleep on the sofa in the living room, curled up uncomfortably, knees almost at my chin. But I am good at sleeping anywhere; it's a long-won habit. I sleep for a bit.

I'm woken by the next-door neighbour knocking gently at the front door. She is a spry-looking older lady with gun-grey hair and shiny red glasses, and it's her who rang 999.

'Ruth Jenkins. Next door. I'm so sorry about Jeanie…'

'Thanks.' I try to shut the door.

'You must be her sister; I can see it round the eyes. Can I offer you some coffee?' she says. 'I've just made a pot.'

I'm about to tell her to get lost, but then I think, *Be nice, Marlena, you owe her.* If it wasn't for her, after all…

'Thanks,' I say again, but if she's come for information or emotion, she's come to the wrong place.

There is no room for grief here. There is only room for answers.

The woman brings the coffee round on a tray and tells me to leave it on her garden table when I'm done, no rush, and she doesn't ask any questions.

I drink the coffee, trying to clear my head. I clean my teeth in the kitchen sink, and then, palms sweating, I ring the hospital.

My fingers are crossed behind my back like I always used to cross them when I was a scared little kid.

No change, they say. She's in a medically induced coma; it's safer for now. The worry is – the worry is – she may be brain dead.

I try to ring Frank; I leave him a message to call me back, but I don't say anything else.

I find myself wishing very briefly that I had someone else to call, someone waiting for me at home, someone who cared, someone to whom I could say, 'I'm really fucking terrified – what will I do if she dies?'

My mind turns to Levi – to his big grin, his teeth very white against his dark skin, his warm muscular arms, the terrible QPR tattoo on his left hip. And then I think away again. We were getting too close – so I finished it last month.

I don't need anyone. Because if I had anyone, they could do this thing that Jeanie's threatening to do. They could leave me too.

I smoke my last cigarette and check the news on my phone – nothing about Matthew. I Google him. Nothing new.

I sit and think for a minute or two, then I text my mate Jez in the ITN newsroom.

Can you hook me up with a stringer who can check out this guy Matthew King; I'll pay ££

Half an hour later I get a call from a Welsh-sounding girl called Sal.

'What do you want to know?'

'Can you get to him? Talk to him?'

'I can try, babe.' Sal is cheerful and efficient sounding. 'What you paying?'

'What do you want?'

She sets out reasonable terms, and I agree.

'I need answers – quickly,' I say. 'And, Sal…'

'Yeah?'

'I need all the help I can get please. Social workers and police, I guess, are the way forward.'

'Sure thing,' she says quietly, and I reckon Jez must have told her why. 'I've got my contacts. No worries, babe. I'll do my best.'

When I hang up, I go back through the cottage, and I open every drawer, every cupboard. I go through everything, through Jeanie's bag, through her phone.

At some point I realise I'm muttering and cursing, sweating as I rush round the tiny house.

I take the phone, and I take the diary, and I put them in my own bag.

I knock on the cottage next door and ask that Ruth contact me on my mobile if anyone *at all* comes to the house. I give her my card.

'I really do hope she's all right,' Ruth says, and she seems quite upset. 'She seemed like a nice lady…' And then she stops, thinking better of whatever it was she was going to say.

'Yeah, I really hope so too.' *Don't cry, Marlena.* 'Can I ask – how come you noticed she was gone?'

'I had a sort of – hunch maybe? I don't know. I saw her on Sunday. She seemed – disoriented. She was walking out on the back fields, and she looked…'

She is embarrassed.

'Go on please,' I say.

'I don't know. I just got the idea something wasn't right. She seemed very – shaky. And I'm afraid – I heard her crying a few times in the night.'

Oh God.

'You can hear everything when the windows are open, we're all so near.' She looked apologetic. 'And when her door kept banging in the early hours, I thought – I'd better go in…'

'Thank God,' I say.

'I just wish…' She trails off. 'Well. I wish I could have helped her more.'

She offers me a lift to the station, but I don't want to talk any more, so I thank her again, as sincerely as possible, and say goodbye.

I walk down to the town square and call a cab. The air here is so fresh and so clean; I can see why Jeanie liked it. She could have been happy here, I can see that. I feel like it might have been the right place.

The cab drops me at the Royal Derby Hospital, and I sit with Jeanie for an hour before I catch the train. There's no change, though I'm sure I feel a flicker of her hand in mine at one point, when I rest my forehead on her fingers.

When I leave, teary and fraught, I head back down south. I research Berkhamsted, the town I will finally visit later. Apparently this pleasant 'commuter town' was once the home of Graham Greene. It has a Waitrose, of course – but Jeanie's no longer there.

And how ashamed am I that it's taken this disaster for me to go? How ashamed am I?

I've got no bloody clue what to do next – that's the truth. I'm so heartsick I don't know what to do with myself full stop. And I haven't managed to get hold of Frankie yet.

The image of Jeanie under that sheet spins round my head, so pale, that plastic thing shoved in her mouth, and all those stupid bloody machines, green lights and beeps. It's unbearable. What will I do – if…

All the way from Derby on the train, my mind jangles like church bells rung by a group of pissed vicars.

As we're pulling into St Pancras, the stringer Sal texts to say she's made contact with her source at Hertfordshire County Council Social Services and started to dig around. She's not seen Matthew yet; she thinks he's still in custody.

She's managed to speak to the investigating officer, who says he can't disclose anything yet – but she knows the allegations have come from someone very close to King.

I get a cab home.

My neighbour catches me as I'm about to shut my front door.

'Package for you,' he says, ridiculous in tight Lycra, on his way to jog through the pollution.

It's a badly wrapped book of some description; my name on the address label – but it's misspelt.

In the flat I light a fag, put the espresso machine on and open it. There's a note: three words. *For safe keeping.*

I realise it's a diary.

It's Jeanie's missing diary.

I flick through it.

Then I shove some clean knickers in my bag, swig my coffee back and I leave again. I walk to the local Avis branch, and I hire a car.

Driving out of London again, exhausted but my brain humming, I think about Jeanie's words; what she wrote about Kaye arriving to get Scarlett. It's hard to get a grasp of the woman's real intentions from my sister's writing. I don't know how much of Jeanie's own disquiet was informing what she wrote. I need to speak to the woman myself.

It's not hard to find Kaye King's address. (Don't ask me how I do it. I can't divulge all my tricks and sources – but I can find an address quicker than you can say 'hot dinner'.)

Kaye King – sounds like some type of poxy singer, some floaty type like Karen Carpenter, doesn't it?

But when I actually meet Kaye, she couldn't be further from that imagining.

Her apartment is in a modern block of expensive flats, set behind gates in landscaped gardens. It's all most out of keeping with the rest of this twee, mock-Tudor town, and the big gates are firmly closed.

I park on the street and walk through the pedestrian gate to locked glass doors. There is her name, all pink and swirly beside number 201: *Mrs Kaye King* it reads.

I press the intercom buzzer over and over – but no one answers.

I'm wondering what to do – wait or go – when a shiny white Range Rover pulls in through the gates, opening electronically.

There's a teenage boy in the passenger seat beside the woman driving. He is different from her blondeness: dark haired, round faced – the apologetic pudding Jeanie described. He sees me, and he says something as she pulls up, so that she looks at me, frowning.

'Hi.' I stand by her car door. 'Are you Kaye?'

'What?' she mouths through the window, shaking her head as if she can't understand me. The boy looks petrified.

'I'm Marlena Randall; I'm Jeanie's sister.' I speak loudly and clearly, as if I'm talking to someone very stupid or very deaf.

'Have you heard what's happened? I'd like to speak to you please.'

'Yes, I got your message. I am sorry.' She lowers the window slightly, the engine still running. 'How is she?'

'Not good. I'm just – I'm wondering what went on...'

'What do you mean?'

'Is your daughter here?'

'She's staying with a friend. She has to be – protected. Because of what's – happened.'

'What's happened?' I know what she means; I just want her to say it.

The woman casts a quick look at her son. 'I don't think this is an appropriate conversation for now, Miss Randall.' She puts huge emphasis on the 'Miss'; coming from her mouth, it sounds like a dirty word. 'Little pitchers, you know.'

The boy is at least fifteen, if not older, staring at his phone, not looking at me. Hardly a little pitcher – and he must be sensing the animosity surely?

Still, I don't want to alienate Kaye immediately.

'Yeah, granted,' I say. 'Is there somewhere we could talk privately? Just for a minute...'

'Not really.' Kaye's face hardens. 'We're going through a really tough time ourselves you know.'

'Yes, I heard. I'm sorry to hear that. But my sister's on life support, and I want to know what the f—' My turn to glance at the boy still mesmerised by Candy Crush. 'What the hell was going on, you know, to push my sister into what she's done?'

As Kaye contemplates me, her perfect manicure tapping the wheel, I'm distracted by a young man jogging towards us.

Kaye sees him too, opens the window further and calls to him, 'I'll see you inside.'

He stops, clearly somewhat confused by Mein Führer's command, poor bloke.

'Yassine,' she snaps. 'We'll be up in a minute.'

'Marlena Randall.' I walk towards him and extend my hand. 'You met my sister Jeanie, I believe.'

He nods, taking my hand in his warm sweaty one. 'She's nice. I'm really sorry. How's she doing?'

'Not too good at the moment.' I swallow the lump in my throat. 'She's unconscious actually – and I'm trying to find out why.'

'I'm sorry to hear that,' he repeats. 'I am sorry she would want to take her own life.'

'Can I give you my number please?' I delve into my back pocket. 'If you think of anything…'

'Anything?'

'Anything at all. I'm trying to understand what drove her to this.' I offer him the card. 'Please. I'm pretty desperate.'

He takes it. A little reluctantly perhaps, but he does at least take it.

Kaye, on the other hand, is not going to get out of her car now, so I give up. I don't want to make a scene here.

Not yet anyway.

As I sit in my hire car on the corner, smoking my fifth fag this hour and thinking, *What is it I'm hoping to achieve by all this?*, something attracts my attention.

I see a girl on the uppermost balcony, in pyjamas and fluffy boots, leaning on the rail, looking down at me. I'm pretty sure it's Scarlett. When she sees me looking back, she retreats quickly.

What is this family hiding? What did they push Jeanie to?

And *who* sent me the diary?

* * *

The next morning I get up really early and finish reading Jeanie's thoughts.

There's a little note on some of the pages, not that many, that says SK. Scarlett King? It makes no sense.

I find some of Jeanie's self-doubt lacerating. Why did I not see sooner that she was in real trouble? Why didn't she say?

After I've called the hospital and they've repeated, 'No change still,' I drive back to Berkhamsted, and I break into Matthew King's house.

Well okay, I don't break in exactly. I let myself in with Jeanie's keys. I set the alarm off – but I'm good with alarms – I learnt at the knee of a master as I was being dragged up – and I manage to disable it quite quickly. Quickly enough, I hope, that it won't alert anyone.

It's cold and empty in this house; this house is cold and empty. There's no heart. Jeanie probably brought it heart – but she's lying unconscious in a hospital bed in the Royal Derby.

The house makes me shiver, even though the day is warm.

I don't know where to begin, but once I do, as in the cottage in Ashbourne, I will go through everything.

I start in Jeanie and Matthew's bedroom. It doesn't look as if she had much to do with the decoration here. It's a grand but impersonal room, with pale blue and gold Chinesey-looking wallpaper and a huge wooden bed that doesn't seem like something Jean would ever choose.

I glance in the other rooms, having a quick swipe round Matthew's study – but his computer is gone, and the filing cabinets are locked. The police have probably got the computer I imagine.

I wonder what it is that he kept asking her to sign.

Really it's Scarlett's room I want to find. I need to know what school she goes to, and it doesn't take long to discover that, through formal school photos hanging on the wall outside her door, and the maroon uniform in the walk-in wardrobe. And she has more clothes than I could imagine owning – quite something for a teenager.

This bedroom is the type of room every little girl dreams of: if you like things flouncy and frilly and pink. The type of bedroom Jeanie and I certainly didn't know existed when we were her age – except for the rich girls in Enid Blyton maybe or, later, that awful Beverley Hills programme about teens with sports cars and too much Gucci.

Does the money make up for the dysfunction? I wonder. We had no money and plenty of dysfunction. Would my errant father and unfit mother have been easier to bear if I'd gone to school in designer labels and holidayed in Barbados?

I'll never know I suppose. At least growing up skint gave us some drive. Just not much security – or enough belief in ourselves, though God we tried. Still, our boundaries may have been blurred sometimes: just look at both our descents from professional heaven…

Enough musing. I have another thought – and I run back downstairs, into the lounge this time. Where is their DVD collection?

Jean mentioned the family home movies in her diary, 'the look on Scarlett's face'. That look had disconcerted Jeanie; she'd found it odd – but I don't know why.

And of course Scarlett's not answered my texts. When I called her earlier, the response from my iPhone made me wonder if my number's been blocked from her end.

On my hands and knees, pulling out old Disney and Harry Potter films, *SpongeBob SquarePants* and some Aston Villa highlights, I hear someone running overhead – I'm sure I do.

I start up – and then someone raps hard on the window, and I bang my head as I try to stand.

A red-haired woman is on the other side of the glass, staring at me, hands on hips as I rub my sore head.

'And who the hell, may I ask'—the redhead raises her voice fiercely—'are you?'

So. This is Alison, the woman Jeanie wasn't sure about.

'I'm a key holder,' she explains on the doorstep. 'The alarm company inform me if it goes off. I only live a few streets away, so I can check it out.'

My sleight of hand failed then. Good thing I didn't follow the master into criminality.

'I'm Marlena.' I offer my hand, trying to pacify her. 'Jeanie's sister. I don't know if you've heard about Jeanie…'

'Heard what? That they've split up? Yes, I did. I'm sorry.'

I turn away from her and move into the house, grabbing my bag to find my cigarettes. Every time I have to say something about what's happened to Jeanie, I feel like I'm going to start sobbing.

I catch my breath. *Pull yourself together, you silly cow.* I go back, fags in hand, and I explain briefly the course of events as I understand them.

'Oh my God…' Alison looks really shocked. 'Poor Jeanie.'

'I need a cigarette,' I say. 'Can we go outside?'

'I wouldn't mind one either.' She indicates my Marlboro Lights. 'If you can spare one…'

Side by side, we sit on the front step together, smoking in silence for a while. It's a pleasant day, too pleasant for what's going on.

'I'm really sorry,' she says eventually. 'Jeanie seemed…'

'What?' I am suspicious. Overly so perhaps, but then none of this lot seemed welcoming to my poor sister.

'I thought she seemed nice. Truly.' Alison must have detected my tone. 'Though we didn't really get a chance to get to know each other. It was awful, that bloody dinner.' She inhales deeply and then coughs. 'God, sorry. Haven't smoked for a while.'

'The dinner when Jeanie got sick, you mean?'

'Yes – only…'

'What?'

'I don't know. It was very odd. I'm a nurse you know – well, I trained as one, a long time ago. Gave it up to go into gardening. Less blood.' She shoots me a look. 'Can I – is it okay to ask you something?'

I shrug to say go on.

'I wondered,' she says. 'Did she – does she have a problem? With drink or drugs?'

'No.' I shake my head vehemently. 'Never. Not Jeanie. She drinks very little.'

'Really? Seems even more strange then.'

'Why? I mean she had a stint on antidepressants, after she had a bit of a – problem at work, a few years ago. But she's never been a party girl. Never a drinker.'

'I see. Well she didn't seem to have drunk much that night; I certainly didn't notice if she had. But she was suddenly *so* out of it. Dramatically so. Like she'd been mixing drink and drugs, I thought, and it worried me. The signs were bad.'

'I see.' I chuck my cigarette butt into the flowerbed. 'So you're a friend of Kaye's?'

'Hardly. I mean I was, once, a long time ago. We went to school together. But…' She pauses. 'We grew apart I suppose.'

'Why? Did something happen?' I could rein it in, I guess, my customary rat-a-tat-tat questioning, but it serves a purpose. It disarms people I find.

'I – I couldn't have kids. And she just got – a bit weird when she had hers.'

'Weird how?'

'Oh maybe not weird then. Maybe just too wrapped up in them. Kind of – obsessive. Or maybe I was jealous. Probably was. Anyway I found it hard. I mean I was very fond of them, the kids; we saw a lot of each other when they were small. Matthew and Sean got on very well – though…'

'What?'

'Oh I don't know. People change, don't they?'

'How did they change?' I try not to seem too keen.

'Matthew made so much money, almost overnight, and then Kaye became all about what car she drove and where they holidayed. All private schools and labels and Mulberry bags you know. Not really my thing.'

'No, well I get that.'

'And Matthew – he was okay, but I started to find him – a bit oppressive. And conservative. Not in a good way.'

'What about the kids?'

'What about them?' Alison grinds her cigarette out in the gravel, hardly smoked.

'I think Jeanie was really struggling – with Scarlett mainly.'

'With Scarlett?' Alison raises a brow. 'I guess – maybe. I mean she's sweet really, but…'

'What?'

'I suppose she always was a bit of a daddy's girl.'

We look at each other.

'I think these allegations are crap myself,' she sighs. 'Matthew mayn't be my favourite person, but I really don't think he's, you know, one of *them*.' She stands. 'It's just been really tough.'

'What can you tell me about the whole Daisy thing?'

'Oh nothing really.' She checks her watch. 'I must go actually…'

'Alison. Please. I feel like something – bad's been happening here, something that's driven Jeanie right to the edge. I need to find out what it is…'

'Well…' She's still hesitating, and I give her an encouraging smile.

She relents. 'It's just Daisy was the twins' kind-of nanny. They got quite attached to her – she was sweet. But she – she had to leave quite… quickly.'

'She had an accident?' It's in the diary, in black and white.

'I can't really – God is that the time?' She rechecks her watch unconvincingly, moving away.

If anyone can read signs of an interviewee with something to hide, it's me. 'Alison, please – it's important.'

'If I think of anything – but I'm sorry, I must go. I hope Jeanie's well again soon.' She hurries down the drive.

'Alison.' I rush after her and put my hand on her shoulder. She has to stop. 'Can I give you my card at least? Just in case.' She's hiding something – and she knows I know. 'I really need to find what pushed Jeanie to this state…'

'OK.' Alison sighs heavily. 'There is just one thing I would say – Marlene, is it?

'Marlena.'

'I was a bit – worried. That Matthew was just sort of – using Jeanie.'

'Using her?'

'For the money…'

'Hardly!' I actually laugh. 'She's the original church mouse; she's been skint for years.'

'I mean, sorry – to sign the money away. To hide it.'

'Hide it?'

'I only know because Sean's his lawyer. Was his lawyer actually. They don't really work together any more. Sean's decided it's not – appropriate any more.'

'Okay. But – why to hide it though?'

'You can guess, Marlena, I imagine. Sean wouldn't really talk to me about it, but he didn't feel comfortable with the way Matthew was starting to move things around.'

And Alison leaves, with a promise I don't believe that she'll get in touch if anything else comes to mind.

I try to ring Frankie again with no luck. So I bite the bullet, and I call the vineyard. If the worst – you know. If the worst comes to the worst, he needs to be here.

In my terrible schoolgirl French, I stumble through explaining my need to speak to Frank Randall; it's urgent, I emphasise, but I don't want to say any more without speaking directly to Frankie myself. I leave my number with the owner, who promises to find him.

I'm on my way to Scarlett's school when Sal rings.

'Matthew King's been released,' she says. 'He's on his way somewhere in a cab, my bloke at the nick says.'

'Have the allegations been dropped?'

'There's been no formal charge, I don't think, so they couldn't hold him any more. I do know this though.' She sounds almost enthused. 'It was the second time he was taken in for questioning.'

God I feel tired.

At the school I know it will raise suspicion if I hover round the gates.

Think, Marlena, think. But my brain is like sludge today.

There's a sweet shop at the end of the road. I go to buy cigarettes and a Coke when two teen girls, in high-tops and baggy jeans, walk in arm in arm, bags full of schoolbooks.

'I like your trainers,' I say to one. 'Dead nice.'

'Thanks.' She looks surprised, and her prettier mate with tightly cornrowed hair giggles.

'I've got some a bit like that. Where are yours from?'

'Er, they're Huaraches I think.' The tall white girl picks up a blue Bounty. 'Nikes.'

'Cool. Do you go to St Bett's? You must know Scarlett King?'

'Oh *her*.' They go all serious and big eyed now. 'Yeah, we kind of know her. We're in the sixth form. She's below us.'

'Poor kid,' I say. 'She's nice, isn't she? She's a family friend actually…'

'Oh yeah, I think so. She's not been in school much since – the thing…' Cornrows whispers theatrically. 'It's deep, what's happened.'

'God, no, I know. Awful. I saw her mum yesterday.' I'm not lying, I tell myself. Much.

'Her mum? She's gorgeous, isn't she? She was an actress, wasn't she? She was in *The Bill*, my dad says.'

'Yeah, gorgeous.' Together we walk out of the shop, and I glance at my phone very obviously.

'Oh damn it! Bloody battery. Can I ask you a favour?'

'Yeah, course.' They are excited to be conspirators.

'Can you get Scarlett a message? I was meant to see her later…' My fingers are crossed behind my back. I swore I'd never lie again, but this isn't work. This is fucking life or death. 'But my mobile's gone flat. Could you give her my number? I'll go and charge it in the park café while I wait. Tell her Marlena will be here? Jeanie's sister?'

'Well…'

'I'm just so worried about her.' I do my best motherly face. 'Poor darling. I don't want her to think I've forgotten her.'

'Yeah, course,' the shorter one says, pulling her sleeves down over her hands. 'Give us your number then.'

'Awesome.' I put it in her phone. 'And could you tell her I'll be in the café for a bit?'

I'm sitting in the park café, scrolling through Safari to find out where the local news agency is when my phone – not flat at all of course – rings. *Unknown,* it says.

I'm terrified it's going to be Frankie or the hospital – but it's neither.

'Is this Jeanie's sister?' the accented voice says.

'Yeah, this is Marlena.' My ears prick up. 'Who's this?'

'It's Yassine, Kaye's… boyfriend.' He hesitates over the word in his strange accent. 'I'm so sorry.'

'About what?'

'She does not know I'm ringing you.' He sounds stressed. 'I had an argument with her about it, you see. It is not a good thing—'

'What isn't?' I'm starting to feel irritated. *Spit it out, man.*

'I told a lie. I'm sorry I didn't say I was there when I was.'

'What? When?' I rack my brains. 'Do you mean at Malum House that day?'

'Yeah, when I took the football boots round. But then she told me to say that I didn't…'

The missing boots. 'Who told you to say that? Scarlett?'

'No.' He drops his voice. 'Kaye.'

'Kaye did? *Why?*'

'I don't know.' Yassine sounds thoroughly miserable. 'She just said not to say I was there; I shouldn't have been there she said.'

'Why?'

But he won't give me any more.

So why would Kaye make her boyfriend lie?

What the hell's going on with these bloody Kings?

And yet I have a feeling in my gut – it's one I recognise from all my days of investigating, of tying ends up – that finally it's starting to make some kind of sense. But the full truth hasn't emerged; it's still hidden, so the dots don't join up – yet.

Yassine won't say any more about why Kaye told him to say he wasn't there; he claims he doesn't really understand. He's extremely uncomfortable, that's obvious. But he does tell me he's moving out of Kaye's for a bit.

'They need some time,' he says, but I get the sense that he wants out of there, and frankly I don't blame him.

'I'm sorry,' he repeats yet again. 'It was wrong, and I feel ashamed for my lie.' His English is very formal, and I tell him not to worry. I don't want to alienate him – though it's a pisser. It certainly didn't help Jeanie, did it? It just made her think she was crazy.

All of these lies.

South Beds News Agency is the most local to here. I put a call in.

'I'm trying to find out about an incident with a Lisa Daisy Bedford, sometime in early 2014,' I make a stab at the date. It can't have been that long before Matthew met Jeanie – it has to be in-between Kaye leaving and him dating Jeanie. 'Nothing is coming up on my searches, but I understand the accident was bad enough for her to have been hospitalised.'

As I hang up, the schoolgirls from the sweet shop hurry into the café, all flicky eyeliner and over-pierced ears.

I wave at them, and they rush over to my table, eyes boggling.

'We did try, but we couldn't tell her to come, cos she got picked up early,' the taller one breathes, full of her own importance.

'Oh yeah?' *Shit.* 'By her mum?'

'No!' Cornrows chews her gum ferociously. 'We weren't sure, cos we were in the common room when it happened, but Sherry Noyce said they reckon it was by her dad!'

If that's true, I think, *there must be no charges.* The school wouldn't release her to him if he'd been charged.

If they knew it was him collecting her of course.

'Sherry gave me her number. I texted your number to her,' the tall one says proudly. 'To Scarlett, I mean. Said you were worried.'

'That's brilliant,' I say, feeling more worried now.

And I have another feeling, as I gather my things and thank the girls.

The other feeling, one that's growing all the time, is that this was never about Jeanie.

That Jeanie maybe just got in the way.

I'm thinking that if I can't get to Scarlett yet, there's one other person I really want to talk to.

The news agency calls me back as I'm waiting for another cab.

'Marlena Randall? I don't have anything for you on Lisa Daisy Bedford, but I *can* tell you why you can't find owt.' The woman is a bored Mancunian. 'There's an injunction on the story.'

'Injunction?' My ears prick up. I love an injunction: it always means there's buried trouble. 'Do you have any more details?'

'You know perfectly well I'll be in contempt of court if I tell you anything.'

'Ah come on…'

'Come on, yourself. You might be Old Bill for all I know.'

'I'm not,' I say through gritted teeth. 'I'm a journalist.'

'Yeah, I know who you are.' She sniffs. 'I recognise your name.'

'Well then, you know I'm not police. And I'm paying for this…'

'Why don't you ask the lawyer who applied for it then?' she suggests. 'There was a minor involved; the name wasn't ever released.'

'Who was the lawyer?'

'Day and Young, it says here. Tenth of March 2014,' she tells me. And then, tartly, 'That's all you're getting, love.' She hangs up.

Day? Why does that name ring a bell?

Appetite whetted, I need to find this girl Daisy – and fast. I text Robo with her name, saying I need an address within the hour.

In the meantime, I contemplate going back to the house – but will Matthew be there now? I never found the home movie before I was interrupted – and I badly want to know what it was that Jeanie thought she saw.

And anyway I want to hear what he's got to say for myself – my sister's husband. What excuse Matthew has for doubting Jeanie, for believing whoever it was that was trying to damage her, over his own new wife, who loved him so deeply. For not seeing she was being manipulated by someone who had it in for her…

And then I think of Alison Day's words earlier, that maybe Matthew was only using her anyway.

Alison *Day*! Of course!

So Day of Day and Young must be her husband, Sean – and he got the injunction for Matthew King.

Before I can make my next move, which is probably to go back to Malum House to challenge Matthew King – Robo's texted back.

No address, but here's a phone number for the family home, I think.

I call the number Robo has sent me. There's just an automated voicemail with no name, so I leave a very polite message asking to be called back.

Then I go back to the King house.

In the avenue there's a tired-looking reporter sitting outside Malum House in a battered old Vauxhall, reading a paperback, and a photographer in a camouflage jacket and cap, leaning on a lamp post, drinking Dr Pepper and texting.

I drive past and down the road slightly.

As I'm parking, a white Range Rover pulls into the drive. I know that the Range Rover is Kaye's, and so I'm guessing this will mean fireworks. But maybe, I think, feeling almost excited, this is the opportune moment to confront Matthew. *Get it all out in the open…*

By the time I hurry across the road, past the two reporters, who are now out on the pavement by the gate, whoever has just arrived has gone inside. I see there's also a big black car parked half in, half out of the open garage, and I open the garden gate.

I hurry up the path with voices ringing in my ears – 'Oi, love, hang on a sec!' – and I feel extremely uncomfortable. The hunter turned prey: all the times *I've* been that insistent voice, shouting at others, begging for their story, whatever their emotional state...

The curtains are pulled at the lounge window, the one that Alison Day knocked on earlier to alarm me.

I go into the open garage, past the black car, and through it, and sure enough, there's a door into the garden at the far end.

In the back garden I creep along the flowerbed until I am adjacent with the patio doors – and I see two figures standing in the kitchen – two figures embracing.

If it wasn't a bloody cliché, I'd double take.

Matthew King – and his ex-wife, Kaye.

Matthew King and Kaye with their arms round each other, and as I stop in my tracks and stare, my mouth agape, she reaches up and kisses him on the lips.

Jesus wept.

So what do I do now?

Do I run screaming forward and yell at them – *you traitors*? Or do I leave quietly and regroup?

You may think I should plump for the former, but I choose the latter. I need to get my head round this, and I need to collate all the evidence I'm gleaning, and I need to try and work out *WHAT THE FUCK IS GOING ON.*

As I retreat down the garden and slip back into the garage, I see a face at an upper window, a pale face, and I think it's Scarlett at first, and then I think no, it's the boy. I find myself putting my finger to my lips.

Who am I kidding?

I get the hell out of Dodge.

I've booked myself a room at the Penny Farthing Inn on the high street. It's quite gastro and chichi, but I'm beyond caring.

I dump my bag, and then I go out and buy myself a bottle of vodka, some tonic, a portion of chips and a pad of A4 paper.

I eat the chips sitting on the bed, then I ring the hospital again. Still no change. And still nothing from Frank.

I pour myself a warm vodka and tonic in the toothbrush beaker, and I lay my own notebook and Jeanie's two diaries out on the table in the corner, and I use the paper to try to make sense of what the hell's gone on here.

And so what I'm wondering now, what I'm faced with, is – if Kaye and Matthew are in cahoots, was Jeanie just collateral damage?

Was Jeanie just about whatever the financial thing was that Alison mentioned? I get the idea Matthew's finances weren't quite what he was making out – that he was in some kind of bother…

Or is it more sinister than that?

The tepid vodka slows my thought processes.

Lying on the bed, exhausted and gutted, I have an idea that Jeanie simply got involved with a man not over his first wife – and it's as straightforward as that.

The only way I will have any idea of the truth, I realise, is by confronting Matthew. But before I can think about how to achieve that, my phone buzzes.

'It's Peter Bedford, Daisy's dad. You left a message?'

Peter Bedford is a short, thickset man with greying hair, sad eyes and a bald spot. He reminds me of a dog; I'm just not sure which breed. A Staffie maybe. He's wary, most suspicious of me – but I explain that I only want to understand what happened to Daisy because of Jeanie's apparent suicide attempt. Bedford seems kind of shocked when I give him the details – shocked that she's in the hospital, that is – but not all that surprised.

'Sorry,' he mutters, in that way with which men often deal with upset. Not head-on.

But then let's face it, who am I to judge?

'Fancy a drink, Peter?' I ask, and he nods. 'Yeah, all right. Cheers.'

We cross the road to the pub opposite, and I buy him a pint, ordering coffee for myself. For once the vodka didn't help anything. That's a first in my book.

'So your sister married Matthew King?' he says and wipes the froth off his top lip. He has a broad West Country accent. 'Good luck to her.'

'Yeah, well she's not had much of that.' I stir sugar into my coffee, even though I don't normally take sugar. 'If it had gone okay, I wouldn't be here now. And I wonder – can you tell me, I mean, I know it's probably not linked – but what *did* happen to your daughter?'

The man drinks half his pint in one go. He bangs the glass down, and then he looks at first the ceiling then at me, as if I were the guilty party.

'That fucking kid ran her over.'

'What?' I can't believe my ears. 'Scarlett did? Ran her over?'

'No.' He glares at me with his hangdog droopy eyes. 'Not the girl. The lad.'

Luke.

'Jesus!' I'm pretty stunned. 'God, I'm sorry. How – is she all right now?'

'Not really.' He shrugs, picks his pint up again with thick fingers. 'She's walking at least. But she's not the same girl; not yet anyway.'

'I'm really sorry. Can I ask then – how did it happen?'

'They swore it was an accident. They'd gone away for the weekend, the kids, that bloody Matthew bloke and he'd taken

Dais to look after 'em – gone to Norfolk to a country place. The kid was allowed to drive the car, that's what they said anyway. They was on private land, and he backed it into Daisy. Didn't see her, he claimed.'

'Who didn't? Luke?'

'Yeah. Cos she was running after the bloody dog. And she can barely remember what happened. All a blur, she always said, when the police got involved.'

'So there was going to be a prosecution? I mean it was going to go to court and then...?'

'Then it got dropped. Don't ask me why, it beat us. But we had the idea Matthew King was – well connected, shall we say.' Peter Bedford looked bitter now. 'He did pay for all her medical treatment at least, King. Paid for Dais to go to America. She's...' He hunts for the word. 'Rejuvenating.'

Recuperating I think he means – but I don't correct him.

'That's good,' I say hopefully. It's no solace apparently.

'But what I want to know is why was he allowed to do that anyway? Drive a big bloody car like that, a little kid like that?'

'I don't know,' I say honestly. The man's pain is palpable. 'But why do you think it was deliberate?'

'Because. Daisy'd already said the kids was messed up. Their mother was a nutter apparently.'

'Really?' My ears prick up again.

'Yeah, leaving her kids like that. Dais only stayed cos she felt sorry for 'em.' He's anticipated my next question. 'Them kids. She's a soft touch, my Daisy. And'—he finished the last swill of his drink—'cos of that bloke, I s'pose.'

This admission seems to pain him even more, but of course it's what I need to know.

'Matthew King you mean? Why? What was their relationship?'

'What you getting at?' he snaps. It's too much for him, and I wince at myself. I know better than this. Don't tread on the emotions of the bereaved or devastated. *Softly, softly*…

'Sorry. I just mean…' What *do* I mean though? How can I phrase it without further offending him? 'I mean how *did* they get on, Daisy and Matthew? Could you say?'

Were they sleeping together? That's what I really mean of course.

'He liked her a lot. Too much, I thought. He was way too old for her though.' Bedford scowls, fleshy jowls creasing. 'He's not much younger'n me, that bugger. But I don't think that mattered to 'im. I mean'—now he pulls an outraged face—'did you see what they said in the paper? About the bloke?'

'I'm not sure it's been proven though,' I try to reassure him. 'I think it might be a mistake.'

'I bloody well hope so.' He brightens slightly. 'Do you want to see her? She's beautiful, my Daisy.'

'I'd love to,' I reply truthfully. I'm more than intrigued.

Her father gets a battered old photo out of his wallet; it's a school photo perhaps, creased and folded. The girl has long blonde hair and a nice smile, but what's rather spooky, I think, is her resemblance to Kaye.

'Beautiful,' I say, though she's not particularly, if I'm honest. I pass it back. 'I'm glad she's all right.' She's beautiful to him, naturally. As all children are meant to be to their parents, only…

It doesn't always work like that, does it?

Peter Bedford zips his old wax jacket up. 'I wish she'd never gone there, to that bloody scary house. Never liked it, she said, used to creep her out.'

'Why?'

'All them dark windows and corners. Whispering walls, she used to say. She heard voices in the night. And them graves in the garden. You wanna ask that King bloke – how the hell did *they* get there?'

'The graves?' I remember Jeanie's entry about the garden, that day she wrote about Yassine's visit.

'All the pets kept on dying, Daisy said. She was freaked out. They said there was a ghost too. A lady what hung herself.'

'Hung herself?'

'That's right. Up in that bloody turret.'

'I'm sorry.' I shake my head, thinking of Jeanie's own terror. 'Was there ever a gardener she mentioned, by the way?'

'Not that I remember. Just her, as it were, on the staff. Oh and some cleaner I think.'

'Thank you,' I say. 'I'm so glad Daisy's getting better.'

He blows his nose loudly.

'One more question,' I say, as we walk to the pub door together. Comedy Gold is on the television in the corner; an episode of *Some Mothers Do 'Ave 'Em* by the look of things.

Some of us have mothers we'd rather not have.

'Did she live there then? With the family?'

'Oh yeah. She had her own room you know. Very fancy. En suite and all.'

The room Jeanie smashed up?

Peter Bedford pulls open the door with a huge wrench. 'She was so proud of 'erself, you know, when she got that job. Good family like that. Wanted her independence you know. Well, kids do, don't they?'

I nod my agreement.

'But my God, I wish she'd stayed working for me in the shop.' His eyes are glassy with tears. 'She'd still be okay then, wouldn't she? She'd not be walking with a limp for the rest of 'er life. She'd not be looking over her shoulder or having them terrible dreams.'

There's not much I can say to that.

As I'm heading back to my room, exhausted but strangely exhilarated – ever closer to the truth, I feel – my phone rings again.

And it's Frankie.

It's reality.

This isn't a case I have to remind myself. This is my sister. This is life and death – and I'm on it too late. If I'd got involved before…

'I'll ring you back in two minutes, Frank,' I say, because I find myself so choked up, I have to prepare myself. 'From the landline.'

I smoke a fag out of the window of my room, like a schoolkid, and then I call him back.

I have to tell him what's happened, where Jeanie is, and he's beyond devastated of course.

And that puts any exhilaration I'm feeling right out of the picture of course.

'I'll get the train tomorrow morning,' he says, voice quivering.

I say, 'Get a flight. I'll pay.' I give him my credit-card details, and I can sense him trying not to cry as he asks where she is and what airport is nearest.

'Can I ring her?' he asks.

And I have to say, 'Well – she's not really talking at the moment, Frankie, not yet.'

And then he does cry.

'Frankie.' I swallow my own grief and fear as best I can. 'She's going to be all right you know.'

'No, I don't know,' he mutters, and I hear the confusion and the anger in his voice. 'I don't know that, and it doesn't sound like you do either, Marlena.'

'Jeanie's really strong,' I tell him. 'She's a fighter.'

Which is true, has been true – up to now. She was always so strong, for me. Look what she did – how she cared.

'But if that's true, then why did she do it? And how…' I hear the little boy that he is. His heart is breaking; I can hear it actually happening. 'How could she leave me?'

Oh Christ.

I can't answer that for her, but I have an idea that, if she did do it on purpose, well, she just couldn't take any more pain, because she loves him so much, she'd never have chosen to go…

And yet, did she do it? Did she try and kill herself?

Or was she pushed?

'She didn't want to leave you, darlin',' I say, 'but she wasn't doing so well. And…' I breathe really, really hard so I don't start sobbing. 'I'm here, Frank. I know it's not the same, but I am here for you.'

'Thanks,' he mumbles, and my own heart clutches painfully.

'You don't need to thank me, you silly sod.' God, he doesn't need to ever thank *me*. 'I'm not going anywhere, I promise you that.'

And I mean it. It's time to stop running.

I sleep fitfully all night, when I sleep at all.

I dream of children running around a big field, screaming, running from someone, a figure in the corner – and I can't tell if the screaming is in pain or pleasure.

When I wake up around 6 a.m., drenched in sweat, I can't think where the hell I am, and then I remember.

I switch on the little kettle on the tea tray and lie back on the pillows, thinking.

I can't go to the house yet – but that's my only plan. There's nothing left to say or do apart from confront this messed-up family and put the blame squarely at their door. All of their doors. I've failed to get hold of Scarlett, and I have no more answers.

If they admit it, will that make me feel better?

No policeman's going to arrest anyone for trying to creep someone else out, are they? No, they're not. Causing someone to try to end their own life, it's not a crime. Not a punishable one anyway, though I make a mental note to check on the CPS website. I'm pretty sure inciting suicide isn't a crime – yet.

Oh sure, I know the kids are probably blameless in this really. I learnt that in my own therapy: we're only playing out our parents' patterns. That's what we learn; that's what we grow up with; that's what we are scarred with and what we repeat.

Or in mine and Jeanie's case, that's what we try to avoid – so desperately that we make ourselves more unhappy in the meantime, denying ourselves relationships and love.

Levi crosses my mind again, and I'm tempted to text him – but I don't. After all, he told me what he thought when I finished it between us. He was furious, said I was a coward.

'If you never let yourself open up, Marlena, you'll end up old and alone.' Normally a pretty cool customer, he was angry and hurt, and I tried to laugh his words off, because it's always easier to do that, isn't it? But I felt like he was right.

I felt like it was a prophecy likely to come true. Alone forever, if I never let anyone in.

I get up to make myself another coffee.

When I switch my phone on ten minutes later, it's flashing with new messages.

I read the first text:

She said it was for the children's sake if they got too close to Jeanie.

Yassine. And he's talking, I guess, about Kaye. She asked him to lie because of getting too close to Jeanie?

There's a text from Frank saying he's booked on to a flight at 2 p.m., direct to Birmingham. He'll go straight to the Royal Derby Hospital he says. There's a train from the airport; he's checked.

I'll see him there this evening I say. Spend what you need to. I text three kisses at the end.

I'm downstairs, about to go to Malum House, psyching myself up for the confrontation, for the horror of saying what I need to say before I go back up to Derby and wait it out with my family, my only family, the only family that matters – when my phone rings again.

'Is that Marlena Randall?' the voice says, a girl – and I realise, with a thumping heart, who it is.

'Yeah,' I say, adrenaline coursing through my veins. 'It is. Is that Scarlett? Are you okay?'

'Yeah,' she says, then there's a pause. 'Well no, not really. How's – how's Jeanie?'

'She's – sleeping,' I say, trying to be kind, though there's a part of me that wants to yell at her, to scream and shout at her for her part in Jeanie's downfall. But I don't want to scare her off. 'She's in the hospital, and she's sleeping still.'

'Will she be okay?' she says, and I swallow hard.

'I hope so. I really hope so. So, Scarlett, what's going on for you?'

'Can you meet me?' she says, and I jump at the idea of course.

'Sure,' I say. 'Now?'

'Yeah.' I hear the shrug in her voice. 'Yeah, okay.'

'Where? Can you come into town?'

'Not really,' she says. 'I'm not meant to go out yet. Can you come near my dad's?'

'Yes, of course. Where?'

She describes a café nearby, near the woods, she says, and I think of that poor bloody puppy.

And what did old Bedford say yesterday? What kept happening to the pets…?

'Scarlett?' I say. 'Did you send me Jeanie's diary?'

She hangs up.

At the café in the woods I wait – but Scarlett's not there. Lots of dog walkers come in and out, and I look for one in a pink Puffa jacket, but there's no Scarlett.

I drink two large black coffees, and then I think, *I can't wait any more.* She's not answering her phone, and time is running out.

I drive to Malum House. I park up and take a huge breath, and I walk up the drive to knock on the door.

The boy, Luke, answers it.

'Are your mum and dad here?'

Up close I see that he doesn't have the looks of his parents – or rather he's the worst combination of them. 'My dad is,' he says, and he looks suspicious. 'Who shall I say it is?'

But his father has appeared behind him in the hallway, and he knows who I am.

'Marlena,' Matthew says, obviously surprised. 'How's Jeanie?'

'Are you bothered?' I say, and Luke looks like he might cry.

'Of course I'm bothered.' Matthew is first taken aback and then angry. 'I've just got off the phone to the hospital. They say she's stable. They say they may try and wake her later.'

This, I won't lie, disarms me. But of course he's next of kin.

'Oh,' I say. 'Can I come in?'

'Sure.' He opens the door to me and leads me to the kitchen. 'Can I offer you a drink?'

'Is Scarlett here?' I ask without answering, and he shakes his head. 'She's been staying with friends. Since the – incident.'

'And all the charges have been dropped?'

'There were no charges…' He's angry again. 'It was malicious rumour.'

'Do you know who started it?' I ask.

'I bloody wish I did.' Matthew is vehement. 'But I don't at the moment. It was a written allegation apparently. The police say it was anonymous. Still.' He has gained weight since I last saw him, no longer the svelte businessman Jeanie met, but a slightly sweaty, middle-aged guy who looks very dishevelled.

'And Kaye?' I keep waiting for her to walk into the room and purr at me, false and proud. 'Where's she?'

'No idea. Why would I know?' he says distractedly, looking for cups. Everything's dirty apparently – no handy housekeeping Jeanie any more.

I don't really want to admit I was poking round the garden yesterday evening, but I'm probably going to have to admit it. As I prepare to make my accusation, Matthew suggests we go into the lounge – 'It's tidier' – and I follow him, annoying plinky jazz playing throughout the house.

'Sit please,' Matthew says, but I don't want to.

I'm about to tell him I'm on to him when a car skids into the drive and pulls up very sharply, just missing the flowerbed.

'Blimey,' I say, 'someone's in a hurry.'

From the window I can see Kaye getting out – as I expected.

'News travels fast!' I raise a brow at Matthew, but to his credit, he looks as surprised as I do. If he has warned her I'm here, he's a very good actor.

The woman comes storming up the front path in full aerobic gear and Luke, who's been skulking round in an anxious, hovering sort of way – as if he's scared he'll miss something – lets her in.

'Is Scarlett here?' Kaye's straight past her surly son, straight into the room, facing Matthew, hands on Lycra-clad hips.

I deduce from Kaye's attitude all is *not* all right between these two. But last time I saw them, they were kissing.

'No.' Matthew rubs his face tiredly. 'She's at Alison's, isn't she? I'm seeing her later.'

'She's bloody well not there.'

I step out of the shadows.

'Oh you! What are *you* doing here?' She narrows cold blue eyes. 'This is Marlena, Jeanie's—'

'I know who she is.' Her purr is laced with venom. 'But what I don't know is *why* you're here?'

I might ask her the same thing exactly.

'I came to talk to my sister's husband,' I say politely, though what I'd really like to do is to order her to *Fuck right off, Beaky-face.*

'Oh.' She slumps a little. 'Right.'

'I'm interested in the campaign of terror waged against my sister since she moved in.'

'Terror?' Matthew pulls a face. 'A campaign? Oh come on!'

'Oh come on yourself, mate.' I'm almost laughing at his denial. 'You didn't notice someone trying to scare Jeanie out of her wits?'

'Oh not again.' Kaye lays a hand on her chest in well-feigned shock and horror. 'Luke? I think we have something to say, don't we, Luke?'

I'm taken aback. I wait for an explanation. We're all waiting: we all look at Luke.

'Lucas?' Matthew frowns. 'What's your mother on about?'

'He can't help it. He's just being loyal, aren't you, baby? You're the one who's made life so miserable recently, aren't you, Lukie – because you were so sad.'

'Oh Jesus.' Matthew emits a long whistling breath. 'Oh for Christ's sake, Lucas.'

Luke just hangs his head and refuses to look at his parents.

'You knew?' I ask Matthew and Kaye, incredulous.

'What is it you've done?' his father asks him urgently. 'Lucas?'

'I didn't mean to,' Luke mutters to the floor. 'It was a joke.'

'Didn't mean to *what*?' Matthew's exasperated.

'You must have had an idea,' I interject, 'and you did nothing. You covered it up, Matthew, like you did with that poor girl, Daisy…'

'But we dealt with that.' Matthew almost looks relieved – almost, but not quite. 'It was an accident, truly, and Daisy's going to be fine…'

'You "dealt" with it?' I think of Peter Bedford's distress. 'Not what her father thinks.'

'He didn't see her,' Matthew interjects.

'Look, sorry, but I'm more interested in Jeanie right now. Tell me, Luke, what did you think would happen if you scared her out of her wits?'

'It was a joke,' the boy repeats pathetically.

'Like killing your own dog was?' I hazard a guess.

'Oh God! I thought you'd stopped murdering animals, Lukie.' Kaye's sigh is as dramatic as her statement. 'We're going to have to go back to the psychotherapist I realise.'

'Murdering?'

'I didn't mean to,' Luke mutters. 'They were accidents…'

'Oh, Luke.' Matthew sits heavily. 'What did you do?'

'Made Jeanie think she was mad, mainly, I think,' I say. 'How did you manage it, Luke? All the whispering walls? The flickering lights.'

He shrugs. 'S'not hard.'

And I'm amazed. He's fessing up; rolling over apparently. 'I just rigged up the Sonos system.'

Of course he did. The sound system in every room; the sound system that Frankie had been so impressed with; the horrible jazz rattling to its end now here and in the kitchen.

'And the porn on Frank's computer? That disgusting porn?'

Luke just stares at the floor.

'And the emails from 'Helpful'?'

'I found the stuff in Scarlett's room. An article about what Jeanie did with that boy.' For the first time, Luke looks more impassioned. It's all coming out like a release. 'I just wrote it down and sent it to Dad.'

'And the school where she'd got a job? Very clever. Know a thing or two about computers do you, Luke?'

'He's very good with programming actually.' For a moment Matthew almost looks proud. 'Natural aptitude.' Then he remembers himself.

'He made it look like the emails were from Frankie, and then when Frankie denied it, he must have changed the address. You made them look like they were from your own sister, Luke! But they weren't, were they?' I demand.

The teenager shakes his head, lower lip jutting.

'Oh sweetheart.' His mother goes to him. 'I know you wanted to do it for me, but it's been very cruel to Jeanie. I just wanted you to make her welcome.'

'Really?' I hear my own disbelief echo in the air. 'I'd say you're a liar – just like your son.'

She was in The Bill, I hear those girls from yesterday say. A born actress.

'But you cried on their wedding day,' Luke speaks to his mother, angry now. 'I didn't get why. I didn't get why – and I just wanted to make you happy, Mum. You left Dad, and then you were meant to be happy, but you weren't nice.'

'It wasn't me.' Kaye's voice has sharpened. Knife sharp. 'I didn't tell him to.' She looks at both Matthew and me now. 'You have to believe me.'

'Do I?' She'd sell her own son down the river for a song. 'You didn't coerce your son into making Jeanie's life a misery then?'

'You said it'd be funny, Mum,' Luke whines. 'You said imagine if she thought that old ghost was around again…'

'Oh for fuck's sake, Kaye.' Matthew stands. 'You child.'

The cards, the emails, the nooses around Jeanie's neck, the photocopies of articles. The dead blackbirds: *the maid was in the garden*. Jeanie – the hired help.

This boy wasn't up to all that – not alone, I don't think.

But I've heard enough; I'm itching to leave.

'I hope you're really proud,' I say. 'How did you do the bird thing incidentally?'

'What bird thing?' Matthew looks confused. 'The blackbirds Jeanie said she saw.'

'She *did* see them.' I want to slap him. 'He knows, don't you, Luke?'

The boy is shrinking further and further into himself.

'Luke?' his father demands.

'I kept them in the attic in a cage. It was just a laugh.'

'Killing birds?' I pull a face. 'A laugh?'

'He thought he was protecting me…' Kaye is half crying now – or trying to. Attempting to squeeze out a tear or two. 'It's just a son's love for his mother. It's natural. Stepfamilies are hard work.'

'It's a completely fucked-up love. Jesus – let them free, if you love them, you stupid woman. Don't use them for your own ends.' I look at Matthew. 'You better get your son some help. Before it's too late.'

* * *

Kaye and Luke are huddled together in the corner, and I'm ignoring them, as I tell Matthew I want to take the last of Jeanie's things with me today. I just want to get the hell out of here before I get sucked into their shit any further. I want to get back to Jeanie's bedside, to meet Frankie, ready for when she wakes up. If she wakes up.

Striding to the door, I say, 'I'll bring my car into the drive, if you can get Jeanie's other boxes.'

'You don't need to take it now,' he's trying to say. 'I'd like to see her, for her to know she's got a home here.'

'A home?' I'd laugh if it wasn't so utterly unfunny. 'God, when has anyone ever been made less welcome? Why would she want to come back here?'

If she ever wakes up.

'Marlena, please…'

'I hope you're all ashamed of yourselves,' I snap. 'You're monsters, the lot of you.' Braver than I feel, I walk out to fetch the car.

But I'm speaking to myself too.

I am ashamed. I didn't realise how close to the edge Jeanie really was. And I didn't realise the extent of the toxicity here.

When I've smoked a cigarette, rung the hospital yet again and checked my emails on my phone, I'm a tiny bit calmer, and I drive the hire car up to the house.

Matthew's opened the garage, looking even more rattled than earlier.

'What's up?'

'The keys are missing,' he says. 'To the gun cabinet.'

'Can't help you there.' I take a box of Jeanie's old vinyl from him.

He walks back towards the garden. 'I'll fetch the mirror. I know she loved it – I want her to have it…'

'I don't think so,' I say – but he's gone.

Kaye appears out on the patio and lights a cigarette, wiping tears away like a scaly old crocodile – purely for my benefit, I'm sure. *Save them, lady*, I don't bother saying. I feel nothing but contempt. I check my phone for messages for the hundredth time this hour. I just want to get on the road up north now.

Matthew and Luke reappear, carrying a hideous big mirror between them, all curly gilt frame.

'I'm pretty sure that's not Jeanie's,' I say.

Kaye's about to object I can see – when suddenly Luke swears loudly. 'Fucking hell!'

I turn at the same time as Kaye.

The girl I know to be Scarlett is standing in the garden, by the back doors. She's wearing a pair of very short shorts, with bare legs and clumpy black ankle boots. Her baggy T-shirt screams **Smells Like Teen Spirit** in neon pink.

And in her hands she holds a long metallic shotgun.

'Scarlett.' Her mother laughs rather hysterically. 'Don't be silly! Put that gun down now!'

'You, mummy dearest,' Scarlett, teeth gritted, speaks loudly. 'You can shut the fuck up right now.' And calmly she levels the gun at Kaye.

'Scarlett!' Kaye says, but she does indeed shut up – thank God. Her voice is nasal and whiny.

Luke is transfixed, staring open-mouthed at his twin.

'I was wondering where that key went,' says Matthew.

'You fool,' Kaye hisses at Matthew now. 'You fucking idiot. You left the gun cabinet key where the kids could get it? Seriously?'

'Oh shut up, Kaye,' he says tiredly. 'I don't think you're in any position to blame others. Put the gun down, Scarlett.'

'Yeah, shut up, Mum,' Scarlett jeers.

The family is imploding cataclysmically right in front of me. If it wasn't rather frightening, if Jeanie wasn't lying inert in that hospital bed, it might almost be exciting. The web of loyalties is getting more complex with every second, and the journalist in me thinks of the story; echoes of Columbine—

But as it is, it's pure alarm I feel as my brain races, trying to work out *who* exactly Scarlett has it in for and what she is planning.

If she really hates Jeanie, then I guess I'm the next best thing...

Out of the corner of my eye, I see Kaye move towards Matthew, desperately whispering to him to call the police – and I realise something.

She's scared of her daughter.

Or of the Beretta – or both, I'm not sure. But I thought they were so close...

'Shop your little girl?' Scarlett levels the barrels at her mother's smooth, tangerine-vested chest. 'That's not very nice, Mummy.'

'Scarlett, baby,' her mother pleads, and I have a horrible premonition of Kaye's perfect, fake bosom exploding, blood and guts spattering everywhere. 'Please, what are you doing, darling?'

'Scar,' Luke says now, rather desperately, 'I really don't think this is a good idea you know.'

'What do you know about good ideas, Lucas?' Scarlett is both withering and tearful now. 'You're the one who fucked it up again.'

'I – I didn't mean to,' he splutters. 'I was just messing around, that's all—'

'I warned you, Luke. I said you were doing more harm than good.' Scarlett levels the shotgun again. 'He likes to rampage through your personal life, doesn't he, Daddy? And I mean it's not like he hasn't done it before, is it? Didn't you notice? The second time he's started a war of attrition, yeah?'

This girl is bright. She has a great future ahead of her – if she doesn't blow us all to smithereens. My palms are sweating now, my own T-shirt drenched.

'I was only messing around,' he repeats. 'Mum told me it'd be funny…'

'And you do everything Mum says, yeah?'

I look at Scarlett's clever, pretty face and then at Luke. It must have been hard for this plain, less-talented boy. Living in his sister's shadow, trying to win his mother's love.

'I liked Jeanie,' Scarlett says. The gun is trained, not at her twin, but at her mother. 'Jeanie was nice to me…'

'I'm nice to you.' Her mother sounds pathetic. 'Aren't I, love?'

'Don't make me laugh.' Scarlett does laugh, and it's a hollow, emotionless echo. 'You just control me. That's all.'

It's starting to make more sense now.

'And you must be Marlena?' Scarlett says to me, but she's still staring at her mother with eyes of steel. 'Sorry I stood you up.'

'No worries.' I feel surprisingly calm, considering the size of the Beretta in the teenager's grasp.

'I was gonna come, but then my mum texted me,' Scarlett says. 'She likes to know where I am, don't you, Mum? At all times. Never a minute's rest, being Mummy's best mate, is there, Mum?'

'Scarlett,' Kaye is pleading, her eyes welling up. 'You're really freaking me out.'

'Not as much as you freaked us out, Mum. You couldn't fucking bear it, could you? You couldn't bear it that Dad had moved on, so you had to mess everything up for everyone.'

'I don't know what you mean,' Kaye says weakly, but her lies are transparent now.

'You wanted us to hate our dad so much.' Scarlett's own steely resolve is fading a little; I can see the emotion taking over. 'But that was the last straw.'

'What?' Matthew's sweating too. 'Come on, Scarlett, hon…'

'You made me hate my dad, you made Luke your little puppet – so desperate to please you, Mummy, he'd do anything. And yet you've always been horrible to him, poor Lukie… no wonder you're a fuck-up.' She actually shoots her brother a look of love now, and I feel some sense of relief. Perhaps she *won't* actually kill us all.

'And then you had the fucking nerve to get back with him. You tried to make me hate my dad, you tried to make me ruin him – and you lied. And then you got back with him.'

'I'm not back with him,' Kaye cries.

'Luke says you are.' Scarlett's eyes narrow. 'He saw you last night, kissing. Don't fucking lie.'

'Kissing?' Matthew says. 'When? We weren't kissing, Luke…'

'I'm not back with him, I swear…' Kaye pleads.

'Not for want of trying though.' Matthew's voice is harsh. 'But we weren't kissing. She hugged me. I was so relieved the allegations were being withdrawn. But she wanted to take it further…' He looks at Kaye as if he's had a sudden revelation. 'God. Scarlett's right, isn't she?' he says very slowly. 'They're both right. I didn't see it…'

'I hate you.' Scarlett suddenly starts to cry, and the gun wavers in her hands for the first time. 'I really, really hate you, Mum.' Snot runs down her face, snot and kohl, and she looks like the frightened little girl she is. 'You were meant to look after us – but you broke it all apart. And then you tried to ruin Dad's and my relationship – you lied…'

Kaye keens. 'I was just looking out for you…'

'You wanted me to hate Jeanie; you tried to make me hate her too – but she was always really nice to me.'

Jeanie; lovely Jeanie. What cesspit did you walk into unwittingly?

'It wasn't till I spoke to Alison properly that I understood.' For the first time the gun looks like it's too heavy in Scarlett's skinny arms.

'Alison?' Kaye expostulates. 'That dried-up bitch…'

'For God's sake,' Matthew snaps. 'She's your oldest friend.'

'You're so fucking jealous, aren't you?' Scarlett takes a step closer to her mother. 'Of other women. You couldn't bear Dad having any girlfriend or us liking them, so you tried to stop each one…'

'It's not true.' Kaye's sobbing too. 'Please, baby. I'm sorry. I can make it all right…'

Jesus, bring out the violins.

I'd really like to go now. Scarlett's little speech has answered most of my unanswered questions. I'm dying for a fag, I need to start heading north – and I'm fairly sure Scarlett's not going to fire the gun.

But what do I know?

She pulls the safety catch back; the click echoes round the summer garden.

'Scarlett!' I croak, and my throat's all dry – there's no saliva at all in my mouth, and I feel like I'm on CSI or some shit. 'Don't ruin your whole bloody life, love, for God's sake – it's not worth it. Prison's shit, I know from experience…'

'Listen to her, hon,' Matthew says urgently. Luke's slumped in his seat, not looking at anyone, and Kaye's sobbing hysterically now.

Kaye's a horrible woman, of that I have no doubt; can't see past her own nose, it's all about her, not her kids – but still, I'd rather not see her pulped to bits.

But…

Scarlett ignores us. Her sharp sapphire eyes sweep the patio as she turns. We hear a second click.

I shut my eyes. I think I'm praying.

There's a scream, and…

She fires the bloody thing.

About thirty seconds later I open my eyes, and very gingerly I look around me.

Scarlett is half sitting, knocked back by the force, the gun between her feet on the floor, her face paper white, two high spots of colour in her cheeks.

Kaye is slumped on the floor.

The shot hit the mirror I realise. That hideous curly-edged gilt mirror. It's shattered into a million tiny pieces.

And Kaye is still breathing. Still crying. Not hurt, it seems. No blood I can see.

Sweat has started properly beneath my arms.

'Scarlett.' Matthew's voice is very calm and sure, and he stands over her. 'Give me the gun right now.'

And finally she does what she's told. She passes it to her father, and he pulls her up to stand and hugs her, and it looks like the normal embrace of a father and daughter to me; though, like I said before, what do I know? Scarlett sobs into his shoulder.

What the hell do I know about fathers myself?

Afterwards I think Scarlett only fired because she wanted to feel the power she was wielding – she'd been impotent in the situation for so long.

She was wielding a whole lot of power, as it turned out.

MARLENA

Like Jeanie said: so often things aren't what they seem.

I mean, take that photo of Jeanie and Otto, uploaded by the kid who wanted to hurt Otto. The photo that started everything. It was all about the angle. From the angle it was taken, it looked like Jeanie was about to start kissing her pupil.

I guess you could say it was the photo that ended it too. And I mean really ended it. With a bang so catastrophic it shook us to our very roots.

And in-between, what was there? If that even matters any more.

It matters a bit, I guess, looking back.

There was love: a spark of hope – a belief that things could be put away into the past, tidied and boxed up. That life could move on; that that was what was right and just.

But in the end it was still there, wasn't it? Always there: malevolent presence and irrefutable evidence, that photo – in black and white if you like. And if you looked at it just so – well yes. Perhaps you could be forgiven for thinking that it was evidence of something.

And it was Jeanie's word, wasn't it? Only her word – and was that enough?

Apparently not.

As I make my way to the M1, I'm trying to tie up the ends in my weary head – but they won't quite go.

Because of this: you realise Jeanie only wrote what she wanted to be seen, don't you?

She didn't want everything to be there in black and white – but it took me a while to work that out.

Stopping for coffee somewhere near Leicester, I receive a text from Sal, the stringer. It says:

Dunno if this is helpful now but the person who made the abuse allegations against Matthew King was a Kaye King.

It's no great surprise.

At the hospital I see two things.

Hurrying through the main reception, the headline of the local paper outside the shop:

PEAKS BIKER DIES IN INTENSIVE CARE

And I think of the brief conversation I had yesterday with Ruth, Jeanie's Ashbourne neighbour.

I hurry up to the second floor in the lift.

The second thing I see is Frankie, before he sees me. He's sitting in the corridor outside Jeanie's room, desolate, drinking a can of pop, staring down at his dusty trainers.

My heart clenches.

'Frank!' I wave, and he looks up – and barely bothers to wave back.

Oh God, what does that mean? I sprint down the rest of the corridor towards him, my soles squeaking on the lino.

'Everything all right?'

'Well'—he stands now—'they're waking her up.'

'Oh God.' I feel the tears spring to my eyes, hot and sharp. 'Are they? How amazing, oh, Frankie, how amazing, oh thank God, thank God…'

And I'm sobbing now, and he's hugging me.

Frankie, my son, who I couldn't look after, who I gave to Jeanie when he was just three months old, because I was scared I'd hurt him, like our mother hurt me.

Because I knew Jeanie could do a much better job than I would. And she took him, and she didn't argue, not after she'd understood that I was buckling. She said, 'It can be temporary,' but I knew it couldn't. Only seventeen myself, I didn't want to mess him up. I didn't want him to feel he'd been rejected. I loved him, of that there was no doubt. But I was too scared of my own black feelings; the post-natal stuff, the savage dog of depression that was hauling me down into the pits, its jaws clamped around my head.

I look into Frankie's freckly face – he gets those off his dad, those freckles. His dad, Sammy, a freethinking musician who didn't believe in bonds, whom I loved fiercely. And whom I could never trace after I told him I was pregnant.

He went to America, I think, Frankie's dad. Vanished. Me, who could trace anyone; I've never found him. Sammy really didn't want to be found.

And I see Frankie is crying too. Tears on his cheeks, sparkling in his eyes, which are so very like mine.

I wipe them away, those tears, from my boy's face, and I think, *However much I want to, however much I'm tempted, I can't tell you the truth.*

I owe Jeanie that much; I can't ever tell him now. I've left it too late.

But I'll love him till the day I drop dead – I'll love Frankie with every tiny sinew, with every cell and vessel of my being.

Take love where you find it I say, if it's the good and pure type.

We hold hands, and we walk into Jeanie's room to see her eyelids flutter for the first time in days.

JEANIE

THE LAST PART

It took me a lifetime to understand that, all too often, people are just plain nasty. They can't see beyond their own stuff. They're scarred forever, and they want to take you down too.

I refused to believe it for so long – too long – and it was painful to accept, but I know now absolutely that it's true.

Marlena *always* knew, of course, and it was natural she would. We are so very different, my sister and I.

She was too hard, sometimes, maybe. It was just a layer of protection. And I was always, no doubt, pretty naïve.

I'd believed in the fairy tale. I'd subscribed to the myth. A bit like – before Otto – the daft way I believed in all the smiling faces on Facebook, all the snaps of blue skies and turquoise seas. The cuddling, kissing selfies; the couples that couldn't live apart. Families having brilliant times.

I missed what lay beneath: I just saw the fantasies and sucked them up. I believed it all and aspired to it.

But when it happened to me, the 'fantasy life', it wasn't long before the beautiful idyllic stuff fell away, shiny and unreal. It all fell apart.

How daft could you be?

As daft as me apparently.

Though I wouldn't have said daft or naïve back then. I would have said… optimistic. Always looking for the best in people.

But actually I always had 'unrealistic expectations', as the doctor in Hove said after I resigned from Seaborne; as he breathed too loudly and, not meeting my eye, prescribed pills I couldn't pronounce the names of.

And I had hidden them away, those pills, a secret stash, and my descent had started again, for a while.

When I got off them that time, I kept the leftovers for a rainy day – just in case. There's always a just in case I think.

JEANIE

19 June 2015

9.35 p.m.

When I open my eyes and see Frankie, I am overcome. He comes into the room, which I understand to be a hospital room, as the nurse and the doctor with me explain.

I'm so groggy, I can't speak; my lips are so cracked and dry – but the sight of Frankie's face is enough, the warmth of his hug is more than enough, as is the kiss he gives me as I see the tears in his own eyes.

The guilt is enormous, but the relief is bigger. I love this boy so much; how could I think I'd let the devil take me down?

Matthew wants to give it another chance. He came to see me just as I left the hospital, took me out to lunch in a nice Derby pub called The Silk Mill. We had fresh pies and thick chips and cider, and spoke little really.

I would never ever go back there again, to the horror of Malum House. Matthew wasn't ready for a relationship when we married; I doubt he's ready now – but I'm sure it won't be long before Mrs King number three is bowled over by the fairy-tale house. Hopefully he'll clear the spare room for her and keep it unlocked this time. Less Bluebeard, more real.

It turned out the stuff in there wasn't Kaye's – it was that poor girl Daisy's. *The maid is in the garden.* Daisy, who Luke may or may not have tried to destroy deliberately. Apparently he swore blind he didn't see her when he backed the car up – and it could have been the last dog that he was aiming for anyway.

I don't know why Matthew didn't sort the room out. Largely because he couldn't bear to admit what had happened I think.

Luke has been signed up for psychoanalysis – the tough sort: an hour a day for weeks and months and years. Maybe there's hope for him. He's not intrinsically bad I'm sure. He's just a confused, lost boy, hoping for his mother's love. I think he'll always be less than – never enough for her expectations.

But maybe now less of a threat than Kaye's gorgeous daughter – whose sheer youth and vitality were driving her mother slowly mad.

Marlena told me what happened and what had been discussed. But I never really understood how much he did of his own accord – because some of it Kaye seemed to know about, and other things, like poisoning the poor little dog Justin and, in the process, accidentally poisoning himself, were all his own ideas, it seemed.

Classic trait of a sociopath – or, worse even, a psychopath: inflicting the pain you feel yourself on something else helpless.

Some time after it all, Luke wrote me a letter. I imagine he was forced to, but I was glad to receive it, all things considered.

I am very sorry, Jeanie, he wrote, *for making things difficult. I didn't think of the effect it would have on you. I didn't mean to scare you so much.*

But I would dispute all of those claims. He made me think I was going insane, and he scared me badly, however misguided his motives were.

Still, he was only a kid – and his mother was filled with such jealousy, undoubtedly she corralled him for her own ends.

Jealous of her own daughter's youth and beauty. That's a terrible place to be. There's no way forward from that, no magic elixir of youth.

Only mirrors, to keep reminding you the clock's ticking on. And Scarlett?

She came to see me one day in London, when Frankie and I were staying at Marlena's – before I moved back up to Derbyshire.

We went to a very cool restaurant in Spitalfields, all square tables and no pictures. I bought her a 'gastro' burger, whatever that was – and I had bangers and mash. We chatted about school. Scarlett told me about living some of the time with her godparents, Alison and Sean, and some of the time with her dad. She was also getting counselling she said.

Scarlett asked about Frankie, and I told her that he was too old for her, and it was too complicated – better they be friends. She picked at her nail varnish and didn't mention him again.

I understood from Matthew that he'd got his police inspector mate, Kipper, to put the fear of God into Scarlett over the gun incident. Kipper 'arrested' her, locking her up in the local police station for a few hours. Then he interviewed her about the shooting. She understood she was on a 'caution', though I don't think it was ever an official one. After all she hadn't actually committed a crime.

But she knew that if she ever did something like that again, it would be far more serious.

I wanted the best for her. I felt sorry for her, and I'd grown quite fond of her – but I couldn't see how our relationship could pan out.

We didn't talk about her mother really that day – she wasn't seeing Kaye much yet – but looking at her shovelling her fries in with alacrity, I remembered what it was I'd seen in those home movies that had bugged me.

Initially I'd read it as admiration for Kaye – but when I'd looked again, I'd seen it wasn't.

It was a look of fear on her face when she looked at her mother: fear and hostility.

I realised that Scarlett's act of violence came from her rage at not being heard. At having her voice and her feelings stifled by the woman who was meant to love her above all else.

I felt sorry for the girl – for both the kids. They had everything they wanted materially, and their lives were still a mess. I hoped that Matthew would be able to be a better father if women were out of the way – for the time being, anyway. There was no doubt he loved his children dearly; they had that security.

'I know you've been cutting yourself,' I said quietly as we waited for our pudding, and Scarlett flushed like her name. 'You can't deny it this time. I saw the blood in Ashbourne, on the carpet. I saw it in Malum House too that time.'

I'm pretty sure she wanted me to see it – in Ashbourne at least. It's usually a cry for help in my experience, leaving a clue.

I'd told Matthew at the time in Malum House, and he'd ignored it; I'd told Kaye before. If I'd not moved out, maybe I could have done something directly, but now I made sure I told Matthew again, told him he needed to watch out for his daughter's mental health. It was his responsibility.

Frankie was mine.

Over chocolate cake and ice cream, I told Scarlett I was learning tai chi and karate, and she grinned.

'You gonna be a superhero then?'

'Hardly. Just keeping fit and learning to defend myself,' I said primly. 'You never know who might be round the next corner.'

I didn't tell her I'd also signed up to a 'self-assertion' course – to learn to speak my mind in the correct way.

It had taken me a long time to learn I had the right to speak. It was something that Scarlett would have to learn too.

It had taken me a lifetime to know it was all right to assert my needs.

Before Frankie returns to France to continue his job for a short while, we go to Brighton for a night.

I want to see the sea; he wants to visit his best mates.

After I drop Frank by the Pier, I drive past Seaborne on the way to Lewes for a drink with some old colleagues.

And I think I see Otto, in his green parka, cycling along the Downs.

My heart is in my mouth – but I don't stop.

I always think I see Otto. Maybe it's because I *want* to see him so much. He has such a pure soul, that boy – despite his dreadful parents and too much skunk. He needed a friend, and in the end that wasn't me. I was his teacher, not a lover, not a mother, and I told him so. I sent him on his way – as you can see in the photograph. I'm sending him on his way.

Ah. You want to know what *really* happened, when the camera wasn't on?

It was a mistake that *could* have happened, but I didn't let it. And it was no one's business – no one's apart from Otto's and mine.

We understood each other. He needed sanctuary; I took him in one night. He slept on the sofa. Two lonely souls.

He was so lost. But I didn't see him like the papers said. I saw him like another child. Another lost boy.

I saw something in him I recognised. Because Marlena and I, we were the proverbial lost girls ourselves.

I saw myself.

MARLENA

I'm striding down Chalk Farm Road, away from Camden, late (as usual), on my way to a gig, when my phone rings.

It's DI Stevens.

'Marlena? I hate to tell you – but forensics have confirmed it *is* Nasreen's body that was found.' He's matter of fact. 'I'm sorry.'

I take a deep breath.

'The good news is we've arrested Lenny Jones.'

I bloody knew it. I knew it when they found the decomposing body of a young woman buried out in an Essex wood a few weeks ago. It's been a long, hot summer and – it wasn't good. They were going to have to run extensive tests – but the odds were high it was Nasreen.

'His DNA's all over her T-shirt – along with her own blood,' the DI goes on. 'It's a no-brainer.'

I knew when there was no trace of her anywhere in Turkey or Syria that something wasn't right, that that boy Lenny had made that ISIS bullshit up. Such a convenient way to cover his dirty tracks, sending everyone in the wrong direction. Rather imaginative for a youth like him.

But I'm not glad to have been right this time. Poor, sweet girl. Poor family. I feel gutted for them.

'You can have the scoop, if you like,' the copper's saying. 'We've ordered a media blackout for tonight. I don't reckon we'd have got him if you hadn't been so bloody annoying.'

'Persistent,' I correct tartly. 'That's the word I think you're looking for.'

On the other side of the road, I see Levi standing outside the Roundhouse.

When he sees me he starts waving madly. I wave back.

'Hurry up,' he's mouthing over Camden's traffic.

'Okay,' I say to DI Stevens. 'Yes, please. But can I come down in a couple of hours? I've got somewhere I need to be right now.'

I hang up, and I hurry across the road to meet my boyfriend. The word nearly chokes me – and I think I mentioned before he has a really dodgy QPR tattoo that I'm not very happy about – but I hurry over with a spring in my step.

I never thought I'd write these words – and I feel a bit embarrassed – but I rush into his arms.

And actually, it feels all right.

JEANIE

3 SEPTEMBER 2015

Jon Hunter's on his way back from Tanzania, so I'm renting somewhere of my own, slightly further out of town: a sweet little place called Pear Tree Cottage. It's very like Jon's home. Red bricked this time, a little crooked, on the top of a dale. Well it is the Peak District after all.

It's got an open fireplace and sage-green window frames. The doorways are low, and the floorboards are a bit creaky – but it's too small to be scary, unlike Malum House.

Jon's emailed me a lot recently; we've chatted back and forth. He says he's looking forward to seeing me; he's got so much to tell me about the kids in the orphanage.

And I find, as I unpack my few boxes and put my clothes away, that I'm looking forward to seeing him too. He's always been a nice man, Jon, and now he's left his shackles behind him, he's so much happier. More free. Free to be himself.

I've got a contract now at the same college, and I'm looking forward to going back. I've been reading some French literature this holiday for a new evening class I might teach in Derby; in particular a book called *Bonjour Tristesse*.

I started to enjoy it – a story about a French girl and her relationship to the various women who might end up being her stepmother – but it has a tragic end.

It was a little close to home.

Poor wicked stepmothers. They always get a bad press, don't they?

Marlena came to stay just before Jon came back.

She'd bought walking boots and a black Barbour – although it was a super-cool, tight-waisted one of course.

On the second day the sun came out, and she suggested, to my enduring surprise, we went for a 'proper, sweaty' walk – so I took her to Thorpe Cloud. It was one of my favourite spots, despite its proximity to where I nearly died. The views went on forever; on all four sides of the summit you could see for miles.

But it wasn't long before Marlena tripped and broke two of her new inlay nails (she was trying to stop biting the real ones). Then she kept moaning about the slopes being 'vertiginous', so we drove on to a less intimidating hill. When we walked through the first village and she spied a homely looking pub, we stopped for a drink.

'Can't we call an Uber?' she joked later – and then I realised she wasn't joking. She persuaded a local guy to give us a lift back to my car, winking at me as she jumped in the front, telling him, yes, she'd met Madonna once and Prince William – and he was tall.

We sat in the beer garden for a while that afternoon before she blagged the lift, enjoying the warmth of the last August sun.

'So. You gonna tell me the truth now?' she said, blowing a plume of smoke into the clear air, and I sighed.

'He came back, didn't he? The devil came back.'

'Yeah.' I put my drink down, my chest tightening. 'He did.'

'The bastard.' Her face darkened. 'I knew it was him. Why didn't you say, Jean?'

It turned out that Ruth had called her when she was on her way back to London and had said, 'I thought I ought to tell someone that man has been around again.'

'Matthew? Her estranged husband?' Marlena had asked. 'Tallish, dark bloke?'

'No, not him. A fair chap…'

'Fair?'

'Stocky; brought her a rabbit for the pot. I heard them arguing once, just before she disappeared.'

So Marlena had known all along.

'It's done, Marlena,' I said. 'It's all done now.'

'I know,' she said simply. 'I saw.'

I hadn't thought he'd ever return. My own devil. I thought he'd had his fun, and he'd slunk back to hell.

Love of my life. I thought I was shot of him after the nightmare that was our break-up, back when Frank was just eight.

When I'd recovered, when Marlena had got me straight again, I'd taken my boy, and I'd left London, and we'd gone to the sea. I thought, *He's destroyed me once, so he's had enough.*

Simon K.

But he found me again. Last year.

It wasn't hard, was it, when my face was all over the press about Otto? He hunted me down, and he found me, the summer I met Matthew.

He wanted money. He told me that if I didn't do what he said, he'd take everything from me.

I told him to get lost. I gave him as much money as I had, and I begged him to leave.

For a while he disappeared again – and I thought that was the end.

You see? Daft and naïve.

Because of course he came back again. He knew so much; too much. He knew about my addictions and my past. He knew I'd got hooked on pills after he started to destroy me the first time. And it didn't take a genius to work out that I hadn't been entirely honest with my new husband.

He threatened to tell Matthew everything – and I couldn't bear it.

Only, when I left Matthew, he had no hold any more. He had nothing to blackmail me with. So then he sought vengeance.

He came to Malum House just after that terrible dinner party, when I collapsed. When Luke might have put something in my drink – or I might have just overdone it myself. I'll never know.

I'd been paying Simon bits of money in instalments – but he wanted more, and I was scared Matthew would notice because I'd no money of my own left.

'I'm inside – you know that? I'm inside the house,' he'd said, and I'd looked at his wind-battered face – the face of a beach bum, a reprobate – those slanty eyes I'd once loved so, those red lips that were too full for a man, and I'd thought, *How could I once have been so in his thrall?*

He'd even got a key somehow.

'You know what, Simon?' I'd said. 'Do your best. It can't get any worse than this.'

I only went to meet him at Dovedale that night because after he attacked Scarlett at Ilam Park, I thought he might hurt her again if I didn't turn up.

I was so tired by then, so exhausted, so ashamed, that I didn't care any more. It wouldn't matter if something happened to me.

I thought, *If I die, he can't do any more. I've won. He's lost.*

I thought Frankie would be better off without me. Marlena would be there for him; I was no good any more.

I drove to the Dove Bridge and got out. I sat by the river, waiting for him in the dusk. I drank the whisky and took a few pills to numb the pain. When he arrived on his stupid motorbike – the bike he'd always loved so – we talked for a bit, walking up the path to the shepherd's hut.

We started to argue when he realised I wasn't going to give him anything else. We had a scuffle near the hut – I remember that – and, spiteful as ever, he stamped on my glasses and threw them into the dark grass.

I didn't cry, I don't think. I used to cry in the old days. But this time I gave him the whisky and told him to finish it. I went outside the hut to pee, near his bike, and soon after that he drove off, and I lay down for a bit in the hut. I must have passed out.

I didn't know he'd come off his bike.

Did I?

I can't remember now.

It's a blur.

The day after we almost walked up Thorpe Cloud, Marlena caught the train back to London. She said she had to go and do a proper interview with Nasreen's parents. The *Guardian* actually wanted it.

'Do you mind if I go?' she asked, and I laughed and promised her I didn't. I just wanted her to do well again. She'd paid her dues. She was doing important work this time – and I could see she loved it.

'Honestly, babe, I love you, but I'm a townie at heart,' she said as we drove through Derby to the station. 'All this fresh air and space makes me feel a bit…'

'A bit what?' I didn't mind. I was enjoying learning to be alone, to my surprise.

'Panicked.' She lit a fag and blew the smoke out of the window. 'I will come again, I promise. Soon.' She kissed and hugged me, smelling of Chanel and cigarettes. The kiss was a second; fast becoming a norm. 'Or you come down to me, yeah?'

And Marlena was gone.

I owed my little sister a lot, but I didn't need to say it, it turned out.

It didn't make me feel panicked, all the space.

It made me feel free.

Just before I left London for good, I did a talk on the subject of stepmothers for my final presentation in the self-assertion class. I went through the fairy tales and the myths, touching on stories like Cinderella and Snow White.

'Where are all the men in this?' I finished. 'What responsibility are *they* taking as they watch their daughters and new wives struggle to meet in a good place? Why are the first wives always pure and innocent? And why is it *always* the girls that have the trouble with these women that replace their mothers? Was Freud right – is it all about the innate jealousy we are born with, wanting to get rid of our same-sex parent? Or is it rubbish – is it just because all the stories were written down by men?'

And the class laughed as if I'd said something clever, all looking up at me. And I said, 'Still, hopefully, step-parent or not, they – and we – *will* all live happily ever after, masters of our own destiny.'

And the group clapped loudly as I stood there beaming – I could actually feel myself beaming – and I took a little bow.

I won't let myself be silenced again.

A LETTER FROM CLAIRE

Hello!

THANK YOU so much for taking the time to read *The Step-mother*. Without you, there would be no point writing stories, so I am truly grateful and indebted to you for picking up my latest novel, which is a bit of a twist on Snow White, as I'm sure you realised.

The subject's one that's close to my heart: we all know families, however close, can be tricky – and in this day and age, more and more of us live in stepfamilies, which can be even more tricky than our natural ones (though that's not a given!). I hope I might have addressed some of the issues that come with the merging of families – though I sincerely hope none of you has had to endure what some of my characters go through!

And if you *have* enjoyed *The Stepmother* then I would be even more grateful – if that's possible – if you could take the time to write a quick review, or tell one of your friends – or family – about the book! Writers are not much without their readers' support, and it's always fantastic to hear from anyone who has taken the trouble to pick up one of my books. If you'd like to get in touch, I can be contacted through Facebook, Twitter or

Goodreads – or my own website, where I sometimes remember to blog! Finally if you'd like to keep up-to-date with all my latest releases, just sign up here:

www.bookouture.com/claire-seeber

And, as always, happy reading ☺

www.claireseeber.com

 @claireseeber

 ClaireSeeberAuthor

ACKNOWLEDGEMENTS

I'd like to thank my sister Tiggy Whitham for her feedback; Verl Dowling for just being Verl and also reading the first draft; Gabrielle Chant for her scrupulous copy-editing, which was invaluable. As ever, great thanks to Keshini Naidoo, for being a great editor and a good friend.

I'd also like to thank Kim Nash, Natasha Hodgson and Oliver Rhodes at Bookouture, as well as the Bookouture authors for their help, friendship and jokes. Huge thanks to all the hard-working bloggers who review so tirelessly for us all.

Finally, thank you to those wily crime writers who know who they are - for making me laugh daily and always lending support, knowledge & occasionally vodka (only when desperate, of course).

37988014R00202

Made in the USA
San Bernardino, CA
28 August 2016